PENNILESS AND PREGNANT IN PARADISE

SHARON KENDRICK

CINDERELLA FOR THE MIAMI PLAYBOY

DANI COLLINS

MILLS & BOON

First Published in Great Britain 2022
by Mills & Boon, an imprint of HarperCollins*Publishers* Ltd,
1 London Bridge Street, London, SE1 9GF

www.harpercollins.co.uk

HarperCollins*Publishers*
1st Floor, Watermarque Building,
Ringsend Road, Dublin 4, Ireland

Penniless and Pregnant in Paradise © 2022 Sharon Kendrick

Cinderella for the Miami Playboy © 2022 Dani Collins

ISBN: 978-0-263-30073-4

03/22

MIX
Paper from
responsible sources
FSC™ C007454

This book is produced from independently certified FSC™ paper
to ensure responsible forest management.
For more information visit www.harpercollins.co.uk/green.

Printed and Bound in Spain using 100% Renewable Electricity
at CPI Black Print, Barcelona

PENNILESS AND PREGNANT IN PARADISE

SHARON KENDRICK

MILLS & BOON

For the effervescent yet droll duo:
Rory Crone & Derek Moran
(Surely worthy competitors for a future episode
of *Strictly*?)
Thanks for helping me capture the beauty of Bali…

CHAPTER ONE

IT WAS LIKE being in one of those nightmares where everyone else was wearing clothes.

Kitty felt exposed. Naked.

As if everybody knew she was an imposter, trespassing on the hallowed ground of the fabulously wealthy.

Her heart was thumping as she glanced around the upmarket bar and noticed what the other women were wearing. Sleek silk dresses which skimmed their slender bodies. High-heeled shoes which complemented their buffed and sheening legs. So what had possessed her to put on a flouncy cotton frock and a pair of cheap espadrilles she'd bought from one of the local markets?

Because it's the only dress you've got. The only outfit which is remotely suitable for drinking expensive cocktails in one of Bali's most exclusive nightspots.

At least for once she'd blow-dried her frizzy hair, so she didn't look like she'd stuck her finger in the light socket—but even so, nervous little beads of sweat were gathering on her forehead.

Because Kitty wasn't the kind of person who walked into bars on her own. Especially not bars which exuded wealth and privilege, despite the low-key and relaxed vibe which Bali prided itself on. Sophie, a nanny staying in the neighbouring villa, had invited Kitty out for a drink with her and some friends holidaying on the island. Kitty was late but as she looked around for Sophie and the others, she tightened her grip on her little rattan bag—another market purchase.

Where were they?

Surely she wasn't *that* late?

She wondered if she should just brazen it out. Order a ridiculously expensive cocktail while she waited, and spend ages sipping it. But then suddenly her body began to tense as she became aware of someone watching her.

It was weird. Almost as if compelled by some powerful outside force, she turned to see a man sitting on the far side of the marble counter, an old-fashioned newspaper in front of him, the narrowed glitter of his dark eyes fixed intently on her. His body was hard and his face was cold. He made her think of winter. Of something bleak and unremitting. She didn't know what made her stare back, only that she couldn't seem to stop—telling herself it was something about his stillness which was so commanding, which made it almost impossible to look away. Or maybe it was his broad shoulders or the stony beauty of his face, which was making the hairs on the back of her neck prickle with something which felt like recognition. Yet how could that be when she'd never seen him before?

Quickly Kitty turned away, bewildered by her reaction and by the inexplicable prickle of her breasts and the rush of heat low in her belly. What was she *doing*, ogling a strange man in a strange bar? She would text Sophie and find out where they'd gone. They must be here somewhere—after all, the Langit Biru was one of the biggest resorts on the whole island and certainly the most exclusive.

Just then her phone started vibrating and she was

about to pull it from her handbag when a female voice broke into the flurry of her thoughts.

'Excuse me?'

A woman seemed to have materialised from no-where—her gleaming hair coiled neatly at the nape of her neck, and a discreet gold badge pinned to her simple black dress announcing her role as the maître d'. The expression on her face was kindly but Kitty's antennae for this sort of thing were acutely sensitive. She'd grown up with people freezing her out, letting her know she was somewhere she shouldn't be, and she waited now for the admonishment she was certain was on its way.

'You do realise this bar is for residents only?'

The woman's voice was friendly enough but her so-phistication only fuelled Kitty's growing feelings of insecurity, which were never far from the surface. It felt like the final straw. An inglorious ending to a day filled with irritating incidents. Camilla's snide remarks. Rupert's sleaziness. Squashed banana in her hair at tea-time. The things they *didn't* tell you when you inter-viewed for a job as nanny to a rich and overprivileged couple. Suddenly Kitty knew she had to get out of there because one thing she didn't need right now was to feel *less* good about herself than she already did. She could easily send her text from somewhere else.

'No, I didn't know,' she said, with the studied calm she had acquired through working with young children. 'But please don't worry. I'm leaving.'

Heart pumping, she weaved her way past the low tables decorated with bowls in which floated pink rose petals, orange carnations and flickering tea lights. But just as she reached the exit, something made her glance back at the bar and Kitty was aware of a stupid feeling of disappointment when she noticed that the man with the broad shoulders had gone. Was she hoping for one final glimpse—a spine-tingling memory from the last night of her holiday to cherish during the grim weeks she suspected lay ahead? And if that were the case then maybe it wasn't surprising that she'd never had a real boyfriend, if she set her sights so inappropriately high.

Acting as if she knew where she was going, she walked past two giant stone dragons which were surrounded by a mass of waxy pink flowers which seemed almost too perfect to be real. Suddenly she found herself off the main route in a long and shadowy corridor which looked as if it could have been an admin section of the resort—but blissfully, it was deserted. She stood there for a moment getting her breath back and then she pulled out her phone.

Sophie's text was brief and to the point.

Gave up waiting. Drinks WAY too pricey and staff VERY snotty! Gone to Kuta. Get a cab and come NOW!

Kitty stared down at the glowing screen as she decided how to answer. Should she travel to the other side of the island to join the three other women who would already be a few cocktails ahead of her, or should she play safe and have an early night? She chewed on her lip, her habit of projecting a worst-case scenario never far from the surface. Because what if she had trouble getting a taxi back to the villa later and disturbed Camilla and Rupert? Was it really worth all the aggro of annoying the bosses from hell, especially as tensions were already running high between them?

She tensed as she heard a soft sound in the distance and tensed even more when she peered into the shadows and realised just who was walking down the corridor towards her. Her heart clenched with excitement as she saw it was the man from the bar—but she could also feel apprehension thundering through her veins. Because she shouldn't be here. She knew that and no doubt he knew it too.

Yet knowing she was trespassing didn't stop her from staring at him, because it was impossible to focus on anything else. As he grew closer he dominated the softly lit corridor in the same way he had dominated the up-market bar, with a quiet and conquering confidence. Now that he was standing in front of her she noticed how tall he was—his towering height and muscular physique making him seem unlike any other man she'd ever seen. Kitty drank in the proud jut of his shadowed jaw. The high slash of autocratic cheekbones. His tangled hair was black as a raven's wing and his eyes looked dark, too—as if they had been chipped from some piece of obsidian. There was a coldness about them. In fact, there was something about him which transcended his delicious appearance and made her more than a little wary. A hint of something hard and impenetrable which lay just below the surface of those near-perfect features.

She knew she should say something—anything—but the words seemed to have become lodged in the tight column which was now her throat. Instead it was left to him to open the conversation and his words were predictable—even a little disappointing, given the way she'd just been fantasising about him.

'This area is marked private,' he said, his richly accented voice underpinned with a note of unmistakable arrogance. 'Can I help you?'

In a way, Kitty felt almost *grateful* for his rather imperious comment because didn't that make it easier for her to be equally cool, rather than blurting out something inconsequential and crazy—like how much she would love to trace her fingers over the sensual lines of his lips, or to wonder how it would feel if they were kissing her?

And because she was completely out of her comfort zone, she didn't have the wherewithal to come up with her usual polite response. Besides, hadn't she just spent two weeks being the model of politeness, only to be treated like a piece of dirt? 'I can read perfectly well,' she answered. 'I just wanted somewhere quiet to send a text after being unceremoniously ejected from the bar.'

'Is that so?' he challenged silkily. 'Yet the maître d' is known for her diplomacy.'

Kitty sighed, because this much was true. 'I suppose she was quite diplomatic,' she conceded. 'It just felt a bit intimidating, that's all. I don't know why the bars aren't open to everyone, why they have such ridiculous policies to keep people out.'

He studied her from between narrowed eyes as if deciding whether or not she was being serious. As if he were unfamiliar with the type of people who didn't understand the unspoken rules which existed in glamorous places like this.

'Because most of our hotel guests don't want to be bothered by curious punters who've saved up all their rupiahs to make one drink last an entire evening,' he answered cynically. 'If corporate giants or European royalty come to stay, they prefer to do so knowing they can relax and let their hair down without censure. Without some eager wannabe capturing their image on their phone and selling it to a downmarket tabloid.'

Kitty was just about to bristle at the implication that she was a curious punter or, even worse, an eager wannabe—no way would she or her friends have taken surreptitious photos of famous guests—until she remembered that one of the reasons Sophie had wanted to come here was because she'd heard a motor-racing champion was staying at the hotel. Hadn't she been hoping to get a selfie with him and use it as her profile picture?

She wondered who the man was because she'd assumed *he* was a resident, yet he didn't sound like one. The silk shirt which rippled over his hard torso and the dark trousers which hugged his narrow hips certainly looked expensive—and at the bar he had seemed supremely comfortable in his own skin, exuding the assurance which Kitty had observed came so easily to the rich and privileged. But maybe she'd got it wrong. Maybe he was a member of security, disguised to look like a wealthy guest. 'You seem to know a lot about the place,' she said suspiciously. 'Do you work here or something?'

There was a split second of hesitation before Santiago answered her question. 'Yes, I do,' he replied without guilt—because there were many variations of fact, weren't there? He might own this thriving eco-resort and several others like it, but that didn't stop him from channelling more hours into the company than just about anyone else on the payroll. So yes, in theory, he *did* work here.

And he was, by nature, a private man. He always had been. At first by necessity and then by habit. He kept his cards close to his chest. He never gave anything away unless he had to. He had been accused of many things in his life but the most enduring frustration for those he associated with—especially lovers—was his indifference. The supposedly icy carapace which surrounded his heart. His lack of interest in forming deep emotional bonds, or settling down. Contrary to the accusations which regularly landed on his ears, this was not an act, designed to keep marriage-hungry women at bay. It was deeply engrained into his psyche—and his fundamental need for isolation from other people was genuine. He gave what he was capable of and no more. And if that caused unintentional hurt along the way—well, he freely absolved himself of any guilt for that, either. He felt the swift clench of his heart. Because didn't he carry enough guilt to last a lifetime?

He met the redhead's gaze. 'And what about you?' he questioned softly. 'Did you decide to come here for a solo drink, not realising that the bar you chose is out of bounds?'

He saw her shoulders tense and as the movement drew attention to her breasts he felt an almost imperceptible beat of heat at his groin. The same beat he'd felt in the bar when their eyes had met across that wide sweep of marble. Which had made him rise to his feet and follow her as if she had cast some siren spell over him. Which was as crazy as it was inexplicable.

'Actually, going for a drink on my own definitely isn't my thing,' she said primly. 'Although there's absolutely no reason why a woman shouldn't go into a bar on her own,' she amended quickly.

He held up the palms of his hands in mock-defence. 'I wasn't suggesting for a moment there was.'

'I was supposed to be meeting some friends here, but my boss kept giving me extra things to do, which made me late,' she explained. 'And my friends have gone.'

'Why?'

'They decided the drinks were too expensive and...'

'And?' he intercepted curiously, when her words faded away.

She shook her head, her magnificent hair gleaming around her pale shoulders. 'I guess it isn't really their sort of venue. Bit too upmarket. So they've gone to the other side of the island and want me to join them.'

Santiago nodded. He knew exactly who she should have been meeting—a clutch of leggy blondes who'd made heads turn when they'd sashayed into the bar earlier with their thigh-high dresses, tanned limbs and loud giggles. It wasn't an unusual sight—beautiful young tourists wanting a brief taste of how the other half lived. Out of the corner of his eye, Santiago had watched them tossing their hair like glossy banners while casting covetous glances around the bar as if searching for someone—someone to pick up the bill, maybe?—before shimmying out again.

But the wide-eyed redhead didn't look as if she was a natural fit with that group. She looked... He frowned as he struggled to find a word which was alien to his vocabulary. Wholesome. *Sí*. That was it. And nothing like the female guests who usually frequented this expensive complex. Not his usual type, no—for she possessed none of the qualities of the sinewy brunettes he favoured. Leggy beauties whose gym-honed limbs could be amazingly acrobatic between the sheets, who treated sex like a deliciously enjoyable sport—which was exactly how he thought of it himself.

She was...uncommon. Pale skin. Curvy, strong body. A simple, cotton dress which looked completely wrong in one of Bali's most sophisticated nightspots. Yet despite her unsuitable attire, she moved with undeniable grace. She had a naturally lissom walk which had caught his attention, in a way no one else had managed to do that evening. In fact, not for many evenings. His mouth hardened. Perhaps he been drawn to her because she was so obviously an outsider and that was how he felt.

How he had always felt.

His gaze roved over her hair, which was nothing short of spectacular. Thick red waves were cascading over her pale shoulders like a spill of fire. She reminded him of that famous painting of Venus rising from the sea. He'd seen it once as a teenager—when he'd been practically dragged to a gallery in Italy. His reluctance to be there hadn't stemmed from a lack of interest in art—it was because he'd found it hard to endure the costly 'cultural' tour of Europe his mother had insisted on, as a price for returning to her fractured marriage. His father had been sickeningly grateful and had spent the entire vacation fawning over her in a way which had turned Santiago's stomach. Particularly as he had known exactly what was going on behind the scenes. His mouth tightened.

She was being unfaithful to the man who was her husband in name only. Already laughing behind his back and preparing to make an even bigger fool of him in the days to come.

But that type of reflection got you precisely nowhere, Santiago reminded himself grimly. Flicking away from the ugliness of the past, he regarded the redhead thoughtfully.

'Are you going to join your friends?' he questioned, aware of being strangely reluctant to see her go. Because she was novel and faintly enchanting? Or because he could feel the sweet stir of desire in his blood and he hadn't felt it for a long time?

'I don't think so.' She shook her head. 'I think I'll just go back to my villa.'

'You're not making that sound like the most exciting proposition in the world,' he observed.

'You could say that,' she agreed, with a resigned shrug of her shoulders. 'But I've got lots to do and I'm leaving tomorrow.'

Was Santiago reassured by those words? Probably. He had always preferred to know where the nearest exit route was and when he could action it. Suddenly he found himself wanting to remove that faint look of anxiety which was still clouding her freckled face. He wondered what she would look like if she smiled. He told himself he was just being benevolent because she'd been abandoned in a bar which was obviously above her paygrade and looked crestfallen at the way her evening had panned out. Benevolence was supposed to be good for the soul, wasn't it—even if the accusation had been flung at him more than once that he *had* no soul?

But deep down he knew it was more than that. It was something fundamental and compelling. He was fascinated by her strange beauty and what was wrong with that? Wasn't he allowed to take some time out for himself, particularly in the wake of his latest deal? He thought back to the blur of the last few days. He'd just been given permission to build one of the largest solar farms on the planet, in an area of western Australia, not far from Perth. It had been widely acknowledged as a stellar feat and he had been lauded by politicians and environmentalists everywhere. He should have been buzzing with a sense of accomplishment. But he just wasn't feeling it.

He had noticed the surprise of the lawyers on his team when he'd left the boardroom abruptly, his celebratory glass of champagne only half drunk. He'd been doing them a favour really, though he hadn't explained why. For how could you tell people who were fizzing over with triumph that you wouldn't add much to the post-signing dinner because you were already hungering after the next deal, and the one after that? Wouldn't they consider it odd if he confessed that each glittering new achievement brought him little in the way of satisfaction?

His mouth flattened.

Few things did.

'What's your name?' he questioned suddenly.

She blinked. 'It's Kitty. Kitty O'Hanlon.'

'Are you Irish?'

'The only thing about me which is Irish is my name,' she said, with a sudden bitter note in her voice that he didn't understand, nor was he sufficiently motivated enough to enquire what had caused it.

'Santiago Tevez,' he said with just enough of a pause for her to make the connection. To say she'd read about him or heard of him. To ask him some of the tedious and predictable questions he was always having to field when people were made aware of his billionaire status. But when she didn't, he continued with a suggestion which was already filling him with a delicious anticipation—the kind he hadn't felt in a long time. 'Why don't you stay and have a drink with me before you go?'

'A drink?' she repeated.

'Is that such a bizarre suggestion? We both seem to be at a loose end. I've finished working and could use a little company. And since your friends have left, I imagine you might be feeling the same way. The terrace bar upstairs has one of the best views on the island.' He paused, and the hint of a smile played around his lips. 'You can see most of Bali from there.'

Kitty felt a rush of something unfamiliar racing

through her as Santiago Tevez studied her with cool invitation glittering from his dark eyes, because things like this didn't happen to people like her. Nobody usually hit on her like this. She was always the one left guarding the handbags if she went dancing with her girlfriends, or the one dishing out tea and sympathy when one of them got their heart broken. The few times she'd dated, the relationships—if you could call them that—had quickly fizzled into nothing. She knew people thought her a prude and she knew the accusation wasn't without merit—but you couldn't change the way you'd been brought up, could you? You couldn't suddenly become a different person overnight. She was hopeless at flirting and certainly had no experience of chatting to a man who looked more like a god than a mortal. She was seriously out of her depth here and knew she ought to leave at top speed. But something was stopping her.

It wasn't just that she recognised having reached a crossroads in her life, or that she couldn't face going back to the villa this early and risking another encounter with her boss's creepy husband, or hearing more snidey comments from Camilla herself. It was more that she was fed up with being Kitty O'Hanlon—the poor, abandoned orphan who'd spent her life being taught to always know her place and be grateful for whatever came her way. Her whole life had revolved around the need for compliance and obedience, and for once she wanted to step out of line. To shrug off the constraints which shackled her and to behave...

She could feel the sudden lure of unknown impulse. Why *shouldn't* she have a drink with this handsome stranger? The opportunity might not come her way again—in fact, she was willing to bet it wouldn't.

Hadn't she just spent two drudge-filled weeks of her life on what was supposed to be a paradise island? She'd hardly seen any of Bali and hadn't even had a chance to do any sketching—which was her normal form of release—the simple and inexpensive hobby which sustained her.

'Okay, then.' She shrugged. 'Why not?'

'Afterwards, I can arrange for a car to take you back to where you're staying.' Dark eyebrows were elevated in question. 'Do you like the sound of that?'

Kitty nodded, even though his words made her realise that *of course* he wasn't hitting on her. He was just being kind, that was all. He probably felt sorry for her. People did. But she wasn't going to knock it, even if it was mildly disappointing. She hadn't experienced a whole lot of kindness of late, so why not just go with the flow? 'A car?' she echoed, unable to stem her momentary sensation of feeling like an actual celebrity. 'Wow. I mean, is that even allowed?'

He smiled at this and Kitty almost wished he hadn't, because for a moment his hard face was transformed into something which made her heart clench with longing. It was like the first rainbow flush of spring flowers after the bleakness of winter. Like getting into a comfortable bed when you'd been working your fingers to the bone all day.

Stop fantasising about him, she told herself fiercely. *Act your age, not your shoe size.*

'Yes, it's allowed,' he agreed softly. 'Let's just say it's one of the perks of my job. Come on, Kitty O'Hanlon. Let me show you the way.'

CHAPTER TWO

THE VIEW WAS to die for.

Santiago hadn't been exaggerating when he'd said it was the best on the island, but Kitty hadn't been expecting this degree of luxury. She tried to take it all in—another memory to cherish when she was back in London amid the noise and the traffic and the endless demands of her employers.

There were long marble floors and walkways which overlooked the dark and glittering sea. The air was thick with the scent of incense and sweet frangipani. A few couples occupied distant tables, although the main balustrade by which they stood was completely deserted. Almost, Kitty found herself thinking a little wildly, almost as if this prime spot had been reserved and was waiting just for *them*. Hidden speakers were pulsing out deliciously sultry music which sounded like jazz, which made her want to kick off her shoes and dance in a way she hadn't done since she was six years old.

Yet the panoramic outlook which captured the beauty of night-time Bali paled into insignificance when compared to the man who stood beside her, looking out to sea. Tonight the landscape was dominated by a full moon which shimmered over the vast expanse of ocean—but it also coated Santiago Tevez's hard profile with a molten sheen, so it looked as if his profile had been hammered out of metal. Like an emperor on the front of an ancient coin, she thought dreamily, before telling herself fiercely to dial it down.

But she couldn't quite hold back her instinctive sigh of pleasure. Was that why Santiago turned his head to look at her in that quizzical way? Like a diligent geography student on a field trip, Kitty shifted her gaze to concentrate on the distant horizon, reminding herself of the reality of her situation. He'd invited her up here to compensate for having been chucked out of the bar earlier. He was probably only doing it to stop her writing a vicious review on some comparative website.

'Impressive, isn't it?' he said. 'I remember the first time I saw it just how blown away I was.'

His words somehow put her at her ease, reminding her that they were both here to work, not holiday— though she thought he must be quite high up in management to have access to a place like this. 'It's wonderful,' she said. 'In fact, I've never seen anything so lovely.'

'That's good to know,' he commented, but she could hear the low curl of pleasure in his voice as he gestured towards a bamboo sofa which was perched on the edge of the terrace. 'Shall we have that drink now?'

'Why not?' agreed Kitty, although this wasn't the kind of thing she would usually have said. Perhaps she'd heard it on a TV show, or read it in a book. It felt much too grown up and sophisticated a statement for someone like her. But then it *felt* very grown up to walk over to a table on which a garland-decked waitress had just deposited two glasses of frosted cocktails, before silently slipping away and leaving them alone again. And despite her lack of a silk dress and expensive shoes, Kitty felt as if she were in an advert as she walked towards the sofa. As if this were happening to someone else. And wasn't that the whole point of doing this? Of *not* feeling like Kitty O'Hanlon for once, but someone else.

She sank down against the soft cushions and the firm thrust of Santiago's thighs was directly in her line of vision as he moved towards her. It wasn't like her to stare at a particular area of a man's anatomy but she couldn't seem to drag her gaze away. His legs were long and hard and strong and once again Kitty found herself flustered by her reaction to him. Her breasts were feeling prickly and uncomfortable—as if they wanted to burst right out of the bodice of her new dress. Her skin felt raw and sensitive and there was a tight, new sensation deep at her core, which was making her feel restless.

Uncomfortably restless.

She knew it was desire. She'd read about it and heard about it often enough. She knew it was indefinable and, for her, rare. She just didn't know what to do about it.

She crossed one leg over the other, an action which did nothing to alleviate the source of her discomfort as Santiago sat down beside her. He pointed to the low table in front of them where amid the flicker of golden tea lights were two glasses shaped like bird baths, filled with a milky pink liquid on which floated a sprig of dark red berries.

'Cranberry martini,' he said, handing her one. 'House speciality.'

Kitty took a sip. The drink was sweet, the berries tart and juicy, but she wasn't really interested in drinking and she noticed he didn't touch his. Just stretched his long legs out in front of him before turning his head to subject her to a lazy stare.

'So. Your last night on Bali,' he said. 'Sad?'

If she'd been having a conversation about Bali a

fortnight ago, Kitty might have answered differently because back then she had still been filled with the hope and expectation which came at the start of every vacation. Even though she'd been working, she had thought—naively, perhaps—that she might get a bit of down time. A chance to swim and to explore some of the beauties of Bali without the constant demands of two toddlers ringing in her ears. But that hadn't happened and since she was never going to see him again after tonight, why not tell him the truth? 'Not really, no.'

'Interesting,' he mused. 'Not the usual visitor reaction. Bali is famously believed to be an earthly paradise and most people can't wait to come back. So what went wrong? Bad hotel?'

'On the contrary. I'm staying at one of the Sangat Bagus villas.'

'But they're...'

She raised her eyebrows. 'They're what?'

'Well...' He appeared to choose his words carefully. 'They're very upmarket and beyond the price range of most people.' He skated his finger around the rim of his glass but still didn't drink from it and now his expression was curious. 'Which wasn't intended to be a value judgement,' he added quickly. 'Just my assessment from having observed people vacationing here, year on year. I thought you were one of those twenty-something young women who flock to the island.' He raised his eyebrows questioningly. 'Probably doing a late gap year, on a budget?'

She leant back on the sofa, finding to her surprise that she was enjoying herself. 'Do continue. This is fascinating.'

'And your disenchantment with Bali was probably because you'd met some handsome Australian or American guy who broke your heart.' His dark gaze glittered with mockery. 'Who promised you the world and left you with nothing.'

'I hate to confound your expectations, but that definitely didn't happen.'

'So why the eagerness to leave?'

Kitty put her drink down, rubbing together the tips of fingers which were chilled by the frosty condensation on the glass. She hadn't confided in anyone about her current problems—not even Sophie—because loyalty was something else which had been drummed into her from her childhood and it was hard to let that go. But suddenly she felt a terrific need to unburden herself. And since he was the one who'd asked the question, maybe she should go right ahead and answer it. It might move her attention away from the distraction of his sculpted features and the disturbing awareness that his muscular body was within touching distance.

'Like you, I'm not here on holiday. I'm working. As a nanny.'

'A nanny,' he repeated, as if he'd never met one before.

'I look after two young children. Sorry, I should have asked before. Have you…? Have you got any children?' she questioned, as the thought suddenly occurred to her that he might be married, with a family. Which shouldn't matter, but it did matter, and she didn't know why.

Yes, you do. You know exactly why.

'No, Kitty. I don't have any children and I don't intend to have any. I'm single. Very happily so.'

She wouldn't have described the expression which had briefly hardened his features as anything *like* happy—and wondered what had caused it. Surely not just her clumsy attempt to discover his marital status? 'The kids I look after are adorable, well, mostly, but…'

'The parents aren't?' he supplied, into the silence which followed.

'They can be…challenging,' Kitty concluded.

'In what way?'

She huffed out a sigh, because talking about her job at length wasn't what she'd had in mind when she'd accompanied him to this fairy-tale setting. 'You're not really interested, are you?'

'I wouldn't be asking if I weren't,' answered Santiago, surprised to discover that he was enjoying her story. He wondered why he found her so fascinating. Because she seemed different from everyone else he mixed with? Or was it more basic than that? The moonlight was shining on her hair, weaving it into a complicated mixture of silver and gold—and he couldn't seem to tear his gaze away from that gleaming spill of waves, or the pale flesh of her shoulders which peeped out from beneath.

Desire was a capricious master, he decided wryly.

Or should that be mistress?

'Tell me,' he urged softly.

She stared at the small dish of salted peanuts. 'My employers are both very high-achieving lawyers, and I don't usually see much of them because they leave at the crack of dawn to go to the gym and don't get home until the children are in bed.'

'Doesn't that make you wonder why they bothered having children in the first place?'

'If people only had children for the right reasons then the human population would have died out centuries ago,' she replied, with a bitterness which almost matched his own abrasive tone, before moderating it a little to continue. 'And even though the villa is massive, it's been pretty intense—with us all being there together.'

'So you've seen more of your bosses than usual and realised you don't really like them? Is that it?'

She nodded. 'That's pretty much it in a nutshell. Their marriage seems to be under a lot of strain at the moment and they seem hell-bent on taking it out...'

'On you?'

She flushed, as if she was suddenly aware of having said too much. 'It's a difficult situation.'

Santiago leaned back, realising that she wasn't attempting to flirt with him and the novelty of *that* was intensifying the heat at his groin. 'So what are you going to do about it?' he questioned, his voice low and husky.

She shrugged. 'When I get back to England I'm going to start looking around for another position and another place to live. It's a live-in job, you see.'

'And do you like that? Changing homes every time you change job?'

Kitty wondered what he'd say if she told him that only once had there been somewhere which really felt like home and that place had been ripped away from her without her consent, like someone pulling out the rug on which you stood. She had a good idea what his reaction would be. He might probe a bit and be fascinated and pitying in equal measure, because that was what people did when she told them about her background and why she never mentioned it unless it was unavoidable. And she didn't want pity from him. She didn't know what she wanted but it definitely wasn't that.

'Variety is the spice of life!' she said, her bright tone lacking in real conviction, but Santiago didn't seem to notice. He was too busy staring at her head as if he'd never seen a woman with red hair before.

'What about you?' she questioned. 'Isn't it your turn to tell me something about yourself now?'

'What do you want to know?'

Kitty shifted on the bamboo sofa, but that persistent ache was still gnawing away inside her. She wanted to know how it would feel if he took her in his arms and kissed her and she wondered if that dark shadow would graze her fingertips if she traced the line of his jaw, but obviously she couldn't say any of *that*. She cleared her throat. 'Do you live here?' she questioned politely. 'On Bali?'

'Sometimes.'

'And the rest of the time?'

'Everywhere.' He gave the ghost of a smile. 'And nowhere.'

'That sounds very enigmatic.'

He shrugged. 'I rent places all over the world depending what I'm working on, and where.'

'So where's home?'

'Home?' He gave a short laugh. 'I'm afraid I don't think of anywhere as home.'

She frowned because he was *definitely* being evasive—she just wasn't sure why. She tried a different tack. 'Not even Spain?'

'You think I'm Spanish?'

Kitty's heart thundered. To be honest, in that pale silk shirt, with his dark hair gleaming silver in the moonlight, he looked like some conquering buccaneer you might find within the pages of an adventure book. 'A bit.'

'Well, I'm not. I'm Argentinian. I was born in Buenos Aires, almost thirty-five years ago.'

She stirred her cocktail with the glass straw and took another sip before putting the glass back down. 'Do you ever go back there?'

'*Nunca.* Never,' he elaborated, a hint of disdain curving the edges of his sensual lips. 'At least, not for many years. But here's the thing, Kitty...'

She tensed at the way he said her name. As if the elongated syllables were composed of honey and velvet. As if he were caressing them with his voice. 'What?' she asked breathlessly, wondering if his boredom threshold had been reached. Was he about to bring the evening to an abrupt end and send her packing? Back to the toxic atmosphere at the villa but, even worse—away from *him*.

'I could answer your questions all night long, but I confess that I'm in no mood for interrogation,' he murmured. 'I've had an extremely busy few weeks and this is the first time I've relaxed in many days.'

'If this is you relaxing, I'm not sure I could cope with you being stressed.'

'And right now I'm being distracted by the moon and the frangipani.' He glittered her a hard smile. 'I suppose you're always being told how beautiful your hair is?'

Kitty hesitated, because wouldn't it sound gauche and somehow *sad* if she told him that no one had ever said that, especially in such a soft and velvety accent? 'I hated it at school,' she confided.

'Because?'

'Because it made me stand out.' Something else to mark her out from the crowd. 'And it inspired a lot of nicknames, none of which were particularly flattering.'

'Then your schoolmates were remarkably unimaginative,' he murmured. 'Because your hair is like fire. Like flames lighting up the darkness of the night.'

If he heard her startled intake of breath, he chose not to comment on it. 'Seriously?'

'I'm being very serious, Kitty Do you know what I want to do more than anything else right now?'

And the weird thing was that Kitty did know. Despite her lack of familiarity with the opposite sex, it was obvious what Santiago Tevez wanted—and not just because he'd started using words which sounded like poetry to her untutored ears. The moonlight was strong enough for her to see the hungry gleam in his eyes and she detected the tension which radiated from his powerful body. And didn't all those things echo the irresistible need which was building up inside her?

She had often wondered what it would be like to feel desire. The kind which apparently consumed you like a fever and left you unable to think straight. She'd wondered if such a thing were possible, because she knew some women were called frigid and she was terrified she might be one of them.

Yet now all those doubts and fears melted away, like a scoop of ice cream dolloped onto a hot pudding. She felt the beat of eagerness and expectation. But more than that, she felt feminine, and that was a first. She knew then that Santiago hadn't been thinking her espadrilles were cheap or her dress was all wrong when he'd seen her in the bar. He didn't care whether she was trespassing, or whether she was rich, or poor. The way he had looked at her then, and was looking at her now, told her more than any words could ever have done that he wanted her. For the first time in her life, Kitty felt beautiful. She was suddenly filled with a sense of her own power and where it might lead her. Of how far she could push back the boundaries and explore what lay beyond them. Because *she* was in control of what she chose to do tonight. Nobody else. Just her.

'I think so,' she said, in answer to his question, and then frowned. 'And do you make a habit of picking up twenty-something women you think might be doing a late gap year?'

He shook his head. 'Never.'

'So what made you follow me from the bar?'

His eyes narrowed into ebony shards. 'I think you know exactly what it was.'

She tipped her head to one side. 'Because you thought I was a security risk?'

Her teasing question was accompanied by the flirtatious saucers of her eyes, and as Santiago realised she was answering the unspoken invitation he'd just issued he was unprepared for his illogical sense of disappointment that she had accepted it so readily. Had he anticipated that it would take longer than this to persuade her into his arms? Yes, he had. He had imagined a prolonged game of cat-and-mouse before satisfying the fierce sexual appetite he had denied himself for so long and which she, inexplicably, had woken in him. And he had *wanted* to endure that wait—knowing that fulfilment tasted all the sweeter if first the senses were starved.

His mouth hardened. It seemed he had been wrong about her. She was not different. She was like a piece of ripe fruit, ready to drop from the tree. A pulse began to flicker at his temple. His lifelong distrust of women ran deep, but he was never anything other than scrupulously honest with them. He did not play games. He did not dish out false hope. His limitations were always understood and mostly unmentioned by the jet-set beauties who moved within his gilded world—but, given the redhead's apparent unworldliness, tonight he might need to articulate them. To spell out for her that he was not the kind of man to feature in her dreams.

'I followed you because I could not resist you, *roja*,' he said. 'Because you sent out a siren call to me, stronger than anything I have experienced for a long time.' He reached out to drift his finger over the silken waves of her hair as he had been longing to do from the moment he'd set eyes on her and he heard her expel a small rush of breath.

She wriggled beside him and he could hear the rustle of her cotton dress. 'What does *roja* mean?'

'It means red—like your hair—but please don't change the subject.'

She was clearly very relaxed now for her eyes glinted. In the moonlight he couldn't make out what colour they were, but he thought they might be green.

'Don't you want to teach me Spanish, Santiago?' she teased him.

'Not right now,' he growled. 'I have things on my mind other than linguistics.'

'Like what?'

'Like kissing you. Do you want me to kiss you, Kitty?'

She nodded and her jokiness seemed to have left her, because her voice became breathless. Husky. 'You… you know I do.'

'*Sí.* I know that. I have known that from the moment I first saw you.' He felt his throat dry as his gaze drifted over the lush swell of her breasts, straining hard against the flowery cotton. 'But you must realise that once I start, I'm going to end up making love to you?'

'Why, is that what always happens?'

'Always,' he agreed gravely.

'And? So what if it does? What if I want that?'

Her nonchalance was unexpected too and Santiago wondered if he'd been guilty of patronising her. She was an adult just like him, wasn't she? She had her own sense of free will, with a body which was quivering with need, just like his.

He leaned towards her, aware of a delicious sense of anticipation surging through his veins as her lips parted for him. She looked up into his face with nothing but soft desire written on hers and it was such a trusting look that Santiago very nearly changed his mind and thought about sending her home.

But his hunger was too fierce and so, evidently, was hers.

And if he started touching her here, he might never stop.

Abruptly, he rose to his feet. 'Let's get out of here and go somewhere more private. The Presidential Suite is just next door.'

'The Presidential Suite?' she echoed. 'Are you sure?'

'Absolutely.' He held out his hand, she took it without hesitation and Santiago felt the sweet pulse of desire as she laced her fingers with his.

CHAPTER THREE

IN CONTROL?

Had Kitty really been naïve enough to think she was in control of *this*? Of the way Santiago was making her *feel*?

As he silently walked her from the snazzy rooftop bar into another, obviously very private terrace, all she could do was gaze around in wonder. This was the Presidential Suite, he had told her, and as they entered an outside space which resembled a grown-up pleasure palace, Kitty gulped as she tried to take it all in.

Amid the tangle of fragrant flowers she could see a hot tub, as well as an infinity pool which was lit from beneath to display tantalising shades of golden blue. Over there was a giant lounger, which looked more like a bed. Again, she wondered if they should even be here, but as he pulled her into his arms her uncertainties seemed to just melt away. Because his kiss was just so…magical.

As Santiago's lips grazed hers—lightly at first and then with more focus—she became aware that he was savouring her, as someone might savour a lavish feast. His exploration was slow and studied. It spoke volumes about his experience and she wondered if it would accentuate her lack of it. But Kitty pushed these doubts from her mind because, as he deepened the kiss, she realised he was capable of making her feel plenty of things besides the pleasure which was slowly rippling through her body.

He made her feel strong.

And powerful.

His tongue slipped inside her mouth and her nipples began to pucker against a bra which suddenly felt too small. Did he sense her physical discomfort? Was that why he drew his head away and peeled down the bodice of her dress, so that her breasts were revealed to him, spilling over the edges of her lacy bra? She saw the appreciative gleam in his eyes and that thrilled her.

'Eres hermosa, roja,' he breathed.

Although Kitty didn't speak a word of Spanish—other than 'red' now, of course—she understood this to be a compliment. 'Oh…' she whispered as he bent his head to graze his teeth over one lace-covered mound. 'Oh!'

'Is "oh" the international word for pleasure?' he questioned lazily.

'I thought you didn't want to talk linguistics,' she replied breathlessly, and he gave a low laugh as he turned his attention to her other breast.

She wondered whether she should be doing something to him—touching him or stroking him—though she wasn't sure what, or where. And besides, she was too dazed by the way he was making her feel to be able to concentrate on technique. How could she think of anything as his hand alighted on her bare knee, other than how good it felt to be touched like this? She held her breath as his fingers began to creep upwards, towards the trembling thigh which badly craved that featherlight caress. Towards her panties, which were now very damp. Sensation after sweet sensation bombarded her. Her body was on fire. She was aware of a beckoning heat as he bent his head and kissed her again, and again, and again.

'Santiago,' she gasped, tightening the arms which were looped around his shoulders.

He drew back, stroking her hair away from her hot cheeks, his ebony gaze raking over her. His autocratic features were painted black and silver by the moonlight and his ruffled hair looked like a darkened version of a lion's mane. He looked so gorgeous that for a moment Kitty wondered how on earth she had ended up here with a man like this—or why he had chosen her—before silencing the insecure voice which was fuelling those vicious thoughts. Hadn't she spent most of her life doubting herself? Judging herself by the standards laid down for her by other people—some of whom she didn't even respect.

Well, she was stepping out of the shadows at last. For once she wasn't going to be ground down by *knowing her place*—for daring to reach out for something she really wanted. And, oh, she wanted this. She wanted him. She wanted him so badly.

'This isn't the ideal place,' he murmured. 'I suggest we get comfortable.'

His hand slid underneath her bottom and suddenly he was scooping her up in his arms to carry her across the marbled terrace.

Kitty felt the clench of pleasure mixed with disbelief at his effortless display of strength. At school she had always been known as a strapping girl—the sporty type you'd always want on your hockey team—but right now she felt small and delicate and very feminine. 'I've never been carried by a man before,' she observed dreamily as he walked across the terrace and laid her down on the giant lounger she'd noticed earlier.

'I can assure you it isn't my usual modus operandi,' he answered wryly.

'Is that Spanish, too?'

'No, it's Latin. Now stop talking,' he growled, and bent his head to her lips once more. 'I want to undress you.'

He took off her espadrilles and set them aside, before turning his attention to her dress. Kitty could feel her heart racing as he peeled the garment from her body and dropped it over the side of the lounger. Now she was down to her bra and her panties, shivering a little despite the sultriness of the Bali air. She wondered if he would be disappointed by her figure or her underwear, but when she risked a glance at him, the appreciation on his beautiful face was unmistakable and she felt the welling up of warmth and gratitude.

'Mujer...' he breathed. *'Mujer.'*

She didn't understand that either but suddenly Kitty didn't care what he was saying—because she was overcome by a fierce need to see *him*. She reached up to his shirt, her usually dextrous fingers shaking as they flew over the buttons until the silken garment was flapping open, and she pushed the shirt from his broad shoulders so that it fluttered to the ground.

'Oh,' she said again, in soft amazement this time, blown away by the vision he presented. His torso was rock-hard, sculpted from moonlit muscle. Ripped arms were tensed as he brushed back the swathe of waves which had fallen over her face. Kicking off his shoes, he removed his trousers and took something from his wallet—before skimming off her bra and panties and tossing them away to join the rest of their discarded clothes.

At last she was naked and so was he and the small moan he gave as he pulled her into his arms seemed to Kitty like the most wonderful sound she'd ever heard.

And then it was flesh. Nothing but flesh. Her softness. His hardness. The slow suck of his mouth. The quick flick of his tongue. A wordless and intricate dance, but like no dance she'd ever done.

'Your skin is so soft,' he said unsteadily, his fingers tantalisingly light as they traced their way across her flesh.

'And yours is...'

He tilted her chin up with the pad of his thumb so that their moonlit gazes clashed and held. 'Mmm?'

She mustn't be shy. Not now. 'So hard,' she whispered at last and, softly, he laughed.

'That's the general idea, *roja*.' He redirected his gaze to survey her chest. 'Shall I kiss your breasts now, for they are such magnificent breasts and they are crying out for me to kiss them?'

'Y-yes. Please.'

He gave a low growl of satisfaction as his lips grazed first one nipple, then the other and she could feel them peak against the lazy lick of his tongue. As his hand explored her belly and beyond, Kitty writhed her hips in glorious expectation, wanting to articulate this fierce new need which was building up inside her but unsure of what to say. She could feel a hot slick between her legs and she shivered when he touched her there—first with his finger and then his mouth. She could feel pleasure wash over her in unremitting waves and his name trembled on her lips.

'I think now,' he said, the unevenness of his voice thrilling her as she responded with a wordless nod.

The sound of tearing foil made her glance down to

see that he was protecting himself. Surely she should have felt shy at witnessing something as intimate as *that*? But Kitty didn't.

She felt as if she were running to catch up on all the years she had missed out on, because of everything she'd been taught to fear. Transfixed, she stared at him—at the pure beauty of his naked form. He was so big, she thought. Not that she had anything to compare it with, but still. Tentatively, she reached out to touch him but he warned her off with a quick shake of his head.

'Not now,' he ground out. 'Maybe later.'

She didn't really understand what that meant either, but by then he was moving over her and she could feel the warmth of his powerful body as he brushed her tumbled hair away from her face. Did it always feel like this? she wondered dazedly. This sense of perfect physical harmony between two people? As if nothing else in the world existed right then except them, and this? His mouth covered hers in a drugging kiss just as he entered her and the sweetness of that kiss made Kitty feel as if she were dissolving from the inside. He claimed her with one long thrust and automatically she choked out her pleasure. But that was when things started to change. His body stilled as he encountered resistance and she heard him mutter something harsh and imprecise in Spanish.

'Santiago,' she breathed against his mouth, wanting to reassure him and to encourage him to continue— because there was none of the pain she'd been told to expect, just a brief sense of him breaking through her tightness and then the incredible sense of him filling her and making her feel complete.

But he had stopped kissing her, was turning his head so that his lips were against her neck, and she could feel the hot rush of his breath as he resumed a delicious rhythm—driving hard and deep inside her, but saying nothing. Instinctively, her hips rose to meet each thrust and she was unprepared for the first sweep of pleasure which built up inside her—growing and growing, before erupting like a fistful of fireworks. She called out his name as she began to convulse around him and that was when he kissed her again, but this time his kiss did not feel tender, or searching. It felt like a kiss intended purely to silence. But then his own body bucked just as helplessly as hers had done and Kitty wondered if she was putting a negative slant on what was happening, because that was her default mechanism.

Just enjoy it, she urged herself fiercely. Claw back some of your newfound confidence and revel in the way he's making you feel. This is Kitty O'Hanlon, going forward. The prude who is now liberated, who has shaken off the shackles of the past. She snuggled into the warmth of his hard body, her head against his chest as she listened to the wild thunder of his heart, and she'd never felt so alive before. As if she could conquer the world.

'Mmm. That was gorgeous.' She sighed against the silk of his skin, but he didn't answer. At least, not straight away.

Santiago lay for a while in silence, waiting for his thunderous heartbeat to return to normal. Waiting for the silken pleasure which was saturating his mind and his body to evaporate, so that he could think straight. He wondered if he had simply deluded himself by bringing her here. If the clues had all been there and he had chosen to ignore them, his hungry body driving them from his conscience—like ashes scattering on the wind.

'You were an innocent,' he said eventually, the word

sounding alien and curiously old-fashioned on his lips. Against his chest he could feel the tickle of her thick hair as she nodded.

'I was.' He could hear her hesitation. 'Does that… matter?'

He thought about it. At a basic level it had been nothing less than sublime. Of course it had, because everyone knew that the novel had an indefinable charm all of its own. But maybe that was because he was more used to deliberate seduction. Lovers dressing up in leather boots with tiny matching thongs, or turning up at the gates of his home, naked beneath a raincoat. Women who would try anything to capture his attention. He had imagined he'd seen it all and done most of it where the opposite sex were concerned, though now it seemed he had been wrong. His initial fanciful assessment of Kitty O'Hanlon as some sort of siren had been completely wrong. She had been a sweet and innocent virgin.

He frowned. Had his irresistible compulsion to follow her from the bar been sparked by a subconscious recognition that she was untouched by another man? Could that be the reason why he'd behaved in an unusually macho fashion—carrying her across the moonlit terrace like some sort of caveman and feeling as if he had just plundered her most delicious treasure when he'd first entered her tight, wet heat?

With an effort he dragged himself back from the dangerous precipice of erotic recall. 'Why should it matter to me about the choices you make?' he returned. 'Though I can't deny being surprised.'

'Oh? Why?' she murmured, snuggling even closer and, once again, that bone-deep feeling of warmth spread over him.

'Because of your age,' he bit out.

He could feel her sudden tension.

'What's my age got to do with it?'

Without thinking, he ran his fingers through her fiery hair and, against his will, felt himself grow harder. 'You are—how old?'

'I'm a twenty-something woman who *isn't* on a gap year,' she reminded him. 'Your words, not mine. Remember?'

'Exactly. And since you've waited this long to have sex, isn't the perceived wisdom that you should have waited a little longer? If not for your wedding night, then at least for a relationship which was going to last longer than one night.'

She propped herself up on one elbow and studied him from between slumberous eyes, but there was no sense of hurt or outrage on her lovely face and that surprised him, too. 'What if I don't want anything that lasts longer than one night?'

'Then you would be a very unusual woman, in my experience.'

'Wow.' She pushed her hair back over her shoulder. 'Have you always been this cynical?'

'Always.'

'Why's that? Did someone break your heart?'

'No, Kitty. Nobody broke my heart. I never allowed anyone to get that close.'

'You were just born that way?'

'Maybe. Or maybe I just learned it along the way.' He shifted his weight a little, intending to get up— perhaps fix her a drink before taking her back to her villa. He wanted to tell her he was no good for someone as sweet as her and it would be better if she got as far away from him as possible. But he also wanted to kiss her and suck on those magnificent breasts and then drive his exquisite hardness into her molten heat again. 'Come on,' he said abruptly. 'Let's get you dressed and I'll take you back to your villa.'

But to his astonishment—and, infuriatingly, to his rapidly soaring joy—her fingers were drifting downwards and feathering the rocky pole of his erection, before curling around it with soft possession.

'Kitty,' he breathed, because her tentative beginner's touch felt insanely good. 'What the hell do you think you're doing?'

'You said later I could touch you,' she began. 'Doesn't this qualify as later? You also said that it was only going to be one night, which by my reckoning means we've got several hours left until sunrise.'

Her bold suggestion was one Santiago hadn't been anticipating from someone so naïve—perhaps if he had, he might have selected a few weapons from his own armoury in order to resist her intoxicating brand of eager shyness.

But who was he kidding, when resistance was the last thing on his mind? One night. How much could he teach her in one night? *How much can she teach you?* challenged a mocking voice in his head.

'I'm not going to change my mind about the things I said to you earlier,' he warned, tilting her chin so that their eyes were on a collision course—though he still couldn't make out what colour they were. 'I'm not going to turn into a knight in shining armour who's going to rescue you. I don't want marriage and I definitely don't want children. I'm happy with my single status and my nomadic life. Do you understand?'

'Do you say this to every woman you have sex with?'

'No, Kitty. But that's because I usually have sex with women with far more experience than you.'

Kitty bristled because she *hated* the thought of him being with any woman other than her. She hated it with a passion which surprised her, even though she knew it was unreasonable to think that way. But, unlike him, she *did* feel vulnerable and that was something she needed to lose because it wouldn't do her any favours. Not if she wanted Santiago to kiss her again, which she did. So she opened her lips and felt a rush of satisfaction as he drove his mouth down on hers and then she gave up thinking about anything as he eased his sweat-sheened body over hers.

She lost count of the times he made her cry out with pleasure, or she him. And that was the incredible thing. That she, a complete novice, was able to make his big body shudder with delight as he husked out broken words in Spanish.

It was a night filled with lazy sensuality, punctuated with practicalities. They moved from the terrace of the Presidential Suite to the vast interior. In the kitchen, he served her chilled juice pulled from a fridge the size of a small planet, then fed her tiny bites of chorizo with shrimp, and tofu with peanut sauce and, afterwards, a creamy coconut sorbet. He took her into a tiled and cavernous wet room and on the way there she caught glimpses of a series of enormous rooms.

That discovery was probably responsible for her one moment of doubt, just before the powerful jets of the shower gushed over them and Santiago demonstrated that making love was just as good when two bodies were slippery wet, though it wasn't quite so easy to get the condom on.

'You're sure we're allowed inside the suite as well?' she questioned tentatively, when she had finished trembling in his arms.

'Don't worry about it,' he drawled, with a carelessness which Kitty would remember all too well afterwards.

The sun was rising by the time she was dressed, her hair drying as the sky turned into a jaw-dropping display of violet and gold as daylight dawned over the island and Kitty realised with a wrench that this was probably the last sunrise she'd ever see on Bali.

'I'd better go,' she said reluctantly.

Santiago heard the trace of flatness in her voice and knew she was sad, but that was inevitable. He didn't want her to read anything into what had turned out to be one of the best nights of his life. He felt the fierce pound of his heart. Far better to remember it that way, than to allow reality or repetition to tarnish it.

He took her to the main reception area and saw her eyes widen as a valet held open the door of the sleek black limo which had been brought to the front of the building, but she didn't make any remark, or ask any predictable questions about why he was driving one of the world's most powerful cars. And her quiet acceptance of her luxurious surroundings fuelled the suspicions which were never far from the surface of his mind.

He drove in silence and waited until he'd stopped outside her villa before asking her, unable to hold back the question any longer—even though he sensed it would probably spoil what had just happened. And maybe that was what he really wanted. He wanted her to be calculating and to have an agenda, because he'd experienced it all too often in the past, and there was a certain comfort to be gained from the familiar. He switched off the engine and turned to look at her. 'So you really didn't know?' he questioned slowly.

A frown pleated her pale forehead. 'I'm not sure I understand what you mean.'

A voice in his head was telling him to leave it. To just lean forward and plant a lingering kiss on those trembling lips and thank her for the memory. But cynicism ran deep in Santiago Tevez's veins. It was like a cold supply of blood which served to maintain the icy temperature of his heart.

'That it is my resort,' he said.

'Your resort,' she repeated blankly.

'Langit Biru. I own it, plus a chain of other resorts. You didn't know?'

'Of course I didn't.' She frowned again. 'How could I possibly know, when you told me you "worked" there?'

'Which I do.'

'Whatever.' And then slowly she nodded, like someone who had been asked a cryptic question and finally worked out what the answer was. 'You think that's why I stayed with you? Because you're obviously rolling in it? You think that?' she breathed, and when he didn't answer, her words were outraged. 'How *could* you?'

He shrugged. 'Easy. I put it down to experience, which I've always found to be the best teacher. I've never met a woman who doesn't want something. And most people will use whatever is available to them as a bargaining tool.'

'I'm not sure where you're going with this, Santiago.'

'You must admit it's surprising for someone to give her virginity to a total stranger during a casual hook-up,' he said silkily.

'The only thing I'm admitting right now is that I made a monumental misjudgement in spending more than a second with a hard-hearted cynic like you!'

Jumping out of the car, Kitty slammed the door more loudly than she had intended, before leaning towards its open window. She knew she ought to keep her voice down, but she was so angry, she couldn't maintain her usual soft volume.

'But at least I won't waste any time pining after you and thinking what might have been!' she hissed. 'Or believe in all that guff about you being happy with your single state. I don't think you'd know what happiness was if it came up and hit you in the face, Santiago Tevez, despite all your apparent privilege. You seem to think you're some kind of prize because you're rich and handsome—but if you want my opinion, I feel like I've had a lucky escape.'

She saw his lips curve and his dark eyes glitter as he turned the key in the ignition.

'You're absolutely right,' he said. 'Every word you speak is true. A very lucky escape indeed. I am the devil incarnate while you are someone who is very special, Kitty O'Hanlon. So go and find a man who's worthy of you. You owe that to yourself.'

His words took the wind right out of Kitty's sails and she stood there for a moment watching his fancy car purr away, wishing he hadn't said that last bit. She didn't want his final remark to be a silken compliment, which had the power to make her want things which were bad for her. Things she was never going to get.

Like him.

Sucking in a deep breath, she tiptoed up the path to the door of the villa and inserted her key as quietly as possible. But as the door clicked shut behind her she could hear what sounded like an expulsion of air from a pair of very angry lungs and there was Camilla stalking towards her, a look of naked fury on her face, while her creepy husband Rupert hovered behind her.

'I was about to ask you where you've been, Kitty,'

said Camilla. 'But the state of your appearance tells me everything I wish to know.'

'Dirty little stop-out,' chortled Rupert, but he was leering.

CHAPTER FOUR

THE FIRST BOMBSHELL exploded two days after Kitty's return from Bali, when Camilla summoned her to the drawing room late on Saturday morning.

It was an unusual summons. Usually, Kitty would be taking her young charges to the playground while Rupert and Camilla ate brunch in a local coffee shop, following their weekly run around Regent's Park. But this morning, Harry and Hattie had gone on a play date, leaving her unexpectedly free.

The drawing room felt even more antiseptic than usual. With its delicate duck-egg-blue walls, fussy furniture and several hideous portraits of some of Rupert's more illustrious ancestors, Kitty always felt like a bull in a china shop whenever she was permitted a rare entry. Camilla was sitting on one of the silk sofas in one of her neat little dresses, her knees pressed closely together, with not a single shining blonde hair out of place. She didn't ask Kitty to sit down or how she was, but that wasn't particularly unusual. The atmosphere in the house had been strained since they'd returned from Bali—with averted eye contact and a chilly silence descending whenever Kitty had walked into the room. Nothing had actually been *said*, but she'd been desperately trawling through job adverts even though it seemed there weren't a lot of vacancies for nannies during the summer.

'There's no point in beating about the bush,' Camilla began, her fingers playing with the lustrous pearls which gleamed at her neck. 'I just want to tell you that we're letting you go.'

'Letting me go?' echoed Kitty blankly.

Camilla sighed. 'We're sacking you, Kitty. One month's salary in lieu of notice. I'm sorry it's come to this, but there you are. We'd like you to pack your bags and leave as quickly as possible.'

Kitty could feel her heart pounding as she stared at Camilla in disbelief. It was all very well deciding she needed to find herself another job—quite another to be told she no longer had a job. She tried to think straight. To drag a few appropriate words from the swirling frenzy of her thoughts. 'But…why?' she questioned stupidly, though afterwards she wished she hadn't given Camilla that particular platform.

'Why?' demanded her boss. 'Oh, come on! I think we both know why! Do you really think the kind of example I want to set Hattie and Harry is to have their nanny creeping back at daybreak when it's perfectly obvious what she's been doing?'

Kitty might have experienced more than one bitter regret about her ill-advised night with the man she couldn't seem to shift from her mind, but her delicious initiation into the adult world of sex had made her feel like a real woman, not a naughty child, and she wasn't going to let herself be treated like one. 'You don't think I have the right to a life of my own?' she asked quietly.

'Not when it impacts on ours!' retorted Camilla shrilly. 'I suppose when Rupert wouldn't take the bait, you decided to look elsewhere!'

Kitty's eyes widened. 'Excuse me?'

'Oh, please don't give me that doe-eyed look of innocence—because it just won't wash. Rupert told me how you kept coming on to him when my back was turned. Parading around in front of him in your swimsuit whenever you got the opportunity.'

It was so unlike what had really happened that Kitty almost laughed out loud. But how could you tell a woman that her husband was a creep with a roving eye who had made her flesh crawl? Would there be any point in exposing him as a liar, if it was Rupert's word against hers? No, there would not. Instead she nodded, knowing that whatever happened she needed to hang onto her dignity. She might not have taken many useful things away from her bleak childhood, but that was one of them.

'If that's what you want.' She blinked, aware of the salty hint of tears stinging the backs of her eyes but determined not to shed a single one. 'I'll go once I've said goodbye to the children.'

'I'm afraid that won't be possible,' said Camilla smoothly. 'We've decided a clean break is preferable, so they'll be out for the rest of the day. The new nanny will be starting in time for tea.'

And that was that. By the time the hour was out, Kitty had no job and no home.

Her heart was heavy and her fingers were trembling as she dragged the large wheely case containing all her worldly possessions past the elegant houses in the street, towards the nearby bus stop.

Now what? Even if she *could* find an agency which was open on a Saturday, it was unlikely there would be a job as a nanny just waiting for her to walk into. Another shaft of fear stabbed through her and this time, despite all her deep breathing, it wouldn't go away. What about references? Would Camilla even provide them? Unlikely, given the nature of her totally unfair dismissal.

She thought about the few friends she had in the city. Not many, because London could be a big old lonely place. But at least there was her friend Lucy—another nanny Kitty had met when she'd first arrived in the metropolis—who offered her a tiny sofa to sleep on until she had fixed herself up with a job.

A couple of days later she had found a compromise of sorts, with a job in a pub. The hours were terrible and The Merry Ploughboy was situated not far from one of London's noisiest A-roads. But it *did* offer a matchbox of a room as accommodation and Gerald and Eileen Flanagan, the Irish landlord and landlady, were very kind. And it had been a long time since Kitty had felt the warmth of kindness.

'Come in, dear,' said Mrs Flanagan. 'And let me make you a cup of tea.'

They made her feel welcome as a steaming brew the colour of tar was placed before her. The kindly pair reminded her of Ellen, Father O'Brady's housekeeper, and for the first time in a long time, Kitty allowed herself a swift pang of nostalgia.

But nostalgia had no place in the life she now found herself living. She was too busy pulling pints and serving hot pies with mushy peas, while the sports channels blared out from the large television, which was always set at top volume. After she had been there for a week, it felt like a whole year. She collapsed into bed at the end of each long day, bone-tired from her exertions. But no matter how exhausted she felt, she couldn't seem to escape those vivid fantasies—all of which involved the man with golden olive skin and eyes which were as black as a starless night.

Santiago Tevez.

Her memories of her Argentine lover were infuriatingly conflicted. He'd been the hottest man she'd ever met. Whatever particular brand of magic he possessed, it had been powerful enough to make Kitty behave in a way she hadn't thought herself capable of. He had taken her virginity with one hard, sweet thrust and it had felt so right. Like the only possible outcome to the most amazing evening of her life. Like it was meant to be.

And then.

It was hard to believe what he had implied with his arrogant question about whether she had given her virginity to him just because he was rich. And although she tried to tell herself that there could be perfectly good reasons for his cynicism—maybe women *were* all over him because he was mega-wealthy—that didn't stop his callous remarks from hurting. Had she stupidly imagined that a special bond had existed between them? Guilty. Maybe that had been her way of justifying such uncharacteristic behaviour and stopping her from facing up to the truth.

That she had been a fool.

Kitty stared up at the cheap lightshade above her narrow bed, knowing she couldn't keep beating herself up about it, because everyone was allowed to be a fool at least once in their life.

Weren't they?

She wouldn't ever see him again. In time, she would learn to focus on something different whenever he popped into her head—and she found that thought very consoling. She would learn from the experience and never repeat it. She would go back to being the Kitty

she'd been before. The tomboy who preferred sport to
the quagmire of human emotions because life felt safer
that way. Or, when her heart had properly recovered,
she would choose the kind of man who wasn't totally
out of her reach. Some sensible office worker, perhaps.
Someone she might have something in common with.

But then the second bombshell came out of nowhere—so hard and so fast that it almost felled her.

At first she could hardly believe it. She didn't think
fate could be so cruel. That one momentary lapse of
judgement could have such far-reaching consequences.
Which was why she did first one test, and then another,
and stared at the blue line which trembled because her
hand was shaking so much.

She was pregnant.

At once, everything changed. The smell of beer in
the pub made her feel sick. She told herself it was psy-
chological but that didn't seem to make any difference.
She told herself a lot of things. She thought about her
own mother. Her birth mother. About the way she'd
dumped Kitty unceremoniously outside a priest's house
one cold autumn night nearly twenty-four years ago. She
must have been pretty frightened to have done a thing
like that. And didn't Kitty now find herself in a similar situation? Alone and scared with a growing baby
beneath her breast. She swallowed. It wasn't quite so
easy to pass judgement now, was it?

So what was she going to do?

Her choices were limited—but when you lived from
hand to mouth, your choices were always limited. She
had a job, yes, but her tenure at The Merry Ploughman
was only temporary. She hadn't told them she was pregnant because she hadn't known and soon she would start
to show. And then what? She had no relatives she could

turn to for help, and Ellen Murphy and Father O'Brady were long gone. She would be out on the street, desperate and afraid. Afraid for herself, but even more afraid for the innocent little baby inside her.

A silent sob ripped through her until she forced herself to remember that she wasn't the only person who was responsible for this tiny life. Santiago Tevez was the father, wasn't he? Despite the finality of his words, would he really want to see the mother of his child destitute?

Sitting in front of her computer in her room at the top of the pub, Kitty thought about the things he had said to her. The words which had stuck in her mind like a fly landing in a sticky jar of ointment.

I don't have any children and I don't intend to have any.

She thought about the way his face had darkened as he'd said it—as if something unspeakable had crawled across his mind. He hadn't made any pretence about his feelings. On Bali, he'd made it clear that he didn't want to see her again and that had come as no real surprise, because she'd known from the start that they were very different. Which made the situation even more complicated than it already was.

Everyone said it was a man's right to know if he was going to be a father and in theory Kitty agreed with them. But in practice it wasn't always that easy. She knew she wasn't like other women. She'd had birth parents *and* adoptive parents and had no illusions about either. What right did she have to foist her baby on a man if he most emphatically didn't want that child?

Remember what happened to you. What you cannot risk happening to your own baby.

Yet her conscience was nagging her to at least give

Santiago Tevez a chance. She couldn't possibly judge his suitability to be a father when she didn't really know him, could she? So maybe she should set about trying to amend that. Even if he subsequently told her he wasn't interested in their baby—wouldn't she have done the right thing by her unborn child?

And Santiago had the resources to help her.

Her fingers splayed out over her flat belly. How else was she going to manage?

Without giving herself time to change her mind, she sat up in bed and grabbed her phone. One o'clock in the morning here, which meant it would be eight a.m. in Bali. Too early to call him? No. He struck her as a man who was driven, who would probably already be at work. Or someplace else. Her finger hovered over the buttons. What if Santiago was lying on that same terrace with a different woman tangled in his arms? Kitty flinched as a sharp spear of jealousy shot through her. But she couldn't afford to think that way. This wasn't about possession or attachment, or yearning for the impossible. It was about trying to discover what kind of man he really was.

And whether or not she told him he was going to be a father.

'I have a woman on the line who'd like to speak to you, Señor Tevez. She says it's a...personal matter.'

Santiago's eyes narrowed as he heard the subtle inflection in his assistant's voice—the implication being that anyone who wanted to speak to him on a personal matter would have his private number. Which was true. 'Did she give her name?'

'She did. It's Kitty. Kitty O'Hanlon.'

Santiago's body tensed, the muscles of his arms

bunching and his groin hardening and there didn't seem to be a damned thing he could do to curtail it. He allowed himself a moment of erotic recall as he remembered the redhead with the tight, curvy body. The fiery beauty with whom he had spent a deliciously blissful night, despite the reservations which had whispered over his skin when he had discovered just how innocent she'd been.

For the first few days after she'd left, he hadn't been able to get her out of his mind and that had rankled. Because she was wrong for him, on so many counts.

She was unsophisticated.

Naïve.

She worked as a nanny in a country many miles away from his main base on Bali. She had been a *virgin*, for heaven's sake, and hadn't bothered to tell him, and that had left him feeling as if she had robbed him of something. Of choice, yes—but more than that. She had taken away the control which was vital to him.

It had been a single night of passion—understandable, but unwise. A powerful physicality which had ignited between two people one moonlit Bali evening—fuelled by his punishing work schedule and a self-imposed period of celibacy. He had acted impulsively. Some might say recklessly. And yet he had been helpless to do otherwise. At moments he had felt as if power were slipping away from him and that wasn't a feeling he liked, or intended to repeat. She had been refreshingly different, yes, but aspects of her personality had disturbed as much as captivated him. With a ruthlessness which was his trademark, Santiago had wiped her from his thoughts, putting her firmly in the past, which he made a point of never revisiting.

But now she had rung him. Despite his words of

warning, she had joined that legion of women who were reluctant to let him go. He gave a bitter smile. When would they ever learn that he was not for reform, nor for changing? That chasing him down or attempting to stalk him would have the opposite effect to the one they wanted.

He thought about having his assistant inform her he was busy, which was feasible. It might hammer home the message that he really didn't want to see her again. But it might not. And wouldn't it be tiresome if she persisted in ringing his office, as had happened so often in the past? Better to crush her hopes now and draw a line under their brief liaison—it would save her heartache in the long run.

'Put her through,' he said abruptly, waiting for the click of the long-distance connection. He sensed Kitty's presence on the other end of the line and he didn't say a word, for he knew the power of silence, but it continued for so long that he was forced to speak. 'Kitty,' he said, in as forbidding a tone as was possible without actually straying into the territory of rudeness. 'This is a surprise.'

'I know it is. I... I hope I didn't disturb you.'

'If that were the case, then we wouldn't be having this conversation,' he answered smoothly. 'But I really don't have a lot of time at my disposal, so...?'

'Of course.' He thought he heard a faint wobble in her voice but quickly hardened his heart against that trace of vulnerability. He was no good for someone like her, he reminded himself grimly. He'd spoken the truth when he'd told her she was better off without him. So he said nothing, just stared out at the azure glitter of the ocean outside his office window and the palm trees which waved their frond-like foliage in the gentle breeze.

'I wanted to tell you that I got the sack.'

His body tensed as he turned away from the scenic view outside, his attention caught by the glitter of the environmental awards which littered his vast desk. 'Why?'

'Because they caught me creeping into the villa at daybreak, after I'd been with you.'

'So? It was your evening off, wasn't it?'

'Even if it was—' her voice grew tight '—it was pretty obvious what…what I'd been doing.'

'I'm not sure I understand, Kitty.' His sigh was slightly impatient because he had somehow imagined her to have a little more resilience than this. 'Did you sign a no-sex or morality clause when you took the job?'

'There's no need to be flippant, Santiago.'

'I'm not. I'm being deadly serious. It doesn't seem fair to fire someone for behaving in a perfectly natural way. You might even have a legitimate case for unfair dismissal. I could have one of my lawyers look into it, if you like.'

'That isn't why I'm ringing you,' she said. 'For *legal* advice.'

Was that determination or desperation he could hear in her voice—and why was his instinct to run as fast as possible in the opposite direction? Because she was expressing *emotion*, that was why. And for him, emotion was just another word for manipulation.

'Then why are you ringing me?'

Another pause. Longer this time. 'Because I'd like you to give me a job. In the crèche at the Langit Biru. Since you happen to own the resort, that shouldn't be a problem.' Her words were coming out in a rush now, as if she were reading them from a rapidly disappearing autocue. 'And I'm a good nanny, Santiago—no matter what Camilla and Rupert might say about me, I am.'

'But why here?' he demanded suspiciously, although he had a very good idea. 'What on earth makes you want to come here?'

'Let's think about that for a minute,' she said, injecting a jokey note into her voice which sounded forced. 'A crèche in beautiful Bali beside the sea—or pulling pints in a noisy London pub? Hmm. Tough call.'

Santiago *was* thinking about it, but, more than that, he was thinking about her. Her hot, tight heat. The soft pliancy of her flesh as it had moulded itself into his. The way her eyes had gleamed with wonder in the moonlight as he had made that first sweet thrust, and then his subsequent discovery of her innocence. It had been mind-blowing sex, despite her inexperience. Or maybe because of it, he thought grimly. His groin was growing deliciously hard as his taunting mind spooled out a series of erotic images and he forced himself to shut them down.

'If you're hoping to pick up where we left off,' he said coolly, 'then I'm afraid you're going to be disappointed, because that isn't on the cards. So if that's your reason for wanting to come here, then the answer would have to be no.'

He heard her shocked intake of breath.

'I can't believe you said that,' she breathed. 'That's so arrogant.'

'I'm being honest with you. Would you prefer me to lie?'

'Do you think I'm some kind of desperado, some kind of *stalker*?'

'I have no idea who you are, Kitty,' he said. 'I don't really know you at all, do I?'

'No,' she answered quietly. 'No, you don't. Nor I you.'

He waited for her to tell him she'd changed her mind, that her request had been nothing but an impetuous whim, but when she didn't—something prompted him to fill the silence again. Was it the nudge of his conscience? The voice of guilt which could never properly be quietened? 'But if you genuinely want a temporary job while you recalibrate your future, then yes, I can speak to someone.'

The pause which followed went on for so long he wasn't sure whether she'd heard him.

'If you wouldn't mind,' she said at last, in a clipped tone which reminded him of a robot. 'I would like that very much.'

'I assume you have references from other jobs?'

'Of course.'

'Then send them over and we'll take a look. If they're okay, then we'll be in touch. But if we decide to take you on, it can be for no longer than a couple of months—to cover a busy period in the hotel. Is that understood?'

'Perfectly,' she shot back coolly. 'And if it's all the same to you, I'd prefer to start sooner rather than later.'

He was about to point out that it wasn't in her remit to set out a timetable, but she cut the call before he could say anything else.

Santiago frowned as the line went dead, because nobody ever hung up on him. Every instinct he possessed was screaming out that this was a mistake and he wondered if his offer was some crude attempt to pacify her. To make amends for having taken her virginity, which had unwittingly got her the sack. He'd warned her not to expect anything else from him and maybe that was enough to give her second thoughts. It might prompt her to change her mind.

He scowled.

Because wouldn't that be the best thing all round?

CHAPTER FIVE

KITTY STARED OUT of the window as the plane began its descent, her heart giving a twist of excitement at the sight which greeted her, despite her almost constant state of worry. For a moment she forgot the bone-deep tiredness which had been seeping into her body for days, because down there was Bali. Beautiful Bali. Studded into the bright blue waters of the Indian Ocean and glittering like a pristine jewel. Even from this height she could make out the creamy gold of the beaches and dark green blur of tropical forests. Inevitably, she started thinking about her last trip to the paradise island. The demanding hours and equally demanding employers. Maybe this time she might be able to snatch some of the rest she so badly needed.

But rest and recuperation weren't the reason why she was here, were they?

Unobtrusively, her fingers fluttered down to lie protectively over her belly.

She needed to get to know the hard-faced Argentinian whose baby's heart was beating inside her.

It had been a long and cramped flight, in economy. An airline ticket had been emailed several hours after her late-night telephone conversation with Santiago, and she had been granted a temporary work visa. For sixteen hours she had been stuck beside a woman sitting in the aisle seat—who had snored for the entire flight—making it difficult for Kitty to negotiate her way to the restroom. It hadn't been the ideal start to a trip she was dreading in so many ways.

Blinking against the bright sunshine, she emerged from the aircraft into the scented air, but it was difficult to concentrate on the natural beauty which surrounded her when Santiago's words were still stabbing into her memory and leaving indelible marks behind.

'If you're hoping to pick up where we left off...that isn't on the cards.'

It had been a brutal rejection, no doubt intended to deter her from coming here. And she wouldn't *be* here if it weren't essential. Kitty pushed back a strand of hair which had fallen down from her hair clip and reverted to its usual frizz. What if Santiago refused to have anything to do with her, as he was perfectly entitled to do? He was the billionaire owner of the resort—which meant he was hardly going to be hands-on at the crèche, was he? He wouldn't have to go within a mile of her if he didn't want to.

What then?

Could she really walk up to a man who was essentially a stranger and announce he was going to be a father?

No. That was something she was never going to do. She knew how ruthless and cruel men could be if they were presented with an unwanted child. Her fingers tightened around the handle of her bag. She knew all about rejection and abandonment—and that was never going to happen to her baby.

Her eyes scanned the faces of the people waiting to greet the plane. Santiago was nowhere to be seen and silently she chided herself for her own stupidity. Of course he wasn't here. Did she think he'd be standing there with a bouquet of exotic Balinese blooms and an eager smile on his face? She was just a nobody who had foisted herself on him. There was no reason for him to provide luxury transport. Not this time. The limousine trip had obviously just been the pay-off for sleeping with him.

Instead, she was directed to a staff minibus bound for the Langit Biru, which was driven by a cheerful young Australian, with colourful braids in her hair. She looked up as Kitty scanned the bus for the nearest available seat and gave her a friendly smile.

'Hi, I'm Emily, your driver, and I'm guessing that since I only have one woman passenger today—you must be Kitty, right?'

'That's right,' said Kitty, wiping her hand over her clammy brow.

'Come and sit up beside me. The air-con's much better in this part of the bus,' said Emily, patting the passenger seat at the front of the bus, and Kitty slid in beside her. She felt hot and tired and thirsty. And nervous. Very, very nervous.

'You English?' said Emily as the minibus drew away.

The true explanation always sparked a lot of unwanted questions, which inevitably took the conversation in a direction Kitty never wanted to go, so she just nodded. Telling someone you were dumped on someone's doorstep as a newborn and you had no idea of your true parentage was always a bit of a downer. 'I'm from England,' she said.

'First time in Bali?'

'I was here a few weeks ago actually. I was working as a nanny and staying nearby.' Kitty had rehearsed this very breezy response on the flight over and thought it sounded convincing enough. 'But then my job in England finished and I got the chance to take a temporary job at the crèche.'

Time to change the subject. To deflect attention away from yourself and find out everything you can about the reason why you're here.

She turned to look at the driver. 'Is it a good place to work?'

Emily brought the minibus to a halt behind a truck of watermelons which had suddenly stopped. 'It's the bomb,' she said, with a sigh of pleasure. 'Paradise location. Great beaches. Plenty of nightlife. What's not to like?'

Kitty nodded, wondering how a private investigator might go about filleting out more information. 'I've heard that the Langit Biru is one of the most expensive places to stay on the entire island.'

'You could say that. But it's also the most eco-friendly, so it's good for the planet,' said Emily cheerfully, as the watermelon truck started moving again and they drove off. 'And the brilliant brainchild of one Santiago Tevez.'

Just the mention of his name made Kitty feel peculiar. Annoying ripples of something which felt like desire had started skating down her spine and her heart was pounding so loudly she was surprised Emily hadn't asked her to turn the volume down.

Jet-dark eyes and hard, autocratic features swam into her memory and she tried to shut the door on them. *This isn't why you're here,* she told herself furiously. *You're not in the market for a romantic repeat.* And then she almost laughed out loud.

Romantic? Surely she wasn't associating what she'd had with Santiago as anything resembling *romance*?

She was going to have to pretend she didn't know him, because what choice did she have? Not unless she wanted her new colleagues to know she'd had casual sex with her new boss. They had left the bar separately and nobody had seen them together when she'd hid in the darkened corridor to text her friends. Even when the waitress had brought their cocktails up to the terrace, she was certain the moonlight hadn't been bright enough for her to make out Kitty's face with any degree of clarity. And besides, maybe she was just one of many different women he entertained like that every night of the week. She clenched her fingers into tight fists, wondering why that should bother her so much.

'Santiago Tevez,' she repeated airily, as if it were the first time she'd ever heard the name. 'He's the boss, right?'

'Mmm. And then some. Billionaire entrepreneur and the hottest man on the island. Some say the southern hemisphere.' Emily tooted the horn. 'I might even go so far as to say the world.'

'Really?'

'Really. Argentinian by birth. Brains to burn. Ex-submariner. Six foot two and built like a male centre-fold.'

'Wow.' Kitty could feel the sudden lump in her throat, knowing that the only way to find out about a man's love-life was to ask the obvious question, even if she knew it to be untrue. 'And does he have a steady girlfriend?'

'Nope. He's so cool, he's icy. They say he breaks hearts as often as the breakfast chef at the Buru breaks eggs for omelettes.' Emily shot her an amused look. 'But he definitely doesn't fraternise with the staff. Believe me, enough of us have tried!'

It was undoubtedly a warning, though a kindly one and Kitty nodded, pushing a strand of untidy hair away from her cheek. She knew how important first impressions were and the last thing she wanted was to come over as some man-hungry female who was hunting down the most eligible man on the island. She stifled the yawn which reminded her she'd been awake for over twenty-four hours. 'I'm not looking for a relationship,' she said truthfully.

'Wise woman. You look like you could use some sleep though,' said Emily, shooting her a side glance. 'Listen, I'll drop you and your luggage off at your room. Key's in the door. Then head straight over to the crèche to get yourself acclimatised. It's a drag when you're tired, but better to get it over with.'

Kitty nodded. It would have been preferable to have had a little respite before meeting her new colleagues, but the most important thing was to make a good impression. Because she wanted them to like her. It was vital that they did. She needed to work hard and keep her head down, and that way nobody would question why she was really there.

She thanked Emily and walked up the gravelled path before pushing open the door to her room. It wasn't big. In fact, it was tiny. Bare walls. Small bed. A couple of framed photos of Bali. The en suite bathroom was little more than a cupboard, and as Kitty washed away the accumulated grime of almost twenty-four hours' travel she contrasted this and the only other part of the resort she knew in any detail. Annoyingly, the memory of that shared shower with Santiago invaded her thoughts, their eager limbs entwined as their slippery flesh met and melded. Despairingly, she closed her eyes and as her eyelids fluttered open again the mirror above the sink told its own damning story.

The sight which stared back at her made her flinch, because she looked awful. Washed out and forlorn. If only there were time to wash her hair and take a nap, before she met the people she was going to be working with...

Briefly, she wondered how long she would be working there but she wouldn't let herself go there. She needed to keep it in the moment, or she would drive herself crazy. So she let herself out of the room and tried to concentrate on the lush green foliage which lined the footpath as she followed a signpost pointing towards the crèche.

The crèche was colourful, bright and airy, with assorted sections designated to differing age groups. Drawing and stories for the older ones. A shaded sandpit next to a small pool, with an old-fashioned picket fence around it. There was a room full of sleep mats and a separate room where musical instruments could be played.

The children were playing happily and Kitty was introduced to three members of staff who were on duty—Dewi, Mawar, and Amisha, who was in charge. Friendly women who looked super-smart in their primrose-yellow dresses and shiny name badges.

'You can start first thing tomorrow. Eight a.m., bright and sharp,' said Amisha with a smile as she handed over a pile of folded uniforms. 'Go over there and choose a pair of matching clogs.'

It was good to have something to think about other than Santiago, less so when Kitty realised how badly the colour was going to clash with her hair. *It doesn't matter,* she told herself fervently. It wasn't the externals which counted. That wasn't the reason she was here.

Maybe if she hadn't been so preoccupied, she might have been paying attention to where she was going—rather than just eagerly trying to get back to her room before she melted in a heap of fatigue. It wasn't until she had almost run straight into the man she hadn't seen on the path in front of her that she realised who was standing there.

Santiago Tevez.

The arrogant Argentinian who didn't want her here.

Over the past few weeks she'd barely thought about him, she'd been too busy fretting about her pregnancy and wondering when she would start to show. The few times his mocking face had made an unannounced visit into her mind, she had quickly pushed the image away again. Which meant she was ill prepared for the reality of seeing him again in the flesh.

Kitty blinked.

Had she really spent a whole night having passionate sex with this man? Looking at him now, she found it hard to believe.

Quiet power radiated from his packed frame. Sunlight was bouncing off the ebony thickness of his hair and gilding his glowing flesh. She could feel the clench of her gut and fierce beat of her heart. A rush of awareness flooded through her and her knees felt shaky. The first time she'd met him he'd had a similar effect on her. But that had been like a chemical reaction. An instinctive response to a handsome stranger in a bar. A weird blip which had felt completely alien. It had been strongly and intensely physical and that was all. As if her body had been programmed to come alive when those dark eyes had raked over her.

But now.

Now something had changed. She was painfully aware that this was no longer just about her staring at the powerful alpha male who had been her first and only lover.

Now she was looking at the father of her unborn child.

And he still didn't know a thing about it.

She could feel the brief ice of terror, because even though she didn't yet show there was still a part of her which was scared he might somehow notice something different about her, and guess.

'Hello, Santiago,' she said steadily.

'Hello, Kitty.'

She was trying to sound normal—but what on earth was normal in a situation like this? All she knew was that she was on a mission and the last thing she could allow to happen was for him to walk away. She needed to *engage* with him. To get him onside and start to discover the sort of man he really was. So, instead of scuttling back to her room to sleep off her fatigue, she fixed him with a smile. 'Did you come looking for me?'

A flicker of irritation crossed his sculpted features. 'I was aware that the newest influx of staff had just arrived from the airport and since your employment wasn't done through the usual, shall we say, *conventional* channels—I thought it advisable to check you were settling in.' He shot a brief glance at the pile of uniforms she was carrying. 'Which I can see you are.'

She thought that was a very long-winded way of admitting that, yes, he *had* come looking for her, but she told herself to dampen down the meaningless spark of excitement which had flared up inside her. She looked at him. 'Yes, I am. Everyone has been very welcoming.' She sighed and then pulled a face as she allowed reality to sink in. 'Look, how is this going to work?'

His dark brows narrowed as if she had set him an unsolvable problem. 'I'm not sure I understand your question. You provide excellent care for the children in the crèche, and get paid top dollar for doing so.'

That wasn't what she had meant, and she was sure he knew it, but Kitty didn't allow her smile to slip. 'Okay. Thanks for pointing that out. What I wanted to know is whether I'm supposed to call you Mr Tevez when I see you around?'

Santiago didn't respond to her question—at least, not immediately. He was too busy getting his head around the fact that Kitty O'Hanlon was on the island and he didn't want her to be. At least that was what his head was telling him, though the heat of his blood was sending out an entirely different message to his body. And why else had his footsteps brought him here? No matter what cool self-justification he might have used, bottom line was that he'd wanted to see her again—with an urgency which had taken him by surprise.

At night she had been invading his dreams, like a fever. Making him wake with an unbearable hardness aching at his groin. He swallowed. Had he been hoping that a second meeting might magically puncture his desire for her? Leaving him wondering what had possessed him to behave in such an irrational way? Because if so, his strategy had failed. Once again this was nothing to do with logic, or reason. This was all about a sweet and powerful lust which was pulsing through him as his senses silently acknowledged her proximity.

Yet she looked terrible.

The brightness and beauty of the Balinese flora only emphasised her waxy pallor and there were dark shadows beneath her eyes, as if sleep had been at a premium of late. Even her hair looked different. The sleek fall of red waves had been replaced by a hair clip from which strands were busy escaping—the frizzy red coils making her appear as if she'd spent the morning in a steam room. And surely she had lost weight.

His eyes narrowed. Had she been pining for him, as women so often did? He felt the fierce punch of regret. Why the hell had he let her come here—wouldn't his rash agreement to give her a job only make it harder for her to get over him?

Well, he had done the decent thing and thrown her a lifeline, but from here on in he owed her nothing.

Nothing.

'It's unlikely our paths ever *will* cross,' he informed her coolly. 'But if they should, it would be ridiculous for you to call me anything other than Santiago.'

She readjusted the pile of yellow uniform dresses she was carrying, on top of which was balanced an ugly pair of clogs. 'You don't think people might find it odd?'

'Odd?'

'For me to be so…' she wriggled her shoulders and he was made uncomfortably aware of the distracting sway of her breasts '…familiar. You know. Newest member of staff on first-name terms with the big boss.'

'You'll find that things are very relaxed here on Bali.' He paused. 'But obviously it won't work in your favour if you start mentioning that you know me. Even worse if you start dropping hints and boasting about having had sex with me. In fact, I would rather you didn't refer to our night together.'

She was staring at him, as if she couldn't quite believe what she'd heard. 'Do you really think I'd stoop that low?'

He shrugged. 'I'm simply trying to protect your reputation.'

'Or your own, maybe?'

He saw the sudden colour which splashed her pale cheeks and as her lips tightened it reminded him of the passion she'd shown in his arms. And suddenly he wanted to change that expression. To melt away the anger and replace it with something else. To see her lips soften and flower as they opened beneath the urgent seeking of his kiss.

He unflexed his fingers, aware that he was unbearably tense. No doubt she considered him cold and arrogant—which he was—but surely it was better she thought of him that way, rather than weaving useless fantasies about him. Just as it was important to draw a line in the sand. To stress that what had happened had been fuelled by nothing but an impetuous lust, which was best forgotten.

Because Santiago suddenly recognised that Kitty's innocence had inevitably spilled over into other areas of her life. She obviously didn't know how to deal with the fallout from a casual hook-up like theirs. She was a stranger to the subtle, often cruel games which lovers and ex-lovers played with each other. And maybe it was better she stayed that way. If she preserved as much of her wholesome purity as possible, despite the fact that she was no longer a virgin.

The kindest thing he could do for her would be to stay away, no matter how much he craved to touch her again.

'So, how was your flight?' he questioned formally.

'Fine,' she said crisply. 'If a little cramped.'

'Oh, dear.' He raised his eyebrows. 'Were you hoping I'd send my private jet to bring you out here in style?'

'Since you've asked, no, I didn't. I've learnt it's better never to have any expectations in life.'

She met his gaze with a look which somehow made him feel uncomfortable and Santiago found himself resenting her for that, too. He didn't want to feel *anything*. Because feelings brought pain and hurt and hardship. He glanced down at his watch, trying to ignore the pulse which was firing at his temple like a canon. Trying to ignore the memory of thrusting into her wet tightness and the low shuddering moan she made when she came.

'I need to be somewhere else,' he said, with a pointed glance at his watch. 'Good to see you again, Kitty. Enjoy your stay on Bali.'

CHAPTER SIX

ENJOY YOUR STAY on Bali.

Santiago's mocking words echoed in Kitty's ears as she slammed the door on the blue-sky day and glanced around at the poky dimensions of her staff accommodation. She hung up her new yellow uniforms, pushed her clogs to the back of the wardrobe and sat down on the edge of the narrow bed.

But her heart was racing because, despite her airy reassurances about having no expectations, hadn't she been hoping for something a little more memorable than Santiago's cool greeting followed by an undeniably dismissive farewell?

Of course she had.

She had prepared herself for the worst but longed for something better. For her baby's sake, if not her own. But the Argentinian had failed to deliver anything other than a grudgingly offered job. He didn't want her here. Why would he? She hadn't missed the look of disbelief which had shadowed his autocratic features when he'd seen her. As if he didn't recognise her. He probably didn't. But this *was* her. The real Kitty. The pared-down practical version in jeans and T-shirt and frizzy curls—not the woman in the flowery dress with the carefully blow-dried hair, who had been dazzled by moonlight and the touch of a man's lips. That had been the best version of herself and he hadn't wanted her then...so why would he want her now?

The question was what to do next.

Or rather, questions.

They buzzed around Kitty's head like a swarm of angry wasps.

If she were him, would she rather know about the baby?

But she *wasn't* him. All she could remember was his emphatic statement that he didn't *want* children. And surely that was the whole point. Why attempt to foist the role of fatherhood on him, if he then callously rejected it? Because Kitty knew better than anyone how that kind of rejection could hurt. How it left a scar which never really healed. And if the voice of her conscience was demanding to know what right she had to sit in judgement of him, then the cruel memory of her own experience was enough to silence it.

Instead, she settled into her new regime and tried to count her blessings.

She had a room which, although small, was ridiculously easy to keep tidy.

She had regular and delicious meals—even if she only managed to pick at them because she felt nauseous for much of the time.

She was working in one of the most beautiful places in the world and the crèche was everything it should be—the staff open and friendly, the children well cared for and happy.

Children.

Sometimes she felt breathless with the enormity of what lay ahead and weighed down by the secret she carried. Apart from her doctor back in England, she had told nobody—mainly because it seemed wrong to confide in other people if Santiago didn't know. Maybe she was half afraid people wouldn't believe her if she let slip that the nobody who was Kitty O'Hanlon was carrying the baby of a powerful billionaire.

And after a few days of working at the exclusive resort, she realised that Santiago had been true to his word. Their paths didn't cross. Not once. Their worlds didn't collide. Why would they? He was the resort owner and she was just one of the many people who worked there. A tiny cog in an enormous wheel. And— she forced herself to face up to something she would rather have ignored—there was the very real possibility that he was going out of his way to avoid her.

And if he was?

She licked her lips.

How long did she give it before she attempted to break this stalemate? Days? Weeks? No, not weeks. This *had* to be resolved before she started to show.

It proved a useful distraction to study the glossy book on pregnancy she'd brought with her, which helped fill the time when she wasn't working or drawing pictures in her sketch pad. The book emphasised the importance of nutrition and exercise and, although she was still finding it difficult to keep much food down, she took the exercise part seriously.

Each day before work, as dawn was breaking over the island, she would put on her swimsuit and marvel at a sky splashed with gold and purple and pink—as if nature were intent on providing her with her own private firework display. Taking herself down to the nearby beach—which was always deserted—she would pad over the soft sand towards the aquamarine waters, before striking out in a steady crawl, following the line of the shore. The rhythmic movement soothed her. It made her feel strong. It made her forget her worries— if only for a while.

It was on her sixth morning at the Langit Biru, with the prospect of her first day off yawning in front of her—that Kitty lifted her head from the water to realise that the beach was no longer deserted. A man was standing watching her and, even from this distance, his powerful physique was instantly recognisable.

He stood very still. Like a rock. Or maybe a statue. Dark and golden, muscular and strong. His thick black hair was ruffled by the breeze and he was standing beside the towelling swim poncho she'd lain out on the creamy sand. She felt the dual leap of excitement and panic—an overwhelming longing to see Santiago again, but also a sinking dread. The heavy weight of her secret was coupled with the knowledge that she meant nothing to him and there was unlikely to be a happy ending to their story.

But this was her opportunity and she couldn't afford to blow it, not if she wanted to stand any chance of getting to know him better. So she waded out of the shallow water and bit back all the predictable things which were hovering on her lips. She didn't ask what he was doing there, or what he wanted. She concentrated on being as agreeable as possible—which wasn't too difficult. Not when his hard body was clothed in a pair of faded jeans which hugged his long legs like syrup, and a close-fitting black T-shirt clung to every pore of his rippled torso.

She walked towards him, trying not to be self-conscious about the fact that he was fully dressed while she was wearing a sodden one-piece and that beneath it she was naked. She could feel her nipples stinging with awareness, as if remembering that here was the man who had given them so much pleasure.

'You're up early,' she observed, her breath catching in her throat as she drew closer.

'So are you.'

'I like to swim before I start at the crèche,' she said, trying not to babble. 'It's one of the advantages of working in a place like this—having a world-class beach practically on my doorstep.'

His black gaze razored through her and Kitty could feel herself shivering, even though the rising sun was warm against her skin.

'But you're not working today, are you?' he probed silkily.

Hurriedly, she bent down to retrieve her towelling robe—mostly to hide the stupid expression of pleasure she was certain must be plastered all over her face. 'How do you know that?'

He gave a shrug. 'All staff rotas are available at the click of a computer button.'

In spite of everything, Kitty felt the irresistible twitch of her lips as she registered his dry observation. 'And you're familiar with the working patterns of everyone on your payroll, are you, Mr Tevez?'

'No. Just yours.'

She forced herself not to look away. To meet the black eyes which glittered with something tantalising and unspoken. Was it that which made her pull on her poncho and wrap it tightly around her—afraid he would notice the tightening of her aching nipples? 'Why?'

There was a pause. A pause long enough for Kitty to acknowledge the sizzle of awareness which was thrumming between them.

'You know why,' he said softly.

She sucked in a breath. He'd done this to her once before. Acted as if they shared some kind of verbal shorthand—a private language which ruled out the need for explanation. But that was misleading because it made her start imagining that what they had was special, and it wasn't. It was just chemistry. And she wasn't going to play that game. Not for a second time. She wasn't going to fall into his arms and have sex with him just because he wanted to. Even though *she* wanted to.

'I'm afraid I don't.' She looked at him questioningly, the silence between them growing, forcing him to speak at last—though with a look of something which was either admiration or frustration glittering in the depths of his eyes, as if they had just fought a silent battle and she had emerged the unlikely victor.

He shrugged his shoulders with a jerk which seemed almost angry. 'Because I can't get you out of my mind.'

'You don't sound very happy about it.'

'I'm not. You're not my type.'

'And you are definitely not mine.'

'You were a virgin, *roja*,' he observed wryly. 'Clearly you don't *have* a type.'

His use of the nickname he'd coined for her pleased her more than it should have done, but Kitty tried not to read too much into that either. He was very good at *replicating* intimacy, she realised, but it had no real substance. It was just banter. It was the kind of thing, presumably, which men said to women they'd had sex with. 'Are you criticising me for my inexperience?'

'On the contrary.' His gaze skated over her. 'I suspect your innocence is responsible for much of your allure.'

'That doesn't sound very flattering.'

'I'm being honest with you, Kitty. I am always honest with women—I find it saves on misunderstandings. The question is where we go from here.'

'Well, I'm going back to my room to change and then I'm catching an island bus to see some of the sights of Bali.'

He looked surprised—as if he'd been anticipating a different response. Had he? Perhaps women usually flung themselves at him without very much provocation. Hadn't she done just that herself?

'Or I could show you around the island myself,' he suggested slowly, as if the thought had only just occurred to him.

Kitty hesitated because, annoyingly, his words reminded her of the ridiculous fantasy she'd woven before discovering she was carrying his baby. Of Santiago realising what a big mistake he'd made and flying over to England to ask her out on a date, before deciding he couldn't live without her. She shook her wet hair and little droplets of seawater flew in all directions. What kind of desperado dreamed up scenarios like that?

Her.

Foolish, inexperienced Kitty O'Hanlon.

If she hadn't been pregnant, she wondered if she would've had the strength to turn him down, on the grounds that she was probably going to get her heart broken. But she *was* pregnant—and that influenced the answer she suspected was inevitable. She had to get to know him well enough to know if she should tell him about the baby. She wanted to know if he was fundamentally a good man. An honourable man. A kind man.

And if he wasn't?

A trickle of foreboding whispered down her spine. She would just have to work that out later. 'Okay,' she agreed carelessly. 'But I'll need to shower and wash my hair first.'

She noticed the pulse working furiously at his temple and the obvious tension in his body. Did that mean he still wanted her? But that wasn't why she was spending the day with him, and at some point during the day she might have to make that clear. She wondered how you communicated to a man that you weren't going to have sex with him, when every pore in your body was screaming its desire? And how did you go about telling him something else he definitely wouldn't want to hear?

'I have some phone calls I need to make first,' he growled. 'I'll meet you at the front entrance at ten-thirty. Wear some sensible footwear.'

And with that he turned and walked away, his bare-footed stride leaving prints in the sand as he created an ever-growing distance between them, so that soon Santiago Tevez was nothing but a dark and indelible shape on the horizon.

Santiago sat in his stationary car, drumming impatient fingers against the steering wheel and glancing at his watch with irritation, even though she wasn't late. Of course she wasn't late. *He* was early—and that was a first. Since when had he turned up for a date with this much time to spare? Two valets and the head of HR had already stopped beside his convertible, asking if there was anything he wanted, or needed.

Yes, to the first of those questions. He badly wanted to have sex with Kitty O'Hanlon again, but he wasn't sure if that desire was powerful enough to morph into *need*.

No. Of course it wasn't. He forced himself to focus—not on the curvy redhead who was doing dangerous things to his pulse-rate, but on the maxim by which he had lived his adult life.

He didn't *do* need.

The drumming stopped as instead his fingers dug into the leather steering wheel, as if they were biting into flesh.

Need made men weak.

Weak and pathetic and, ultimately, losers.

Like his father.

Briefly he closed his eyes, willing away the image of the man who had reared him for much of his life, but sometimes those shadows were just too stubborn to shift and they lingered in the corners of his mind like a stain he couldn't quite remove. Just like the memories of his childhood, and his mother's terrible deception.

In many ways, the brightness of Bali had helped eradicate much of the darkness which had lingered in his soul for so long. It was one of the reasons he had chosen to spend so much time here—as well as the fact that nobody had known him. At least, not from before, from the supposedly privileged existence he'd led amid the upper echelons of Buenos Aires society. People here wouldn't have recognised the Santiago Tevez he had once been. The rich boy who had joined the Argentinian navy and then excelled in every aspect of it. The man who learnt to hide his pain behind achievement.

But at this precise moment he wasn't quite sure *who* he was. He hadn't flown to Australia this morning as planned, to liaise on the giant solar farm he was building, and—although it pained him to admit it—he knew exactly why. A strange new restlessness had infiltrated his blood and it was all down to Kitty O'Hanlon. To knowing she was here. Close. Close enough to touch. And, oh, how he wanted to touch her. He wanted to stroke his hungry fingers over her firm flesh. To feel himself deep inside her again.

He'd tried to reason himself out of the wild trajectory of his thoughts. He told himself it was simply a physical itch which needed scratching. So why not flick through his address book and find someone eager for a no-strings hook-up, rather than a wide-eyed innocent who made him feel stuff? He could have enjoyed a mutually satisfying interlude, which might have morphed into a long weekend. Flown his plane or sailed his yacht to Kangaroo Island and booked a suite at his favourite hotel. Taken advantage of a vast bed overlooking the crashing sea while revisiting old pleasures with one of his many ex-lovers. But as he'd scrolled through the numbers none of the supermodels, lawyers or cattle-ranch heiresses had tempted him. He scowled. He couldn't seem to shake off the memory of Kitty and the best sex of his life.

When he'd given her a job here—a job *she* had asked for—he had feared she might prove to be something of a nuisance. He had sensed her disappointment when he'd warned their paths were unlikely to cross and had waited for the inevitable 'chance' meeting, or the sight of her mooning around the place, hoping to bump into him.

But that hadn't happened. She hadn't featured anywhere on his radar. A casual enquiry to his chief assistant—who had worked for him long enough to know never to ask questions—had elicited all the information he needed about Ms O'Hanlon. She was popular with both staff and children and kept herself to herself. She hadn't spent her evenings off frequenting some of the livelier bars on the other side of the island with other staff members. Instead, she'd spent much of her time sketching flowers at the far end of Langit Biru's extensive tropical gardens, or taking a regular swim in the sea as the sun was rising. Apparently, she'd even offered to do an unpopular shift when one of the other staff members had gone off sick. Was she too good to be true? he had wondered moodily.

Her disinclination to contact him had intrigued him, because Santiago was used to shameless pursuit from the opposite sex. And in a way, he liked that kind of woman better. At least you knew where you stood with them. Better the brazen seductress than the sly types who used manipulation as a silken snare.

'I'm not late, am I?'

He had been so lost in his thoughts that he'd failed to see Kitty appear and suddenly she was pulling open the passenger door of his car, causing consternation on the face of the nearest valet, who clearly thought that should have been *his* job.

'No,' Santiago said, amused. 'You're not late.' He shot her a quick glance as she slid onto the passenger seat. She'd taken him at his word regarding footwear and was wearing a pair of sturdy trainers. Surprisingly, she was also wearing shorts—a practical knee-length pair which would prove perfect for scrambling up steep inclines, but their sensible design did nothing to disguise the slim contours of her athletic legs. Just as her plain T-shirt failed to conceal the lush thrust of her breasts. Was it his imagination, or did they seem larger than he remembered? 'Put your seat belt on,' he instructed huskily.

'It's okay, Santiago. I have been in a car before, you know.'

'I do know. You were in the limo. Remember?'

He watched colour steal into her cheeks. 'It wasn't this car.'

'No, it wasn't,' he agreed evenly. 'Top marks for observation.'

'Just how many cars have you got?'

'This one is mine. The other belongs to the hotel.' He shot her a glance. 'Why, would you like me to list all my assets before we set off?'

'You think I care that you're rich?'

'You would be a very unusual woman if you didn't.'

'Huh. You could have a million cars and it wouldn't impress *me*!'

'That wouldn't go down particularly well with my stated position as an environmentalist, would it?' he observed drily.

'I don't own a car,' she said thoughtfully. 'In fact, I haven't even passed my driving test,' she said.

'Seriously?' He started up the engine. 'How is that even possible?'

'Quite easily. Even if I could afford a car—which I can't—I live in the middle of a city where parking is at a premium and lessons are crazy-expensive.'

Her defensive words only highlighted the huge gulf in their lifestyles and reminded him of how mismatched they were as a couple. Santiago glanced in the driving mirror, angered by the haphazard nature of his thoughts. He liked to be in control of all elements of his life, but his emotions most of all. These he had pruned vigorously and, at the first sign of life, cut them back with a ruthlessness which had always proved immensely satisfying.

Until now.

It was difficult to define the impact the freckled redhead was having on him, only that it was profound. And disturbing. Maybe it would lessen once they'd slept together again. His mouth hardened. Of course it would. Why else was he here, if not for that?

'Ready?'

There was a pause. 'Of course,' she replied, but he thought her voice sounded strained. As if she was also aware of their powerful chemistry and resented it almost as much as he did.

CHAPTER SEVEN

'YOU'RE LOOKING BETTER.'

Kitty stared a little guiltily across the restaurant table as Santiago's richly accented voice broke into her reverie, wondering if she had deliberately zoned out because he was making her feel uncomfortable? Possibly. It had certainly been easier to concentrate on the gorgeous Balinese landscape than on the distracting company of her companion. She had been on a curious knife-edge of excitement and fear all day. Excitement about the way he was making her feel yet fear about what she hadn't yet told him. A secret which seemed to be growing more momentous with every second that passed. Which was why it seemed safer to stare at the captivating scenery rather than look at the man seated opposite her, whose arrogant beauty had turned every head in the restaurant when they'd first walked in.

With the dappled sunlight glancing off his ebony hair and his skin glowing like burnished gold, the magnetism he exuded was off the scale. But that faint edge of danger hadn't gone anywhere. It was there in the hard glitter of his eyes and the new growth shadowing his jaw, making her wonder whether he'd shaved that morning. And that element of danger unsettled her—

warning her never to underestimate the breathtakingly handsome Argentinian billionaire.

Yet despite her misgivings, she'd spent the day feeling curiously *alive*. It was as if her senses had been fine-tuned, making everything seem more intense than usual. The colours seemed so vivid. The birdsong was piercing and sweet. The food tasted heavenly. At times she had wanted to pinch herself—wondering if this island could actually be for real.

They had driven past verdant rice terraces and craggy mountains, and the lush, impenetrable beauty of the jungle. They had stopped at flower-decked temples, where curvaceous statues spilled water into smooth ponds. She had seen huge green embankments covered with small plants and picturesque bridges, which straddled silver rivers. And everywhere they went, she was welcomed by the hospitable islanders, while the scent of incense permeated everything with its spicy perfume. Bali truly was a paradise, she concluded dreamily.

But there were always serpents in paradise. Everyone knew that. Didn't matter how brightly the sun shone, or how perfect the beaches were—you could always rely on shadows lurking in the background. And the darkest shadow of all was the secret which beat beneath Kitty's breast.

They were currently sitting on low seats in a chic and breezy restaurant at the top of a hill, which enjoyed matchless views over the jungle, and where a feast had been placed before them. Griddled pancakes heaped with mango and coconut and glistening slices of dragon fruit. Kitty had surprised herself by tucking into the food with enthusiasm, her recent haphazard appetite making an unexpected return.

But Santiago's remark made her wary.

'Better than what?' she echoed cautiously. 'What was the matter with the way I looked before?'

Narrowed black eyes glittered like jet. 'You want me to be honest?'

'Feel free.'

'When you arrived, you seemed washed out. As if you haven't been sleeping.' He frowned, the two dark wings of his brows knitting together. 'And you've lost weight, I suspect.'

Kitty could feel her throat dry, because his assessment was scarily accurate. What would he say if she came right out with it, if she was as honest as he had been?

You're right. I have. Several kilos, to be precise— though weirdly my breasts are larger than before. And I've been sick at odd times of the day, which apparently is perfectly normal when you're pregnant.

But how could she? It would be too bizarre to admit it now and here, in a setting like this, when he seemed like a stranger to her.

Because he *was* a stranger.

So find out more about what makes him tick. Find out what kind of man he really is.

'I lost my appetite when I lost my job,' she explained, which was sort of true.

'I see.'

She leaned back against the cushions, trying to disguise her sudden rush of nerves. Because how on earth did she begin interrogating someone like him—a billionaire whose life could not be more different from hers? A man who owned resorts and planes and employed gazillions of staff.

Yet their lives were now linked, whether she liked it or not, and surely they had progressed beyond the fluent commentary he had provided while they were driving around the island, coolly supplying fact after fascinating fact whenever she had breathed her appreciation about the scenery. To her, he was more than a tour guide and she was more to him than someone he'd employed in her time of need.

He just didn't know that yet.

'So...' She was aware of how nervous she sounded, so she smiled, trying to inject her attitude with a bit of confidence. 'How did you end up living in a place like Bali?'

He leaned back against the cushioned bamboo seat, his black gaze reflective. 'Maybe I found the island as magical as you seem to have done today.'

'Is that what it was? A simple love affair with the island?'

'No, Kitty.' He gave a cynical laugh. 'I require something a little more concrete than scenic attractions, no matter how many a place has to offer. I saw an opportunity and I took it.'

'You mean a financial opportunity?'

'Is there any other kind?'

'I wouldn't know. I've never really understood the world of business.' She wriggled a little on her chair. 'Tell me how you got started.'

'But surely you researched me before you came out here?' he probed, stretching his arms along the back of the seat so that the movement highlighted the hard ripple of muscle beneath his silk shirt.

Kitty nodded. 'I tried,' she admitted. 'But there was remarkably little about you online, which was surprising, considering you're obviously so successful.'

Santiago regarded her from between shuttered lashes, noticing the dappled light which flickered over her bright hair. He'd figured that a dash of his habitual cynicism might stem her sudden rush of curiosity, because he didn't like talking about himself. But she'd been honest enough to admit that she'd tried to find out more about him, and didn't such honesty merit some kind of reward?

'I pay people a lot of money to control my online profile,' he said. The facts which were out there were true, but bare. Father and mother dead. His unexpected direction after growing up in the lap of luxury was dealt with in a single spare sentence: Distinguished military career.

It was the one thing in his life he could be truly proud of.

'I was in the navy. But you probably know that part already.' As she nodded he watched her lips part and wished he hadn't, because it made him want to kiss them. 'Were you surprised?' he asked, trying to drag his attention away from the hard throb at his groin.

'I was. A bit.'

'You can't imagine me in uniform, Kitty, is that it? Or perhaps you can...'

Her answering blush was enchanting. Its warmth seeped right into his flesh, like sunlight beating down on his skin. He felt the quickening of his pulse.

'And did you like it?' she continued, as if she was determined to ignore the allusion, or the sexual tension which was sizzling between them. 'Being in the navy?'

Santiago sighed. This was way too definitive a question for such a complex subject. The military rules had been all-encompassing, and some men had found them too tough, but he had thrived in that fiercely spartan culture. He had enjoyed the rigorous daily exercise regime, which had made his body like iron and which he

had continued ever since. He had even welcomed sublimating his natural desire to dominate by obeying the
rules. Because hadn't those rules provided the discipline
and routine which had been missing from his supposedly privileged life for so long?

'I saw what I needed to do to get ahead. I became a
submariner.' He gave a short laugh. 'A position which
is highly prized within the navy hierarchy—something
which has always struck me as curious, considering it
involves months at sea in a windowless craft, isolated
from all interaction with the outside world.'

She snaked the tip of her perfect little tongue over
the curve of her lower lip and once again he wanted to
kiss her. 'You didn't get claustrophobic?'

'Strangely enough, never. I liked the challenge of
surviving in such cramped confinement.' He hadn't
been daunted by the monotonous routine of submarine
life either, with its prolonged and unpredictable sub-
mersions and ongoing awareness of the mortal consequences of mechanical failure and human error. It
had reinforced his certainty that he could exist happily without relationships. He had graduated top of his
class—informed by his superiors that he possessed
the qualities necessary to make him a master submariner. Basically, he was an emotionally detached workaholic—traits which had served him well in the life he
was to choose for himself.

When he'd left the navy the expertise he'd acquired
had proved invaluable. He'd started laying cables on the
ocean floor—and seen an opening on the other side of
the world, which he had pursued with his usual tunnel-
vision focus. The fact that the opportunity had been in
the Indian Ocean had been an added enticement to his
ambition. Anything which was a long way from Argen-

tina had suited him just fine and he'd all but cut ties with his homeland.

Kitty was winding a lock of red hair round and round her forefinger and Santiago allowed himself to be mesmerised by the movement, though he suspected it was mostly to distract himself from the lush thrust of her breasts.

'So how did you make the jump from submariner to—?'

'Businessman?' he supplied mockingly.

She shrugged. 'If that's what you like to call yourself.'

He frowned. Was that a faint reprimand he could hear in her soft voice? Surely she wasn't suggesting she wasn't enjoying the benefits of his success—or that she would have preferred her round-island bus hop to riding around in a luxury car. 'I started out in telecommunications,' he said slowly. 'The industry was in its infancy and I was lucky. The right place. The right time. I made a lot of money and channelled it into the emerging eco-leisure industry.'

There was a pause. He wondered if she was about to let it go, but no.

'Your parents must have been very proud.'

'My father was dead by then,' he said flatly.

'And did you...did you have a good relationship with him?'

It wasn't what he had been expecting. Perhaps if he had, he might have been better prepared to answer it. To deflect it. To wonder why she had asked such a bizarre question when they barely knew one another. 'I thought I did,' he said roughly. 'But I was wrong.'

'And your mother—'

'No, Kitty.' He could feel a sudden tension invading

his body as he shook his head. This wasn't why he'd brought her here. He had no intention of letting her peel back all the layers to discover what lay at the core of him, because even if he did—she was bound to be disappointed. He hadn't changed since those golden days in the navy. He was still a detached workaholic—or a heartless machine, as he had been called more than once.

This island tour had been the sweetener. The sociably acceptable prelude to what had seemed inevitable from the moment he'd seen her on the path outside her staff accommodation, with a pile of yellow dresses in her arms and the sunlight setting her hair on fire. But she needed to know that nothing had changed. He wanted to have sex with her—badly. But that was all. And if she could admit to wanting the same, then nobody would get hurt. 'I'm done with talking about the past, Kitty,' he said roughly. 'In fact, I'm done with talking altogether. Have you had enough to eat and drink?'

'S-sure.'

'Then let's go.'

He saw the crestfallen look on her face as she rose to her feet and suspected she thought he was tiring of her. But that was a deliberate strategy on his part because she needed to understand that, essentially, he was fickle and to accept that he was never going to be a stable feature in her life. He didn't want to hurt her and there was something so soft and gentle about her, which made him realise she could be easy to hurt. She had been innocent—the most innocent woman to grace his bed—and some bone-deep instinct told him that there had been nobody since him.

And wasn't it the same for him? Didn't the thought of undressing any other woman than her fill him with something akin to revulsion? He remembered her body opening up for him—like the petals of a flower beguiled by the warm light of the sun. Santiago frowned.

Petals? Sunlight?

Why were such thoughts entering a mind which had never fallen prey to sentiment before? He wondered if her allure was down to a primitive sense of possession. Or maybe it was just fascination, at observing something new. Because although he was used to women who used sex as a weapon or a bargaining tool, Kitty hadn't realised her potential. She had yet to grow into the true power of her sexuality. And although Santiago wanted to experience all that sensual wonder again while it was still fresh and unexplored by anyone other than him, she needed to realise he could take or leave her. That his fail-safe way of controlling any relationship was by making it clear where the boundaries lay. His mouth hardened. And his boundaries definitely excluded in-depth analysis of the most damaging relationship of all.

Parenthood.

He waited until they were back by his car before turning to look down into her upturned face. Her green eyes were wary, but her unpainted lips remained deliciously kissable. If he'd been the type of man to indulge in public displays of affection, he might have bent his head and done just that, because the pulse of heat in his blood was overpowering.

With an effort, he dragged his thoughts away from the clamour of his body. 'I think we've seen enough for one day, don't you? Would you like me to take you back to your room, or shall I drop you off somewhere else?'

Kitty resisted the urge to gnaw on her bottom lip, afraid it would make her look anxious—which was exactly how she felt—and not just because Santiago was obviously eager for the day to come to an end. Because she had achieved very little. In fact, she'd found out almost nothing about him that she didn't already know. He had opened up—a bit—then clammed right up again. But she had seen his face change when he'd talked about his father, before silencing her when she'd dared mention his mother. It had struck an instant chord inside her and for a moment she had forgotten her reason for being there, because his tight expression had been underpinned with a fierce and elemental pain she recognised all too well. She had wanted to go to him and put her arms around him. To hold him close and hug him tightly and tell him that sometimes she felt that pain too.

Yeah, sure. That was the only reason she wanted to hug Santiago Tevez—to offer him comfort.

So now what? Well, she certainly wasn't going to *throw* herself at him.

'Time to head back to my room,' she said carelessly, telling herself there was bound to be another opportunity to get to know him better. 'It's been a long day.'

'Or you could come and have a sundowner with me?' He turned his eyes dark and inscrutable. 'I'm sure I don't need to tell you just how magnificent the sunsets are on Bali.'

'Actually, you probably do, because I hardly saw any when I was here before. The sun always sets so early that it used to clash with the children's bathtime and Rupert and Camilla's gin and tonics,' she explained, feeling stupidly triumphant at having made him smile like that. 'Did you mean, have a drink with you back at the... Langit Biru?'

'No, Kitty,' he said drily. 'I don't think that would enhance your professional reputation any.'

'But I thought...' She furrowed her brow. 'I thought that was where you lived. In the Presidential Suite. Where we...we...'

'No.' He cut across her obvious confusion. 'That's where I sometimes stay when I'm at the resort, should the need arise. I have another place on the other side of the island.'

'Which is your proper home?' she verified, still puzzled.

'I don't have a *home*, Kitty,' he said, his voice as brittle as burnt sugar. 'I have places I rent. Places where I stay.'

'In Buenos Aires?' she ventured.

He shook his head. 'No. Not there. I haven't been back to Argentina for years.'

The irony was that if Kitty weren't pregnant, she would have run a mile, because it was obvious from what Santiago was saying that he didn't want any kind of permanence—not with anyone, let alone with her. But she *was* pregnant. With his baby. And she still hadn't told him. She licked her lips. She *had* to tell him.

'Actually, I'd love a drink,' she said and couldn't miss the responding glint in his eyes. Or the brief curve of his lips and the tension which suddenly made the muscles in his arms bunch as he opened the passenger car door so she could step in. Did he view her answer as a tacit acceptance they were going to have sex again—and if that were the case, then wasn't she putting herself in a difficult situation? She needed to dampen down the desire which was spiralling up inside her because she was determined not to send out the wrong message. In Santiago's eyes she should never have been more than a one-night fling and she wasn't going to repeat that mistake.

Her fingers crept over her belly.

She couldn't afford to.

But everything seemed to be conspiring against her. As he got in the driver's seat, he turned on the engine, and flicked on the music—and although it was unfamiliar, Kitty's senses fizzed with sensual recognition when she heard those first sultry notes drifting out. Then there was the villa he took her to—the rented place which was emphatically *not* a home. A sprawling villa surrounded by water and sky, giving Kitty the impression of it being just the two of them, alone with the elements.

Tonight there was no garlanded member of staff bringing them cocktails on a tray. Instead, Santiago went into the kitchen to fix her a drink while she used the washroom, her heart racing as she shut the door and looked around. There were mirrors everywhere. Nothing to look at but herself. Kitty had never been given to vanity—that was something else which had been frowned on, first in the presbytery and then when she'd been adopted—but for once she couldn't seem to tear her gaze away from her own reflection.

Who was that woman with a face so pale that the freckles seemed to stand out in stark relief? Or whose eyes looked so green and glittering that they appeared almost…wild. She wished she hadn't chosen to wear shorts. She wished her feet were covered in something other than a sturdy pair of sneakers, which made her feel clumsy and heavy. But most of all she wished she didn't have this terrible secret ticking away inside her, like an unexploded bomb which could be detonated at any moment.

She washed her hands and face, pulled the scrunchy from her hair and raked a comb through her tangled curls. And then she drew in a deep breath as she prepared to go and face Santiago Tevez.

She still didn't know much about him but the overriding impression she'd got from him today was that he seemed... She put her wide-toothed comb back in her bag. Despite his occasional arrogance and undeniable detachment—towards people *and* places—he seemed decent enough. He couldn't be blamed for not behaving as she would have wanted him to behave. Very few people did that, she thought bitterly.

He'd told her he was happy with his single life. Well, that was fine—she wasn't expecting a gold band on her finger. He'd told her he didn't want children. That was more of a problem. Or not. It just depended how you looked at it. He hadn't planned a baby and neither had she, but the baby was a fact now. He might not want anything to do with it—but even if he didn't, mightn't he offer to help support the child he had fathered?

She needed to think about the future. She couldn't just hang around here, doing a temporary job in an exotic location. Sooner or later she was going to have to think about practicalities. About where they were going to live, and how. And wasn't that something which Santiago could help with? The security of his wealth could cushion their child's start in life. She wasn't thinking luxury yachts or diamonds, or penthouse homes in fancy apartment blocks—more the fundamental stuff. Like four walls and warmth and food on the table.

In her head she had planned to get to know Santiago better before she decided whether or not to tell him about the baby, but now she could see that might not be so easy. How could she discover what sort of man he really was, if their paths rarely crossed? Was she planning to just pitch up at his fancy office, wearing her hideous yellow dress with the matching clogs, and announce her news?

And he had been good company today, hadn't he? Thoughtful and considerate.

Was there ever going to be a perfect time?

Maybe she should tell him sooner rather than later...

Sucking in a deep breath, she pushed open the door and went to find him, but the air left her lungs in a disbelieving puff as she drank in the vision which awaited her.

He was standing silhouetted against a backdrop of coral and gold and red—the sky set on fire by the flames of the setting sun. Beside him, on a small mosaic table, was an ice bucket containing a bottle of champagne and two glittering crystal glasses. Once again that feeling of unreality swept over her because it was like looking at a cinema screen, as if all this were happening to someone else, not her.

But the expression on Santiago's face was real enough and Kitty could see unmistakable appreciation glinting from his eyes as she began to walk towards him. She told herself she was just going to savour the beauty of it all for a minute or two longer. The last few dying seconds before the time bomb exploded.

Afterwards she wondered if she'd been stupid—but what else could she have done? She still hadn't properly decided and even if she had—she was hardly going to yell her news at him across the terrace of that fairy-tale setting, was she? And by the time her footsteps came to a halt and she was standing looking up into the hard and perfect beauty of his face, it was too late. The raw hunger which blazed from his ebony gaze must have matched something he'd seen reflected in her own, because he reached out and pulled her into his arms and looked down at her for one long, intense moment. And suddenly he was bending his head to kiss her and her heart was melting as fast as her body and there wasn't a thing she could do to stop it.

CHAPTER EIGHT

SANTIAGO CLAIMED KITTY'S mouth with a hunger which had been building inside him all day. And she was kissing him back—her lips just as urgent—as if she had been sharing his erotic fantasies. Her fingers dug into his shoulders for support, as if she might just slide to the ground without it and his heart pounded because didn't he feel a bit like that himself? As if this hot rush of desire were something new. Something outside his realm of experience.

He skated an unsteady hand over the swell of her hips, turned-on but mystified. While at sea it had been necessary to go without physical intimacy for long periods—at a time when his hormones had been rampant—and Santiago had dealt with those frustrated yearnings with an icy control envied by his crewmates. Sublimating his desire had been just another test to set himself and he had triumphed over it, as with all his other self-imposed challenges. Yet it had been only weeks since he'd been intimate with Kitty and somehow it felt like for ever—as if a great empty void had opened up in his life. And wasn't part of his reason for wanting this so badly his certainty that the second time would fail to live up to his heated expectations? He'd thought he would never again experience that overpowering reaction she had provoked in him, and yet now…

Now.

It was inexplicable, but it was happening all over again and he was on fire.

On fire.

And so, it seemed, was she.

Santiago's throat dried as she writhed in his arms with an urgent, gasping hunger. Her body was soft but her nipples were like bullets—jutting against his chest through the thin silk of his shirt as he flicked his tongue inside her mouth and met her shuddered moan. How could a preliminary kiss be so damned *hot*?

He palmed one breast, stroking his thumb over the puckering peak before turning his attention to the other, and her little mewls of satisfaction spurred him on even more. Sliding his thigh between hers, he could detect the subtle scent of her sex in the warm air and never had a perfume been so evocative or so musky. As she continued to murmur with helpless provocation, he was tempted to reach for the button of her shorts and let them slide to her ankles, along with her panties. To unzip himself and tumble them down on one of those nearby loungers, so that he could thrust into her tight wetness as soon as possible and rid himself of this unbearable ache in his body.

But he didn't want another al fresco coupling, no matter how much privacy this exclusive villa offered. The sky was still on fire, not yet cloaked with the concealing black velvet of night. And wasn't there always a chance they could be seen by one of the long-range camera lenses which often pursued the images of the wealthy and powerful for the ever-voracious appetite of the downmarket tabloids?

'No. Not here,' he bit out, scooping her up in his arms and carrying her inside the villa, barely aware of anything other than the urgent need to get her horizontal. Impatiently, he peeled off her T-shirt and shorts, undid the laces of her unattractive trainers and tugged them off, before tearing off his own clothes until he was as naked as she. He stood for a moment, just looking at her, transfixed by the fiery tumble of her curls on the pillow, splashed red-gold by the setting sun. 'You are as beautiful as I remember, Kitty O'Hanlon, and now I want to kiss you.'

Her lashes fluttered open, her green gaze luring him in. 'So what's stopping you?' she husked.

Her incitement threatened to drive his desire off the scale but as Santiago bent his head towards her, he forced himself to temper his hunger, his tongue slowly laving over her soft skin as he slowly reacquainted himself with her delicious body. Each lick of his tongue elicited a shudder. A helpless sigh or a murmured word he couldn't quite make out. It occurred to him that this felt brand-new as well as achingly familiar—because he'd only ever seen her by moonlight before. And, oh, this redheaded beauty was born to be lit by the fire of a Balinese sunset.

Her fingers were tiptoeing over his back and sliding over his flesh, her movements a little tentative at first and yet somehow managing to be intensely seductive. For a moment, Santiago drew back to look at her, his gaze raking over her naked body. It seemed his initial assessment of weight loss had been correct for her hips seemed bonier than before but ironically, her breasts were lusciously full. A faint cloud swam into his mind, but it was gone the moment he reached between her legs to find her molten heat, and his hand was unsteady as he reached for a condom. As he stroked on the protection, he thought he saw a fleeting shadow cross her green eyes and she opened her lips as if to speak.

'Santiago—'

But he silenced her with another kiss. He didn't want questions. He didn't want her asking where this was going because he didn't know. He didn't know anything right then, only that he wanted to be inside her and his heart felt as if it might stop beating if that didn't happen soon. Her trembling thighs were already opening and she made a choked little sound as he moved over her and entered her.

'Kitty,' was all he said. And then again. 'Kitty.'

His unsteady words shafted their way straight to her heart and Kitty closed her eyes with a mixture of despair and delight as Santiago filled her, knowing it was too late to stop him now.

But she hadn't even tried, had she?

No. She hadn't. Because the truth was that Kitty didn't want to stop him, even if deep down she knew this was wrong. How could she prevent what seemed inevitable when this burning need was rushing over her in a thick, hot tide and threatening to swamp her? How could she possibly resist something this earth-shattering? Which made everything else seem inconsequential—as if satisfying this mighty physical hunger which raged between them were the only thing which mattered. Blindly, she turned her head to seek his mouth and he answered with a kiss which was sweet and drugging and addictive.

In a way, she wanted it to go on all night, because the sensation of feeling Santiago deep inside her body was pushing reality to the sidelines—but already she could feel the insistent flicker of pleasure which quickly became a demanding flame. Her thighs tightened as she accommodated each hard thrust with the eager tilt of her pelvis and didn't his corresponding moans make her feel as if she'd just won a prize?

Because at that moment he was hers and only hers. She possessed Santiago Tevez just as thoroughly as he possessed her—with an elemental need which dominated everything and made the rest of the world recede. All too soon she began to pulse around him—and maybe he'd been waiting for her surrender, because immediately he began to shudder out his own satisfaction, biting out something hard and helpless in Spanish.

And then it was over. Her heartbeat slowed and Kitty felt as if she were floating. He wrapped his arms tightly around her and she could feel his dying spasms as he slowly pulsed to a halt inside her. She ran her fingertips over the sheen of sweat which coated his skin, and when she moved a little beneath him, he began to grow hard again.

'I think you liked that, didn't you, *roja*?' he murmured against her ear.

And it was that—that single word of supposed intimacy which made Kitty realise exactly what she'd done.

She'd had sex with him again, despite vowing not to.

She had behaved impetuously. Thoughtlessly. Stupidly.

And he still didn't know.

She felt a wave of heat washing over her skin—but this wasn't the good kind, like when she'd been craving him so badly just a few minutes ago. This heat was composed of guilt and regret. And something else. Something which had become all too familiar in the preceding weeks. A prelude to the wave of nausea which rose in her throat and had her scrambling from the bed.

'Where...where's the bathroom?' she demanded urgently.

He looked surprised by her question as he pointed to the far side of the enormous room, which had grown darker while they'd been making love. Maybe he wasn't used to women who wanted to vomit straight after sex.

'The nearest is over there.'

She didn't want the *nearest*. She wanted the one which was furthest away—from him and from the sounds she was terrified of making. But the demands of her body were too insistent and the churning, burning of her stomach too urgent to ignore. She dashed across to the bathroom door, with no time to shut it behind her as she slid down in front of the toilet, her bare knees cold against the marble floor as she began to retch.

It was over very quickly, and Kitty wanted to just curl up on that cold floor and close her eyes. To spirit herself away from there and the situation she had created. But that wasn't an option. Shakily, she rose to her feet and staggered over to one of the washbasins, sluicing her mouth out with cold water and washing her hands, before splashing the sink clean.

At first she didn't see him. She certainly hadn't heard him enter the bathroom, but she guessed she had been otherwise engaged. It was only when some sixth sense alerted her to his presence that Kitty slowly raised her head and saw Santiago's reflection in the mirror as he stood in the doorway watching her.

It was difficult to describe what he looked like, only that it was nothing like the naked man she'd left in bed, and not just because he had dragged on a pair of jeans. Gone was all that urgency and passion and hunger. Wiped clean away—as thoroughly as she had just wiped the sink. In its place was cool inscrutability and a thoughtful deliberation which made whispers of fear tiptoe over her skin. She swallowed. Had he…had he somehow *guessed*?

'Put some clothes on,' he said.

Kitty realised she was still naked and it was like being back in the middle of that recurring nightmare, especially when his voice sounded like that. So icy. So mechanical. 'My clothes are all next door.'

He grabbed a robe which was hanging from a silver hook and draped it around her shoulders, as if he couldn't bear to look at her for a second longer. 'Wear this,' he instructed abruptly. 'And then come and find me.'

And although she was grateful for the sudden warmth, Kitty didn't want to wear a robe which enveloped her as this one did. A robe which was obviously his because his scent was all over it and it felt as if she were being mocked by the memory of how close they had just been but no longer were.

She found him in a room which overlooked the sea. The sunset had been blotted out by the indigo darkness of a sky now studded with the diamond glitter of stars. As soon as he heard her approach—and his hearing must have been very acute, because her feet were still bare—he snapped on a switch and light flooded the vast space. It emphasised the tight lines of his face and stony glint of his eyes and Kitty felt as if she had been transported to an interrogation cell.

'Sit down,' he said, indicating a squashy-looking leather chair beside a table on which stood a glass of water. 'And drink.'

'Thanks.' Eagerly, Kitty sank down into the chair and grasped the delicate crystal tumbler, thirstily gulping the cool water into her parched mouth. She drained the lot and put the glass back down with a shaky hand as she forced herself to meet his eyes. Still cold, she thought. But was it her imagination, or had some of his initial iciness melted?

'Are you okay?' he questioned.

She nodded, pathetically relieved, thinking his solicitous question meant that maybe he *hadn't* guessed and that she would get to be the bearer of the vital information she carried. As if again, that sixth sense was warning her how important it was that *she* be the one to give him her news, rather than have him prise it out of her. 'Yes, thanks. I—'

'When were you planning on telling me, Kitty?'

The voice which cut through her words was totally devoid of any emotion—and wasn't it strange how, in times of extreme stress, you reverted to the patterns of childhood? So that suddenly she was back to being the child whose strict adoptive parents hadn't allowed her to eat between meals—*'It's for your own good, Kitty'*—and whose hunger had once let her down, and she'd been caught with cake crumbs around her mouth and a doomed hope she could bluster her way out of it.

'Tell you what?' she hedged.

Santiago's mouth tightened. Perhaps if she'd answered his question truthfully, then this smoulder of rage wouldn't have been quite so intense. But why should he be so surprised by her evasion and her secrecy? The only real surprise was that he had allowed himself to be fooled by her. He had stupidly believed her to have a refreshing honesty, but he had been wrong. She had been deceiving him all along. And she was *still* trying to lie through her manipulative teeth. His mouth tightened. How could he really have thought she was different from every other woman he'd ever known?

'Perhaps you'd like some time to reconsider your answer?' he suggested icily.

She nodded then. As if she were all out of places to hide. 'I'm... I'm pregnant,' she whispered.

Santiago flinched as the pieces of the jigsaw finally came together and a profound shock reverberated through him forcefully. And although he was a man who liked answers to perplexing questions, he felt his hot rage increase as he realised this was the very last thing he wanted. 'I know you are,' he snapped.

'But...*how*?'

'Because it all adds up. Now.' He shook his head, unable to believe he hadn't worked it out sooner. But he had been too blinded by desire and by the urgent need to satisfy that desire. Hadn't he thought that another night with Kitty O'Hanlon would subdue his inexplicable hunger for her? Yes, he had, but he had been wrong about that, too.

'Your eagerness to return to Bali when I made it quite clear I had no desire to see you again. Even the most desperate of women is rarely *that* desperate,' he bit out, ignoring her pained look. 'The way you've obviously lost weight, yet...' He couldn't continue. The last thing he needed right now was to start focussing on her body. With an effort, he dragged his thoughts away from the luscious new shape of her breasts. 'And then there's the way you looked at me when you arrived last week.'

'The way I *looked* at you?' Her eyes were very big and very green. 'What do you mean by that?'

Unable—and unwilling—to explain the connection which had targeted his solar plexus when he'd seen her standing in the sun-dappled gardens, Santiago shook his head. She was biting her bottom lip and even now— *even now*—he found himself recalling how good it felt to trail his tongue over that soft cushion of flesh. But he blocked out that thought too, along with the realisation of how small and vulnerable she seemed, swathed in his robe, which reached almost to her feet. He told himself it was just lingering sexual hunger which made him want to take her into his arms and cradle her—to smooth those snaky red curls and tell her it was all going to be okay.

'It doesn't matter,' he said roughly, before forcing himself to address the more pressing matter of her deception. 'So how long were you going to wait before you told me, Kitty? I'm trying to imagine what must have been going on in your head today when you were gurgling with delight at all the sights on the island, and yet all the time you knew—'

'It wasn't easy.'

'Was it *easy* having sex with me again *before* you told me the truth?' he taunted. 'Was that supposed to make me more sympathetic towards you? Perhaps you thought that a satisfied man might be more inclined to be generous towards you.'

Kitty could scarcely take in the cruel lash of his accusation or the way he was glaring at her. He'd freely admitted to being a cynic and she had witnessed his detachment and now his fury for herself—but was he really suggesting she'd had sex as some kind of cunning plan, to extract as much as possible from him?

'I can't believe you just said that,' she breathed.

'You can skip the gushing incredulity because, in the circumstances, it's completely unconvincing. What is it you want from me, Kitty?' he continued remorselessly. 'Money?'

He said the word as if it were poison—as if it were something bitter and unpalatable—which was ironic considering he had so much of the stuff. And the truth was that although she didn't want money, she certainly needed it right now and she would be a fool to forget that. Because Kitty knew the difference between idealism and realism. What good would it do to tell him she wouldn't take anything from him and would manage perfectly well on her own? Life wasn't that simple. She knew that better than anyone. Her baby wouldn't thank her for a self-serving show of defiance which might leave them both cold and hungry and at the mercy of social services. So she swallowed her pride and looked at him steadily. 'Yes, as a matter of fact, I do think you should provide some money.'

'Why? So you can get rid of it?' he demanded, the words tight and taut.

A wave of nausea rose in her throat again and if she'd had a missile to hand, she might have hurled it at him. 'Don't you ever *dare* suggest such a thing,' she hissed.

She wondered if she had imagined the relief which briefly flickered across his face before he answered.

'So, if that isn't your preferred option,' he continued, 'then what is?'

She realised he was the first person other than the doctor to have addressed this question. *Because he was the only other person she'd told.* Saying it out loud not only made the situation more real—it also made Kitty realise how alone in the world she really was.

But now was not the time for self-pity. Now was the time for affirmation. And gratitude. A little heart was beating beneath her breast and no matter what the circumstances of that conception—it was a miracle.

'I'm going to have my baby, of course! And I'm going to love that baby with every fibre of my being.'

'A commendable sentiment,' he offered coolly. 'But one which throws up many practical dilemmas.'

She thought how forensic he sounded—like a scientist examining something underneath a microscope, with an impartiality devoid of any emotional attachment. Which happened to be true. And as the reality of her situation hit her, all the fight drained out of her. She tried to summon up some energy to figure out what she needed to do next. 'I'm all done here, Santiago. I can't talk about this any more. Not tonight. I need to get back.'

'Back where?'

'To my room at the Langit Biru, of course. I've got work in the morning.'

'Don't be so ridiculous,' he snapped, his composure momentarily slipping. 'If you think I'm driving you halfway across the island at this time of night, then you're mistaken.'

'Don't worry. I'll ring for a taxi.'

'You will not. You will stay here,' he reaffirmed, with a powerful air of finality. 'You've been sick and we have a lot to talk about.'

She wanted to say: 'Like *what*?' but her mouth couldn't seem to get the words out. She felt weightless. Boneless. As if her body were composed of nothing but feathers and if she attempted to stand up, she might just float away. 'I've got work,' she croaked.

'One of my assistants will find someone to replace you. Do you really think you're going to continue at the crèche as though everything's normal, when you're having my baby?'

And Kitty hated the stupid spring of hope in her heart when he said *my baby* like that, because surely it didn't mean anything. Not when his voice was so distant and his eyes so remote. It was just an expression. A slip of the tongue. A fact made cruelly clear by his next words.

'Go back to my room and try to get some rest. I'll sleep nearby.'

But Kitty shook her head as the implications of his command sank in. If he thought she was going to crawl in between those sex-rumpled sheets and be haunted by memories of what they'd done—then he was very much mistaken. 'No, you won't,' she answered and saw the flare of surprise in his eyes. 'You can show *me* where the guest room is and I'll sleep there.'

She rose from the chair with a tight smile, as if to reassure him that she would be fine on her own in an anonymous room which was lacking in comfort and company.

Because hadn't she spent most of her life that way?

CHAPTER NINE

KITTY WOKE UP not knowing where she was, which wasn't a particularly unusual experience of late—but this time it felt surreal. Because this wasn't a narrow bed in one of a series of small rooms, befitting her position as humble employee—this was a bed as big as a football pitch with fine linen sheets and unbelievably soft pillows, which made her want to snuggle down and cocoon herself there for ever. While outside…

She gazed out of the window at the unbelievably beautiful panorama which lay before her, thinking how tired she must have been not to have been woken by the dawn. Unshuttered floor-to-ceiling windows dominated two sides of the bedroom and flooded the room with natural light. Through one she could see the wide blue sweep of the ocean and through the other, the waxy green leaves and kaleidoscopic flowers of the tropical gardens beneath.

She glanced at her phone, whose battery was just about to die, and blinked at it in disbelief. Nine o'clock. How could she possibly have slept for so long? She should have been at the crèche an hour ago and hoped Santiago had made good his promise to get someone to stand in for her. But now she needed to get dressed and get away as quickly as possible. Yes, they needed to discuss the baby, but it didn't have to be this morning.

The shower was deliciously powerful, and she lingered longer than she'd intended and the toiletries—sumptuous with hibiscus leaves and lemongrass—were so amazing that she ended up washing her hair, even though drying it was always such a mammoth task. Emerging from the bathroom twenty minutes later, Kitty felt like a new woman—though she was dreading having to put on yesterday's clothes and underwear.

But it seemed her reservations were redundant because a solution to her dilemma had been found, even though it made her feel slightly uneasy. There, on a dressing table on the far side of the room, was a pile of clothes she hadn't noticed before. A perfectly respectable pair of wide linen trousers in a sludgy shade of green, along with a T-shirt in a slightly paler colour. The fabrics were exquisite, and the colour perfectly complemented her hair, and her eyes.

Kitty's heart contracted as she surveyed the neat stack. Not just clothes, but a pair of dainty jewelled flip-flops along with a frothy heap of lingerie. Delicate lacy panties in subtle hues of peaches and cream, along with a matching bra, which was the most beautiful thing she'd ever seen.

Her heart was racing like a train because now she felt compromised. But what else could she do other than put them on? Attempt to find her discarded clothes, when the last she'd seen them they had been littered over Santiago's bedroom floor? No. There was a time for defiance and pride and that time was not now. She needed all the protective armour she could find. So she pulled on the beautiful garments, took a deep breath and pushed open the door, working out some kind of strategy. Santiago might already have left for work and mightn't that be best? She could call a taxi and leave him a note saying, yes, they could meet—and talk—of course they could. But neutral territory might be a better place to discuss the future.

But she didn't know the address, did she—so how could she ask for a taxi? She quickly explored the large villa, but it seemed empty, so she stepped outside into the gardens, the air thick with the scent of gardenias. She heard the distant sound of a splash and Kitty found herself following that noise in the direction of the swimming pool. She could see the turquoise glitter of the water from here—and, as she approached the vast pool and saw who was just hauling himself out of the water, wished she could turn around and go back inside the villa.

Who was she kidding?

She could have stood and watched him all day.

As Santiago levered his gleaming body out of the pool, he was the embodiment of power and perfection. Broad shoulders. A rock-hard torso. Narrow hips above long and muscular legs. Droplets of water were streaming over the bronzed surface of his skin, so that he resembled a statue someone had spent a lot of time polishing. Wet black hair was plastered to his head and his eyes were narrowed against the sun so she couldn't really read their expression. But surely she wasn't expecting them to be anything other than cool, and calculating? She had told him something he hadn't been expecting. Something he'd told her from the beginning that he didn't want.

This was not going to be an easy meeting.

'You're awake,' he observed as he reached for a towel and began to rub it over his head. His cool gaze swept over her linen trousers and T-shirt and, despite the highly practical nature of her outfit, Kitty felt curiously exposed beneath that narrow-eyed scrutiny. 'And dressed.'

'Obviously.' She cleared her throat, not wanting to appear ungrateful but unsure how one went about accepting unsolicited gifts from a billionaire. 'I ought to thank you for providing the clothes. It was very... thoughtful of you. I'll make sure they're laundered and returned to you as soon as possible.'

'Don't be ridiculous, Kitty.' His voice was mocking. 'Unless you think the Langit Biru boutique will be able to sell them after you've worn them.'

'No. I suppose not.'

Why on earth were they talking about clothes? Why wasn't she putting some space between them so she could get her head together, instead of obsessing about how delectable he looked in a pair of swim-shorts which were clinging to him like a second skin? And why had neither of them yet referred to the baby? She wondered if it was because this was the first morning they had ever spent together—which meant yet another social hurdle to overcome. Kitty swallowed. 'Could you organise a taxi for me?'

'I could, but I'm not going to.' He rubbed the towel over the black waves of his hair. 'We need to have a conversation and you need to eat breakfast—not necessarily in that order.'

'So I'm to be kept prisoner here?'

He threw the towel down onto a nearby lounger. 'Please don't test my patience by using melodrama.' He pointed to a large area on the other side of the pool, which was shaded by an inviting-looking canopy. 'Go and wait for me on the terrace over there. Ambar, my housekeeper, will look after you and I'll join you as soon as I can.'

Despite his undeniable bossiness, Kitty thought it felt strangely comforting to have someone else take charge, after so long of doing everything on her own. Just as it felt amazing to be picking her way along a path lined by streams of flowing water, to the accompanying sound of exotic birdsong. A table had been laid for breakfast, a shallow dish of flowers at its centre—the creamy orange blooms exquisite and intensely fragrant. It was, she realised, a long way from the pub in Chessington.

She sank down on the nearest chair, trying to second-guess what sort of 'conversation' Santiago wanted and how best to respond, when a beautiful young woman appeared from inside the villa. She was wearing an embroidered ankle-length dress and bearing a tray, on which stood a teapot and delicate cup.

'Good morning,' she said, with a smile, before beginning to pour a pale brew whose unmistakable fragrance scented the air. 'I'm Ambar and the Señor Tevez asked me to bring you some ginger tea.'

Señor Tevez. The deferential way the housekeeper said his name made Kitty stiffen with wariness because didn't it reinforce Santiago's authority as well as his undeniable influence on the island? And *she* was carrying his baby. His *heir*, she thought suddenly. A wave of fear washed through her as she thought what that might mean to someone like him. Would this unbelievably wealthy man want to possess the one thing his money could not buy?

She watched Ambar go back inside the villa and took a tentative sip of tea. Her usual preference was for builder's brew with a splash of milk, but the gingery liquid tasted perfect. She sat back, trying to relax, but all thoughts of relaxation fled the moment she saw Santiago walking across the marble tiles towards her.

Backlit by the bright sun, which threw his powerful body into silhouette, he looked in total command and as beautiful and as remote as the sunrise.

He pulled out a chair and sat down, his black gaze unreadable. 'How's the tea?'

'Very good.' It wasn't the opener she had been expecting and maybe her expression conveyed her curiosity.

'I understand it's recommended for pregnant women. I asked Ambar to make some for you.'

'Did you tell her I was pregnant?'

He raised his eyebrows. 'You think I'm required to provide an explanation to my housekeeper for requesting a certain type of tea, Kitty? Of course I didn't. I discovered online that ginger tea was good for nausea in the first trimester—'

'You were researching pregnancy online?' she questioned incredulously.

'I'm someone who likes to equip myself with as many facts as possible,' he said, only now his voice was clipped and hard.

There was a pause. *Don't ask it,* Kitty told herself fiercely—then went ahead and asked it anyway. 'I suppose Ambar is used to providing breakfast for your... guests?'

Santiago registered the familiar spike in her voice and gave a brief nod of satisfaction. Usually, he abhorred jealousy and the possessiveness which inevitably accompanied it, but for once he could see that such an emotion might work in his favour.

'Actually, she isn't. As a rule, I prefer not to bring women here.'

There was another pause, and her voice sounded a little strangled. 'You prefer to go to them, I suppose?'

'Usually. But your staff accommodation presented something of a challenge, since I've never had sex with one of my staff before,' he mocked, when the sudden colour which splashed across her freckled cheeks gave him a momentary sense of contrition. This was all new for her, he reminded himself. New for me too, he thought grimly. 'You should learn not to ask questions if you can't deal with the answers, Kitty,' he warned softly.

'I can deal with them perfectly well,' she said, with an airiness which didn't quite come off—but just then Ambar appeared with a large tray of food, and by the time she'd gone, he found he was more preoccupied with Kitty's air of frailty than establishing boundaries.

'Eat,' he instructed and almost obediently she nodded and picked up her fork.

For once Santiago had little interest in his own food, watching through veiled lashes as she devoured papaya with lime, followed by pancakes covered with transparent slices of banana and the sticky local jam. He was used to wafer-thin women who saw food as the enemy, and it was curiously satisfying to watch Kitty eat with such gusto. For a moment he enjoyed a small window of unexpected peace until he reminded himself of the unwanted reality, and why she was here.

The only reason she was here.

He had been awake for much of the night as—again uncharacteristically—he had been unable to get his head around the fact that this unknown Englishwoman was pregnant with his child. They had been careful. He always was. And then he remembered the incredible sex they'd had in the shower. The way she'd made him feel out of control as the warm water had gushed down on them and his impatience to cover himself with a condom. His mouth dried. Maybe they hadn't been so careful after all.

'Thanks,' she said eventually, dabbing at her lips with a napkin. 'That was delicious.'

She sat back with a quiet question on her face as if waiting for him to take the lead, and Santiago realised he needed to be objective. He mustn't think about curls which glinted like fire, or breasts which looked lush and heavy against her soft T-shirt. Far better to concentrate on the lies she had spun him, like the rest of her sex.

'So why the subterfuge?' he demanded, his voice low and rough. 'Why not just come out with it on the phone when you called me from England? Wouldn't that have been simpler?' His eyes narrowed. 'Or did you think I would deny all responsibility and slam the phone down?'

She shrugged. 'That was always a possibility, yes.'

'But that wasn't the reason which brought you out here?'

'No.'

There was a pause. 'So what was it, Kitty?'

She looked down at the napkin still on her lap and when she lifted her face, her eyes were very bright— as if a lifetime of unshed tears were glittering in their emerald depths—and despite all Santiago's best intentions, he felt the sudden inexplicable clench of his heart.

'I wanted to know what sort of man you really are,' she said slowly. 'To discover if you were…'

'If I was what?'

'Fit to be a father to my child, I guess.' She shrugged. 'There's no other way to put it.'

'You mean you were subjecting me to some secret

personality test?' he verified, his mouth hardening. 'I guess I'd already passed the financial check with flying colours. What else were you looking for, Kitty? Did you want to establish my IQ? Find out if I was kind to animals?'

'There's no need to be sarcastic. It was nothing like that.'

'So what was it like? Why don't you tell me what gives you the right to stand in judgement of me? I'm curious.'

Kitty heard the anger in his voice and knew she'd touched a raw nerve. But what had she expected? That she could plot and scheme and draw up her own timetable of events, blithely imagining she wouldn't suffer any consequences as a result? She hadn't thought it through properly, she could see that now.

'I did it with the best of intentions.' She hesitated. 'Because my own experience has made me, well…suspicious, I guess.'

'I thought the whole point of this was that you haven't had any experience,' he came back at her witheringly.

'Not of lovers, no. I don't. But I…'

'You what, Kitty?' he snapped, the harsh lines of his face emphasised by a deep scowl. 'Get to the point, will you?'

Kitty puffed out a sigh, knowing he had her cornered and there was nothing she could do about it. She knew she needed to come clean about her past, yet she never talked about it—because in her situation, who would? But Santiago Tevez was looking at her with expectation—and she had to tell him. Because he of all people had a right to know.

'Let's just say that I find it difficult to trust people.'

'Join the club,' he said, with a bitter laugh. 'Why?'

'I was...' Her words trailed off. Would she ever find them easy to say? 'I was abandoned as a baby,' she said, and when he didn't comment she continued with the faltering delivery of someone speaking in a foreign language. 'I was dumped on the doorstep of a priest's house in south London. The priest was called Father O'Brady,' she added, as though such extraneous detail were necessary. 'Who lived there with his housekeeper, Ellen.'

Did she imagine the flicker of compassion which briefly softened his cynical expression, or was that just wishful thinking?

'Go on,' he said.

'I'm told it was an unseasonably cold autumn evening and Ellen heard a squawk outside. Father O'Brady said it was a fox, but Ellen wasn't so sure, and when she opened the door, she found me on the step, wrapped in a blanket and lying in a hessian carrier bag, covered in fallen leaves.'

'Me estas cargando—'

'No!' she interjected fiercely, before he got the chance to pity her—in any language—because she had been *poor Kitty* throughout all her school years and it was a nickname she hated. 'I was lucky.'

'Lucky?' he echoed, pursing his lips together in disbelief. 'Are you kidding?'

Kitty nodded, because this had been drummed into her time and time again by dear Ellen. To count her blessings. To think how much worse it could have been. And, oh, her imagination used to run away from her if she allowed her mind to go *there*. 'I was taken in by two very kind people and spent six very happy years with them, until...'

'Until?' he prompted as her words faded away.

Kitty shrugged, as if that might distract her from

the sudden stab to her heart, thinking how weird it was that it could still hurt, even after all this time. Her whole world had changed overnight and she had been powerless to do anything about it. A bit like now. 'But then Ellen had to go back to Ireland to look after her sick mammy and obviously I couldn't stay with Father O'Brady. So they found a couple in the parish who hadn't been able to have any children of their own, and they took me in.'

'I'm guessing that wasn't quite so happy?' he said, into the long silence which followed.

In a way Kitty admired his perception although part of her resented it. It would have been easier if he'd just dismissed the rest of her story with a bored expression and wave of the hand, so she wouldn't have to talk about it. 'Not really, no,' she said flatly.

He picked up the silver coffee pot and poured himself another cup of the inky brew. 'Why not?'

When had she last said it out loud? Had she *ever* said it out loud? Yet there was something very *persuasive* about Santiago Tevez, despite his anger of earlier. 'They were a very uptight couple. The sort who hid their lives behind net curtains. Mrs Bailey—Mum,' she added awkwardly, because the word still felt like a dry stone in her mouth, 'had always wanted a baby of her own, her husband less so—and he quickly discovered that I got in the way. And he didn't like it. He wanted his old life back. But, of course, they couldn't send me back, not after they'd adopted me. I wasn't like a sweater you decided you didn't like once you got it home.' She gave a hollow laugh. 'Or a dog you'd mistakenly bought as a Christmas present.'

'And did you ever try to find out who your birth parents were?' he questioned curiously.

'No.' She shook her head. 'I couldn't face it.' Or, more accurately, she couldn't face the possibility of any more rejection. But she didn't tell him the other side of the coin. The side she'd witnessed within her adoptive home, which had made her wary of relationships. Of a woman so in thrall to a man and so eager to please him that she was able to ignore the muffled sobs of a lonely little girl. In that household, the husband came first because 'Mum' loved him. And if that was what love was, then Kitty didn't want any of it.

But Santiago wasn't interested in her views on love, or why she'd steered clear of men until she'd fallen into his arms, driven by an impulse so powerful she'd been unable to stop herself. He had warned her from the outset about all the things he didn't want—and a baby was one of them.

She cleared her throat. 'Look, I know we need to make some decisions about the future—'

'What is it you want from me, Kitty, hmm?' he interrupted. 'A capital sum? A big house in the country? Marriage?'

'I'm not expecting anything you don't want to give,' she said fiercely, her fingers linking protectively over her stomach and the arrowing of his dark gaze told her he hadn't missed the movement. 'You don't have to be a hands-on father. If you don't want to put your name on the birth certificate, that's fine by me. You don't need to be involved at all.' She hesitated. Why not make it easy for him, by giving him the let-out clause he was probably praying for? 'In fact, it would probably be better for everyone if you aren't.'

It was that which made Santiago sit up straight, his breakfast coffee growing cold. And even though he'd felt an inevitable tug of compassion when he'd heard about her childhood, this was eclipsed by a sudden surge of emotions which he had repressed for so long.

He felt outrage.

Exclusion.

Worst of all, he felt powerless.

Shadows of the past began to filter through his mind and once they had taken root there, he couldn't seem to get rid of them. Was this what always happened to children? he wondered bitterly. That they were used as pawns within the toxic relationships of their parents?

'Run that past me again, Kitty,' he instructed softly. 'You think you have the ability to permanently exclude me from this baby's life?'

'But you told me you liked being single,' she protested. 'You told me you didn't want parenthood, or a permanent relationship, or marriage. I was just taking you at your word.'

'So why did you come to Bali, if you knew all that?'

'Because…' He saw her swallow, the movement rippling down the long pale column of her neck, and he wondered why it was now, of all times, that he should find himself recalling how soft her skin was.

'Because I felt you had a right to know you were going to be a father,' she continued shakily. 'But if you'd turned out to be really…'

'Really *what*, Kitty?'

Distractedly, she ran her fingers through the wild mass of red curls. 'I don't know.' She shrugged. 'Cruel or mean—then I wouldn't have mentioned the baby at all. I would have gone away and managed, somehow.'

'So what happened to change your mind?' He gave a hollow laugh. 'Did you decide I wasn't too bad a person after all—or was your sexual hunger for me too insatiable to resist, meaning that I found out anyway? Did desire win over judgement, Kitty? Because that's sure as hell what it looks like from here.'

'Does it matter?' she blurted out. 'We can't change what's happened. We can only decide where we go from here.'

Santiago could feel the violent pound of his heart, but he kept his expression as neutral as it had been at any time during the most dangerous moments of his naval career. How many people had told him he should take up professional poker? 'And do you have any idea where that might be?'

He saw her features relax. She thought he was giving her a choice, when in reality he was laying out a silken trap for her.

And she walked straight into it.

'I can go back to England,' she said. 'That would probably be best.'

A memory sunk deep into the recesses of his mind returned now—knife-sharp, and painful, as he was reminded how biology allowed women to control men. 'For you, maybe,' he iced out. 'But this isn't all about you, Kitty.'

'So what do *you* want?'

And for once in his life, Santiago didn't know. He was a master at determining the outcome of business situations—it was the emotional ones he found so unmanageable. He lowered his voice and for a moment had to concentrate very hard to remember to speak in English and not Spanish. 'I have learned to my cost to follow my own instincts, which at the moment are telling me not to let you out of my sight.'

'What are you suggesting?' she whispered.

'I have to travel to Australia on business,' he said. 'And you're coming with me.'

'You can't just *order* me to accompany you,' she breathed.

'Oh, believe me—I can,' he negated grimly. 'Because what's the alternative, Kitty? Maybe you do have the air fare to take you back to England. But even if that were the case, do you really think I would just let you…go?'

CHAPTER TEN

'YOU'LL NEED CLOTHES.'

Kitty turned away from the window of the luxury car to find Santiago looking at her and, despite the cool detachment of his gaze, it still had the annoying effect of making her skin prickle with something she didn't want to acknowledge as desire. A woman with pride might have demanded to know what was wrong with the outfit she was wearing and all the others which she had hastily assembled in her tired little suitcase back at the Langit Biru—but why ask a question when you knew what the answer would be? Her practical, high-street wardrobe certainly wasn't suitable for accompanying one of the world's most successful men on a foreign business trip—even to a place as famously relaxed as Australia.

The staff on his private jet had already looked her up and down as if an alien had just landed in their midst, and the driver of the limousine who'd been waiting for their arrival at Perth airport had failed to hide his surprise when he saw her. And yet somehow Santiago himself didn't make her feel like a gate-crasher. Hadn't he shown her glimpses of thoughtfulness and care, which were just as seductive as his hard kiss? More dangerous, too—because those things made her start longing for the impossible.

Of course they were impossible.

She closed her eyes and tried to bat away the idea that she was falling in love with him, because only the biggest fool in the world would admit to that.

'I suppose I can go and buy a few things when we get there,' she said, trying to work out how much money she had in her current account and how best to prioritise some new outfits which were going to have to span two continents and a pregnancy.

'Don't be ridiculous.' His voice was faintly impatient. 'You don't know the city and I don't have the time to take you shopping myself. I'll arrange for a stylist to bring a selection of clothes for you to try on at the hotel and, naturally, I'll pick up the bill.'

'Should I be grateful?'

'It would make a pleasant change if you accepted my gifts with something other than a scowl.'

'I might feel like smiling if I knew what was going on. You still haven't told me why I am being forced to fly to Australia with you.'

'You know exactly why.' He stretched his long legs out in front of him. 'I want you where I can see you because we have a lot of decisions to make.'

Kitty was trying very hard not to stare at the fine material of his suit trousers, taut against the muscular bulk of his thighs. With an effort she dragged her attention back to his face, but in terms of easing her racing heart—it didn't really have the desired effect. 'And what am I supposed to do while you're attending all these high-powered business meetings?'

'We're staying at the finest hotel in the city. You should find plenty to amuse yourself there. The spa is world-famous, and most women would jump at the opportunity to use it. Get your nails done, or something.'

'I'm not used to lazing around the place and dunking myself in and out of a hot tub,' she objected, because surely everyone in an upmarket spa would be thinner and prettier and cleverer than her. More than that, she found his tone more than a little patronising 'I'm used to working.'

'I know you are,' he said, and suddenly his voice softened. 'So why not give yourself a break for once?'

Kitty swallowed. Again, that distracting glimpse of softness. Of kindness. *Stop it,* she thought helplessly. 'I suppose so,' she said.

'Good. Tonight there's going to be a party at my lawyers' offices to celebrate signing the financial investment decision papers for my new solar farm, and I'd like you there.'

'Why?'

'You mean, apart from the fact that it would be a shocking lapse of manners to bring you out to Australia, then leave you alone? Then let me be extremely shallow for a moment.' His mouth flickered with the hint of a hard smile. 'When you're not glaring at me, you're very easy on the eye, Kitty O'Hanlon—isn't that a good enough reason?'

It was undeniably a compliment and it made Kitty glow with pleasure. In the back of the limousine his eyes glinted and something fragile yet powerful seemed to shimmer through the air between them. For a minute she thought he was going to lean across and kiss her—furious with her subsequent wash of disappointment when he didn't. *Why would he kiss her?* He hadn't touched her since he'd found out about the baby, and couldn't have made it clearer that sleeping with her had been a big mistake. All he was doing now was working out how best to deal with the consequences of that mistake. Which was what successful people did. They saw problems and they found solutions.

But the contemporary hotel he took her to was gorgeous enough to make Kitty temporarily forget her woes. With tall, curving lines of glass overlooking the Swan river and sporting a myriad turquoise pools—the palm-fringed Granchester WA was an urban paradise. A glass elevator whisked them up to a vast suite, where the hotel manager was waiting to greet them. Kitty blinked as she tried to take in their very own private pool, a terrace hot tub, four bedrooms and a sprawling movie room—as well as its own sleek kitchen and dining room.

'And, of course, don't forget our famous twenty-four-hour butler service.' The manager smiled at her as he fractionally moved a bowl of scented apricot roses which were sitting on a Perspex table.

'Thanks,' said Santiago, depositing his suitcase beside a vast desk which overlooked the city skyscrapers.

Their suite was so unlike anything Kitty had ever seen that she was still in something of a daze once the manager had left, glancing up at the high ceilings and the modern chandeliers which captured the light and sent it dancing in bright patterns across the walls.

'Why are we staying somewhere so huge?'

'Privacy,' he answered succinctly. He flicked a glance at his phone before looking up again. 'You don't like it?'

Kitty looked around again. Who could fail to like it? But it was a bit like setting foot on Mars, it was so big and so strange. She wanted to ask Santiago about sleeping arrangements but it didn't seem the right moment. She knew the most sensible outcome would be for him to direct her to a separate bedroom, as he'd done on Bali, but she realised she no longer wanted that. She wanted him to hold her again. To comfort her and make her feel safe. A rush of unexpected mockery spiralled up inside her. Yeah, sure. Comfort and security were the only things she wanted from Santiago Tevez. It had absolutely nothing to do with simmering lust or the way the sunlight was gilding his autocratic features into a mask of sculpted bronze.

'Nah, it's a dump,' she joked, stupidly pleased to have coaxed a smile from his hard face.

'I need to be on the other side of town for my first meeting,' he said. 'My Australia assistant is called Megan. If you need anything—call her. She'll be li-aising with you about the stylist. I've left her number next to the roses.'

'You noticed the roses?' she questioned in surprise.

'I'm not completely immune to beauty, Kitty,' he said wryly. 'I'll see you later. Anything you want to ask before I go?'

Throughout her life, Kitty's default mechanism had been to ignore anything awkward and hope it would go away—or learn to live with it if it didn't. But she was discovering that this situation was different from any other she'd ever found herself in. She couldn't afford to bury her head in the sand. As Santiago had said, it wasn't just about her any more. She had to stop think-ing about all the things he represented—which had the potential to intimidate her. It didn't matter that he was rich and powerful. What mattered was that they be-haved like grown-ups. She still didn't know him, she realised. She didn't know him at all.

'Are we just here because you want to keep an eye on

me and make sure I don't do a runner? Are you planning to remain a stranger to me, or are you willing to face up to the fact that I'm carrying your baby and I'd like to find out more about you?'

His automatic recoil spoke volumes and Kitty sensed that maybe they were more alike than she'd thought. Perhaps he also found it easier to sideline reality, than to deal with it head-on.

'What kind of "more"?' he demanded.

'The normal stuff. What goes on inside your head. What sort of man you really are.'

But to her surprise, he nodded. 'We'll talk later,' he promised. 'Whatever you need to know, we'll discuss. But right now, I really do need to be somewhere else. I'll be back around five.'

Resolutely, Santiago turned and headed for the glass elevator, not relaxing until he was in the waiting limousine and heading for St George's Terrace, to sign the pile of legal documents which awaited him. Actually... He sighed. Who was he kidding? He wasn't relaxed at all. He was tense—in mind *and* body—without a clue about what best action to take. Yet the answers had always been there for him after the teenage tragedy which had set in motion the austere trajectory of his life, where nobody was permitted to get close enough to hurt him ever again.

He stared at the back of the driver's head.

Should he just settle a sum of money on Kitty O'Hanlon? An amount vast enough to make her accessible to the demands which would inevitably accompany his offer. She certainly hadn't objected to the new clothes he'd offered to provide. No surprise there. All women liked *things*, he reminded himself grimly. He heard a buzzing and looked down. Someone was calling his phone—the CEO of one of Australia's biggest mining companies—but he let it divert to his assistant because, for once, it didn't seem important.

He guessed he could have his lawyers draw up a water-tight contract dealing with the baby's future. It would have to be carefully worded, of course. There would have to be a confidentiality clause—a non-disclosure agreement, forbidding Kitty from ever giving interviews to the press. They would also need to agree on the child's schooling and place of residence. His eyes narrowed. Should he insist on the acquisition of Spanish as a second language?

But his heart was pumping violently in his chest as he realised there was one way to guarantee that particular scenario—by ensuring the child grew up with a native Spanish speaker.

Like himself.

The thought flew at him like a curveball—the first time he had thought of the baby as essentially *his*, rather than as something theoretical.

The car drove past Perth's magnificent skyscrapers—tall structures of glass gleaming like golden monuments in the Australian sunshine—but all Santiago could focus on was the single, burning question which dominated his thoughts.

What did Kitty really want from him?

Fortunately, he was able to switch off his immediate concerns as he stepped into the boardroom, because right now he needed to concentrate on his bold new solar project just north of the city and the reason for his presence here today. A smattering of applause greeted him as he began to sign the documents and he saw undisguised pleasure on the faces of the lawyers and bankers as he scrawled the final signature. But as usual, his own sense of joy was perfunctory. He wanted to get back to the hotel, he realised.

To make a few hard decisions?

Or to pull Kitty O'Hanlon into his arms and lose himself in the softness of her body?

But as the limousine drew up outside the hotel and he got into the elevator, he could feel irritation vying with lust. Surely sex would be nothing but a distraction in their current situation. His mouth tightened as the doors slid soundlessly open. Which meant it was best avoided. Shrugging off his jacket, he stepped into the suite and was just thinking about taking a shower, when he stopped in his tracks.

It was Kitty, and she hadn't seen him.

She was sitting out on a terrace which was splashed with sun, for the Australian winter was mild. A large straw hat was shading her face, a sketchbook lying face down on her lap, and a jug of water sat on a table by her side, along with a row of pencils. Her polka-dot dress was diaphanous and beneath the straw hat her red curls spilled like a glorious banner. He stood there for a moment just watching her, because she looked so relaxed and so…yes…beautiful. Once again he experienced a rare moment of peace—though woven in with that was the bright thread of desire, which made him aware of the heat at his groin. And although he was standing perfectly still, she must have sensed his presence because slowly she turned her head to look at him. Her eyes darkened and her lips parted as if she was about to smile but she seemed to change her mind and replace it with a cloak of wariness.

'Hi.' She made as if to rise, but he shook his head.

'No,' he commanded softly. 'Stay right where you are. I'll come and join you.'

He went inside and stripped off his suit before heading into the stadium-sized wet room, where the icy jets of the shower failed to cool his heated blood. Afterwards, he slid on an old pair of jeans and a T-shirt, wandered into the minibar and flipped the lid on a frosted beer, before wandering back out onto the terrace.

This time she was anticipating his arrival and sitting up in expectation, the sketchbook now closed and lying on the table.

'Was it a good meeting?' she said, her uncertain smile betraying her nerves.

He was unused to a woman being there to greet him on his return from work and as he met the green glitter of her gaze Santiago wondered if this was what most men had, or wanted. Or thought they wanted. If this was what being in a relationship was all about. For surely this was domesticity—with all its unthreatening ease. The considerate question. The absence of anger and recrimination. All these had been missing during his childhood—although occasionally he had caught glimpses of serenity within the humble homes of his father's servants. Before he'd trained himself not to, he had sometimes wondered why all the money in the world couldn't buy the simple pleasures which seemed to fulfil the lives of most people. For him, home life symbolised dissent and deception. Perhaps that was why he had spent his adulthood avoiding it.

Yet he recognised an attempt at a truce underpinning Kitty's polite question and, though it was tempting to converse in these unthreatening niceties, Santiago was aware that he'd made a promise to her and, strangely, found himself wanting to honour it. Maybe if she'd been nagging him or demanding answers, he might have baulked—but she was doing neither of these things.

She was like the soft fan of the breeze on your face after you'd walked many miles in the punishing heat of the midday sun.

'I'm sure everyone there today would have agreed the meeting was a triumph,' he said. 'But I'm guessing that's not the kind of thing you had in mind when I agreed we would talk.'

Twisting her fingers nervously together, Kitty shook her head. Santiago's expression was mocking as well as questioning—as if daring her to ask the things which had been bubbling inside her for weeks. She'd wanted more than anything to discover more about the father of her baby, but now the moment had come, she was scared. Because she knew all too well that knowledge wasn't necessarily a good thing. Sometimes it was preferable to imagine the best, rather than know the worst. She had preferred to think of her adoptive father as a shy man who'd found it difficult to engage with an awkward young orphan—not that he resented that child and wished her gone. That had been the truth and it had been a hard truth to live with.

'I told you about my own background,' she said, her voice faltering a little. 'I don't imagine yours could be any worse.'

His black eyes hardened. 'I would hate to disenchant you, *roja*, but I suspect I'm going to.'

She waited, despite the temptation to grin stupidly when he used his pet name for her. She didn't say a word—as if the bubble of what he was about to confide could be popped at the slightest provocation and she might not get another chance to hear it.

'I was born in Buenos Aires,' he began. 'To a father who was unimaginably rich, and a mother who was very beautiful. But beauty comes from within,' he added, and now his voice sounded harsh—like a rusty nail being scraped across a piece of fine crystal. 'Isn't that so, Kitty?'

Kitty nodded, noticing the sudden tightening of his jaw. 'That's what they say, all right.'

'My father was much older than my mother.' He shrugged. 'Such interactions between men and women are age-old and well-documented—fabulous beauty offered in exchange for fabulous amounts of wealth. Less of a relationship—more of a transaction.' He stopped speaking for a moment. 'I was born very quickly after the marriage, but as soon as I became aware of the world around me—I discovered that theirs was not a union made in heaven.'

She looked at him and still she said nothing, because Kitty realised that her choice of questions might not give her the answers she was seeking.

'It took a long time for the true picture to emerge because as a child you see the world through a prism and you're not sure how it's supposed to work.' His gaze settled on a pot of flame-coloured blooms at the far end of the terrace. 'I can't remember how old I was when I realised that other mothers didn't speak to their husbands with contempt, nor treat them with disdain. Or take other lovers—younger lovers—and then flaunt them in his face. Nor have as little as possible to do with their own child and constantly pass him over to the care of servants.'

Kitty flinched and suddenly she could no longer retain her air of impassivity. 'Oh, Santiago. That must have been awful. For all of you.'

'Sí,' he agreed, almost flippantly. 'It was. But as you know yourself, I had nothing to compare it with. It was all I knew and so I accepted it.' There was another pause. Much longer this time. 'And then she left him. And me, of course.'

'How old were you?'

'Twelve.'

The silence which followed became such a bleak vacuum that Kitty felt compelled to fill it.

'You must have missed her.'

His face twisted but there was no sadness there. Only anger. 'Is it mandatory to love your mother?' he demanded harshly. 'If you want the truth, my life felt infinitely better without the constant rows and mind games and deceptions.' He gave a bitter laugh. 'My father was a different matter. He went to pieces.'

'So he wasn't able to be a good parent to you?'

He shrugged. 'He did his best and I was fine with that. Most boys on the brink of being teenagers would welcome being given a loose rein and eventually we forged our own kind of compatibility.' His voice took on a hard and steely note. 'The real difficulty came several years later, when my mother decided she wanted to reconcile.'

Kitty sat up a little straighter. 'And how did...how did that pan out?'

Santiago hesitated, because these were places he never went to. The humiliation and subsequent horror had been bad enough without having to take himself back there. But he had promised Kitty and he prided himself on his honesty. And couldn't this particular memory be useful to him? Wouldn't it remind him that life was so much simpler if you didn't place your trust in anyone else?

'My father was...' he breathed out a ragged sigh '...*pathetically* grateful that she was back. He bent over backwards to accommodate her every whim, no matter how expensive or outlandish. It sickened me to see him behave that way, and every time he did, her contempt for him grew. I was the unwilling onlooker. The helpless spectator. We took a cultural trip to Europe and I remember people looking at them and laughing.' His words tailed off and he waited—no, he *hoped*—for some simpering sympathy which would aggravate him, so he could walk away and pour himself a strong drink and bring the conversation to an abrupt conclusion.

But Kitty said nothing. She just continued to look at him with that same air of calm expectation, her green eyes shaded by the wide brim of her hat, and Santiago could feel the unexpected clench of his heart, because he wanted to kiss her.

'It ended messily, of course. How could it end any other way? It was like watching a disaster movie. We returned to Buenos Aires, which was when my mother moved her younger lover into the house.'

Some of the calmness had gone. 'Excuse me? *She moved her lover into the house? How does that work?*'

'It was big enough for my father not to have known about it.' But then Santiago was all done with flippancy and in its place came something long suppressed. Something like sorrow, but it was something else too.

Ask me, he thought. *Go on, ask me if I knew.* But she didn't ask and—inexplicably—he found himself telling her. As if the weight had now become unendurable. Or maybe it was the guilt. So many different layers of guilt.

'But I knew. I knew and I didn't tell him. Perhaps if I had, things might have been different. As it was, he found them together.' His mouth twisted. 'I believe the Latin term is *in flagrante.*'

Her fingers flew to her lips. 'Oh, Santiago.'

'He told her to get out,' he continued, trying to forget the rage he'd felt—much of it directed at himself. 'I thought he would divorce her, drag her through the courts and publicly humiliate her, but he didn't. He acted as if nothing had happened. Nobody knew a thing—not then and not afterwards. He didn't tell and my mother certainly didn't. He just turned in on himself. Became a broken shell of a man. It was painful to watch.' He paused. 'And then, one day, he told me we were going on holiday and I thought the tide had turned—that we were back to where we used to be. It was just the two of us. We went to Rio de Janeiro, to the most amazing beach resort. My father seemed interested in going out—to bars and restaurants.'

For Santiago, it had been as if someone had switched a light. Secure in the knowledge of his father's re-emergence into society, he had felt free for the first time in his life. He had played volleyball on the beach. Become aware of the many beauties who had looked at him with open hunger in their eyes. And then fate had stepped in to deliver its devastating curveball.

He tilted his chin, still searching for some perceived fault in Kitty's expression which would make him dry up—but her soft understanding only seemed to encourage him to articulate the few stark facts which could convey so much.

'We flew back to Buenos Aires, and things felt better. Certainly better than they'd been before. And then, a couple of days later, my father didn't come home when he was supposed to.' He had sat in that colossal mansion until dawn broke over Argentina's premier city and, in a funny sort of way, the knock on the door had seemed almost inevitable. 'The police arrived a couple of hours later to tell me he'd been involved in a traffic accident and had died at the scene. And there was a part of me which wondered whether he had wanted that,' he husked. 'Whether deep-down he would rather be dead than be without her.'

'Oh, Santiago. I'm so sorry,' she breathed.

He inclined his head.

'Did your mother—?'

'She came to the funeral but we barely exchanged a word,' he said. 'And I never saw her again. She was a cold-hearted bitch who humiliated both me and my father—why would I ever want to see her?' He answered the silent question in her eyes. 'Since they had never divorced she inherited his fortune, which she lavished on a series of increasingly unsuitable young men before she died, her body wrecked by too much high living. So there you have it, Kitty. You see—you don't have the monopoly on lousy childhoods, after all.'

Kitty nodded, but his air of bravado failed to hide the faint crack in his voice and her heart went out to him. She knew what it was like to have the kind of background which sounded like something you'd see on a downmarket reality show and realised there was nothing she could say to ease the pain he was so obviously trying to hide. Nothing she could do, either.

Or was there?

She understood more about him now.

She understood why he was so opposed to marriage and fatherhood and why he was so cynical about women. Who wouldn't be, in his situation? She could see why her news must have been like his worst nightmare and why he would despise her for keeping the baby secret from him. His mother had deceived and kept secrets, hadn't she? And even though Kitty had felt justified in not telling him straight away, Santiago might not agree with her.

Every bit of reason she possessed was telling her that the safest thing would be to keep him at a distance. To continue with this no-touch, very adult way of addressing their problems.

Yet she hesitated. Earlier, she had wanted comfort from him, but it seemed Santiago might be the one who needed it more. Could she give him that? With all her innocence and inexperience could she help this man who was trying so hard to disguise his pain?

Rising to her feet, she was aware of him watching her, his muscular body tensing as she walked across the terrace towards him. She could feel the filmy fabric of her new dress swishing around her thighs until, a little breathlessly, she reached him and stared up into his face. His eyes glittered like polished jet, his bronzed skin stretched tightly across the high slash of his cheekbones. Never had he seemed more remote or untouchable.

'I don't want your pity,' he ground out.

'And you're not getting any. Not from me,' she whispered. 'I hate pity with a passion.'

For a moment she thought he might be about to turn away because his body became completely rigid, as if he were testing himself. When suddenly all that resistance evaporated and was replaced with a different kind of tension.

'That seems an awful waste of passion,' he observed unevenly.

'Does it?' she questioned, without missing a beat.

His black eyes were unreadable as he studied her face for what felt like a long time. Then he pulled her into his arms and drove his lips down on hers. And Kitty shuddered because his kiss was hard. Almost brutal. But that didn't matter. Because on some newly awoken level she recognised that maybe it needed to be like that.

It certainly didn't impact on her helpless moan, nor the warm rush of anticipation which flooded through her as Santiago picked her up and carried her into the luxury suite, like a victor about to claim his spoils.

CHAPTER ELEVEN

THIS WAS WRONG.

As he carried Kitty towards the bed, Santiago *knew* it was wrong, but somehow he couldn't seem to stop himself.

His mouth hardened. Who was he kidding? Did he really believe he had some kind of *choice* in the matter? As if he could have stopped himself from doing this when soft invitation was exuding from every pore of her delicious body?

As he set her down he wondered why he had told her so much about himself. Surely providing that kind of information was giving her a unique power over him. But it was easy to block out his conflicting thoughts when Kitty's tongue was in his mouth and she was writhing eagerly in his arms. When he was taking off her dress and dropping it to the ground before tearing off his T-shirt and jeans. His throat was dry and his heart pounding as he pushed her onto the bed and a pent-up breath hissed from his lips as he raked his gaze over her.

Usually he was the master of restraint. He could make a woman scream her pleasure over and over again before allowing his own satisfaction to engulf him—yet today he seemed at the mercy of a hunger so overwhelming that he wanted to just plunge inside her liquid heat and lose himself in her sweetness.

He forced himself to temper his desire, slowly removing the delicate green lingerie which complemented her eyes and which, presumably, he had paid for. As the tiny lacy thong fluttered over the side of the bed, it was a timely reminder of everything he knew to be true. *She's no different from the others*, chanted the cynical mantra inside his head.

But *she* felt different.

This felt different.

It was as if a layer of himself had been torn away—leaving him exposed and aching, her body the sweet balm he needed in order to heal himself.

He moved onto the bed and took her in his arms and she was stroking his shoulders and his back and her lips were soft and seeking as they whispered over his skin. Her touch was electric, pure and simple, and he groaned. How could someone so inexperienced be so damned good?

He shuddered as he entered her, luxuriating in the way her body tightened around him. As if it were her first time. As if it were his. And then he rode her—cautiously at first, but soon she was urging him on with the persuasive thrust of her hips. Was it because she was carrying his baby that his senses seemed to have gone into overdrive, or because she knew more about him than anyone else had ever done?

The two were inextricably linked, surely.

And then it became all about movement and sensation. He wasn't thinking any more. He was lost. Lost in something he didn't understand. He could feel the clench of her muscles as she coaxed out the wild rush of his seed and he choked out something broken and incomprehensible against her neck.

As his heart slowed, so did the universe. The only thing he could compare it to was floating down to earth on a parachute. That sense of quiet and calm and peace. Her head was lying on his chest, the rapid rhythm of her breathing warm against his skin and, absently, he ran his fingers through the tangled spill of her vibrant curls.

'Fue increible,' was all he said.

Kitty didn't ask for a translation. Even if one of the words wasn't remarkably similar to its English counterpart, the lazy satisfaction in his voice told her everything she needed to know.

Or did it?

Good sex was all very well, but it only went so far, and in a way it was a distraction. What happened now? They still hadn't talked about what lay ahead.

But sleep was beckoning her with beguiling fingers and she must have drifted off because when Kitty's lashes fluttered open, it was to see Santiago on the other side of the room, with nothing but a small white towel wrapped around his hips. The moist sheen of water on his shoulders indicated a recent shower and for a moment she couldn't speak, and not just because he looked so amazing. They'd just had sex, which was surely about as close as two people could get, yet there was something even more intimate about seeing him in such a careless state of undress. It implied a relaxation and a closeness which took companionship to a whole new level. And she wanted that, she realised suddenly. She wanted that more than anything.

Like her, he'd opened up and revealed some of the things which had left him with deep emotional scars and Kitty figured that a man like Santiago wouldn't have done that lightly. Didn't his disclosure imply that on some level he trusted her, as she did him? Would it be crazy to hope they might be able to forge some kind of future together, even if it wasn't a terribly conventional one?

She licked her dry lips and saw his eyes darken. 'Santiago?'

'You need to get dressed,' he said abruptly.

She was confused and maybe she showed it.

'We're going to a party. Remember?'

It hadn't been top of her list of priorities but, yes, of course, Kitty remembered now. 'How long have I got?' she questioned calmly when inside she was screaming, *Why haven't you kissed me?*

A single drop of water trickled down over his bare torso. 'Will an hour be long enough?'

'Sure.' Trying not to be self-conscious about her nakedness, Kitty walked towards the bathroom, hoping she didn't show her disappointment that he was acting so distantly when he'd been so passionate just a while ago. Maybe this was the way people behaved, in his sophisticated world. As she angled the shower over herself and tried not to get her hair wet, she tried convincing herself that his reaction was entirely rational. They'd had sex, that was all. *That was all.* It might have been good sex—even she knew that—but it hadn't magically turned Santiago from a commitment-phobe who mistrusted women into the kind of ardent lover who never wanted to let her go. If she started expecting things, or making unreasonable demands of him, she was going to end up either hurt, or disappointed. Or both.

And if she'd learnt one thing in life, it was never to have expectations.

She emerged from the shower and peered into the

wardrobe at the row of new clothes hanging there, each with their own matching accessories. The stylist had been sweet. She hadn't tried to put her in yellow and had gently steered Kitty away from worrying about the cost.

'Señor Tevez can afford it,' had been her gentle advice.

Of that Kitty had been in no doubt, though she had rejected all offers of accompanying jewellery. But as she selected a dress she would never have chosen for herself—a ridiculously flattering sheath of navy silk—she couldn't help wondering just how many other women had been the beneficiaries of Santiago's generosity. Did he dress them all up this way—like those paper dolls she'd made as a child—so he wouldn't be ashamed of being seen with them in public?

But then she chided herself for her own stupidity as she remembered some of the articles she'd seen about him on the Internet. The supermodels and heiresses he'd been photographed with in the past certainly wouldn't need an urgently acquired wardrobe.

She was a charity case.

She had always been a charity case.

Her fingers were unsteady as she applied mascara to her lashes and a slick of lip gloss, before sliding her feet into suede heels which were higher than anything she was used to. But when she walked into the main living area, Santiago looked up from his computer and brought his lips together in a long and silent whistle.

'Is this okay?' she asked.

'Is this okay?' he repeated slowly as he rose from the desk and came towards her, his pale silk shirt open by a couple of buttons at the neck, revealing a glimpse of gleaming bronze skin. 'No, it is more than *okay*. You look utterly spectacular, *roja*, and I would like more than anything to kiss you, but if I do I don't trust myself to stop and that will inevitably make us late.'

If only she'd had the nerve to say that surely it didn't matter if they were late and ask him to kiss her anyway. But she'd come onto him earlier, after he'd told her all that brutal stuff about his past—and wasn't there a perceived wisdom that a woman shouldn't always be the one to do the running? Kitty wasn't sure and she had no template to fall back on. Nobody had ever taught her how to be confident. And if you'd never been in a real relationship, then how did you know when it was okay to express your needs?

But she relaxed a little as the limousine whisked them through the pristine streets of Perth and Santiago pointed out some of the spectacular sights of Western Australia's capital, dominated by the glittering Swan river—home to the city's iconic black swans. His lazy commentary meant there was little time for any doubts to accumulate and before long they had arrived at the hotel where the party was being held and were riding the glass elevator to the rooftop bar.

'So if people ask me who I am and what I'm doing here, what do I tell them?' she ventured nervously as the elevator pinged to a halt.

'You tell them you're with me.' His lips curved mockingly. 'Anything else I leave to your discretion.'

She tugged at the skirt of her dress with nervous fingers. 'I'll do my best.'

'Just be yourself,' he advised suddenly, meeting her eyes, and she found herself wanting to grab hold of that statement and hug it to her chest, because wasn't that just about the nicest thing anyone had ever said to her?

Santiago watched as Kitty walked into the bar with her head held high and saw the gazes of his lawyers and various investors fixing on her, as if taken by surprise. Maybe they were. Although the velvet banquettes, golden chandeliers and sweeping views of the surrounding skyscrapers ensured a glitzy setting, this was essentially a business party and not the kind of function he would usually have taken a date to. Certainly not a date like Kitty O'Hanlon.

He thought how stunning she looked in her expensive new finery, a dark blue dress accentuating the firm curves of her body and lush swell of her breasts. Her thick curls were captured in an intricate style on top of her head, although tantalising tendrils dangled by her cheeks, like spirals of fire. Yet despite her polished new image, that air of sweetness and innocence shone through and he realised the last thing he wanted to do was to hurt her.

How was he going to manage that?

Didn't every woman he'd ever been involved with claim that he'd inflicted pain, because he was unable to give them what they wanted in terms of emotional commitment?

Unable? he found himself asking, with an uncharacteristic degree of self-insight.

His jaw tightened.

Or just unwilling?

With one hand lightly cupping her elbow, Santiago introduced her to a couple of people and then listened while she charmed two of the most successful lawyers in the state with her naiveté and genuine interest. Feeling confident enough to leave her to her own devices, he worked the room, before giving a short speech thanking everyone for their hard work and raising his glass to them. He could see Kitty applauding his words, clapping her hands with the enthusiasm of a football supporter celebrating a season-clinching goal. No attempt at coolness there, he thought with wry amusement, but a warm rush of pleasure flooded through him.

In the car on the way home, he looked at her curiously. 'What was Jared Stone saying to you?'

She turned her head. 'That he was thinking of buying a puppy.'

'You're kidding me?'

'Why should I be kidding?'

'That man's so tough they say he eats iron filings for breakfast.'

'I think he's come to a sort of crossroads in his life,' she said thoughtfully.

He couldn't wait to get her back to the hotel, where he tumbled her straight into bed and, after he'd made her come three times, he ordered buttered eggs from room service and fed them to her with a spoon.

He thought how dazed she looked as she slumped back against the pile of feathery pillows afterwards.

'Are you okay?' he prompted, more softly than was usual for him.

'I think so.' She bit her lip and nodded. 'That was...

'Mmm?'

'Incredible,' she said at last.

'The sex, or the eggs?'

'Well, both, actually.' Her cheeks went very pink. 'I don't think I've ever eaten a meal in bed before, except for when I was ill.'

Her words were those of someone whose childhood had been devoid of many of life's pleasures, and, despite the almighty contrast in their backgrounds, he experienced a sharp clench of identification. 'When did you last have a holiday, Kitty?'

Her emerald eyes narrowed with suspicion. 'When did *you*?'

It was a good point. 'I've been thinking,' he said slowly. 'Why don't we go up to the Northern Territory for a couple of days?'

She fiddled a bit with the rumpled sheet, before looking up at him. 'Why?'

He shrugged. 'It's the dry season. It's warmer than Perth. It's an amazing part of the world, like nowhere else you'll have ever seen. I don't know how you feel about crocodiles and snakes, but I promise to keep you a safe distance from both.'

But the wariness in her green eyes hadn't gone anywhere and she was still pleating the edge of the sheet with her fingers. 'No, I meant why do you want to take me on holiday?'

Aside from the fact that he wasn't used to having his invitations greeted with such a lukewarm response, it was a seeking question and the kind he usually would have deflected. But Kitty was pregnant, and he couldn't keep concealing his motives behind his usual armour.

Pregnant.

A tingle of something inexplicable whispered down his spine.

Usually he had all the answers, but this time they were eluding him.

'I think we do need to get to know one another better,' he said finally, and then, just in case she started building foolish fantasies inside her head, he subjected her to a cool look. The kind of expression he might have adopted if he were about to begin negotiations with a land-owner and wanted to keep things amicable. The quick smile which followed was his only concession that this wasn't business. This was personal. 'We have a child's future to navigate, don't we, Kitty?'

CHAPTER TWELVE

SILHOUETTED AGAINST THE thick canvas of the tent, Santiago was just pouring a glass of iced water when his attention was caught by a folder lying unobtrusively on a table nearby.

'What's this?' he questioned curiously.

'Nothing,' answered Kitty quickly.

'Doesn't look like nothing.' A pair of jet-dark eyebrows were raised in question. 'May I look?'

Kitty shrugged a little self-consciously but nodded all the same. 'Sure. Why not?' she agreed reluctantly, because she'd never intended him to see the drawing she'd done of him—not in a million years. Lying back against the rumpled sheets, she watched as Santiago slid out the sheet of paper and looked at it.

'It's me,' he said slowly, and then frowned as he studied it more closely. 'Wow. Do I really look like that?'

'Sometimes,' she said.

He was still frowning, and she wondered if he was offended by the sketch. She had done it during their flight from Perth to Wallaby Wilderness—an upmarket glamping spot close to a wide river in the far north of the country. They had been travelling in some luxury on Santiago's private jet but he had been immersed in a complicated business deal—his promise of taking a holiday from work seemingly forgotten.

Having seen as much as she wanted of the vast landscape which stretched endlessly outside the porthole window, Kitty had started to draw—her pencil flying swiftly over the paper as she had depicted him exactly as she saw him that day. But now she was aware that his features looked stony. Stern. Almost fierce. The sensual lips unsmiling, his jaw shadowed. It was the portrait of a beautiful but remote face—with emotional distance etched on every pore—and that was why she'd hastily concealed it in the folder when she'd finished it. She certainly hadn't meant Santiago to stumble upon it.

'It isn't a particularly flattering portrait,' he observed.

'Possibly not. The truth is rarely complimentary.'

'You think so?' He put the drawing down and began to walk across the tent towards her, gloriously and unashamedly naked, his dark eyes glinting, his glass of water forgotten.

Kitty's heart raced, because she knew that look on his face so well. 'That's what they say.'

'Do they?' He sat down on the edge of the bed and reached for her exposed breast, rubbing the nipple between his thumb and forefinger so that it puckered into instant life. 'What if I were to tell you that you're beautiful—would you believe that, Kitty?'

'No.' She shook her head. 'Because I'm not.'

'Or that I want you again?'

Now that part *would* be easy to believe because he seemed to want her all the time. As he bent his head to place his mouth where his fingers had just been, Kitty had to fight the desire to sink into the delicious sensations he was inciting with his tongue. Because sex could be all kinds of things, she was beginning to realise. It could muddle and obscure the truth. It could make you forget what you were doing or why you were here, inside a tent the size of a small house.

With his dark head still licking deliciously at her nipple, she looked around. The stilted canvas tent actually had *rooms*. A dressing room. A bathroom which, although nothing like as fancy as the one they'd left behind in Perth, was still pretty sophisticated. In the enormous living/sleeping space there was a giant bed on which they now lay, surrounded by gauzy pale mosquito nets which somehow managed to give it a retro vibe. Above the bed whirred a giant fan.

She thought how easy it would be to suspend disbelief and pretend they were a couple of normal lovers, here on holiday.

Except they weren't.

'Santiago,' she whispered.

He lifted his dark head, his eyes smoky with desire. 'What?'

She wanted to remind him that they couldn't keep allowing their incredible chemistry to distract them like this. That they were supposed to be talking about their baby. Yet deep down she was afraid of having that discussion. Afraid of the unforgiving light it would shine on their relationship? Maybe she was just scared of the future because she suspected it wasn't going to involve Santiago in any major way, which she'd known from the start. But that was the trouble with getting involved with a man. You had no idea how you were going to feel about him, or that your feelings might change. She hadn't planned on being continually captivated by him. She didn't want to laugh at his jokes, or find herself admiring his quiet charity work, which was something else Jared Stone had told her about, in Perth. She swallowed. Or to feel safe and protected whenever he was around. She wanted to be able to take him or leave him—because she suspected that the latter was going to happen before too long.

'We haven't done very much talking.'

'Talking is overrated,' he growled.

She smiled, in spite of everything. 'I know, but—'

He pulled away from her, surveying her belly cautiously. 'You're feeling okay?'

The words were solicitous but she wished he would *touch* her there. That he would splay a possessive palm over the warm flesh and acknowledge the tiny life which was growing inside. But Santiago only ever touched her in a sexual way and even the most oblique reference to her pregnancy was always greeted with detachment. And *that* was the reality, she told herself fiercely. Not the ever-hovering fantasy of shared parenthood, which was ready to spring to poignant life if she allowed it to. 'I'm feeling fine.'

'Not sick?'

'No. Not sick at all. Feeling great, as a matter of fact—as I have been since we got here.' She sucked in a deep breath. 'But the thing is—'

'Later, *roja*,' he instructed throatily. 'Just not right now.'

Santiago stemmed what he suspected was coming by the simple expedient of kissing her because, as he had acknowledged on more than one occasion, her honeyed lips were sweeter than anything he'd ever tasted.

But he associated honey with traps.

With deceit, and with cruelty.

He whispered his fingertips over her silken flesh and heard her murmured response, but still those caustic thoughts plagued him. He knew what he wanted. Or rather, what he *didn't* want—to tie himself down to one woman and open himself up to the possibility of manipulation and deceit.

But lately he had experienced an aching in his heart he hadn't been expecting, along with a fierce desire to protect the child which Kitty carried.

His child.

Like a dark spectre which lingered on the edges of his mind, he thought about responsibility. Should he do the right thing by offering Kitty the security he suspected she really wanted? His jaw tightened. Just as long as she understood—and accepted—his limitations.

He waited until dinner. Until they had eaten barramundi fish with pepper berry and bush tomatoes and the last of the blood orange sorbet had melted in pink puddles in the rustic pottery bowls. He had just announced they were due an early start in the morning but brushed aside her ensuing questions, because the matter in hand was of far greater importance than the surprise trip he had organised for her.

But now that the moment was here, he found himself strangely reluctant to speak, suspecting that, once he did, things would never be the same again. He stared at the red wine he'd barely touched, then lifted his gaze to the woman sitting opposite him. Her fiery curls spilled down over her shoulders and she wore a silky dress the colour of forest leaves. She *was* beautiful, he thought. And that was the truth.

'We need to discuss where we go from here,' he said. 'Don't we?'

Her emerald eyes became hooded. 'I'm assuming you're not talking about where your plane is going to take us?'

He heard the faint nerves which tremored her attempt at a joke. 'No, Kitty, I'm not.' He fingered the stem of his wine glass. 'I have a couple of suggestions to put to you.' He spoke carefully because, although known as a master of negotiation, never had he been so aware of the potential for his words to be misconstrued. 'Obviously, I'm in a position to fix you up with an income, which would enable you to have your own house, or apartment. And obviously, I'm prepared to be very generous towards you and the baby.'

'That's very...kind of you,' she said stiffly.

He narrowed his eyes as if to detect sarcasm but there was nothing but wariness on her freckled face, giving him the fuel he needed to make his additional and unprecedented offer.

'But I have an alternative proposition which may appeal more.'

The flicker of candlelight was gilding her pale cheeks. 'Go on.'

'I suspect the most straightforward way of dealing with this situation would be for us to marry.'

'To marry?' she repeated, as if she wasn't sure she'd heard him properly.

He shrugged. 'It makes sense. It will give you and the child the security you both need.'

'I know, but...*marriage.*'

He didn't know what he had expected. Gratitude? Delight? Yes, certainly. But her face seemed to grow even paler and there was no answering smile, no gushing thanks. Nothing other than a glint of caution glinting green fire from the hooded beauty of her eyes.

'Someone has to inherit my fortune, Kitty.'

'That sounds very...contractual.'

'Of course. I deal in contracts.' He removed his fingers from the stem of his glass. 'It's how I live my life.'

'But always as a single man,' she pointed out. 'You made that very clear—even on the night we met.'

'It's true I'd never planned to marry and, now you know more about me, you can probably understand why. The example set by my parents was less than...' he felt his mouth twist '...*aspirational*. It wasn't a tough choice because I'd never met anyone who I thought would make a good wife.' He paused. 'And then I met you.'

He could see the sudden flicker of hope in her eyes.

'That was one of the reasons I brought you to Australia with me, from Bali,' he said. 'I wanted to see whether you could fit into my world, and it seems you could. You are personable, and kind. People like you. I have watched them warm to you. I like you.'

'Wow,' she said.

'You don't even seem particularly interested in my wealth,' he continued, deciding to overlook what definitely *did* sound like sarcasm. 'The stylist in Perth told me you refused to accept any of the jewels which were entirely at your disposal. Believe me when I tell you there aren't many women who would do that.' He gave a short laugh. 'Who would refuse a rich man's diamonds?'

For a while she just sat there, nodding her head in comprehension. 'So you've been testing me,' she said slowly. 'All the time we've been in Australia, you've been subjecting me to some sort of silent character assessment. That was why you brought me here.'

'Didn't you do exactly the same with me, when you flew out to Bali to decide whether or not I would make a suitable father?' he challenged softly.

Awkwardly, she shrugged. 'I guess.'

'So what's the problem?'

Her voice had started to tremble. 'Because marriage is about more than a piece of paper, Santiago, or ticking a load of boxes. It's about fidelity and commitment and...and *love*, surely.'

'Won't two out of three suffice?' he questioned silkily. 'I can promise fidelity and commitment. But I don't do love.' His voice had become harsher now—his smooth negotiating skills momentarily forgotten. But surely the truth was better than the alternative of broken dreams and unfulfilled expectations. 'I don't know how to, if I'm being honest.'

'And you have never been anything but honest, have you, Santiago?'

He studied her for a long moment. 'Is that a criticism, Kitty?'

She shook her head. 'No. It's simply a statement of fact. And it's okay. You've told me what was on your mind. You've put marriage on the table and I'd like... I'd like to think about it.'

'You'd *like to think about it*?' he echoed, unable to hide his incredulity.

'Don't tell me you expected an instant answer? Ah, I can see from your expression that you probably did.' She gave him a funny look. 'A proposal is a lot to take on board, Santiago. I'm sure you'd hate me to rush a decision as important as this.'

Kitty knew she sounded calm as they rose from the table, but calm was the last thing she felt. She was glad to leave the faux romance of the restaurant—with its gleaming candles and fairy-tale views of the star-studded sky. As they picked their way over the walkway towards their stilted tent, she remembered that they'd spent most of the afternoon in bed, so it didn't feel particularly significant for them not to have sex, when eventually they sank down beneath the gauzy mosquito nets. But as they kissed goodnight, her mind was still seething with unresolved thoughts.

As the careless hand Santiago had slung around her waist relaxed and his breathing deepened into the regular rhythm of sleep, Kitty felt relieved not to have to talk any more, because even now she could hardly believe he'd asked her to be his wife. Another woman might have been satisfied with the cold-blooded terms he had offered. But not a woman with her experience.

It took a long time for her to fall asleep because, no matter how hard she tried to silence it, the sound of Santiago's stark declaration echoed round her head like a discordant bell.

I don't do love.

Of course he didn't. She'd known that all along. But *she* did, and therein lay the problem. Because somewhere along the way she had fallen for him. Stupidly, yet irrevocably. The thunderbolt which had struck her when she'd first seen him, combined with his kindness and consideration, had been too much for her to resist. Far easier to withstand his appeal when he had been arrogant and judgemental—than when confiding how much people liked her.

He woke her just before dawn and Kitty gazed up at him through drowsy eyes, still heavy with sleep.

'Time to get up,' he said.

'What?'

'I promised you a surprise, remember?'

'But it's the middle of the night,' she grumbled, as the memory of last night's conversation slammed into her thoughts, like a bird flying into a window.

'Get dressed, *roja*,' he said softly. 'It'll be worth it.'

'Where are we going?'

'Wait and see.'

Now that she was properly awake, that heavy stone of dread had taken up residence in her heart again and Kitty wished more than anything that she could pull the sheet over her head and block out the world. But she dressed in a long-sleeved silk shirt and a pair of cargo pants and hopped aboard the mud-splattered four-wheel drive which was waiting for them, commandeered by an enthusiastic female guide named Dani.

She drove them to a billabong—a wide, serene pool, strewn with waterlilies and lit by the pale rose of the dawn sky. They boarded a sturdy boat and Kitty held onto the rail tightly as it moved through the quiet water. It was beautiful, she acknowledged. So beautiful. She just wished it didn't seem so *romantic*, because it wasn't. It might look that way, but the effect it created was as insubstantial as a stage set—like last night's candlelight and starlight and all the amazing sights she'd witnessed back on Bali. Because Santiago didn't *do* romance—he couldn't have made that plainer when he'd laid out his coldly contractual terms of marriage last night. Despite the fact that she thought they'd grown closer, the fundamentals were exactly the same. Just because she *wished* things could be different didn't actually change anything.

Even so, it felt surreal to be drifting across the glossy billabong as the sky grew lighter, even more so when Dani silently pointed towards the water and Kitty saw a dark shape slowly emerging from beneath the millpond surface, its scaly dimensions instantly recognisable from a myriad children's books and films.

Her heart pounded with excitement and fear. 'It's a crocodile,' she whispered.

'Sure is.' Dani smiled.

'I hoped we'd see one but there's never any guarantee,' said Santiago, spanning his hands protectively around Kitty's waist. 'You're not scared, are you, *roja*?'

Kitty shook her head. No. Not of the beast whose scaly head she could see with such clarity. The only thing she was scared of was the see-sawing of her own emotions.

'Largest reptile on earth and related to the dinosaurs. That saltwater croc you can see over there has the strongest bite of any creature on the planet,' said Dani. 'And unchanged from two hundred and fifty million years ago. Pretty incredible when you stop to think about it, isn't it?'

Trying to get her head around these mind-blowing facts, Kitty nodded, and as the prehistoric reptile sank silently beneath the surface she suddenly found herself feeling very small and insignificant.

But she wasn't either of those things.

She thought about Santiago, because in many ways he reminded her of that crocodile. Not because she thought he was a bit of a dinosaur—even though she'd heard women throw that accusation at men if they didn't think their outlook modern enough. No. What disturbed her was his power—perceived and very real. It was part of what made him so attractive and it was also what made him so dangerous. Certainly to someone like her, who had little defence against his formidable charisma. He moved in a high-octane world and was the personification of success. People looked up to him. They envied and admired him. She remembered snatches of deferential comments she'd heard about him during that celebratory party he'd taken her to in Perth—the way Jared Stone had commented that Santiago Tevez put other entrepreneurs in the shade. For a man like the

Argentinian billionaire, everything was always on *his* terms. It always would be. And wouldn't someone like her always struggle to keep up with him?

She realised something else too—that her feelings for him had changed and grown. She felt ease in his company as well as longing, and that brought a whole new threat to their relationship, because women who cared too much made themselves vulnerable. She stared at the water—the disappearing ripples the only indication that the crocodile had ever been there. And she knew her options were running out.

'Can we go back now, please?' she questioned, in a low voice.

'Of course,' Santiago said, though he didn't ask why.

Kitty was silent during the return to Wallaby Wilderness and her instinct was to clam up and turn in on herself, as she had learned to do as a child. Maybe she could prevaricate for a little longer—tell Santiago she needed more time to think about his proposal. Mostly she wanted to fly back to England—in essence, to run away from the problem and hope that somehow it sorted itself out.

She drew in an unsteady breath. She needed to talk to Santiago but first she needed to eat. She mustn't come out with wild and emotional statements provoked by a drop in blood sugar. For their baby's sake, they mustn't become enemies—that was more important to her than anything. So she waited until room service had delivered breakfast and they'd eaten fruit and pancakes and drunk a pitcher of iced tea, then they sat on their veranda and watched the wallabies at play.

For a few seconds Kitty held onto that outward moment of companionable contentment, before reminding herself that it was nothing but a mirage. 'I can't marry you, Santiago.'

He didn't protest. His façade remained as detached as it had ever been. Yet still she longed for him to put his arms around her and hug her tightly. There was still no place she'd rather be than in his arms.

You fool, Kitty.

'Why not?' he questioned coolly.

Kitty chewed on her lip. She couldn't afford to let herself be swayed by her own desires. She needed to make him understand the bigger picture.

'You remember when I told you about my growing up?' she said slowly. 'That after I left the presbytery, I was given a home by a married couple who were supposedly desperate for a child?'

His nod was brief. 'Yes, I remember.'

'What I didn't tell you was that my adoptive mother loved my father absolutely, but he didn't feel the same way about her. He tolerated her but he didn't love her and her way of coping with that was to do everything in her power to make him happy. To ensure he would never stray, I guess. And when—very quickly, as it happens—she realised how much he resented my presence in their home, she decided that I needed to be hidden away.'

'Hidden away?' he echoed, only now a faint note of horror had crept into his voice.

'Oh, I don't mean they locked me in the basement, or anything—nothing like that,' she amended hastily. 'I was just encouraged to stay in my room, out of sight and out of mind—and to keep away from my father. I didn't need a lot of encouragement because, believe me, when someone resents your very presence you start wishing you were invisible. That's when I first started sketching things—it was something I could do which didn't cost very much. It's why I left school so young and went off to be a nanny. To escape, I suppose.'

'A harsh experience,' he conceded. 'But I don't understand what any of this has to do with us, Kitty.'

Kitty swallowed. She wanted to say *There is no us*, but she didn't want to come over as volatile. Calm and rational were what she was striving for—the building blocks for their future relationship. 'That's why I was reluctant to foist the role of father on you if you didn't want it, because I've seen the damage that can do. Just like I've seen the damage that emotional inequality can cause. And...' She drew in a breath but instead of bringing the comfort of much-needed oxygen, it felt hot and raw as it scorched its way into her lungs. 'And I'm terrified of doing the same thing, Santiago. Of history repeating itself. Because now I find myself in a similar situation to the one I so despised in my adoptive mother.'

'What the hell are you talking about, Kitty?' he demanded.

It hurt that he didn't know, or wasn't even able to make a guess. That she was forced to own up to it, like somebody who had been caught out in a crime.

'I've fallen in love with you, Santiago. I didn't mean to. I didn't even want to—but somehow it crept up on me when I wasn't paying attention. And you don't do love—you've told me that more than once. Even if you did, you probably wouldn't choose a woman like me.' She stared at the remains of iced tea in her glass. 'And I don't want to spend my life tiptoeing around you, trying to please you, or worried that I'm annoying you— which is inevitable when one person cares much more than the other. I don't want to be shushing my child because Daddy wants peace and quiet, like my adoptive mother did. We would be coming to this marriage from very different places, which is why it won't work, and why I can't marry you. It's why I need to go back to England to give us space to think about what's best for the baby and why…why we need to stop this affair of ours right now.' Her breath was so tight in her throat she could barely get the last few words out. 'Do you understand what I'm saying?'

She saw how tense he had become while she'd been speaking. The skin had stretched and tautened over his autocratic cheekbones, and the shadowed lines around the unsmiling slash of his mouth had grown deep. Yet still she hoped. That was the craziest thing of all. Because wasn't there a little bit of Kitty O'Hanlon who prayed for a fairy-tale ending? At least, until he began to speak, firing out his words with the steely precision of bullets.

'How could I fail to understand?' His eyes glittered like dark fire. 'You tell me you love me, then threaten to leave. That sounds awfully like an ultimatum to me.'

'But—'

'Sorry, Kitty, but I'm not going to bite. A long time ago I made a rule never to engage in clumsy attempts to manipulate my emotions—and, believe me, enough women have tried in the past.'

'And is that what you want—what you *really* want?' she demanded. 'To keep running away from your feelings? To allow yourself to be defined by the past?'

'Excuse me?'

But Kitty didn't flinch beneath that steely gaze. He had asked the question, so he would damned well listen to her answer. She might never get another chance to tell him all the things he needed to hear. 'You're not really living at all, are you, Santiago? You're trapped by your own emotional shutdown. Scared of taking risks.' Her voice shuddered a little. 'And scared of feeling.'

'How dare you speak to me this way?'

'How *dare* I? You're the father of my baby and if that doesn't give me the right, then what does?'

'That's enough!' He stood up and went to stare out over the scrub and the sudden movement caused the wallabies to scatter and when he turned back to face her again, all that tension was gone. He looked composed. In control. The mighty billionaire with all the answers at his fingertips.

'You want to return to London?' he continued coolly. 'Then so be it. Let's get that arranged as quickly as possible, shall we?'

CHAPTER THIRTEEN

IT WASN'T SUPPOSED to be like this.

Like a fitness fanatic obsessed by their daily step count, Santiago paced up and down the sun-drenched terrace of the Presidential Suite. But he registered little of the ocean's blue glitter, or the verdant panorama of Bali, which was spread out before him. Usually he was delighted to return to the island, but for once the beauty of his surroundings was completely lost on him. He might as well have been sitting in a darkened room for all the notice he took of it.

All he could think about was Kitty.

She haunted him.

Day and night she haunted him.

He couldn't stop thinking about the way she had opened her arms and her heart to him. The way it felt to kiss her. To wake up with her silky red curls tickling his chest. To hear her soft voice and sweet laugh. Kitty. Kitty O'Hanlon. She had told him she loved him and he had thrown it back in her face. He had accused her of emotional blackmail, then arranged for her to be ferried out of his life as quickly as possible.

His throat tightened. He recalled the last time he had seen her, just before she had boarded his plane for England. Looking glorious in a vibrant dress which echoed the Balinese landscape behind her, he'd noticed the first hint of a baby bump. The sight of that bump had made his mouth grow dry and as he'd touched her elbow to guide her onto the jet, a silent look had passed between them, along with the sizzle of pure physical chemistry. In her eyes he'd seen hurt and pain and regret. But he'd seen hope, too—lingering in the depths of that shimmering green gaze—and he had been unprepared for the fierce clench of his heart as he'd acknowledged it. All it would have taken from him would have been a single word or touch to make her stay, but he had done nothing and she had crammed on a pair of dark glasses with trembling fingers, and turned away.

And he had let her go.

He had wanted to brush away the things she had said about loving him and her accusations about his emotional cowardice—as if her words were nothing more than an inconvenient shower of rain which had fallen onto his overcoat. He had wanted to be free again. Not answerable to anyone, as he'd been in the days before she had shot into his life like a fiery comet.

But it hadn't worked out that way and his 'freedom' had been an illusion.

Without her he had been left...

What?

Empty?

Aching?

Missing her with a pain which was almost physical?

He scowled, because he didn't want to feel *anything*.

As usual, he had thrown money at the problem, informing his assistant that there was to be no financial limit on the home he intended buying for Kitty. But, infuriatingly, the temporary accommodation his ex-lover had insisted on acquiring in a place called Rich-

mond had been ridiculously modest by his standards.
And didn't it rankle that *she* had been the one to call the
shots on terminating their physical relationship, something which had never happened to him before?

His pride had been hurt—he freely admitted that—
but he had thought she would change her mind. He'd
imagined she would succumb to their undeniable chemistry and tell him she'd been too hasty in turning him
down. But that hadn't been the case. He'd waited in vain
for a phone call which had never materialised.

Fourteen days after she'd left, he realised how little
work he was managing to accomplish and decided that
enough was enough. He needed to have a discussion
with her about the future of the baby.

Their baby.

Surely once that had happened he would be rid of
this deep sense of regret.

'Clear my diary,' he told his assistant. She had
glanced down at his diary in horror. 'But you've got—'

'And prepare a flight plan for the UK,' he concluded
grimly.

He didn't warn Kitty he was on his way. He wanted
to take her off-guard, although he didn't stop to ask
himself why. It wasn't until he was being driven towards
her rental house in Richmond that he realised he didn't
know what he was going to say to her.

The cottage was situated close to the river and overlooking a small green, the garden filled with the fragrant honeysuckle and lavender he remembered from
the time when he'd hired an English stately home for the
summer, just for the hell of it. Flowers brushed against
his legs as he walked up the path and he could hear the
buzzing drone of bees. There was no bell, just an old-
fashioned brass door knocker, and when he lifted it

and let it fall he could hear the sound echoing through the house.

There was no answer and Santiago cursed himself for not giving prior warning, wondering if he should ring her and go to wait in the nearby pub, nursing a glass of unspeakably warm beer. But then, just as he was about to turn away—there was Kitty, standing in the open doorway, her hair a loose spill of red curls which tumbled around her shoulders. She was wearing shorts and a T-shirt and now the swell at her belly was very definitely there and he felt a sudden stab to his heart. She looked as fresh and as blooming as the flowers in the garden and he found himself resenting the cool and questioning look she gave him.

'Santiago,' she said, carefully. 'This is a surprise.'

'Can I come in?' A thousand demons entered his thoughts and took up residence there. 'Unless you are entertaining someone?'

Her mouth tightened and he saw a spark of anger in her eyes and for some reason this pleased him far more than her composed look of before.

'Is that why you didn't bother warning me you were coming?' she demanded. 'So you could try to catch me out? Yes, come in, Santiago. Go ahead and search the place if you like—I've got nothing to hide!'

He had to dip his head to enter and the interior of the cottage seemed unnaturally dark after the brightness of the day outside. He could see that she'd been sketching because some of her pencil drawings were spread over a table next to a window. But she seemed to have been concentrating on trees, not people, and there were certainly no portraits of *him*.

'So, should I offer you refreshment?' she questioned

spikily. 'Or is your car waiting to whisk you off to some fancy lunch?'

'I don't want *refreshment*,' he growled. 'And I'm not going anywhere else.'

'Because I'm wondering just why you've turned up here like this, unannounced,' she continued, as if he hadn't spoken.

He realised he didn't know either, because he hadn't allowed his mind to go there. He wanted to pace the room as was his habit when something was troubling him, but the dimensions of her rented cottage were so limited that he could have circumnavigated the place in a few seconds. And suddenly Santiago recognised that he was trying to avoid the seeking survey of her stare, afraid of what she might read in his face.

Had she spoken the truth when she'd left? *Was* he running scared? Terrified of exposing his failures, his flaws and his fears? 'I have missed you,' he said carefully. 'My life has not been the same since you left Bali.'

'I see.'

But she did not seize on this uncharacteristic admission to hurl herself into his arms, as he had expected. She just continued to subject him to that steady look and Santiago knew he was going to have to give her more. But it was hard to break the habit of a lifetime. Hard to connect with emotions he'd spent his whole life burying. The most dangerous submarine mission would have felt like a breeze compared to what this stubborn redhead was asking of him.

'You made me realise that, yes, I was being defined by the past. Inhibited by it. For all my self-professed love of freedom, I discovered to my surprise that I was completely trapped.' He sucked in a breath. 'And you made me realise what I *could* have. A good life. A real life. With the things that matter. With a woman who cares, who tries to understand—and an innocent baby who is looking to us to give him or her the kind of unconditional love which neither of us ever had.'

Still no rapturous thanks, he thought. She just continued to look at him with that same, steady look.

'You say you love me. I think…' His words faded, but still she didn't prompt him or feed him the line he was so reluctant to say. 'I think I love you,' he said finally and was rewarded at last with the glimmer of a smile. 'But I don't know if I'm capable of giving you the love you deserve, Kitty. The last thing I ever want to do is to hurt you—when you have been hurt so many times before.' She opened her mouth to speak but he raised his hand to silence her because he was on a roll now and he still hadn't finished. 'Just like I don't know if I'm capable of being a good father,' he concluded huskily.

The lump in Kitty's throat was so big that she could barely breathe as she stared at him, shaken by the things she could hear in his voice and see on his face. Pain and guilt and regret, and something else too. Something she could identify with, which was the fear which lay in the heart of every human.

She drew in a deep breath. 'You think I have all the answers?' she questioned unsteadily. 'I can assure you, I don't. Because love doesn't come with a rulebook, Santiago—not for partners and not for babies either. Sometimes you have to learn it as you go along. All I know is what I feel for you, which is…'

'Which is what?' he demanded urgently as her words tailed away.

Kitty's throat tightened and she could feel the race of her pulse. Like Santiago, she had never openly spoken of the emotions which lay inside her heart. Nobody had ever been close enough for her to want to try. Even now, she was a little apprehensive about saying the words out loud, as if they would crumble to dust when exposed to the daylight.

But love was the great equaliser, surely.

You had to believe in it—and yourself. You had to put aside your pride and push away all your stupid fears. Santiago had always been honest with her and she had valued that, even if sometimes the things he'd told her hadn't been what she wanted to hear. Now it was her turn to be honest.

'You make me feel as if I'd spent my life half asleep before I met you—as if you'd woken me from a dream. When I found out I was pregnant I was scared, yes—but there was a part of me which was jubilant about having your baby. I can't describe the feeling adequately, only that it felt primitive. Primeval.'

'Kitty—'

But she silenced him with a shake of her head. 'I thought we were finished when I flew back to England. I thought maybe it was best that way and I'd get over you. But I don't think I ever will, because I can't.' She shrugged and her mouth wobbled into something which was intended to be a smile but instead heralded the tears which began to slide from her eyes. 'You see, no matter what I say or do, I can't stop loving you.'

He made a small hissing sound, like the releasing of a pressure cooker, as if he had been holding his breath for a long time. With a single step, he moved to take her into his arms and the warm contact of his powerful body was like the best homecoming she'd ever had. The only homecoming.

'So you'll marry me?' he demanded, raking his gaze over her, eyes blazing ebony fire. 'We will do this properly. You will be my wife, for the rest of my life. Because I warn you that once I put that ring on your finger I am never letting you go, Kitty O'Hanlon.'

'Yes, Santiago. I will be your wife.'

For a while he just stood there, pillowing his face in the soft coils of her hair, and Santiago realised he was trembling. Or was it her? Fractionally, he pulled away and saw that her cheeks were wet with tears and he set about drying them with the gentle caress of his finger, and that made her tremble some more.

After a little while she led him up a narrow staircase to a snowy white bedroom, which overlooked the flowing river at the back of the house, and as she moved breathlessly into his arms he closed his eyes as countless feelings washed over him. And for once, he didn't block them. He embraced them. Revelled in them.

He closed his eyes because now there was not a single doubt inside his head.

He didn't *think* he loved her.

He loved her.

Unequivocally.

And in a while he would tell her that.

EPILOGUE

THE SKY WAS a bright and blinding blue and the distant murmur of the sea sounded hypnotic. Screened by lush foliage which showcased bright flowers, the pool area was completely private, and in the branches of the surrounding trees birds sang exultantly. Kitty, shaded by an enormous sun hat, thought she knew exactly how they felt.

Putting down her pencil, she gave a sigh of satisfaction as she sank back against the cushions.

Bali truly was a paradise.

She looked at the man stretched out on the lounger beside her, his powerful body gleaming with the ripple of bronzed muscle. A battered straw hat was perched on top of the unruly black hair and, as always, her heart turned over with love, and longing.

Santiago had just put their little son upstairs for his afternoon nap and Kitty had stood silently in the doorway of the nursery, because just watching them together made her feel so grateful that her heart felt it could burst open with joy. How could he ever have thought he wouldn't make a good father when there was so much untapped love inside him, just waiting to get out? He was the best father that their rumbustious two-year-old son, Alex, could have wished for.

And he was the best husband in the world.

They had married in England and honeymooned in Argentina. Kitty had expressed her desire to see the country of Santiago's birth, but deep down she'd thought he needed to confront the last of his past, in order to properly let it go.

It had been an emotional journey. They had stood outside the huge French-style mansion where Santiago had spent his lonely childhood and his face had been a bitter mask as he'd peered through the wrought-iron gates at the soaring white building. But afterwards, he had seemed calm. Calm enough to visit that ornate graveyard and place a bunch of white lilies before the cold, marble headstone of his father. To remember some of the good times, as well as the bad.

Their son Alex had been born in Perth, but when he was six months old, the family had moved permanently to Bali, where they had settled into a new house—the first place Santiago had ever called home. Whenever Kitty got the opportunity, she continued to draw—and her sketches were selling like hot cakes in one of the art galleries in Ubud. All proceeds went to charity and for some time she'd been thinking about illustrating a story about a lost little girl who eventually found great happiness. To try to convey the simple message that everyone should always have hope in their lives.

She gazed down at Santiago and sighed once more. She could have looked at him all day long and never grown tired of it.

'I'm not asleep, you know,' he murmured lazily. 'I know exactly how long you've been staring at me.'

Kitty felt the clench of excitement. 'I've been drawing you,' she said primly. 'That's the only reason I was staring.'

'Is that so?' he mocked, partially opening his gleaming eyes. 'It wouldn't have anything to do with wanting a siesta?'

'Well, there is that.'

'May I see?'

Santiago held out his hand for the sketch she'd just finished and, as he studied it, he felt a warm rush of satisfaction. He remembered the first time she had drawn him—depicting a face which had looked hard and cold, even cruel. But this was nothing like that version of himself. It was as though she'd drawn a different person—for the black and white portrait showed a man radiating a contentment and happiness he'd never imagined could be his.

'Do you like it?' she asked, a touch anxiously.

'I love it.' Their eyes met. 'Just like I love you, Kitty Tevez.' He began to whisper his hand up over her thigh, slowly alighting on the skimpy bikini bottoms she wore, and he loved the way her lips parted as his finger skated over that moist panel. 'Perhaps I need to show you just how much.'

'Santiago,' she breathed.

'Time for that siesta, do you think?'

'Oh, I think so.'

He suspected they must have looked almost demure as they walked hand in hand towards the interior of the sprawling villa.

Home.

Something which had eluded him for a whole lifetime, but not any more.

Because Santiago Tevez had found his place in the world, even though he hadn't realised he was looking for it. All the riches he had acquired hadn't been able to buy it for him, but it had been there all along.

Waiting for him one beautiful balmy Bali evening, when Kitty O'Hanlon had walked into the bar.

* * * * *

CINDERELLA
FOR THE
MIAMI PLAYBOY

DANI COLLINS

MILLS & BOON

To all the readers who asked me if Everett from
Confessions of an Italian Marriage
would get his own story.
This one's for you! xo

PROLOGUE

New York, six months ago...

EVERETT DRAKE WAS in the worst possible mood for a man like him. He was *bored*. Bored was one step away from making trouble purely to stay awake.

You're lucky. *You'll enjoy it*, had been the refrain from the few people who knew of his retirement. *I'm so glad you're out of it*, his mother had said of the end of his career handling agents and informants for the U.S. Government.

He was not glad. He was livid. Men twice his age moved to Miami to tinker with cars. He was in the prime of his life and ought to be doing something more meaningful, but he couldn't. Wouldn't. He was punishing himself and that was as it should be. He would live quietly. *Authentically*. The way normal people lived.

Well, normal people with buckets of wealth from multiple sources. Given his deep pockets, he could do anything he wanted, even be the dissolute playboy he had used as his cover for the last fifteen years.

Nothing about any of that appealed, though. Not the travel, not the parties. It was all empty as hell. He couldn't even race cars or hydrofoils. His mother would drag him out by the collar and run him over herself.

Given his current ennui, that didn't sound half-bad.

He gave up his overnight bag to the flight attendant

as he climbed aboard the executive jet. The automotive parts he'd come to New York to source himself—because he was that desperate for something to do—were already stowed below.

Old habits had him glancing at the manifest to read the names of his fellow passengers. Only one. Bianca Palmer. The name was unfamiliar, and it didn't matter, he reminded himself. He was no longer on guard against those who might seek to unmask him, or digging to find those who carried secrets like smuggled cargo.

He stepped into the main cabin, glanced at the woman in the luxury armchair on the left and a thousand impressions hit him at once, many of them the visceral reaction of a healthy male spotting an apparently fertile female. Alluring curves on a lithe build. Slender calves beneath a narrow skirt. Her ankles were crossed carefully to avoid scuffing her designer shoes. Her silk blouse was open at her throat, providing a view of her honey-gold upper chest, unadorned by any chain or locket.

That other more analytic part of him noted that her clothes were priced comparably to the bespoke suit and Italian shoes he wore. He judged her age at seven or eight years younger than his thirty-five. She was a professional, but not in a conservative career like banking. Something creative, given the way her rich brunette hair was side-parted and woven into a braid from one ear around the back of her head to the other, ending in a wavy waterfall behind her hoop earring.

She understood the value of appearances and how a style like that conveyed an eye for beauty and attention to detail. Sophisticated makeup emphasized her features. Bronze dusted her eyelids and playful cat tails decorated the corners of her eyes. Her complexion was a flawless, golden tan, almost olive. Her nose held an elegant curve at the bridge and her jawline was strong yet very feminine. Merlot-colored lipstick coated her wide mouth, glossy enough that her lips looked kiss-dampened and pillowy. Inviting.

Her dark chocolate gaze lifted absently from dropping something into her handbag and locked with his for no reason other than that they were sexually compatible. He wasn't coy about such things. He had been told many times he was handsome, and he had zero problems dressing well and shaving daily to heighten that impression. She was vibrant and beautiful, and chemistry was a wonderful thing when it struck both parties equally, as it was doing right now.

A satisfying billow of desire moved through his chest like smoke before sinking into his belly and groin.

He watched her throat flex as she swallowed. Her eyes widened slightly before her gaze flickered all over him like an indecisive butterfly, leaving tickling touches at his shoulders and the middle of his chest, on to his tense abdomen and lower, following the sharp crease in his trousers to his freshly shined shoes.

As her gaze made its way back, the delicious tightness of arousal invaded the flesh behind his fly and climbed his spine, releasing an urge to pursue into his blood.

"Good morning," he greeted.

"Good morning." Her voice held a husky note. He wasn't sure if it was natural or because they were having such an effect on each other. She dropped her gaze into her lap, where she was twisting her fingers.

A fresh impression struck him like a slap, one that was an even sharper cat nip than carnal hunger. He read tension, vulnerability, wariness. *Secrets.*

The hair on the back of his neck lifted, and there was a tang in his nostrils like the whiff off an extinguished match.

His ability to scent danger had kept him and others alive

more often than he could count—and that one time when he had ignored it—

No.

He brushed that incident aside, staying in the moment because that's how you stayed alive when this happened, but his sexual interest had collided straight into that part of him he had severed like a limb. The part that chased intrigue and answers and knew that knowledge was power. The part that *liked* that power and enjoyed skating on the edge of icy cliffs.

He was an addict. That's what he was. Whatever was going on with this woman was nothing to do with him. *Ignore her. Go live your life*, he ordered himself.

What life, though? The banality of his existence was likely to kill him quicker than his old life might have, but he had made his choices. He would live with the consequences.

"May I bring champagne? Mimosas?" The flight attendant arrived behind him and accepted the jacket he removed.

"Nothing for me, thank you," Bianca said in her sensual voice.

"Coffee," Everett requested, and seated himself across from her, resisting the urge to swivel his chair so he could see her better. Not for him. Not today. Not ever.

Bianca turned her face to the window and knotted her hands in her lap.

Ringless hands, Everett noted. Why couldn't there be a band or a diamond there? He would have dismissed his attraction without another thought. Even in his previous life, he only lied as much as he absolutely had to. Entangling himself with a woman who happened to be cheating on her partner fell into unnecessary deceit.

But given the absence of rings or last-minute texting or chatty *I love yous* before switching to airplane mode, his libido urged him to make a pass. He didn't get nearly as much sex as the profligate playboy he pretended to be. If she was amenable, why the hell shouldn't he spend a night with her? He could stay at a hotel rather than take her home. Keep it to one night.

Just one drink. Just dinner. Just enough to find out what her story was.

It truly was the rationalization of someone with a substance abuse problem. Just *no*.

He was so damned aware of her, though. It was as if he sat next to a radiator that softly pinged as it baked his right side.

The ladder came up and the seal of the door locked them into a bubble of charged air. He knew she was chewing her bottom lip. Her head was still tilted toward the window, but he knew she was as aware of him as he was of her. A special sort of tension emanated off her. He knew she was sliding surreptitious glances from the corner of her eye because he was doing the same.

Nope, nope, nope.

Was he even reading her correctly? Or was his latent horniness tasting all this electricity and turning it into something it wasn't? Maybe she was just a nervous flyer.

As the plane taxied and the attendant buckled into her own seat for takeoff, he remarked, "I use this charter company all the time. These jets are very reliable. You won't feel any turbulence."

In fact, he owned shares in the company. In his previous life, he would volunteer a detail like that. He had always liked to nurture the impression his fortune was inherited, passive and mildly obnoxious. That way he avoided inconvenient questions about what he did for a living. People presumed "nothing."

That's exactly what he did now, but he balked at this woman viewing him as shallow and aimless. He wasn't sure why. It rarely bothered him what anyone thought of him.

She shot him a culpable glance, seeming briefly rattled before she visibly took hold of herself, stacking her hands and relaxing her shoulders, pasting on a smile.

"Am I that obvious?"

Wow. That blanket of false calm was such a deliberate application of control, as though she were sitting in a high-stakes poker game and realized she was betraying herself with a tell. His most sharply honed synapses fired in his brain.

Definitely not this one, his logic brain said firmly.

His lizard brain shifted his ankle onto his knee, hiding the fact he was growing hard. She was caressing all his buttons with that serene mask that disguised a mystery and the way her breath subtly hitched, causing her breasts to quiver.

"Allow me to distract you," he suggested. Because if he was going to fall off the wagon, it ought to be with premium, hundred-year-old Scotch, right? *Look at her.* "Are you heading to Miami for business or pleasure? Visiting family?"

Surprise bloomed behind her eyes as she realized he was hitting on her.

He didn't like to waste time, he informed her with a sideways pull of his mouth, but how could she be surprised? Women with that much sex appeal were inundated with advances. They knew how to shut them down very quickly and he always respected that, but he found himself holding his breath as he awaited her reaction.

She blinked in disconcertion, and her finger and thumb worked the spot at the base of her naked ring finger as she considered how to handle his attention.

Ah. There was no ring, but there was a commitment in

place, one that typically shielded her from sexual interest. Pity.

It was for the best—he knew it was—but he couldn't remember ever feeling his inner animal rising so urgently with desire. He made himself sip his hot coffee to burn away the pall of disappointment in the back of his throat.

She didn't mention a partner, however. Nor did she grasp at the armrest or show any sort of nerves as the engine roar grew and the plane gathered speed. She seemed perfectly relaxed as they were pressed into their seats by the climbing jet.

He didn't take credit for taking her mind off her trepidation, though. Flying wasn't what she was afraid of. He knew that in his gut, but all his willpower seemed to have been left on the ground. His entire being was awake and alive in a way he hadn't been in months.

"I'm not sure how to answer," she confided as they leveled off, forcing his mind back to the question he'd asked. "It's a little bit of all of those. Business, pleasure and family. My grandmother passed recently."

"I'm sorry," he said politely.

"I didn't know her," she dismissed, but the corners of her mouth briefly tilted down. "She stopped speaking to my mother when Mom got pregnant and wasn't married. We reached out a few times, but we never heard back. Then, out of the blue, I got a letter saying my grandmother had left me her apartment. I'm going to Miami to sell it."

Her glance reflected resignation and… Damn. He knew that cagey look. She was hoping he was satisfied with what she'd given him. She was holding something back.

They were strangers, though. Sometimes that allowed a person to open up without reserve, but not all the time. Family was complicated, and convoluted stories didn't always reap useful information. He left room for her to elaborate by saying, "That sounds troubling."

"It is. Thank you for acknowledging that." Her brows came together with annoyance. "Everyone seems to think I've won the lottery. All I can think is that I would have preferred a relationship with her. I mean, she didn't even send me a card when her *daughter* died, but she made me her beneficiary? That's bizarre, isn't it?"

Perhaps that was the source of her tension. Her conscience must be bothered by accepting a windfall from someone who had hurt her mother.

"You can never be sure why someone holds others at arm's length. Shame. Anger. Secrets." Self-loathing. Guilt. Everett eschewed intimate relationships for all of those reasons.

"I know, but..." Her mouth twisted with frustration.

This time, as their gazes met, a deeper curiosity crept into her expression, one that stoked the heat in his gut. Her attention strayed over his clean-shaven face again and reassessed his shoulders and chest and thighs, all of which he ruthlessly kept in fighting form.

She tellingly eyed his left hand, which bore neither ring nor tan line.

Everett had tried long-term relationships. They had always withered from neglect, mostly due to work getting in the way. He had all the time in the world now, though, and a soft blush of attraction had risen under her skin, one that pleased him immensely as did the implied interest in her next words.

"And you? Why are you going to Miami?"

I live there. That's what he should have said, but old instincts had him prevaricating.

"There's a yacht I'm thinking of buying. I'm only in town the one night—" He always liked to be clear about his limitations and in this case, he should have shut his mouth ten minutes ago, but there was a war going on inside him. He knew, *he knew* not to ignore the way his scalp was tightening, but his interest in her was galloping like a wild stallion, determined to catch her and have her.

Lust won over logic.

"I'll be free by six and dining alone unless you'd like to join me?"

Her head tilted as she considered his invitation. For one second, he had the impression of looking in a mirror. She was definitely hiding more than she was revealing.

Tension invaded his muscles. He ought to be hoping for a rebuff. It rarely happened, but when it did, it didn't bother him. If she turned him down, however, he would be more than disappointed. He'd be thwarted.

Her guardedness relaxed a few notches as she offered a shy smile. "I would like that." She leaned out to offer her hand. "I'm Bianca, by the way."

As he took her hand, a punch of desire struck his middle. Her breath caught as though she experienced a similar impact. He swept his thumb across the back of her knuckles before releasing her, absorbing the fact she posed a type of danger he hadn't ever experienced.

He really should retract and retreat. This was madness.

"Everett," he provided. "I'll make a reservation at my hotel."

CHAPTER ONE

Present day, Miami

BIANCA PALMER HAD what anyone would consider an ideal job, especially when one was hiding from the law, reporters and the white-collar criminals she had implicated when she had blown the whistle on them.

She hadn't known what to expect when she had pulled a number off the We Can Find You Work flyer at the bodega near the sketchy room she'd been renting by the week, but Miami had a thriving underground economy. There were tons of companies that placed undocumented workers in domestic positions. Her desire for cash-only employment hadn't raised any eyebrows and when she had offered a generous bonus for "extra privacy," the manager had taken her payoff as a sweetener and sent her to interview for this cushy gig.

Despite the blue pixie cut she'd given herself when she had abandoned her old life, she'd been terrified she would be recognized, so she had also worn gray contacts and appropriated an old school friend's Puerto Rican accent. After spinning a story about supporting her ailing grandmother, she had landed the position.

She lived in the pool house of a mansion on Miami's Indian Creek. It wasn't the most extravagant house in the neighborhood, but it was very swanky with two cabanas next to its free-form pool, five bedrooms in the main house, nine baths, a home theater and an elevator to a rooftop bar. The six-car garage held a motorcycle, an SUV, a modern sports car in pristine condition and two vintage ones in different states of restoration. The last bay was taken up with shelves of tools and parts.

Those fancy cars, virtually the only personal items she'd seen here, were extremely well protected. Every door and window of the house was wired and alarmed. A high brick wall surrounded the property and surveillance cameras monitored every exterior angle, including the path to the private beach where no watercraft were moored.

That always made her wonder. The dock was built for a large yacht, but there wasn't even a little runabout. Of course, no one came or went from the road, either. The woman who had hired her—a housekeeper who had possibly hired Bianca for cash so she could take time off while her employers were away—had said the house was being held in trust while the owners were in divorce proceedings.

Bianca hadn't asked for more information than that. It was too sweet a deal. Her accommodation was part of her compensation and her duties consisted of dusting, vacuuming, mowing the small patch of lawn and polishing the windows.

There were *so many* windows, probably with a square footage equal to the house. They all looked onto stunning views and were all tinted against the intense Florida sunshine. Bianca was well shielded from view if she wanted to stand in the main lounge next to the grand piano and speculate on what all those people in those skyscrapers in Miami Beach were doing as they went about their very normal lives.

She tried not to do that. It made her yearn to drag heavy bags onto the crowded subway and overhear lively conversations in languages she didn't recognize. She wanted to drink in spicy food aromas mixed with the gritty stench of city streets and walk through a door calling out, *"I'm home!"*

She wanted someone to answer her back.

Instead, she skimmed the pool or did her yoga practice beneath the weighted branches of the orange trees and tried to convince herself this isolation was a gift. She was paid well *and* had a generous budget for groceries and household incidentals. Deliveries were left at the gate, allowing her to live expense-free and undetected.

It was a bizarre arrangement that she had leaped on when she'd been desperate for a means to support herself while staying out of sight. Now that she'd had time to dwell on it—seriously, nothing but time to dwell—she wondered if she had leaped out of the frying pan of financial fraud only to land in a roaring fire of something equally unsavory. That would make her not only an accessory, which she was trying to avoid, but also the world's biggest hypocrite. Who exposed crimes only to assist in different ones?

Was the owner of this house a criminal? Wealthy people could be felons. Bianca knew that from her experience with Morris and Ackerley. Her fiancé had been a charming, Ivy League alum with generations of wealth behind him, but he'd still cheated average citizens out of their life savings.

She felt like such a fool for getting involved with him! For believing his flattery and letting him take advantage of her grief.

Thanks to her poor judgment, she didn't have much choice even if she *was* being paid with dirty money. She'd made her bed and would have to keep sleeping in it.

With a sigh, she picked the ripe oranges and took them to the main kitchen, as she did every morning. She made her toast and ate it while she squeezed juice that she would freeze in ice cube trays. They made a nice addition to a glass of water or white wine, but she didn't have enough room in her small fridge to keep it all there.

As she worked, she daydreamed about where she would go if she could leave. It was one of her preoccupations every single day, along with what sort of career she should retrain for since she had nuked her old one. Where and how could she start over, and would anyone want anything to do with her?

It was hard being inside her head all the time. She was hideously lonely. Aside from answering the intercom when drivers notified her of deliveries, she hadn't spoken to anyone since the day she'd taken this job. She barely interacted with the outside world at all, staying offline and buying paperback romance novels and DVDs with her groceries.

At first, she had watched the news incessantly, but she could barely make herself do even that these days. Morris and Ackerley were being investigated, which was what she had wanted, but progress was glacial. The company was denying and deflecting and throwing mud on her name at every opportunity.

It was exactly what she had expected them to do, but it was hard to watch her character being assassinated. It made her want to defend herself, but no matter how tempted she was, she never, ever, *ever* reached out to anyone or checked her social media feeds.

Or checked up on *him*.

Everett.

Her eyes drifted shut in a mixture of reminiscence and mortification. After meeting him on the plane to Miami, she had looked him up at the library while making her final preparations toward abandoning her old life. She'd still been of two minds as to whether she should meet him for dinner.

According to the tabloid articles, his father had been a renowned automotive engineer from Switzerland, who suffered a brain injury during a test drive. His French mother had been an interpreter at the UN. There had been scads of family money that had mostly come to Everett in his early twenties.

With all that gold falling out of his pockets, he had become a playboy in the most iconic sense. He traveled the globe on spontaneous adventures, seeing and being seen. There had been links to nightclub appearances and ski holidays and affairs with this or that socialite. For a time, he had raced cars. There had been a youthful photo of him in Monte Carlo, shirtless and with his arms around two extremely beautiful women dressed in gold shorts and eyelet bikini tops.

I wonder what he would think of those cars in the garage, Bianca sometimes mused.

She thought of him far too often, almost as if he was her companion here. It was an odd trick that her mind played on her, probably because she was so starved for company and because he was the last person with whom she'd had a meaningful interaction.

Meaningful, Bianca? For her, perhaps, but it had been obvious from the first moment that he was a serial pickup artist. Joining him for dinner had served her own purpose, but she had meant for it to only be dinner. Hookups with strangers weren't her style *at all*.

He'd had a charming way about him, though, one that disarmed and encouraged her to trust him. He had fascinated her with his intelligence and nuanced opinions while drawing her out with what seemed like genuine interest in her. It had taken superhuman effort not to blurt out what she was about to do. Only her lifetime of keeping secrets had allowed her to compartmentalize and leave him in the dark.

Even so, she'd been in a heightened state, fearful of what she was about to do and eager for the distraction he offered. Given the huge step she had been about to undertake, it made sense that she had taken another uncharacteristic risk of letting a stranger seduce her.

Maybe she'd simply needed to be held.

Either way, that interlude should have made her feel empty and used, but she had reveled in it, letting go of herself completely. It had been a unique experience where the outer layers of her persona had seemed to burn away in the heat of their passion. When she had left his room, she had walked away altered at her deepest level. Centered and confident. New.

Or she was completely delusional, and he'd just been really good in bed.

She longed to see him again and find out. A far more sensible part of her suspected she would be hideously disappointed if she met him again. She doubted he had spared a single thought for her. He might not even remember her, which would be humiliating in the extreme.

Leaving here wasn't an option anyway. She would be mobbed by paparazzi, if the way reporters were badgering Troy was any indication. All the letters of the alphabet seemed to be looking for her—SEC, FBI, DOJ. From what she'd seen of other whistleblowers' experiences, she could face prosecution or be persecuted for leaking information. If she was offered protection, she would likely wind up exactly as she was, cut off from the world but with less agency. Most importantly, if Troy Ackerley and his partner, Kirk Morris, got their hands on her, the outcome could be life-threatening.

No, she was safest exactly where she was, even if she was claustrophobic and lonesome and bordering on despair.

She twisted the orange half with excessive force, trying not to cry.

Oh, stop it. She jammed the last of her toast into her

mouth, not caring that her juice-coated fingers gave the PBJ a weird, tangy flavor. Pity parties solved nothing. She swallowed away the lump of toast and reached for the last orange.

As she touched the knife blade to the skin, a soft, measured sound came to her ears, a muted, rhythmic pattern of thumps.

That wasn't the neighbor's sound system. What was it? She held very still, listening, trying to place it. Not a bird or—heaven help her—a gator? One couldn't get in here, could it?

With a lurch of her heart, she realized it was growing louder, coming toward the open sliding door to her left, the one that led onto the courtyard and the paved, poolside dining area.

She never left doors open, only this one, and only when she crossed into this kitchen from her cabana. She always felt safe leaving the screen in place because the courtyard was completely enclosed—except for the single locked gate that accessed the path down to the beach.

That gate was on the same circuit as everything else. She glanced at the computer in the nook beside the pantry. The monitor showed the screen saver, not the view from the cameras the way it was supposed to if motion had triggered the system to start recording.

Something was definitely out there, though. Some*one*?

As the sound closed in, Bianca's breath backed up in her lungs. The wait became macabre. It was timed like footsteps, but that's not what it was. It was longer and slower with a tap and a rest, a tap and—

A man on crutches appeared behind the screen and froze as he spotted her. They stared at one another.

He wore a gray-green shirt with a subtle palm leaf pattern and pale gray shorts, both tailored. His knee was bandaged and so were his knuckles. His cheekbone wore a garish purple shiner, and his eyes narrowed, projecting the warmth of an Ice Age glacier.

Despite all that, buoyant delight slammed through her.

"Everett!" She was ecstatic to see a familiar face, even as concern lurched through her at how banged up he was. She was glad to see *him*, flattered even, after thinking about him so much since—

Reality arrived in a breath-punching tackle. He shouldn't be here. He was from her old life. This was her new one. How had he found her?

Her heart kicked into an unsteady gallop. Her scrambled brain tried to tell her body what to do. Adrenaline seared through her veins like a bullet train, but her muscles turned to stretchy rubber. Think, Bianca. *Run.*

She had a go-bag packed in the cabana, but Everett was swishing the screen open, hitching himself into the kitchen, placing himself between the screen door to the courtyard and the door to the lounge. He sucked all the oxygen from the room with his presence. His gaze flickered around as though searching out hidden dangers.

"Hello, Bianca." His voice was harder than she remembered. His gaze came back to hers, and the easygoing confidence of a lothario had become a force field of power.

Some basic, primitive female in her absorbed that he had become even more appealing. His shoulders seemed broader, and his biceps bulged where he braced on his crutches. The other part noted his scowl was pure Hollywood hit man, sexy enough to turn her bones to pudding, but sending her into survival mode.

She spun and ran through the door into the garage. No bag, no cash, but she had a contingency plan in place for such an emergency. It was a terrible plan, but it was a chance. Her only chance.

She snatched the fob off the hook and ran for the fancy sports car—

"Bianca!" His thunderous shout was accompanied by a clatter.

She reflexively looked over her shoulder, stumbling into the coupe and crashing her hip into its side-view mirror.

"Do not steal my car," he warned in a deadly voice. "That would annoy me, and I am already very annoyed." He was using his shoulder to hold open the door to the kitchen, slouching as he tried to pick up the crutch that had fallen.

"*Your* car." Her brain was trying very hard to think through the miasma of shock and disbelief, fear and compulsion to escape. The thump of her own heart deafened her ears.

"Yes. My car. My house."

But— That wasn't possible. The sheer coincidence meant he would have known who she was before she got here. Was he a mind reader? Had he known what she planned even as they had made love? Then somehow tricked her into coming here?

No one had known what she had planned.

None of this made sense, but all she could blurt was, "*How*?"

An exhale of tested patience left him. "Come inside. We need to talk."

"No." She blipped the fob and moved to open the car door.

"I'm serious. Do not steal my car." He got both crutches under his arms and swooped fully into the garage, allowing the door to slam shut behind him.

They were in a standoff in the filtered light through the row of small windows across the top of the big doors. She might be able to leap into the car and lock it before he reached her, but then what? He could disable the front gate in the time it took her to pull out of the garage and get down the short driveway.

He must have calculated all of that himself. His posture eased slightly while his gaze flickered over her face and shoulders.

"How are you? You look good."

She doubted it and suddenly wished she looked like her old self, not a runaway from a punk rock band. Her brown hair with its faded blue ends hung around her face in air-dried frizz. She no longer owned makeup and her threadbare shorts and T-shirt had been secondhand when she had bought them from a Goodwill store six months ago.

"How—" Her throat kept going dry. He looked very disreputable and dangerous with his blackened eye and air of watchfulness. Murderous. "How did you get in? The security system is on."

"I came by boat and used my phone to disable it before I walked up." He drew his phone from his shorts pocket and tapped. His mouth twisted in a very poor imitation of a smile. "It's fully armed again now."

Meaning the garage doors would scream bloody murder if she opened one.

In the months of talking to herself without anyone around to be offended, she had developed quite a potty mouth and let one slip without thinking.

His brow went up. The corner of his mouth dug in with dark amusement. "I usually prefer some foreplay first, but I'm happy to accommodate if you're feeling an urgent need."

It wasn't funny. All of this was deeply distressing. Her veins were burning with adrenaline, her chest tight at being trapped. Then there was that other betraying part of her that was overjoyed to see him again. All those bunched muscles that had gathered her up, those sexy lips set between the carved hollows of his cheeks. He had kissed her *everywhere*. The hot light in his eyes seemed to recollect it as vividly as she did, freshly burning those kisses into her psyche.

She had spent *way* too much time replaying their night together. Often, in the dark of night and the privacy of her bed, she had let herself imagine they had had more between them than pheromones and a free evening.

In stark daylight, confronting him, she acknowledged that she had been played by a player. He had been way too good at sex to be anything less, and he had clearly been ten steps ahead of her the whole time.

"I thought this house belonged to a couple in divorce." Her voice wavered despite her best efforts to steady it. "The housekeeper—"

"Wanted time off. Her daughter was expecting."

She blinked as she absorbed that. "Okay, but how did you arrange for me to come here?" She already knew. The offer had been too good to be true and she'd fallen for it anyway. "*Why* did you? Oh, God, do you work for Troy?" Her stomach bottomed out.

"No." The smug amusement that had hovered around his mouth disappeared. "Your story broke a few days after we met." His jaw hardened and the curl in his mouth became very cynical. "Once it became clear you had disappeared, I made it my job to find you."

"Why?"

His brows winged up. "Why did you go into hiding?" The note of challenge in his tone suggested he knew the answer.

"Snitches get stitches." She tried to shrug it off, as if her knees weren't knocking with terror that she'd been located. And because it was true. People hated a tattletale. "A lot of rich, powerful people are either implicated or lost a chunk of their fortune." Maybe Everett was one of them? She hugged herself. "I don't imagine anyone is happy with me right now, but I can't afford a bodyguard.

My only choice was to disappear." Even her last resort strategy offered no guarantee she would survive it.

"Don't forget the paparazzi," he said with mocking helpfulness. "There's a six-figure price on your headshot."

"You don't have to make it sound like a bounty!" Her skin was clammy. She couldn't even swallow, her throat was so dry and tight.

"That's what it is." He started to approach her.

She set one foot inside the car. If she jumped inside, she could get the door slammed and locked, hopefully pop out the other side before he had time to get around.

He only moved as far as the motorcycle, where it stood on its kickstand near a utility sink. He lowered to balance his weight against the tilted seat, releasing a small sigh as though relieved to take a load off.

It was a sneaky move, one that put him a lot closer to her and trapped her in the V of the open door. Rather than a whole car, now there was only the corner of the car's short trunk between them.

He could probably move a lot faster than he was letting on. She remembered *exactly* how powerful his legs had been, hard as sculpted oak between her own.

She looked away, not wanting him to guess what she was thinking. Feeling. Tendrils of yearning were unfurling in her belly. Her blood had become molasses, making her breaths heavy and her movements slow.

"You did a good job of covering your tracks." He sounded as if he admired her for it. "Took me over a week to find where you were staying."

"You found me in a *week*?" Her stomach cramped. She had tried so *hard* to disappear. It was demoralizing to have failed so quickly.

In the next second, she wondered what it meant that he had looked for her, but as quickly as her heart lifted, it dropped like a stone. If he had wanted to see her, he

would have appeared a lot sooner than six months after
their night together.

"I'm better at finding people than they are at getting
lost." He spoke as if it was an absolute fact. *I'm taller than
average. I bench press two-forty.*

The way he slouched on the motorcycle was like an old-
time poster of a rebel hero with his stubble and bruises
and pensive scowl. She'd never had a thing for that type.
Not until right this moment. Why? It was self-destructive.
Her mother had fallen for a bad boy and had been in hiding her whole life as a result. Bianca had stumbled into an
engagement with a white-collar criminal, who had wanted
to use her up then throw her to the wolves. Men with dark
hearts were not worth the bother.

But all she could think about was Everett's mouth in
the crook of her neck, his hands on her arms and the small
of her back. His weight on her and his thickness moving
powerfully within her, filling her with tension and intense
waves of pleasure.

Was there a carbon monoxide leak in here? She couldn't
catch her breath.

"When reward money climbs that high, landlords and
employers grow tempted to line their own pockets. I had
to draw you out and tuck you somewhere safe."

"I got the number from a flyer in a bodega! How could
you know I would call it?"

"I didn't. It's a numbers game." He shrugged. "You
didn't have any income sources that I could discern so I
put in listings with all of the under-the-table outfits. Dog
walking, childcare, computer work… Anything that might
catch your interest. My criteria made me sound racist as
hell and kind of a pervert, but it filtered out ninety percent
of the applicants. Within a week, you turned up."

"You don't even have a dog," she noted with annoyance.

"I would have got one."

If only she'd known, she might have had company all this time.

"You found me, then went to all that trouble to get me here without speaking to me or letting me know?" Her mind was derailing all over again, trying to calculate how much time, effort and money he had put into that. "Why? Are you a private investigator or something?"

His mouth opened, shut, then, "Not anymore."

"What does *that* mean?"

"It means I'm off the clock. This is more of a hobby."

"A creepy one!"

"I gave you a job and a safe place to stay. You were free to leave anytime. It's not like I watched you on the cameras."

"Did you?" she screeched.

"No." He rolled his eyes as if she was the one being a weirdo.

"And I'm supposed to believe you," she scoffed.

"Whether you believe me or not is your choice. If you decide to leave, go forth with my blessing. Not with my car," he added, pointing a warning finger. "But walk away if that's what you want to do. Understand by doing so, however, that I will get what I want, and you won't get anything except a lot of attention, much of it negative. Dangerous, even."

She clenched her fist at her side, asking warily, "What do *you* want?"

"For you to come out of hiding." With a flat smile, he waved at his state of injury. "I've been implicated in your disappearance, Bianca. My name must be cleared."

He'd been attacked because of her? She felt ill.

"How could *you* be implicated?"

"You left your luggage with the concierge at my hotel. Eventually, your... Have I got this right? Troy Ackerley is your fiancé?"

"Ex," she assured him, but a hollow feeling opened up behind her breastbone. She couldn't really see the color of his eyes in the low light, but she suspected they had turned frosty and forbidding. His voice sure had.

"I'm not sure he got that memo. He's still feeling very proprietary." Everett curled his lip. "His people were delivering a message as much as squeezing me for your whereabouts."

She clasped the edge of the car door so hard she should have bent the metal.

"Did you…" Her tongue felt as though it had swollen too big for her mouth and her head grew light.

She couldn't blame him for telling them where she was, but stark fear poured into her bloodstream, dampening her eyes. She looked to the wide garage door, mentally planning the route she would take to that *other* mansion if she was able to get out this gate. She was far more comfortable risking Everett's wrath by stealing his car than that of Troy if he caught up to her. She would definitely need protection if that happened.

"I'm not an amateur, Bianca," Everett said indignantly. "Of course, I didn't tell them where you are."

"Even though…" She looked to his bandaged knee. "Are you okay? Is it broken?"

"Swollen. I'll mend. The men who jumped me will be out of commission much longer."

He had fought them off. She shouldn't find that sexy. It wasn't. Violence was never a solution, but she was wavering in this space between worry for him and guilt that he'd been attacked because of her, yet he was brushing it off, confident that he had come out ahead. She couldn't help being affected by that.

"If they think you and I are involved, they'll come to your house," she noted, blood turning cold.

"All my houses are held by numbered companies. Ackerley's clown show took six months to draw a line from your abandoned luggage, through the hotel registry, to the fact we were on the same flight. I'm not worried about them finding us anytime soon, but they've become very annoying, trying to dig up dirt on me that doesn't exist. You and I need to plan how you'll come forward, so they'll get off my back."

Panicked at the mere thought, she vehemently shook her head. "I *can't* come forward."

CHAPTER TWO

SHE WAITED FOR him to argue, but Everett held his position in silence, as though there was no debate because in this case there wasn't. Plus, he found people filled a silence in a very revealing way if he let them.

Besides, it gave him the chance to take a long sip, drinking her in like fine brandy. Her lack of makeup only accentuated how lovingly her features had been crafted. And those lips. She was biting the bottom one, making him want to suck it. Again. He wanted to bite his own lip and groan out his six months of celibacy.

He wanted to touch her. Her shapeless T-shirt and low-slung cutoffs were sexier than any French lingerie, making his palms itch. Her braless breasts lifted the cotton off her tanned stomach providing a glimpse of her navel. Her golden-brown thighs were smooth and soft and went on for miles. All of her was like that. Endlessly, sensually pleasing. He'd spent way too many nights reliving exactly how hedonistic and generous and responsive she was.

Yet he had forgotten this effect she had on him, the one where desire dragged all his brain cells into a knot of craving in his groin. Actually, he had underestimated it, thinking he could control it the way he controlled most everything else, but this yank on his inner animal was even more potent than he recalled.

This was the reason he had let desire override his instincts, buying her dinner and sleeping with her against his better judgment.

No. He had to be honest with himself. He had relapsed and *embraced* the risk in seeing her. The nature and level of risk had been a mystery, which had been part of the appeal, but rather than heed the prickle down his spine, he had given in and scratched his itch, arrogantly certain he could weather any repercussions that came from their night together.

And this damned sexual heat had muffled the signals. When her voice had thinned, or her gaze had dropped, he'd seen it as a reaction to the brush of his foot against hers or the fact their stare had already been locked too long as a moment ripened with anticipation. She had licked her lips and stammered, but only in response to his most innocuous questions. *Should we order dessert? Are you cold?*

That last had been in response to how her nipples had stiffened beneath the silk of her blouse. Such a physical sign of arousal wasn't something she could fake, and she hadn't realized where his gaze had strayed when she answered, *Not at all.*

He'd been on fire himself, skating on an edge between fascination and caution, as though she was a tigress who could turn on him, but since he was close enough, he was compelled to reach out, pet and stroke.

She had captured all his attention, lighting up when she laughed and challenging his opinions and growing wistful as she talked about her future. *My work situation is complicated. I just broke my engagement, and he was my employer. I'm facing a life change.*

He had already done a cursory search and knew where she worked. There hadn't been a reason to linger on that dispiriting topic, so he'd ordered dessert. They'd shared it and held hands as they walked through the hotel grounds to the beach. They had kissed beneath the moonlight, her back shifting beneath his palms, hips tilting into his in a way that still heated his blood when he thought of it. He'd invited her upstairs and she had proceeded to reset his bar for one-night stands, making it impossible for him to settle for any of the pale imitations he'd been offered since.

Never once through all of that had she given away the enormous step she had been about to take.

When her face and name had hit the headlines a few days later, he'd been surprised, yet not. He had waltzed into her minefield on his own two feet, but he'd been angry at himself, feeling foolish and wondering if he'd been taken in by a pro.

He couldn't imagine how, though. Nothing in her background suggested a history like his own, which had left him with an irritating amount of concern for her. She was a woman of limited resources pitting herself against a well-financed corruption machine. His conscience had compelled him to help her even though he had left the dark underworld of espionage so he wouldn't be responsible for other people's lives anymore.

Ensconcing her here had been his compromise. He'd stayed in New York, keeping half the Eastern Seaboard between them, digging into the Morris and Ackerley charges to better understand it. To help.

Because she'd haunted his thoughts no matter how hard he tried to dismiss her.

Then, yesterday, he'd been dragged into an alley and found himself fighting for his life. And hers. That's what had given him the strength to put those men on the ground. Everett had been terrified for Bianca. He hadn't breathed easy until he'd seen for himself that she was safe.

Which didn't make sense. How could he care so much what happened to a woman he'd slept with *once*? Okay, they'd made love three times, but he barely knew her. And she'd pulled him into a rat's nest of trouble, one to which he was rapidly becoming an accomplice. That peeved him deeply.

Worse, she was causing him to backslide into unraveling conspiracies and protecting sources. It wouldn't do. He'd made promises to his mother. To himself.

Now that he knew she was unharmed, he would insist she clear his name, put some distance between them, and he would never see her again.

His stomach reflexively clenched in resistance, but he ignored it.

"Could I…" She finally broke, folding her arms and hunched her shoulders defensively. "Press releases are my forte." Her head came up. "I could issue a statement, make it clear that I don't really know you." Her expression was sincere, as if that was a genuinely helpful suggestion.

He snorted.

"It's *true*," she said defensively, but her cheeks stained a darker pink. The way her chin dipped and her lips rolled in suggested she was recalling exactly how well acquainted they were.

That was gratifying, at least. If he was still hostage to this pull between them, at least he had a cellmate.

She tucked her jaw-length hair behind her ear, and even the fact it was rich brunette at the roots and distressed as old denim on the ends was sexy as hell.

He absently closed his empty hand, recalling the satisfying give of those thick, springy waves between his fingers. It was a lot shorter now, but he bet it still smelled of almonds and citrus. He wanted to pick it up and set his mouth in the hollow at the base of her skull, feeling her squirm, and push her bottom into his groin in response.

So damned stupid. He gave his head a shake to dispel the fantasy.

"I'm not dismissing the idea because we know each other in the biblical sense." There had been nothing puritanical about that night. It had been delightfully debauched. "It's a very naive offer from someone who struck me as intelligent. Have you not seen the news?"

"Not lately." Her mouth twisted. "I stopped watching. It was too depressing."

No doubt. Still, "You haven't happened across any head-lines?"

"I don't go online. I was afraid of leaving digital foot-prints. I even put tape over the camera on the computer." She chucked her chin toward the door to the kitchen, then sent him a baleful look. "I didn't think of the security cam-eras, or I would have covered them, too."

"I didn't even peek at you today." He had reviewed the map of sensors to see which house doors were open, sur-mising from there that she was in the kitchen. Then he had disabled all the cameras so he wouldn't activate them as he entered.

"Look, Morris and Ackerley are pretending all is well, but they're imploding. Their legal bills are mounting, and anyone who was able to pull their money out of the company already has. Their assets are frozen, employees haven't been paid, more victims are coming forward and most are going to the press with their complaints. The fact that the whistleblower is missing is stirring up swarms of hashtags. Your fiancé—"

"*Ex*," she reminded, teeth clamped on a nip of her cu-ticle while her fixed gaze impelled him to keep talking.

"Ackerley suddenly realized he could be on the hook for murder charges if you don't turn up alive. He doesn't know that I'm helping you, but he doesn't care. Now that he's fig-ured out I was the last person to see you, he has issued an ultimatum. Either I tell him where you are or take the fall for your absence. It would make a nice distraction for him to sic the media and authorities onto me, and it would be highly inconvenient for me. Therefore, you have to reap-pear, make it clear I had nothing to do with your decision to expose them and draw the fire back where it belongs."

"I'm really sorry." Her tone held the placating tone of, *I'd like to help you, but I can't.* "I wasn't trying to set you up for anything like this."

"No? Why did you sleep with me then?" Because, as she'd briefly evaded him with skills he usually only saw in a fellow operative, he had begun to suspect ulterior motives in her spending those erotic hours with him. Had she meant to entrap him?

She looked away, hugging herself as she flushed with embarrassment, mouth pinched with reluctance to speak.

"Because you made it sound as though you'd recently broken your engagement and wanted to move on, yet you were still engaged." Everett didn't know why he was so outraged by that. When he'd brought her to his room, he hadn't planned to see her again. He sure as hell hadn't expected to feel this roil of indignation if he did, especially one stained with such a dark green of possessiveness. But spiky barbs of jealousy sat sharply under his skin.

"I did want to move on. I was angry with Troy, but that wasn't why I—" She cleared her throat before admitting in a strangled voice, "I was attracted to you."

He wanted to cage her face in his palms and look into her eyes. He wanted to get right up against her to learn if this thing between them had been as real as it had seemed, but he kept his distance. His focus.

"That's the only reason you slept with me? Attraction? You weren't deliberately drawing me into your plot?"

"What? No." Her eyes flashed wide with shock. "Why would I?"

Why indeed? It wasn't as if he had a secret past that she might have discovered and thought she could weaponize.

She held his gaze, earnest tension sitting across her cheekbones.

"I knew I shouldn't have dinner with you." Her voice was tight with mortification. "I was planning to land, send my files and disappear, but when you asked me to dinner..." She showed him a pensive profile. "I was anxious to get away from Troy and everything else, but I was scared." Her hands were flexing in remembered anxiety. "I wasn't sure how to get rid of my luggage, but I realized that if I met you for dinner, I could leave it at your hotel as an insurance policy. If I chickened out on sending the files, I could pick up my bag and my life in the morning. If I went through with it, it would take the concierge some time to wonder why I hadn't come back for it."

Smart. And it rang true. "But you spent the night."

"That wasn't part of my plan. Truly. I don't sleep with men I don't know or like or, you know, want to sleep with." She was blushing again.

He took a similar approach with his intimate partners, but had to ask, "Does that mean you were sleeping with your fiancé or not?"

"I wasn't." She shook her head in an urgent reassurance, as if it mattered as much to her as it did to him. "I was desperate to break the engagement, but if I had, he might have realized I was about to set fire to his great-grandfather's firm so I made excuses for why I couldn't spend the night with him."

"Headache?" he guessed dryly.

She grimaced and her shoulders came up to her ears. "I claimed so many migraines, he booked me for an MRI."

He refused to laugh, but a gust of relief left his lungs. This was what had transfixed him that evening. There was no chance for boredom when everything about her was unexpected. She veered effortlessly from introspective to playful, from sincere to sarcastic, then dipped to warm and sensual as her expression softened. A rueful smile touched her lips.

"Why did you get engaged in the first place?" It was the last question he should be asking, but he wanted to know. "Did you love him?"

"No. Not really. It just sort of happened." She wrinkled her nose as though she still suffered regret. "When he hired me after I interned, I was really flattered. And yes, I realize my credentials were less a factor in my landing that job than the fact I fit the image they wanted to project." She rolled her eyes.

No false modesty. She knew she was beautiful, knew it was an advantage, but didn't wield it like a weapon. He liked that about her, too.

Focus, fool.

"Troy took a personal interest in my professional development. He kept giving me more responsibility and shifting me into different departments. My specialty is marketing, but my degree is business, so I thought I was elevating my skill set. Eventually I realized I was doing his work so he didn't have to, but Mom was sick, and when she passed, he was really kind. He sent flowers and said my absence had made him realize I deserved a raise. Looking back, I see he was making sure he didn't lose my 'elevated skill set.'" She made air quotes. "But it felt good to be taken out for fancy dinners when I was feeling so blue."

"It felt good to be taken advantage of when you were vulnerable?" He had nothing but contempt for men like that.

"I didn't see it, but yes, that's what he was doing. By the time I was plotting my escape, I was certain he had been keeping at least one woman on the side the whole time he was romancing me, but it felt genuine. I wasn't thinking it would lead to marriage, though. Not until he took me into a corner office and said, 'This can be yours if you say yes.'"

"And went down on one knee? What a tool." He was so embarrassed by his own sex sometimes.

"Right? But considering how hard I'd been working I didn't see it as nepotism or even a condition of our engagement. I had earned that promotion. He told me I had. He said he didn't want to lose me to another firm *or* another man. I thought all these big gestures meant he loved me. My mom was gone, and I wanted a family one day. He seemed like a caring man who was a good provider. I thought grief was holding me back from deep feelings and decided, why *not* him?"

"Then you realized why not," Everett deduced grimly.

"I did," she said somberly. "I came across some transactions that I had done for him and… Basically, they were stealing. He was getting me to do his work so he could keep his own hands clean."

"Plausible deniability."

"Exactly. He wanted me to take the blame if it came to light. Which is why I had to expose it." She took hold of the open door of the car, wavered as though trying to decide whether to get in or close it. "It feels good to talk about it. *To talk.* To a human. But be honest." She sent him a look of consternation. "Are you here to find out how much I really know? Or, like, hang me out to dry in some way?"

"I'm not an assassin, if that's what you're implying," he said dryly. "I'm not a cop or a reporter, either."

"What, then? What are you 'not anymore?'" she amended, eyes narrowing as she recollected his earlier remark.

"We'll save that for another time." Like never.

"But I'm supposed to trust you?" She tsked and shut the car door, coming to the back of the car, where she leaned her hip next to the taillight.

He tried not to wince. The paintwork could be buffed.

"Is there a reason you don't want to trust me?" he asked.

"Aside from the fact that you tricked me into staying here?"

"Where you've been very safe and comfortable," he pointed out.

"It's suspicious, though. What do you get out of it?" She crossed her arms and tilted her head.

"A housekeeper. And the knowledge I did a good deed." It had been so much more complex than that, but he rose and tucked his crutches beneath his arm, having learned that standing was a great way to close a topic and take command of pretty much anything.

Her solemn gaze met his black eye. "If ending up on crutches is what happens to someone who knows where I am, what will they do to *me* if I come out of hiding?"

His heart lurched.

"Nothing." He swallowed the ashes that came into his mouth. "I'll arrange protection. Security, a lawyer, a PR agent, a safe place to stay. Anything and everything you need."

"Why? Do you have a grudge against Morris and Ackerley? Were you an investor?"

"No."

"This is just to keep your name out of it?"

"Yes."

"It's that important to you."

Obviously.

"What happens when someone realizes you've paid for all of those things?"

"They won't."

"Who will they think paid for it?" she asked with exasperation. "The woman who claims she didn't have anything to do with defrauding all those people of millions of dollars?" She pointed at herself.

"I have work-arounds." He shrugged that off. "How do you feel about a six-figure book deal? If you don't want to write it, I can hire a ghost writer."

"Where does *that* money come from?" Her hands went up in bafflement. "Are you a drug dealer? Arms? What?"

"No." Good guesses, though. "Are you always this suspicious?"

"I just want to know what's going on! You're such a good Samaritan, you want to give me a six-figure book deal to hide the fact that you've been helping me. Heck, you hid that information from *me*. Why? Oh, God." Horror washed across her expression. "You're not married, are you?"

"No." If he wasn't so aggravated with her, he would revel in the way she looked ill at the thought of him being committed to someone else. "When you started making headlines, I realized our night could surface and bite me, so I tucked you out of sight. That's all."

"So this was *never* about protecting me and always about protecting *you*?"

So smart and so maddening. "Yes."

Barbed hurt flashed in her eyes, causing a pinch behind his heart.

"You've gone to a lot of trouble and expense to keep our night hidden." She tossed her head. "It's not like I was ever going to tell anyone that we hooked up. It was a one-time thing that didn't mean anything to me, either. That's why I left as soon as you were asleep."

"I wasn't asleep."

Her head snapped around, appalled hurt flashing in her wide eyes.

He bit back a curse, annoyed with himself. He hadn't liked hearing their night meant nothing and had struck back.

"Thanks, but no thanks," she said frostily, pushing off the car and starting toward the door to the house. "I'll take Option B, the one where I take my chances with the paparazzi and my fiancé."

"Bianca!" He moved so fast lurching to catch her arm, he dropped a crutch, stupid damned things.

She yanked free of his touch and whirled to confront him.

"I wasn't ashamed of being so easy that night until right now, when you made me feel like I curdle your image like sour milk. You shouldn't have asked me to dinner if you're embarrassed to be associated with me. Did you think of that? And don't tell me to trust you! You could be leading Troy to me right now for all I know."

Ah hell, she was shaking. Scared.

A cool space opened behind his breastbone. She wouldn't be this close to falling apart if she had some master plan in place. She was flying by the seat of her pants and was running out of fuel.

"I'm not embarrassed we slept together," he said quietly. "My life is very complicated—"

"Really? What's that like?"

He licked his lips, still enamored with that snappy wit of hers, but it struck him how hard these months must have been for her. In the past, when he left someone in a safe house, they had caretakers and he visited as often as he could, keeping their spirits up.

"I had the means to help you and I wanted to. I still do." *Don't get further involved*, the nagging voice in his head reminded. *Clear your name, get her out of your house, never see her again.*

She rejected his offer with a lost shake of her head, blinking and pressing her lips flat to hide their trembling.

"Bianca," he chided. Pure instinct had him holding out an arm. "Come here. You don't have to do this all by yourself. That's why I'm here."

Fool, that voice said, but when she gave a sniff and looked so damned slight and vulnerable, he couldn't take it. He stepped closer and nudged the back of her arm.

A sob left her and she turned herself into his chest. Her arms went around his waist, hugging tight. She hunched close as though sheltering from the elements and a small shudder went through her.

The impact on him was cataclysmic.

He had thought about her constantly, wanting the feel of her narrow back under his hand and the tickle of her hair under his chin. He smoothed her spine, saying nothing while she took unsteady breaths, trying to keep a grip on her composure.

"You're still very safe," he assured her. "We're only talking about what might happen. Nothing has changed. Not yet."

"I kept thinking about you." She drew back enough to look up at him. Her lashes were spiky with unshed tears. "I wished I had been honest with you. That I had given you my side before I turned up on the news. It's like a hallucination that you're even here. That I've been in your house all this time. I want to trust you, Everett. I do. But I don't know if I can."

Same, he almost said, but his senses were taking in her perfume of oranges and sunshine. He liked the press of her curves against his chest and abdomen and thighs. She was a puzzle piece that fit exactly into the landscape of his own shape, blending heat and sensation, filling his vision with color, blurring the space between them into nothing.

The atmosphere shifted. Her searching gaze drifted to his mouth. She swallowed.

They each nudged their feet a fraction closer, bodies leaning more firmly into one another.

Careful, Everett. Not in a million years would he make a move on a woman who was only seeking comfort, but as he drew a breath and started to pull back, the light in her eyes dimmed. Her beautiful mouth, which was *right there*, trembled with rejection. She firmed it and her chin crinkled. Her weight shifted away from his.

His arm instinctually tightened, trying to keep her from dissolving like loose sand through his fingertips.

Her gaze flashed up to his and, damn it, he'd been thinking of kissing her again for *so long*.

As he slowly, slowly let his head lower, she stayed right where she was. In fact, her body inclined more into his, melting and receptive, warm and welcoming.

He touched his mouth to hers and a tingling dance slid across his lips. Smooth, plump flesh gave way as he settled deeper into their kiss. A soft noise throbbed in her throat, one that added to the moans and sobs and cries of ecstasy that echoed in his erotic dreams.

There was a worth-the-wait quality to this kiss, but he groaned thinking that he had known where she was all this time and could have had a thousand of these kisses by now. He shouldn't have wasted any of that time. She opened her mouth further and he drew her closer, sliding his arm around her as he rocked his mouth to deepen their kiss.

He became so lost in her scent and taste, he didn't immediately catch the flavor on her tongue or the faint aroma clinging to the hand she raised to touch his cheek, not until his lips began to burn.

His lips began to burn.

He grabbed hold of her upper arms and set her back a step.

"How did you know?" he growled.

True fear sent his heart slamming with the force of a wrecking ball, nearly cracking his ribs. The prickling sensation was already spreading into his mouth and down his throat.

A clock began ticking in his head. He would never make it to the boat. Was there a first aid kit in the house? Why hadn't he grabbed his pen? He always had one in his pocket, but he'd been fiddling with the security system on his phone and too impatient to see her. *Idiot.*

"How did I know what?" she asked as he swiveled away and hopped with one crutch toward the door to the kitchen.

"That I'm allergic to peanuts."

This time it might actually kill him.

CHAPTER THREE

"Is IT SEVERE?" Bianca rushed ahead of him to hold the door, afraid to touch him again. "Do you have a pen? There's a first aid kit in the laundry room."

Her mind raced. She'd had a classmate in middle school who had had a deadly allergy to bee stings. The whole class had learned how to administer the epinephrine, but she had never actually jabbed anyone. She didn't even know if there was a pen here.

Everett began to wheeze and grasped at the doorframe. He was likely winded by hopping on one crutch as his windpipe closed. Behind the determination in his eyes was angry despair.

Reacting purely on instinct, she slapped her hand across the garage door buttons.

As she had suspected, the moment they began grinding upward, the security system bleated its alarm.

Everett flashed her a look of disbelief.

"You need help." She didn't let herself think of what might happen after. "The ambulance can reach you fastest if you stay out here. Lie down before you fall down." She grasped his arm because he was already sinking to the floor.

As he crumpled to the concrete, she released him and ran inside to look for a pen. She would make one if she had to.

Over hidden speakers, a woman's voice identified herself as working for TecSec, the security company. "All cameras are activated. Your movements are being recorded."

"We have a medical emergency. Anaphylaxis. Order an ambulance *now*." Bianca banged through the cupboards in the laundry room and grabbed the red kit with the white cross. She dumped it unceremoniously onto the top of the washer. Bandages and scissors and antiseptic... Where was the damned pen?

"An ambulance has been dispatched," the voice said calmly. "It should arrive in four minutes. The gate will open when it nears. Our notes indicate there is a stock of self-injectable epinephrine in the master bedroom. Emergency personnel are asking if this is an insect bite—"

"Peanut allergy." Bianca leaped up the stairs two at a time, tearing down the hall and into the master bathroom where she quickly found a box of two needles. "For God's sake, cut that siren. It's killing my ears," she shouted as she raced back to the garage.

The noise silenced and the disembodied voice began reading instructions on how to administer the needle, reminding her to check the date.

Everett was on his back on the concrete floor, one arm thrown over his eyes. His lips were blue, his chest shaking as he strained to breath. He lifted his arm as she appeared. The tense resignation in his expression flickered to surprise.

"Nice opinion you have of me," she muttered, fumbling to scrabble the needle from the box. The date was fine, thank God.

She pulled the ends off and lifted the edge of his shorts so she could press the red end against the outside of his thigh. He didn't flinch at the sting of the needle going in, only held her stare while a hazy curtain seemed to descend over the shimmering blue of his eyes.

"Don't you dare, Everett." She finished counting as she held it against his skin, then covered the needle and set it aside, rubbing the spot on his leg with her other hand.

She was about to ask the disembodied voice if she should give him another, but she heard the ambulance siren approaching. The gate was rattling open.

She started to cup Everett's face, wanting to rouse him and see if he was just closing his eyes or actually falling unconscious, but she remembered she hadn't washed her hands.

The soap at the utility sink was an industrial grease remover, but she used it anyway, hurrying to wash her hands to her elbows and all over her face, rinsing her mouth and spitting, then using the nearby paper towel before discarding it.

As she came back to check Everett's pulse—he had one, but it was faint and very fast—the ambulance stopped in the cobblestoned forecourt. She waved and called out, then stepped back as one of the attendants ran up to crouch next to Everett, checking his vital signs.

Beyond the gate a dog walker paused to peer at their commotion.

Run, a voice of self-preservation urged her. *This is your last chance.*

Bianca looked to the other paramedic, who was bringing oxygen, then to Everett's limp form. She couldn't leave him like this, not when she was responsible for putting him in that state.

She hovered tensely, worried at how swift and grave they were being about packaging him for transport.

"Are you coming in the ambulance or—" The paramedic glanced at the sports car.

"I'm coming." She was in no fit state to drive. "Security, alarm the house as we leave."

"Of course. TecSec is pleased we could be of service today. A full report will be issued shortly."

She should have stayed at the house to clean it, Bianca thought several times over the next hours. Everett couldn't go back there until all traces of peanuts were gone.

If he went back there.

The EMTs had been forced to insert a tube into his windpipe to ensure he was receiving enough oxygen. Twice they had thought they would have to administer CPR.

When they arrived at the hospital, someone asked if she was his wife and Bianca had unhesitatingly said, "Yes." She had signed every piece of paper they put in front of her.

A short while ago, they had decided his blood pressure was strong enough and the swelling in his airway reduced enough, that they had removed his air tube. Now he only had a tube resting in his nostrils, continuing to provide extra oxygen. He was still hooked up to IV and a number of monitors. He was still unconscious.

As she sat curled in a chair beside his bed, she kept trying to think of herself and her situation, trying to work out the best course of action for *her*, but her mind wouldn't cooperate. It wouldn't even stick to all that had happened this morning and the revelation that he had been her employer all this time.

No, her brain insisted on conjuring memories of their night together, the way it had for months, lingering over the slow seduction of a dinner and strolling the boardwalk, the night air caressing her shoulders and arms, then his light touch following those same paths. A kiss that had drawn her so far from this world, she had felt drugged when he had lifted his head and said, "Come to my room."

It had been both invitation and command. She'd been incapable of resisting either.

She hadn't known lovemaking like that was possible. For her, sex had always been a pleasant if tame and awkward encounter. She knew men thought she was attractive, but they'd always looked at her like a prize, making her feel removed, as though she was being made love *to*, not *with*.

Everett had definitely ensured she was with him every step of the way. He had been in no hurry and he had brushed her hair behind her shoulder and said, "Your hair is beautiful. It smells like you," he added. "Run it across me. I want your scent all over me."

He had touched and kissed her everywhere, along the base of her neck and down her back, inside her elbow and even her ankle. "Your skin is so soft. Do you like this? Move my hand. Show me what makes you feel good." Instead of telling her what he wanted her to do to him, he had asked, "Do you want my mouth here? Do you need me to do this harder?"

She had grown emboldened with her own caresses, doing things she'd never done, rubbing her breasts on his erection and licking her way down his body purely to hear him groan with tortured anticipation.

Time had stopped as she became immersed in the experience, each caress so sharply exquisite it nearly hurt. Twice he had brought her to the brink and backed off, continuing to pleasure her in a slower, more indirect way, keeping her on that plateau of heightened arousal while building them toward even grander pinnacles.

When he had finally thrust into her, she had nearly wept at how badly she had needed his penetration. All inhibitions had been abandoned by then. She was completely his, reveling in his slow, deep, powerful strokes. She had moaned her encouragement without any sense of decorum or restraint. She'd said filthy things, telling him what she wanted. *Needed.* More. Harder.

Still he had made it last, rolling them across the bed, encouraging her to ride him, then pinning her beneath him again, determined to wring every last sensation from every stroke.

When the tantalizing stars of orgasm had begun to coalesce behind her eyes, when her breath shortened and her body was one live nerve, he had done exactly what she needed and given her more. Harder.

She had shattered. The crashing waves of orgasm had shot all the way into her fingers and toes. Through the storm, as her body ceased to belong to her and her consciousness was devolved to its most primitive form, she had felt him pulsing within her. Shuddering upon her, skin adhered to hers. He had released jagged noises with his hot breath against her ear, matching her unintelligible cries of ecstasy with his own.

They had been together. United. For the first time in her life, she had felt as though she was truly connected to another person. Broken down to her most basic level, but unbreakable because she had him. They were one.

Then he'd done it again. And once more after they'd dozed.

As the sky had turned pearlescent, she had made herself rise. It had been harder than all the planning and plotting she'd done to leave the man she had been engaged to, but she'd left, aware pieces of herself would stay with Everett, but she was leaving everything behind, and she was deeply glad he held *those* pieces.

Then.

Now she knew he had feigned sleep and let her go.

Had he been relieved by her departure?

My life is very complicated.

She had hated him for a minute there. She had hated

herself. Their night had become tawdry, and she had felt cheap.

Then he had hugged her. *You don't have to do this all by yourself anymore.*

Those words, the way he'd held her... Profound relief had nearly buckled her knees. His promise to stand by her had been everything she had dreamed of while she'd been rattling around in that empty house, wishing she knew what came next. Had it been a rescue fantasy? Perhaps. But he was the man she had wanted to rescue her this whole time and here he was.

Then she had nearly killed him.

She sat at his bedside, earning double takes from nurses and other hospital personnel as they recognized her. She didn't have so much as a spare coin in her pocket for a phone call and only one person to call if she did. Would her father even take her call? Believe her? Welcome her? Or reject her?

If she possessed one ounce of self-preservation, she would leave before Everett woke, but until he woke, she couldn't seem to make herself leave this chair, let alone his room or the hospital. She needed to know he would be okay.

She desperately hoped he wouldn't hate her.

"Hello." A male voice forced her to drag her gaze off Everett and glance to the door.

A very handsome man of thirty-something had appeared in the open doorway. He was in a wheelchair, but not one of the hospital ones. It was streamlined and clearly custom made for him, given he showed no sign of illness and wore stylish linen trousers draped over the ends of his amputated legs. His shirt was a collared polo in a berry brown that clung to his extremely well-built chest and biceps as he smoothly rolled in.

Her next thought was that he possessed an air of confidence similar to the one Everett exuded, especially when the man casually leaned down and released the doorstop, letting the door fall closed behind him as he came up to the bed.

His face hardened as he took in Everett's black eye and bandaged hands.

"That's not a peanut reaction. What happened?" The way his hardened glare turned on her and pinned her through the heart had her pressing into her chair.

"He showed up like that." She scratched her neck, not sure how much to say. She had told the doctor the peanut contact had been the fault of a gardener because who would believe the man's wife didn't know about his allergy? Then she had quietly washed again with antiseptic wipes *and* brushed her teeth with a toothbrush that would likely be added to Everett's bill.

She instinctively knew not to lie to this man, though.

"I ate some peanut butter, then kissed him," she admitted in a mumble.

"On purpose?" The deadly way his voice dropped sent icicles jabbing into her plummeting stomach.

"*No.* I mean, it was consensual. *He* kissed *me*, if you want to be technical about it." She rubbed her clammy palms on her bare arms. "I didn't know about his allergy, or I never would have brought anything like that into his house."

He gave a snort of mild disgust and came around the end of the bed, so they weren't speaking over Everett's unconscious body.

"He only told me about it a year ago and downplayed how bad it was."

"And you are?" she prompted.

"Giovanni Catalano." He offered his hand. "A friend of Everett's, which makes me wonder why I wasn't invited to your wedding. Bianca."

"Um…" She had started to offer her name and hold out her hand, but she was so disconcerted, her fingers turned to limp celery as he closed his strong grip over them.

He was gentle, though. Brief.

"That's what they told me at admin. That his wife was with him." And he knew who she was. His delving gaze was trying to put together how his friend had wound up married to the Morris and Ackerley whistleblower.

"I only said that so I could sign the papers for his care." It belatedly occurred to her that he might be a reporter or investigator. She set her feet on the floor and rose, feeling as though she was peeling off her own skin as she said, "But I guess if you're here to speak for him, I can leave." She didn't want to leave him, though. And she had nowhere to go.

Giovanni made the smallest adjustment to the angle of his wheelchair, but it was a very loud, *Thou shalt not pass*.

She lifted her brows, cornered between the bed and the window, but not afraid to vault over the hospital bed and the man she had put in it, if that's what it took to maintain her freedom.

"Someone has tipped off the press that you're here," Giovanni said. "You won't get out without help."

That wasn't much of a surprise. She was tempted to peek through the blinds but decided she'd better not. She sank back into the chair.

"Are you offering to help? Why?"

"I'm Everett's friend." He shot another look at the man that held shades of impatience and exasperation. "Thankfully, you've laid the groundwork. It's an easy spin to say you kept your marriage a secret to avoid media attention. We'll issue a statement that doesn't mention the allergy. A Jet Ski accident," he decided. "To account for his injuries. I'll order a change of clothes, so you'll be camera-ready when we walk to the car. We'll leave the minute he's awake and able to walk."

"And go *where*?" She had so many questions, she was tripping over her own tongue. "You can't just come in here and take control."

"Someone has to. I need to make some calls. Stay put." He neatly spun his chair.

Panicked belligerence had her saying, "I will not."

"Bianca," a voice rasped from the bed. "Do as you're told."

"I thought you retired," Giovanni said.

"I thought you did," Everett grumbled back.

He felt as though he'd been thrown down a flight of stairs and turned inside out. He sat on a lounger in the shade, his only true friend seated beside him. Bianca and Giovanni's wife, Freja, were in the far end of the pool catching the couple's twins as they jumped off the ledge into the water.

Bianca laughed as she was splashed by the energetic two-year-olds, her mood a complete one-eighty from how sullen she'd been in the SUV as they had left the hospital. She'd pulled on a simple wrap dress and chic sandals, coiled her blue-tipped hair under a floppy-brimmed hat and covered her eyes with huge black sunglasses. The bold red on her lips had emphasized her mouth's downward curve. She had used Everett's limping body as a shield as they passed the gathered photographers.

They had arrived to a cleaning crew wiping every wall and surface of his mansion. Everett had messaged his housekeeper from the hospital, and she had hurried in a service. She was quick to ask Bianca where the workers should make extra effort to remove traces of peanut butter. Then, because the twins had been begging to go in the pool, Bianca had been commandeered by Freja.

"Why are you even here?" Everett heard how ungrateful he sounded, but he could barely face the man as it was. Giovanni had done him a huge favor when he ought to have cut Everett out of his life completely by now.

"Our good friend at TecSec thought I might be interested in the security video that had just come across his desk. He was prepared to fly in himself, but I was closer. We were in New York, preparing to come for Freja's premiere this weekend. We moved up our trip and here we are."

"I meant why did you bother?" Everett said, but Giovanni was speaking over him.

"Was your reaction this dangerous when you ate those peanuts—"

"What's done is done," Everett cut in, not wanting to talk about the time he had deliberately ingested peanuts to clear his conscience where Freja was concerned. It had done nothing to square things with the man beside him.

Giovanni sighed. Annoyed. "It wasn't your fault, Everett. I wish you'd get over it and accept a dinner invitation now and again."

It *was* his fault, though. He and Giovanni had been friends in their school years, when Giovanni had kept him sane through a very dark time. Years later, Everett had recruited his friend into the spy game. They'd been a sort of dream team, but Everett hadn't forced Giovanni to stand down when he had known Giovanni was not at his mental best. His best friend had nearly been killed and it still turned his guts to gravel.

He loathed himself for endangering his friend and couldn't understand why Giovanni didn't.

"Freja never would have asked you to risk your life for her," Giovanni said quietly. "But thank you. What you did means the world to her."

"Don't get maudlin." Everett couldn't take it right now.

Ever, really. "And don't expect me to thank you for your assistance today." He waved toward the pool. "I don't *want* a wife."

"Don't knock it till you try it."

Everett shot him a glower, but Giovanni only grinned, then chucked his chin.

"Seriously, are you working again?" he asked in an undertone.

"No."

"Then what are you doing with her?" Giovanni looked to Bianca.

"We crossed paths. She needed help. My involvement would have stayed between the two of us except…" He swirled a hand to encompass the farce of a day this had turned into.

"Judging by that pretty black-and-blue eye shadow you're wearing, it's not just between the two of you. If it's that dangerous, should you *stay* involved if you lack backup?"

This was why Everett had wanted to keep Giovanni on the payroll as long as possible. He never missed a thing and always drilled straight to the heart of a problem.

"What's my alternative? Leave her to face it alone? I'm in it now." According to the headlines, he was married to it.

"But can you trust her? After today?"

"She didn't know." And she had saved him.

An emotive vibration hit his sternum as he recalled that harrowing moment when Bianca had run into the house, leaving him collapsing on the garage floor.

He'd been furious at her for catching him off guard *again*, but it served him right. He had known she was dangerous from the get-go. Even when he learned how much trouble she was in, he had waded right in. He had spooked her with his surprise arrival and even though she had tripped the alarm, he had fully expected her to save herself, leaving him to take his chances on the ambulance arriving in time.

Part of him had wanted her to get herself into the clear, but in the twilight of fighting for enough oxygen, he'd been worried about her. Who would look out for her if he wasn't there to do it?

She had reappeared then, breathless, and jabbed him without any squeamishness. Her eyes had been shiny with fear, her mouth tight with determination.

Everything had fogged after that. He'd come back to Giovanni's voice, which hadn't been much of a surprise. Everett was a terrible friend, but Giovanni was a good one.

Everett might have let himself sink back into unconsciousness, safe in good hands, but Bianca's voice had pulled him back to wakefulness. He hadn't expected her to be there. That meant she had broken her cover. For him.

"Okay, but if you need anything—"

"I won't," Everett said flatly. "Stay out of it."

"*Dio, sei testardo,*" Giovanni muttered in Italian, calling Everett stubborn.

There was a pulse of silence where only the splashes and squeals of the children sounded, then Giovanni continued in Italian.

"Fine, but this doesn't add up. Why did she stay in Miami?"

"Because I gave her the means," Everett replied, also using Italian.

"Why did she want to, though? She could have hopped a yacht, got work on a cruise ship… Why did she stay where her fiancé sent her?"

Everett had wondered those things, too. While he'd been apart from her, he had focused on looking into her employer's background to bolster the case against them, only running a cursory background check on Bianca.

She had been born in New York, her mother had been a

nurse and Bianca had been an exemplary student. Her CV had checked out as had the grandmother in Miami leaving her money—although the timing had been off with that. The probate had finalized two years before Everett had met her. Beyond that, there hadn't been anything untoward.

"Finito?" Giovanni smiled as Freja and Bianca approached. "I'll help get them changed." He reached for his wheelchair.

Bianca cradled one of the towel-wrapped toddlers. The girl's lips were blue and her teeth were chattering. Bianca wore a white T-shirt over her bikini, the wet cotton plastered to her hips and upper thighs. Neon green showed through and beneath the hem, and her honey-gold thighs were sparkling with dripping water.

She's doing it again. Giovanni had just given Everett good reason to question her motives, but all Everett wanted to do was lick each of those drops off her skin.

"We should get to the hotel," Freja was saying to Giovanni. "Unless you two need more time?" She glanced to Everett with a glimmer of optimism.

"We're finished talking," Everett said crisply.

Giovanni settled into his chair and exchanged one of those married people looks with Freja, the kind that communicated a dozen thoughts at once. Everett couldn't interpret all of it, but he caught the part where Freja's mouth pressed flat with empathy.

Did she not realize Everett didn't deserve their forgiveness? He was poison. She ought to know that better than anyone.

"I didn't realize you weren't staying here," Bianca said with a wary flicker of her glance at Everett as she stooped to hand Louisa to Giovanni.

"We have such an entourage—it's best if we pay people to put up with us," Freja joked.

And this house wasn't really set up for Giovanni. Most

of Everett's homes had at least the ground floor remodeled to accommodate his friend's chair, but Everett hadn't got around to making those changes here, which made him feel like an even bigger jerk.

"Lars is with us," Giovanni said, mentioning his physiotherapist. "Do you want me to send him over to look at your knee? Give you some exercises?"

"I'm fine." *Quit being nice*, Everett told him with a glare.

You could try it, Giovanni told him with a cocked brow.

"Oh! I had tickets set aside for you, for the premiere," Freja said to Everett. "That was before…" She rocked her head. "Today. But you hadn't seen it yet so I thought you might…"

She trailed off as she took in his stonewalling expression.

"No pressure. Whatever you decide. Yes, I know you're hungry." Freja nuzzled her nose against Theresa's as the little girl whispered an entreaty. "We're going to dry you two off and get you a snack for the drive to the hotel. Then we'll have a nice big dinner. Thank you so much for your help today," Freja said to Bianca. "I'll leave my number. Let's stay in touch."

"Oh. Yes. Thanks. It was my pleasure. Truly." Her smile faded as the couple retreated into the house. Bianca hugged herself against the chill of her dripping T-shirt. "Those girls are adorable and she's so nice. I didn't have the heart to tell her I don't even have a phone." The spark of wry humor in her eyes winked out as she met his eyes.

Everett was fighting to keep his gaze above the way her breasts swelled against the translucent fabric of her shirt.

It was a fair question. Why *had* she stayed in Miami?

"Well, I guess I'll, um, go change." She turned toward the cabanas.

"Your things are in my room. I had the housekeeper move them."

"Why?" She blinked her wet lashes in astonishment.

"Because we're married," he reminded pithily.

CHAPTER FOUR

BIANCA FINISHED REMOVING the lipstick that had smudged in the pool and stared at her clean face, almost able to convince herself that she was exactly as she had been this morning. Nothing had changed.

Yet everything had. This wasn't even her small oval mirror in the cabana. It was the huge, well-lit mirror in the Hers side of the master bathroom.

She hadn't argued with Everett about sharing his room. She felt awful for what he'd endured at her expense. He had barely got himself into the SUV to leave the hospital, moving as though he had been hit by a car. Plus, she hadn't wanted to stand there arguing with him, half-dressed, when she could come up here and take a few minutes to collect herself.

If only she didn't have to face him alone.

When they'd first returned to the mansion, there had been a chaos of people here. Some had been cleaning, others had been guards ensuring the mansion was secure, holding off reporters trying to take photos from the road and the water.

Freja had been anxiously waiting for them. The Italian couple clearly cared about Everett, but he had some kind of wall of resentment erected against them. Bianca had thought he was just being grumpy when he gave Giovanni one-word replies in the car, but Freja had briefly hugged him and when she had searched his expression, he had avoided her gaze and extricated himself, claiming he needed to sit down.

The couple had exchanged a resigned look that could have equally applied to one of their toddlers having a tantrum. It had been intriguing enough that when Freja asked Bianca if she would help her in the pool with the children, Bianca had agreed, hoping to learn more.

She had realized very quickly that she was being managed. Freja was providing the men a chance to speak privately, and it had gone against Bianca's best instincts to let Everett make any more decisions about her future without her input, but honestly? Cooling off in the pool with a pair of exuberant girls who were generous with affection had been an enormous stress reliever. When had she last laughed so unreservedly? Or chattered about daily life with another woman? Before her mother had died, she suspected. It had been nice. Normal.

Plus, Freja was so lovely, Bianca couldn't resent her machinations, especially when she asked her to reveal exactly what had happened to Everett, then grew choked up hearing it.

"He purposely put himself in hospital a year ago, so he could get a message to my foster mother. I didn't know he nearly *died*."

Bianca had wanted to hear more about that, but the children had distracted them.

Now the family was gone, along with the cleaners. The housekeeper was rearranging the kitchen back to the way she liked it and the guards had shooed off the worst of the photographers.

Bianca was cowering in this bathroom like a virgin on her wedding night.

She sighed, accepting that she couldn't hide forever. Not from the outside world and not from Everett.

With a twanging sense of exposure, she acknowledged how much she had already revealed about herself. Maybe she had kept the whistleblowing from him that night they'd made love, but she had talked candidly about her life, telling him about her mother and her school years. Then she had completely given herself over to him.

At the time, she'd felt safe doing it, maybe because she had never expected to see him again, but now it felt like something he could use against her, leaving a shivering knot of apprehension sitting low in her belly.

She sighed, wishing they could go back to when he had held her in the garage. In that moment, she had started to think coming forward might be okay, if she had him on her side. She had started to trust him.

Oh, who was she kidding? She had thought him as handsome as ever, even with the stubble and black eye. Maybe because of it. His arms around her and his hard frame, so solid against her own, had felt exactly as good as the first time—reassuring and strong and tantalizingly hot. She had desperately wanted to know if he could still make her blood sizzle and her body soar the way he had six months ago. The only thing in her head had been, *Please kiss me again.*

He had. And it had been everything she remembered.

For a few seconds.

Now he probably wanted to throw her out on her ear.

There was only one way to find out. She pulled on a well-worn, halter-style sundress and combed out her hair, then went back outside to the patio.

For a second she thought he was dozing, but he turned his head and, *bam*, his blue gaze hit her like a tropical surf, crashing over her and filtering a soft tingle down her skin as his gaze went from her bared shoulders to her bare feet in cheap flip-flops.

She touched her damp hair, brushing a wet strand off

her cheek that the breeze had picked up. She wished she had tied her hair back to hide the fading color. She wished she possessed makeup so she could have applied a small shield. The way she looked only emphasized that she had been living off his good graces all this time. She had very few assets and resources while he had a seemingly infinite amount, judging by the meal that had appeared like magic on the patio table.

"Are you hungry?" He swung his legs off the lounger and rose with a small wince.

"I am, actually." She pulled out her own chair, stomach pinching at the aroma off the paella still sizzling in its pan on the trivet. "No, thanks," she said of the wine he reached for. Best to keep her wits.

He left the bottle in the ice bucket and they both sat. His breath left him in a small grunt and her conscience was tugged yet again.

"I'm sorry. Truly." She waved him off from serving her and picked up his plate to serve him. "I'm sorry you were assaulted because of me. And the allergy, obviously. I didn't know about it, but now that I do, I'll be so careful in future." Did that sound as if she expected a future with him? The filled plate wobbled as she set it in front of him. "And the fake marriage," she added with a grimace, filling her own plate. "In my defense, I was trying to save your life, but I realize that I've made things awkward for you."

"You could add an apology for that colossal understatement," he said dryly. "It's the opposite of·what I wanted to happen. All of those things are."

"I know. It's perplexing." She wrinkled her nose. "I've never been one of those people who is a walking disaster, but apparently that's my brand where you're concerned. Hashtag rom-coms are real."

"Are you seriously trying to make me laugh? My organs feel like they're dangling by threads inside my body."

"Sorry," she said, biting her lips. She scooped a morsel of chicken and rice and blew across it. "It's just I'm sure you're hating my guts by now and..." She didn't want him to hate her. The thought made her lonelier than she'd been all this time without anyone. Which made it even harder to say, "I would, um..." Her voice faltered. "I would completely understand if you wanted me to, um, do what you wanted me to do in the first place and say we don't know each other, then get lost." He wouldn't help her the way he'd offered. That was a given.

"It's too late for that," he dismissed tersely.

She had suspected it was an empty offer, but she had had to put it out there and there was no relief in his dismissing it. He was looking at her with that incisive gaze, making her own internal organs feel jiggly and hot-cold.

"What do you want me to do, then?"

"Help me sell this image of being happy honeymooners."

"Really? How?"

"We'll start with upgrading your wardrobe and fixing your hair. Then we'll make some appearances—"

"I meant how can we pretend to be happily married when we don't even know each other? But back up." A clang of alarm began ringing in her ears, making her voice quaver. "I realize a man like you can't have a wife who looks like a stranded castaway, but I can't afford a pile of new clothes." She had a small nest egg she was saving for legal fees and a little cash to bolt with. "The wardrobe I had in New York has probably been burned in effigy by now." If not by Troy, then by the flight attendant from whom she sublet.

"I'll take care of it," he dismissed, as though her interruption was inconsequential.

"That's very kind, Everett," she said through her teeth. "But I let a man give me expensive gifts and polish me up once before. Things didn't work out as well as I'd hoped. Don't tell me to do as I'm told," she held up a finger and waggled it. "You got your one free pass with that one."

His eyelids drooped with boredom. "Do we really need a long discussion on why you're uncomfortable with this arrangement only to arrive back at this point? You asked me what I want you to do. I'm telling you."

Her inner shaking increased, spreading into her hands as a burning tremble.

"So none of this is up for debate? Tell me, does the patriarchy issue union cards?" She tilted her head in facetious curiosity. "Can I see yours? Does it ever expire?"

"We're taking the long route through unnecessary argument, then?" He huffed a small noise of tested patience. "I am extremely wealthy, Bianca. I can afford to trick you out with the latest fashions. My image expects that you wear them, and your situation demands it. Think of it as armor. Troy Ackerley will exploit any sort of weakness you present. David and Goliath is a very heartwarming story, but Ackerley believes that might makes right. You need to match his wealth and power. Exceed it. Otherwise, he'll turn you into roadkill."

"Nice."

"Truth."

"And what do you get out of this? What do I owe you in exchange for a new wardrobe?" Her abdomen tightened as she anticipated a demand for sex.

"Nothing." His cheek ticked. "Play your part well so this looks like a love match."

Was that pang inside her disappointment? Good grief, she was far too desperate for company if that was the case. Maybe she had lost all chances with him, given today, but did she even *want* a chance with him?

"Where does your wealth come from?" she asked.

His face blanked with surprise. "Family, mostly. Both

of my grandfathers were successful industrialists. One was married to a princess, the other to the daughter of a real estate baron. My father patented some automotive technology that still pays out to me. Aside from squandering some of my fortune on cars—" he tilted his head toward the garage "—I invest wisely and live off the dividends."

"You've never held a real job?"

She saw a brief flash in his eyes before he dropped his gaze to his plate. "Like a paper route?" he drawled. "No." He chased it with a bite.

"No, Everett." She clapped her fork onto the table, sensing misdirection. "If you want me to trust you and go along with all of this, you have to be honest with me. I won't associate with someone who makes his money through immoral means." Couldn't and wouldn't. Her mother had set that example and she followed it. "That's why I had to expose Morris and Ackerley."

His gaze came up and she saw another flash, one that was his dominant personality surging to the fore, wanting to quash her for her outburst. But he pressed his mouth flat and ran his tongue over his teeth behind his lips. She watched a flicker in his expression as his mind seemed to weigh scales of pro and con.

"I did have a real job. For a decade and a half, working for the government. You'll have to accept that I can't tell you much, but that's why I can't have reporters digging around in my private life. This entire situation is *extremely* awkward," he pronounced facetiously.

She sat back, taking that in. "Can you tell me which part of government?"

"The part that gathers intelligence."

She lurched forward to hiss, "You were a spy?"

"Don't get excited." The corner of his mouth curled. "It was a lot of boring travel and a lot of boring paperwork. I could care less whether my martini is shaken or stirred."

"No," she dismissed, instinctually knowing that. "If it was boring, you wouldn't have done it. There must have been risk. Money. Power?"

He gave a small snort, as if he'd been caught before he'd found his hiding place.

"There was a certain amount of all those things," he downplayed. "And there was a competitive aspect. You have to think of information as a resource like any other. The first to discover it gets to exploit it."

"And sell it?"

"That happens," he allowed. "I was paid well enough I didn't need to extort anyone."

"Why did you quit? Not because of me?" She pressed a hand to where her belly began to churn.

"No, I quit before we met." He blinked and any sense of openness in his expression was gone. In fact, it darkened with displeasure. "Your situation became a gateway drug back into that work. Much as I didn't want to be connected, I thought it best to know exactly what I was mixed up in. I've spent the last six months gathering intel on Morris and Ackerley, following the money. When we sit down with your lawyers, I'll hand over the package. It should bolster the case against them. Maybe some funds will be recovered."

She opened her mouth to thank him but could see he didn't want her gratitude.

"You're anxious to put that work behind you? Why? Because it was dangerous?"

"Sometimes." He shrugged that off.

"Did Giovanni work with you?" she asked with sudden insight.

"See, these are the sorts of questions I don't want to be asked." His voice grew terse. "That's why you have to be my adoring wife for whom I would do anything, so people will believe that's the only reason I'm involved in your little tempest."

His sarcasm stung, telling her he disparaged such devotion, but she longed to be someone's adoring wife. She yearned for someone to be willing to do anything for her, even more so now she'd seen that Freja and Giovanni had exactly that.

She looked down at the fragrant, saffron-infused dish and didn't think she could take another bite.

The few options she still had left—going to her father or going on the run—were even less appealing than what Everett was offering. At least Everett would provide her the physical protection she needed along with legal help that could end the investigation more quickly.

And she owed him what protection she could provide in return. The way he'd brought her into this house was sketchy, but she was grateful for the security she had enjoyed these last months. She hadn't been scraping by, constantly looking over her shoulder.

On the contrary, she had been very comfortable aside from a thirst to see him again.

She blinked in a small wince at that piercing truth. She had wanted another chance to be close to him, to *really* get to know him. She still did, but she had to wonder if that was even possible. When she glanced up, he was looking at her with aggravation.

She was an encumbrance, dependent on him the way she had been on her mother, but at least her mother had loved her.

The fact Everett resented her could make their time together excruciating.

"How long would we have to pretend to be married?" she asked, voice rasping with vulnerability.

"A few weeks. Once things calm down, we can issue a statement that the media attention put too much pressure on our marriage and we're taking a break. Fade to a divorce announcement during a busy news cycle."

Her fake marriage was already dissolving? Bianca's brain tripped over her heart, trying not to hit the rough gravel of how quickly he was planning to dump her.

"And what—" She cleared her throat. "What are the rules?"

"Rules?" His brows went up.

"I realize you don't want sex, but if we're sharing a room—"

"I never said I don't want sex. I said I didn't *expect* it."

Her pulse swerved while he regarded her with that inscrutable look on his face.

Did she want to sleep with him again? Yes. But no. She wanted to sleep with the man she'd met six months ago, the one who wasn't so enigmatic and remote and shadowed by a secret past. She wanted to be the woman she used to be, the one with a life and a career, friends and a home. One who knew who she was. Not a stray. An orphan. A pariah in some circles. A ghost of the woman she'd been.

She wanted him to make her feel as though she excited and fascinated him. As though she was real and important, and he *liked* her.

Maybe some of her conflict showed on her face because he said abruptly, "Let's keep it simple. What are those rules for prom? No touching above the ribs or below the hips?"

"Perfect," she lied as her heart fell like a stone. She forced a smile and ate a bite of paella that coated her mouth like chalk.

"Now you tell me something. Why did you stay in Miami?" His voice was casual, but there was such an underlying lethality, her breath stalled in her lungs.

"I—You gave me a job and a place to stay." She found a shrimp and shoved it in her mouth.

"Oh, no, Bianca." His tone was gentle, but that note of

danger remained. "Look me in the eye and tell me why you wanted to stay in Miami."

The poor little shrimp sat in her throat as a sharp lump.

She lifted her lashes. They were heavy as cast iron. Meeting his gaze sent her stomach roiling. Her fingers tightened on her fork.

If she hadn't trained her whole life to compartmentalize this topic, she wouldn't have been able to prevaricate so blatantly. She had a brief thought that maybe he deserved to know, but this particular secret had been locked so far in her personal vault, it could never rise to bite him. He didn't need to know the whole truth, only the part he was asking about.

"This city feels like a connection to family. My mother grew up here and…" She forced the shrimp down with a sip of water. It lodged behind her heart. "As far as I know, my father still lives here." True enough. She hadn't looked him up lately. "Not that he knows I exist. Mom left him without telling him she was pregnant. She never liked to talk about him." She had, though. And when she did, she had impressed on Bianca that it was *their* secret, never to be repeated. "I can't tell you his name but believing in the possibility that I could meet him makes me feel…less untethered."

His brows went up. "I could find him for you."

A sting of alarm shot through her arteries. She didn't doubt Everett could find anyone, given his bizarre skill set. She would love to think he was motivated by a desire to help her, but she had a feeling it was more about the challenge.

"What would I do?" she asked with a pained smile. "Turn up on his doorstep? Interrupt whatever life he's made with a new family?" That was a genuine reason she had never reached out to him. That and the fact her father was a Mafia kingpin whose life and family were in constant peril.

Even so, curiosity chewed at her deepest id. Her mother hadn't wanted to be associated with ill-gotten wealth, but Bianca constantly wondered what moral compromises were worth accepting if it meant she could finally meet her long-lost father.

What if he wanted nothing to do with her, though? She would be jeopardizing her own anonymity for nothing.

"Why the ruse about your grandmother?" Everett asked.

"Pardon?" She was jolted back by his question.

"I know your inheritance was real, but when we met, you made it sound like it had just happened. Why?" The quiet command in his tone told her he was determined to get every last grain of truth from her.

"Oh…um…what I told you on the plane was mostly true. Mom was estranged from her mother and when I called to tell her that Mom had passed, she hung up on me." Bianca didn't mean for her voice to quaver when she said that, but it did. She stole a moment to push that particularly agonizing genie back into its bottle.

"I'm sorry, Bianca. That's cruel." His expression softened slightly, making the backs of her eyes grow hot.

"Someone told me once that people have all sorts of reasons to keep to themselves." She gave him a wobbly smile.

"Someone exceptionally wise, I imagine." His lips twisted in self-deprecating humor.

She dropped her gaze, not wanting him to see that she knew the elderly woman had most definitely had good reason to cut her daughter out of her life.

"About a year after Mom passed, I got the notice that my grandmother had left me her apartment. Troy and I were involved by then, but I didn't tell him." She had feared there would be questions about her father. "It sounds weird, but even though I didn't know yet that his business was dodgy, I didn't want him to pressure me into investing with Morris and Ackerley. Mom had always preached to me about how important it was for a woman to make her own financial decisions. To never let myself wind up in a position of being dependent."

Like now. She waited for him to say it, but he only watched her.

She took a slow, burning breath. "When Troy went away on business, I nipped down here, liquidated all my grandmother's assets and used most of it to pay off the last of Mom's medical bills. When I was getting ready to bolt, the apartment story made a good excuse to leave town. I doctored the original letter, mailed it to myself and acted super surprised. Troy was excited that I wanted to sell the apartment and use the money for our wedding and honeymoon. He couldn't put me on a plane fast enough."

His cheeks hollowed. "You're very sly beneath that sultry, damsel in distress persona, aren't you?"

She pretended that didn't sting, but it did. Deeply. Especially because she had to wonder if that wasn't her father's cold blood showing through in her veins.

"Not unlike a playboy who seduces a woman, then maneuvers her into living in his house. But married couples need something in common. Slyness can be ours." She smiled with false brightness.

"Along with not trusting one another." Cynicism coated his smile. "How fun."

CHAPTER FIVE

THEY NEEDED WEDDING photos to support their story.

Everett knew that doctored images would be disproven quicker than it would take to mock them up, so he called his former PA. She sent over a stylist for Bianca, a selection of gowns and a discreet photographer, who didn't hesitate to set his camera with an alternate time stamp. Everett tasked his housekeeper with sourcing a cake and spent an hour perusing jewelry, choosing a ten-carat Asscher Cut diamond in a platinum setting. The matching wedding band was coated in pavé diamonds. He also bought a matching necklace and earrings, sending those up to Bianca after the jeweler left.

He didn't know why people made such a fuss about organizing a wedding. He had everything arranged by the time he'd finished his lunch. All that was left was the honeymoon, according to the online checklist he consulted.

If only.

I realize you don't want sex...

For a moment, he had feared he was overplaying his hand, letting her know he was up for sex. Then he'd seen the hesitancy in her expression. As much as this attraction might still be burning brightly between them, she was too dependent on him for a no-strings affair, and her longing for family reinforced that he shouldn't lead her on.

Unfortunately, the more time he spent with her, the

more he wanted her in every possible way. He wanted the secrets she wasn't telling him and her sarcastic little asides. He wanted to *touch* her. He wanted *her*.

Don't, he ordered himself, but his eyes were closing, and he was picturing her as she'd been that night they'd spent together, skin glowing with perspiration from their energetic lovemaking, lips swollen, eyes glazed with lust. He was thinking of her heat, her taste, her moans and the way her hips had danced as she straddled his hips.

A knock on his bedroom door brought him to an awareness that he'd been standing here brooding over her, proving how thoroughly she derailed his usually excellent concentration. Disgusted with himself, he finished pulling on his tuxedo and let in the stylist, who efficiently applied makeup to hide his black eye.

A short while later, he went outside where Freja and Giovanni waited. A wedding needed guests, and Giovanni would have been Everett's best man if Everett had ever legally succumbed to marriage, so Everett had invited them. Giovanni wore a tuxedo, Freja was in a lovely off-the-shoulder gown in pale blue and the twins had matching dresses covered in frills.

Did Giovanni work with you?

Damn Bianca was smart. And good at lying. She had shamelessly suckered her fiancé on more than one occasion and threw out falsehoods like, *Yes, I'm his wife*, without hesitation. She hadn't been completely honest with him about her reason for staying in Miami, either. His well-trained ears had been crackling, trying to decipher the nuance in her voice, certain there was more to catch beneath the faltering way she had relayed how alone she was in the world.

That had got to him, despite his best defenses. He had seen the melancholy in her.

Didn't she realize that human connections were nothing but anguish? His mother was alive and healthy and lived a quiet life, but Everett's father had put her through hell. He'd put Everett through hell, first as a child who had worried about him alongside his mother, and later as an adult, when he had realized he resembled the man too closely.

Even Giovanni, who knew Everett better than anyone, had put him in an impossible position that had forced him to make some terrible choices with painful consequences. He still carried a heavy weight on his conscience over that.

No. From the first time he had *looked* at Bianca, he had known he shouldn't approach her, that she would get under his skin, yet here he was, more worried about her than about what she could be doing to him. He was pretending to marry her, for God's sake. Not just forging some paperwork but putting on a romantic pageant to bolster the image.

He looked around at the way the setting sun filled the courtyard with golden light. Candles floated on the pool's still surface. Fairy lights adorned the umbrella that sat over a cake decorated with seashells and sea stars.

And they all waited for a bride, just like at a real wedding.

He opened his mouth to point out what a farce it was, but Bianca stepped from the house. He caught his breath.

She was all the more impactful for her subtlety. The strapless silk of her gown hugged her breasts and waist, then poured over her hips in frothy ivory, pooling around her feet.

Her bare shoulders gleamed like dark honey, setting off the diamond necklace around her throat. The earrings winked as they swung from her earlobes. Most of her hair was pulled up and interwoven with a string of pearls, but ringlets of tarnished bronze framed her face.

Bianca paused to take in the candles and atmosphere, and Louisa said in a breathy voice, "*Zia è molto carina, Mamma.*"

"She is very pretty, isn't she?" Freja smoothed her daughter's hair.

Bianca ducked her head shyly, then accepted a bouquet of orchids from the housekeeper. The photographer stepped onto a chair and asked them to stand so the pool would form a backdrop.

Bianca picked up her gown as she walked toward Everett. Her steps slowed as her gaze met his. Maybe it was his imagination or maybe time itself stretched out. A soft breeze played with the fine strands of hair against her cheek and her breasts lifted against the confines of her dress as she drew in a breath.

It's fake, Everett kept reminding himself, but music was playing in his head as she approached. Not the pedestrian wedding march, but something from the night they had met—a lazily paced, sexy, moody song. Violin strings sauntered as Etta James's powerful, emotive voice crooned "At Last"…

He tried to ignore it. Tried to look away from this vision approaching him, but the damp sheen on her eyes shot out like an arrow to pierce his breastbone.

"What's wrong?" He instinctively reached for her hand, hearing that his voice was far too thick for his liking.

Her self-deprecating smile fell away, and her expression flinched.

"This wedding isn't even real, but I can't help wishing my mother was here." The candles reflected in the poignant sadness that filled her eyes. The corners of her mouth trembled.

Without conscious thought, he cupped the side of her neck and caressed beneath her ear. Damn, he'd been aching to touch her again. Kissing her had nearly killed him, but he was staring at her unsteady mouth and wanted to press his own against it with reassurance. He wanted to draw her in and protect her from sad ghosts and wistful wishes.

"That's really good," the photographer murmured. "Step closer and put your hand on his chest. Look smitten."

A small flinch crossed her expression. It bothered him, too. She might withhold some things, but her heartache was real. It shouldn't be misused for a lie they would feed to the press, but as she shifted closer, her pulse grew rapid against his palm. Her lashes lifted and conflict swirled behind her eyes—yearning and defensiveness, desire and memory.

So many hot, delicious memories.

"Pretend you're about to kiss?" the photographer prompted.

Everett slid his arm behind her back. She was pliant, allowing him to draw her closer. In fact, she leaned into him in that delicious melting way that short-circuited his brain. His hand found her tailbone. Her body heat radiated through slippery silk to brand his palm. His heart began to thud even harder.

Her fingers came up to play with his ear, sending the most exquisite shivers across his skin. A groom ought to desire his bride, but that's not what either of them was. He shouldn't be twitching and swelling, reflexively dragging her closer so her breasts flattened tantalizingly against his chest. He shouldn't be fantasizing about carrying her over the threshold of his bedroom and placing her on his bed.

Her breath shortened and she tilted her chin to offer her mouth.

Pretend. He bent his head but made himself stop short and held the position as the camera clicked and his whole body turned to concrete with tension. They were already breaking the rules they'd set. His hand was splayed on the top of her bottom. His other was against her rib cage, the heel of his palm resting against the side swell of her breast, fingertips tickling at the edge of her gown where the warm skin under her arm beckoned.

When her light touch found the hollow at the base of his skull, and twitched in subtle invitation, he broke and crashed his mouth onto hers.

This was the kiss he had wanted this morning. Electrifying heat shot through him, and she arched as though she'd been struck by lightning. Plush lips clung to his. The damp tip of her tongue grazed the inside of his lip, and he stole a deeper taste of her. She quivered and pressed harder into him. He hauled her closer, consuming her.

They had an audience, two of them children, but he didn't care. Maybe the photographer even said, "That's good," in a way that suggested the kiss could end.

Never. Everett ignored everything except the sensation of Bianca's hands roaming across his back. He greedily ravished her, filling his hands with her, thinking only one thing. *At last.*

"Theresa, no!"

If they had all stayed exactly as they were, nothing would have happened. The toddler would have run up, grabbed Bianca's dropped bouquet and handed it back to her. That's all the little girl was trying to do.

But the photographer was coming off his chair and instinctively tried to protect his precious equipment. He stumbled and caught himself on the table. The scraping sound of the table legs triggered Everett's most sharply honed reflexes. He jerked up his head and, while his one arm tightened around Bianca, securing her against him, he pressed out a hand to guide the toddler away from the edge of the pool.

Even that would have been fine. He would have stepped back and caught his balance, and it would have all been completely fine.

But Bianca was also startled. *She* tried to place herself between the little girl and the pool edge. She collided into Everett. Their feet tangled. The lip of the pool edge provided exactly the right slope for her sharp heel. She slipped and lost her footing.

That was it. Her weight landed against him. His injured knee buckled and they were falling. There was nothing Everett could do except catch his breath before they hit the water in a mighty splash.

The photo was tracking really well, Bianca noted as she checked her new smartphone.

It had been two days since the doomed photo shoot, four since Everett had shown up so unexpectedly. In that time, he had provided her with all the latest gadgets along with so many clothes she spent half the day in fittings. The rest of the time, she sat in meetings with lawyers and PR specialists. She rarely had a moment alone, especially with him.

So she didn't know what he thought of the photo. Probably that it was insult to injury after a previous injury and one before that, she thought dourly. But after viewing the staged almost-kiss that the photographer had managed to take before they fell, they decided this one looked the most authentic with its candid lack of elegance. Most of the candles had been gutted by their splash. Their clothes were soaked through and ruined, but with the underwater lights glowing behind them, she and Everett were silhouetted in waist-high water, the backlighting hiding his injuries really well.

It also showed him reaching for her. He'd been doing it as much to steady himself on his one leg as to ensure she was upright and breathing. He'd been furious, growling, "First rule of this marriage is no more attempts to kill me."

It had been wrong to laugh, but she had. In the photo,

her head was thrown back, her profile one of unrestrained delight. Her exposed throat was vulnerable and trusting. Everett was grasping her possessively, head tilted in a way that dominated, but also suggested protectiveness. Tender, almost.

He'd been *so* annoyed, which shouldn't have made it funnier, but it had. Thankfully, none of his impatience came through in the image. He was starkly beautiful, seemingly mesmerized by her.

Judging by the comments, everyone thought they were deeply in love.

Bianca nearly believed it herself when she looked at the photo. Or rather, she wanted to believe she could experience love like that, love that was unforeseen and grand and joyful. A love that loved her back even when she was messy and clumsy and ruinous. Love that was willing to save her when she was in trouble.

She knew that sort of love was a figment created by Hollywood to sell popcorn. Dating had been enjoyable when she had made time for it, but she had never been so moved by anyone that she couldn't take or leave that particular person. Troy had been her most intense relationship, and she had always felt a little manipulated by his over-the-top romantic gestures, as though he was using them as leverage to guilt her into whatever he wanted from her. It hadn't felt like what she wanted love to be.

Of course, she had always heeded her mother's advice to keep her heart well guarded. Her mother had loved her father her whole life. Her heartbreak had always been obvious when she talked about the difficult decision she'd made in leaving him. *I was immersed in his life, and it was a life I didn't want. One I feared I wouldn't survive.*

That was the real reason Bianca had been compelled to expose Troy's crimes. She had started to repeat her mother's history, attaching herself to a man who broke laws for his own gain. She hadn't even loved Troy, not the way her mother had loved her father. Her mother had already been gone, but the guilty knowledge that Bianca was letting her down had far outweighed any affection or loyalty she'd felt toward Troy.

She had thought that tepid mix of gratitude and companionship was all she was capable of feeling toward a man.

Until she met Everett.

She couldn't say why their connection had felt so profound and real from the very beginning. It *wasn't* real, she scolded herself. It was a trick of lust and isolation. She had played a hoax on herself by reliving their night again and again, allowing herself to believe his feelings ran deeper than they did.

Whatever he had felt that night hadn't been mentioned again. Sure, he'd kissed her before their dunk in the pool, but he avoided her during the day, came to bed after she was asleep and rose before she woke.

His indifference reinforced the impression that he would rather leave her on the bottom of a pool than pull her out of one.

She tried not to let his lack of interest bother her, but it did. She felt as though she had disappointed him, or he begrudged her. If he hadn't been providing the protection and advisors she needed, she might have struck out on her own.

Her mother had never prepared her for this, she thought ironically. Rather than becoming dependent because she'd fallen in love, it was the opposite. She had no choice but to rely on him, and he didn't seem to give two hoots about her.

"Is that the Montrachet Grand Cru?"

Everett's voice startled her into dropping her phone into her lap. She usually spent this hour before dinner curled up on the sofa with only her phone and glass of wine for company.

"I wanted to try it before I order a few cases." He poured one for himself.

"Order me one," she joked. "I really like it." She picked up her glass and drank in the aromas of earth and pear, then let the cool lick of smoky butterscotch pour across her tongue. There was a tang of orange peel before it finished with smooth vanilla.

"It's five thousand dollars a bottle."

She nearly spit her wine back into her glass. Instead, she took a big gulp to catch the ice cube she'd dropped into it because she had let it grow warm.

As he came to sit across from her, nerves closed in on her. She had been wanting one-on-one time with him, thinking it would clear the air in some way, but the air became charged and weighted.

Fortunately, her phone pinged, allowing her to duck her head to read the message as she swallowed the half-melted ice cube.

"Freja," she said as she set her phone aside. "She's been checking in with me a lot. I guess she has some experience with being reluctantly famous."

Freja's father had been a renowned travelogue writer. Freja's memoire-turned-movie had made her a celebrity in her own right, not to mention the surprising fact her husband had been pronounced dead for a time.

Bianca was dying to ask Everett about that. She had read what she could find online, but a lot of links were broken—which struck her as suspicious, but the one photo she'd found of the press conference when Giovanni reappeared showed Everett by his side.

"Freja asked me if we were going to her premiere," Bianca continued, chattering nervously. "I said I didn't think it would be a good idea. I'm too notorious and would steal her thunder. She said this is actually the fifth opening after viewings at film festivals and a big thing in Hollywood.

She said that, if anything, the film would benefit from the buzz we would cause, but she didn't mean that as pressure for us to turn up."

"I've been thinking about it." Everett was swirling his glass and poked his nose into the bowl before sipping. The face he made couldn't have been in reaction to the wine. It was excellent. "Given all the celebrities, the security will be very tight. It's an ideal place to debut as a couple. Showing up is the least I can do for Freja."

He cared about that family; she knew he did. She had caught him smirking affectionately at the little ones, even though he kept his distance.

"I asked Freja about the work you used to do," she admitted. "She said she couldn't talk about it, but that she understands how curious and frustrated I must feel. I guess that means Giovanni did work with you."

She didn't make it a question and she wasn't surprised by the hard stare of warning he sent her.

"Can you tell me how you met him, at least? Or is that classified, too?"

"No. It's just painful." His expression turned stoic. "His brother, Stefano, was a close friend at boarding school. I met him when some older boys thought it would be a funny prank to sneak crushed peanuts into my soup. I would have died if Stefano hadn't got me help."

"That's horrible! But how did Giovanni not know of your allergy until last year?"

"Because I became very careful about who I told," he said in a hard voice. "I thought that was the best approach, managing it myself, discreetly, until you exploited that weakness the other day."

He didn't give her a chance to defend herself, continuing on.

"Giovanni was younger, not there when it happened. Their father was a diplomat, and they moved a lot, but I stayed in touch with Stefano until he died in the same car crash that killed their parents. That's how Giovanni lost his legs. He was alone in hospital for months after. I visited him as often as I could."

"Oh." She clapped a hand over her breaking heart. "He must have been so lonely. That's really nice that you were there for him."

"I wasn't being nice. I was grieving, too. Not just Stephano, who was my only real friend, but my father." He looked into his wine. "After his brain injury, I lost the man I knew. Half the time Giovanni and I played video games without speaking more than ten words, but it got us through a difficult period."

"Yet you're borderline hostile toward him now. What changed? Do you resent that Freja came between you?"

"I know she calls me his ex," he said pithily.

Bianca hadn't heard that and bit her lips to hide her amusement.

"My feelings toward him are not, and never have been, romantic. Even if they were, how could I resent her? She's his perfect complement and he deserves to be happy." He drank deeply, expression faraway and contemplative.

"Do you envy him that happiness?"

"No." That came out prompt and firm. His cool gaze snapped to hers, seeming to carve his next words indelibly into her soul. "The higher you soar, the farther you fall. I saw how wrecked he was by loss. More than once." His gaze shifted to the darkening sky beyond the windows. "I wouldn't subject myself to that. Ever."

"*That* sounds lonely," she said with a catch behind her heart. "I ache for a family. I feel empty not having anyone." That's why she had yearned for her grandmother to embrace her after her mother had passed. That's why she was tempted every single day to reach out to her father and half siblings.

"You can have one," Everett said, making her heart swerve. "When this is over."

With someone else. That's what he was really saying with that dispassionate look.

She swallowed the lump that rose in her throat. It stuck itself, jagged and hard, behind her sternum.

"But pretend that's what you and I are embarking on now?" she asked with a creak in her voice.

"Yes."

It was exactly as she had known things were, but hearing it, absorbing it, made the ache in her chest all the harder to bear.

CHAPTER SIX

THEY ATTENDED THE PREMIERE. Everett's conscience wouldn't let him snub his friends again. *You're borderline hostile toward him.*

Everett hadn't meant to come across that way. He had been giving them space to push him out of their lives as he deserved. He chafed at the way Bianca kept pulling them back into his sphere so he had to constantly confront his guilt.

As if he didn't wear self-loathing as a cape all day, every day.

It had a new lining, though. One that was slippery as satin, hot and cold in turns. Bianca.

He'd been trying to ignore her since the poolside kiss. Thank God they'd fallen in, or they may never have stopped. He'd been avoiding her as much as possible, trying to dodge further temptation, leaving her in meetings with interview coaches and spending his own time ensuring the circle of security around them was impenetrable.

He couldn't ignore her tonight, though. He could barely take his eyes off her.

His tux had been replaced after the photo debacle and Bianca was in a stunning, sequined gown. Her hair had been corrected to a rich brunette that fell around her face in screen star waves. Her makeup was subtle, allowing her natural beauty to shine brighter than the diamonds she wore.

"Is my makeup smudged?" she asked with a trace of dread as she glanced across the back seat of the SUV and caught him staring. Her hand came up.

"No." She was breathtakingly perfect. "I was thinking that you'll be asked who you're wearing."

"The stylist told me Versace."

"The jeweler is local." He told her the name.

"These are real?" she hissed, touching the necklace. "I thought all of this was costume. I've been leaving them lying around like old shoes."

"I noticed," he said dryly. "But the house is secure. We'll put them in the room safe tonight."

"Why are we staying at the hotel?" she asked with a distracted frown.

"Appearances."

"Hmph. Still, why don't I just give them back to the jeweler, so I don't have to worry about them?"

"Because I bought them."

"You did not." She glared at him.

He lifted a negligent shoulder. "Appearances." And he had thought they would suit her. They did. The warm tones in her complexion were emphasized by the platinum setting and her electrifying presence was amplified by the sparkle of the stones.

"Well, I don't accept that burden of worry," she informed him. "I have enough of those on my plate, thanks." She leaned to peer through the window as the limo slowed.

They had joined the queue approaching the red carpet out front of the theater. Her profile grew apprehensive.

Everett had been in his share of media scrums, but Bianca was new to this. When they emerged a few minutes later, the roar of the crowd rolled over them as a reverberating wave. Her fingernails dug through his sleeve, and he noted how she tried to use him as a shield against the flashing cameras.

A surge of protectiveness had him pulling her close. He brushed off the request that they pose and make remarks and drew her into the theater.

"Are you all right?" he asked as he found a quiet corner. For the most part, she was very self-possessed and confident. It hadn't occurred to him she would be so overwhelmed.

"I'm feeling a little like Cinderella, going from only having the birds as company to this." Her stark gaze took in the melee of celebrities and VIP guests. Waiters with trays of champagne circulated and they each accepted one.

"Is Cinderella the polyamorous one who took up with seven small-statured miners?" Everett asked conversationally.

"Do brush up on your fairy tales, Everett. She's the indentured servant who dropped a shoe and turned into a pumpkin."

"The one who dropped her *luggage*." He nodded. "That tracks."

"Hilarious." But she suppressed a smile, and that pleased him since he'd been trying to put her at ease.

He was sorely tempted to kiss that smile. She would be a lot easier to resist if he wasn't constantly picturing her wet lashes and dripping hair and chilled nipples pressing against silk. If he wasn't hearing her laughter when she got a video of the children from Freja or wasn't forced to stand so close right now. The heat of her body was radiating against his while she wore a look of wonder.

"I have to say, you do know how to impress a girl. If I forget to tell you later, I had a good time tonight."

"You have a crystal ball in that little purse of yours?"

"Seriously?" Her cheeky smile faded. "It's a movie

quote from that other well-known fairy tale, *Pretty Woman*. You must have seen it at least once. Julia Roberts?"

"Is that the one where she sues the company for poisoning the water?" He knew it wasn't.

"You're hopeless," she declared, but they were both hiding smirks of enjoyment.

Their flirting was interrupted as they were ushered to their seats. They watched an engaging movie that had him sincerely complimenting Freja when they saw her at the after-party in the hotel ballroom.

She and Giovanni were much in demand, so they only spoke to them for a moment. Then Everett kept hold of Bianca's hand as they circulated.

In maintaining his cover, he had attended thousands of parties like this so it was inevitable that he would bump into people who knew him as a globe-trotting playboy. A few even knew him from his other role in intelligence. They all wanted to congratulate him on his marriage and meet his notorious wife.

Everett introduced her but kept all the interactions very brief while behaving as solicitously as a newly married man ought to seem toward his bride. Did he take advantage of the excuse to touch her? He tried not to, but the way her voice faltered when his hand absently drifted to her lower back, and pink rose under her cheeks, made him realize he was having an effect on her.

At that point, it took all his discipline not to draw a line up her spine to explore the sensitive skin at her nape, to see if he could deepen her blush. His gaze wanted to travel to the swells of her breasts, to see if they were lifting in an uneven rhythm against the line of her gown.

It was a tipping point, one where he ought to have called a halt to the evening and saved them both. Instead, he let it go on and, a few minutes later, the music started. It was not the staid waltz of a charity gala. It was loud and lively, and Bianca glanced with longing to where the crowd began bumping and grinding to the beat.

"Do you want to dance?" He could see she did.

Eagerness lit up her expression. "Do you? I haven't gone dancing since college."

He couldn't deny her. No, that was a lie. He didn't want to deny himself. It was only dancing, he chided himself as he shrugged out of his jacket and hung it over the nearest chair. He waved an invitation for her to lead him into the flailing bodies.

She set down her drink and her arms were already climbing over her head as she entered the fray, hips swaying hypnotically.

Everett danced the way he did everything else—with competence and without drawing undue attention, but Bianca was genuinely good. She had natural rhythm and the way she moved was sinuous and sexy as hell.

As she loosened up, she picked up her skirt at the top of the slit, exposing more of her thigh while she stepped and shimmied. Half a song later, she took hold of his shoulder and made a figure eight with her hips, dipping and climbing, then trailed her hand down his chest and around his waist as she circled him.

He felt the vibration of a groan in his throat, one drowned out by the pounding music. Whether she was playing a part or was simply lost in the moment, he couldn't tell. It didn't matter to the flesh behind his fly. He responded as though she was working him up for their mutual pleasure, and the more she lost herself to sensuality, the harder it was to remember why he didn't want to give in to this incessant tug of want.

She wanted things he didn't, he recalled. They might be sexually compatible, but their lives and aspirations weren't. She was dependent on him.

She came back around, and he watched her turn twice

before he gave into temptation and closed in on her, pulling her back into his front. He pinned his hips to her rocking bottom, letting her feel his arousal so she knew exactly how he was reacting to her.

She didn't balk. Her hand climbed to curl behind his neck, and he pressed his jaw to her temple, following her every move. Her stomach was tense against his splayed hand. The backs of her thighs rubbed hotly against the fronts of his. Her hair got him drunk on the aroma of almonds and orange blossoms and her bottom ground into his erection.

He started to think maybe none of those other things mattered. Maybe, they could keep it physical.

Maybe he was dancing with danger and maybe he didn't care.

Before Bianca realized it, their lighthearted fun became foreplay. One moment laughter was bubbling in her chest, the next her pulse was thudding with the music, her skin sensitized to every sensation.

With each brush of their bodies and skim of his hands, desire unfurled a little more within her, overriding her inhibitions while her memory of their night teased her to, *Do it again. See if it's the same.*

The way Everett touched her was reminiscent of their lovemaking—as though he was worshipping her with his hands. As though their bodies were in such perfect accord, they moved as one. As though he wanted her more than he wanted anything else in life. She was the only thing that mattered.

It was so intoxicating, she turned to face him and curled her arm around his neck, then touched the back of his head, urging him to bring his ear down to her mouth. He was tense and his expression forbidding, but the intriguing thickness pressing into her abdomen encouraged her.

"Do you want to go upstairs?"

His hands on her hips tightened deliciously before he lifted his head and looked at her from beneath hooded eyelids. His nod was barely perceptible, and his hands fell away.

A flush of nervous excitement engulfed her. She led him through the writhing bodies back to their table, suddenly feeling drunk even though she'd only had a couple glasses of champagne.

She glanced over her shoulder as they walked to the elevator. His expression was unreadable, but he carried his jacket in front of him, filling her with amused, heady power.

As they stepped inside the car, she pressed herself to the side wall, expecting him to crowd against her and kiss her passionately the way she was longing for him to do.

He used his key to activate the *P* button and leaned on the far wall, regarding her with a flinty look. Her buzz of arousal stumbled into uncertainty. A prickle of inadequacy began to cool the sultry heat that gripped her.

"Is something wrong?" She knew they'd agreed to different rules, but...

"I want to be sure you're not still caught up in fairy tales. Everything that has happened tonight has been part of our act. You know that, don't you?"

Her heart lurched.

"Everything?" The banter? The way he had held her hand and solicitously asked if she was all right? The way he had just danced with her as though they were already making love?

Her ego took that straight on the chin, but she lifted it the way any good boxer did when they still had some grit left in them.

"Your body should win an award for its performance then. Why bother hiding it if all of this is for show?"

He kept hold of her gaze. The air crackled as he absorbed her scathing remark.

"My erections are biology. They're not a promise or a sign of growing affection or an attempt to make that family you said you long for."

The elevator arrived at their floor with a gentle halt, but his words jolted with the force of an earthquake. As the doors opened, guards immediately requested their identification.

She stood there dumbly while Everett took care of it.

If she had had any choice, she might have walked right back into that elevator and out the front doors of the hotel, but all she wanted in this moment of mortification was to hide. She subtly kept Everett from touching her elbow and accompanied him down the hall. They passed guards stationed at all the doors of these top floor suites, so she didn't speak.

"We swept when we placed your luggage inside, sir," the one at their door said. "We can do it again now if you'd like."

"I'll do it." Everett used his key card to open their door and stepped inside to hold the door for her. Then he moved methodically around the room, running his hand beneath shelves and table edges, following sight lines to the sofa and into the bedroom and bathroom.

"Do you really think someone would bug our room?" she asked with equal parts disbelief and mockery.

"Allowing yourself to believe no one would is how you wind up compromised."

Hmph. She should probably be grateful for his vigilance. Being in the headlines was invasive enough. She didn't need nude photos undermining her credibility where Morris and Ackerley were concerned, but she was still affronted by his attitude in the elevator.

She sat to remove her shoes, throat aching with something worse than rejection. Humiliation. She only wished she could claim she'd been acting, but it was too late for that, not when she was the one who had suggested they come up here. She didn't even want to face him after being so blatant about her desire.

"Clear." He came back from the bedroom and headed straight to the bar, where he cracked a bottle of Scotch. "What were we talking about?"

"I don't remember," she said dourly.

"No?" He sent her a sideways look, one brow cocked. "That's fine." He set out two glasses and poured the drink into the first. "Will you have Scotch, or do you want something else?"

"I know the difference between fantasy and reality, Everett."

"Oh, *that's* what we were talking about. Let's make it a sober conversation, then." He set aside the bottle and came to the sitting area empty-handed. He took the armchair like a dissolute king, dropping into it and studying her as though she were some lowly petitioner.

Her skin tightened and her throat dried, but she managed to ask, "What's there to talk about? You were acting as though you wanted to have sex with me, but it was just an act. My mistake." She picked up the skirt of her gown so she could get her knees under her and resettled with a huff.

"Is that all you want? You're horny so you want sex?"

"Excuse me?" Her chest and cheeks were already scalded with ire. Now they burned hotter than the backs of her eyes.

"There's no shame in it. You're coming off a dry spell. That's also biology."

"Just because you pick up lovers like frequent-flyer points doesn't mean *I* don't know how to be alone." She rose, too offended to face him.

"It's been a spell for me, too," he said flatly. "One of the exact duration as yours."

She faltered, turning around with disbelief.

He cocked a brow.

She shook her head and looked out the window. Much as she wanted to believe his celibacy had something to do with her, she wasn't that delusional.

"Spending time together, pretending to be in love, was always going to put us at risk for this, Bianca. All I'm saying is, don't start believing we have anything more than we do."

"You have to know a person to fall for them. We're still practically strangers."

"Why do you want to have sex with me, then?" he asked gently. "Because you don't have sex with strangers. I knew that the first time we were together."

"When I had sex with a stranger?" she asked caustically, then sighed. "I like the way you make me feel, okay?" It wasn't quite true. Emotionally, she felt so much yearning it was rending her apart.

She drooped her forehead against the cool glass, hating herself for being so susceptible to him because when he touched her, she condensed like a supernova, becoming a ball of light and energy and glittering joy. The way he'd shaped her waist and hips as they danced had sent tendrils of need climbing upward from her belly. He had guided her in ways that made her think every move was her own, then he had perfectly matched each step, as though they were intrinsically connected. The flex of his muscles, the way he'd watched her as though she was the only person in the room, had made her *want*. Want to touch him, want to kiss him and strip for him and take him inside her.

No one else had ever made her feel like that, and it hurt, physically opened a cavernous ache inside her, to think she would never feel that way again.

"I've spent six months wondering if we're still as potent a combination as we were that night." The lust in his voice matched the sizzling embers sitting in the base of her throat and the bottom of her heart and the pit of her stomach. It made her breath catch.

Her shoulder blades tensed and tingled, and her gaze was pulled from the view to lock with his, but there was no smile there. No warm glow of affection in his burning gaze.

He wasn't any happier with this pull than she was.

"When you were pushing up against me on the dance floor I wanted to take you into a stall of the men's room. I would have had you over the edge of a table if I could have."

Neither of them moved, but her whole body began to quiver. His blatant talk sent a spike of fresh arousal into her, one that made her feel loose and drugged. Dizzy with carnal hunger.

Truth was, it hadn't really gone away. It had only been veiled by petulance and denial on her part, thwarted by his ruthless self-discipline and annoyingly tough demand to be in control of everything, including her.

That realization made her heart lurch. He was far better at resisting his reaction to her than she was to him. He had been three steps ahead of her from the first time they spoke, and still was. She was hopelessly outmatched, which meant that any loss in this relationship would be borne by her.

"I will happily make all of your sexual fantasies come true, Bianca." His tone was both a licentious promise and a grim warning. "But that's all it will be. You have to know that and accept it before we do anything in that bed besides sleep."

She curled a fist, trying to find a semblance of self-protection. Trying not to betray that she was willing to accept any terms, so long as it meant he would touch her.

"Be careful what you offer." She leaned her shoulder against the glass and glanced out, trying to find an idle tone. "You're talking to a woman who has spent six months reading romance novels. I have thousands."

"Of fantasies?" In his translucent reflection, he sat taller. His voice lowered an octave, so it was deeply intimate and darkly curious. "I've never read one. Tell me what happens."

Her knees weakened. She locked them and forced herself to say facetiously, "A lot of virgins are seduced by ruthless tycoons. Which one do you want to be?" She turned her head to bat her lashes at him.

His head went back, and his eyes narrowed with consideration. "My first time wasn't my best look. That's when I learned that success doesn't always mean arriving first."

She bit her lip, hating him a little when he was like this—human and endearing.

"I've never actually seduced a virgin and since I already have the costume, I'll be the tycoon." He loosened his tie. "What happens?"

"I was joking." She cleared her throat and sent a look of desperation out the window, but her body was reacting to everything. His confidence and command. The way his body radiated power and the way his expression had settled into watchfulness.

She was becoming his sole focus and it made her skin tighten. She had to cross her arms and hug them against breasts that began to swell and tingle. Her pulse was tripping and quickening.

"Tell me," he insisted softly. "I'm ruthless, remember? I'll get it out of you one way or another. Why am I ruthless, by the way?"

"You tell me," she said with false brightness. "It's also not a great look. You might want to work on that."

A slow smile stretched across his lips. "I like that you're already getting into it. Tell me about your first time. Is it worth reenacting?"

"*No.* It was me trying to find out why everyone thought sex was such a big deal. I never really got an answer to that."

"No?"

Her heart lurched. Until him. That's what she should have said.

"Let's fix that," he suggested in that compelling tone.

He was all the way across the room, and she was practically melting the glass with her body heat, thinking she would fall through it at any moment.

"Why am I deflowering you?" he asked.

"Stop." She ignored the nervous excitement slithering into her middle. "This is silly."

"It's a fantasy," he said quietly. "One that we can stop anytime. If you want to stop now, that's fine."

His words rocked her to the soles of her feet. She set splayed fingertips on the window to steady herself, but maybe he was right. Maybe it was the best way to ensure she didn't take their lovemaking too seriously.

And maybe she was rationalizing so she didn't have to deny herself something she wanted with every cell in her body.

"You want to seduce me into giving up my virtue as revenge against my father. I'm trying to save his business, but you'll probably ruin him the way he ruined you. You're willing to use me to humiliate him."

"I want to send you back to him guilty that you slept with his enemy and *liked* it."

Oof. He caught on fast. She swallowed. "I don't care

about myself, but my secret half sister will be left penniless if my father loses all his money. You don't know that part."

"Then why tell me?"

"Exactly. You're too contemptuous to care. All you think about is your quest for revenge. You'll be merciless in exacting it."

"I will."

He rose and adrenaline soared up through her arteries. A rush of fight or flight burned in her muscles as he came toward her.

His expression was so carnal and pitiless, she pressed her back to the window and held her breath. Her hand came up to his chest as he caged her by leaning his forearms on either side of her head. His lips were so close to hers, her mouth felt sparks of static jumping between them. Her breasts rose and fell unevenly, *almost* brushing his shirt.

"Your father consigned my best friend to a wheelchair. Mention his name and I will walk out and take my vengeance in other ways. Perhaps on your poor sister."

Her scrambled brain tried to catch up. "Did you just give me a safe word? Everett."

She covered her heart, weirdly moved beneath her lewd excitement. She'd never had a safe word, never imagined needing one. She hadn't imagined it would feel so profound. It forged an immediate bond of trust between them, which was silly. This was a *game*.

"Do you have one?" she asked.

"No," he said simply, and somehow, that didn't surprise her a bit.

He took hold of her chin. "But if you mention any other man's name when you're in my bed, I assure you I'll leave you panting in a state of heat." He scraped his thumb across her bottom lip. "Now quit trying to play on my sympathy. I have none. This is a transaction, and you'd better do exactly as I say or the deal is off."

He released her and rocked back on his heels.

She was pinned by a fearful thrill, heart pounding. "Really?"

"Find out. Get in that bedroom and wait for me." He jerked his chin toward the door.

"N-naked?" Her head swam.

"No. I like my toys in mint condition. I'll unwrap you myself." He didn't look at her as he moved to push a hand into the pocket of his discarded jacket. When he noticed her still leaning weakly against the window, he commanded, "*Go.*"

CHAPTER SEVEN

THE PUNCH OF thrill that sent her into the bedroom faded to nerves once she was there. Why was he making her wait for him? Left alone, her head began filling with tumbling second thoughts and hurry-up anticipation. Not knowing what he intended to do to her was excruciating.

She had been thinking about their first night for six months, yearning to repeat it. On that night, he had seduced her slowly with small gestures that she could have easily rebuffed if she hadn't been into it. A light caress on her wrist, a slip of her hair over her ear, a kiss on the boardwalk. She'd been more than a willing participant by then, moaning when he'd kissed her neck in the elevator. She had been weak with want.

Since then, she had longed to be swept away again. For possibility to become probability, then reality.

This was different. It was happening, yet it wasn't. She had no doubt she could back out, no hard feelings, but she wasn't so much afraid of what was about to happen as jittery at the uncertainty of not knowing. She had never role-played a fantasy. In that respect, she did feel like a virgin. Would she do it right? Would she like it? Would he?

He had grasped onto his part with such brutal ease, she was daunted. She knew the point was to commit to the role and play it out to its conclusion. She wanted that, but it meant giving up control to him. Letting him guide and take the lead and *have his way*.

Another shiver of dread-filled anticipation went through her, followed by a rush of incendiary heat.

The door clicked and he entered. His shoes were gone. His tie still hung loosely around his neck. He made a point of closing the door with a firm click, then stood with his arms folded, shoulders straining the fabric of his shirt, weight balanced evenly between his braced feet. He was a potent man intent on ravishing her and her knees nearly buckled in capitulation.

He sauntered toward her, pulling his loosened tie over his head as he closed in.

"Cross your wrists."

"Are you serious?" she gasped, tucking her fists beneath her neck.

"It's only to remind you who you belong to." He met her gaze as he took hold of her wrist, slowly drawing it down, watching closely and giving her plenty of time to refuse.

Her heart was crashing around in her chest, but he was watching to make sure she was with him, exactly as he had the first time. It was weirdly reassuring.

In a small daze, she let her other arm come down and crossed it over the first. He wound the loop of silk around her wrists and gave it a tug.

She wriggled slightly. It was snug, but she could pull herself free if she really wanted to. At the same time, the small constraint seemed to tug her deeper into the game they were playing. She threw her head back to glare at him.

"Now lie back and think of England?" she challenged.

"I will not have a sacrificial lamb in my bed." His smile was cruel. "Your pleasure will very much be my pleasure. Harder to meet your father's eyes that way." His fingertip traced her lips in a tickling caress that had her rolling them inward, unable to erase the sensation. "Which you would know if you weren't so inexperienced."

She was. In this moment, she was confronted by a man who far outclassed her in worldliness. In willpower. Whatever she thought she knew about men and sex and herself would be completely rewritten tonight. She knew that as a fact.

"Where is the zipper on this thing?" His arms came around her, drawing her into bumping against his front as he felt along her spine.

Her arms were trapped between them, and his erection brushed the back of her wrist. He slowly released her gown so it gaped across her breasts, nearly exposing them.

She gave a small gasp and reflexively tried to catch it.

"Shy? I haven't even started." His breath tickled a few loose strands of hair against her ear.

A shiver trailed down her nape. She tried not to sway, but the press of his palm against her bared spine tilted her into him. His other hand brushed her hair back from her cheek and his mouth went to the side of her neck.

As he opened his mouth to lick and suck against her skin, a pleasurable frisson streaked into her erogenous zones. Her lips felt swollen and so did her breasts. Their tips stung. Eddies of need began to swirl in her middle and more intense trickles of excitement grounded like electricity between her legs. She couldn't seem to catch a full breath.

Nor could she think of much else beyond that implacable evidence of his own arousal, undeniable against the back of her hand. He was soothing his fingers up and down her bared spine while his other hand moved to her hip, then traced the crevice of her bottom cheeks through the sequined silk, erotically rubbing the lining of her gown against her skin.

She could hardly breathe; she was so overwhelmed by

sensations. She unconsciously cupped her throbbing mons with her hand, trying to ease the ache pulsing so insistently there.

"That's mine, Bianca." He nipped her earlobe in small punishment, hand sliding to brush hers aside and replace it. "Do I have to tie your hands behind your back?"

She couldn't answer. Starlight exploded behind her eyes as he pushed his hand into the notch of her thighs, palm wide and possessive against her mound. His other arm stayed around her, pinning their arms between them as he said, "Give me your mouth."

She tilted back her head and his mouth captured hers, unceremonious about claiming her. She was fully involved in the flagrant kiss before it had barely started, reveling in the dragging heat of his lips across hers, the sweep of his tongue and the flex of his hand between her thighs.

A throaty noise left her, then another. She was growing wet, and she wriggled, needing more pressure. A more purposeful rocking of his hand. She wanted to run her hands over him but was unable to express her desire or to encourage him except to grind herself into his palm and suck on his tongue.

"Don't peak too early, darling." He loosened the arm that was around her and removed his hand from where he'd been caressing her. "I want you naked and begging when that happens."

"You're a bit of a bastard, aren't you, Everett?" She wasn't joking.

"I'm a lot of a bastard," he assured her as he worked the gown's fitted bodice off her breasts and nudged it down her hips.

The weight of the sequins dragged the fabric into a stiff circle on the floor. She wore only her strapless bra and a pair of matching pink knickers. He made short work of them and helped her step out of the gown.

Now she was naked, forced to stand there as he took his time looking her over. He used one bent knuckle to draw a light circle around her nipple. It was stiff with arousal and bright pink at the tip while the rest of her areola was a pinkish beige. The caress was so light as to be disappointing but made her sex pulse and release another rush of dampness.

He touched her shoulder in a silent urge for her to turn. She did and his hot hand cupped her bottom. "Why are you bruised here?"

The harshness in his tone jolted through her lassitude, making her stiffen.

"I don't rememb— Oh. You scared me. In the garage. I bumped into the mirror of your car."

"Be more careful. Cars can be fixed. You can't." He lightly caressed what had to be a fading yellow mark, then shocked her by kneeling and clasping his arm around her waist as he bent to kiss it better.

She reeled, almost losing her balance, but he straightened and dragged her backward into his chest. His fingers sought the tangled hair of her mound and she felt the rumble of gratification when he discovered her folds were slippery and plump.

She wanted to say she could do that herself, but she couldn't speak. She could only shake and groan with abject need that emanated from the pit of her belly, where the fire he stoked was dancing upward. She rolled her head against his shoulder, nearly mindless with desire as he teased and tantalized, grazing the best spots, but refusing to settle in to properly appease her.

"Everett," she moaned with a pang of frustration.

His caress slowed, drawing out each sensation. "What do you want, lovely?"

"You."

"You're not really in charge here," he reminded, forcing her to endure his lazy caress a little longer. When she was biting her lip, straining for the release she longed for, he eased his touch up her belly, bracing her as she tried to catch her breath. "Have you seen a naked man before, sweet thing?"

She almost said, *Of course. You.*

But this was a game, she recalled. None of it was real, even though she felt truly vulnerable and aroused and very much at his mercy. Of which he seemed to have none.

She had never been so caught up in a need for sex. Wanton craving had her watching him as he unbuttoned his shirt and pulled it from his trousers.

Her reactions were the furthest thing from pretend. She was nearly overcome by the sight of his strong shoulders and wide chest. Oh, she ached to cling and press her mouth against him and taste the salt of his skin. To lick at his abdomen and kiss across his washboard abs. She recalled far too well how his flat hips and those firmly muscled thighs had felt when she straddled them.

And that. His erection. Thick and dark. He slid his hand over and around, comfortable and unabashed as he stroked himself.

"Have you ever touched a man like this? Tasted?" he asked with wicked interest. "Give me what I want, and I may be persuaded to give you what you want."

She flashed her disbelieving gaze up to his. Did he realize she wasn't actually a virgin?

"You'll have to untie me." She was trying for defiant, but her voice was papery and thick with excitement.

"I don't think so." He sat on the edge of the bed and dropped back onto his elbows, knees splayed. "Take your time."

With a small jab of arrogant I'll-show-him, she sank to her knees between his feet. His eyes gleamed with salacious pleasure.

"Need any tips?" he asked.

"I'll find the one I want when I'm ready," she said tartly, pleased by the wolfish flash of his teeth.

She found a convenient bed rail ledge to balance herself and tilted her head so her hair fell against his inner thigh. She swept it back and forth across his leg, then turned her head and did the other.

His breath deepened and rattled in his chest.

She blew softly all over the flesh before her, then gave him a few dampening licks before doing it again.

His next noise was a deeper inhale, one that seemed a little more pained. His erection bobbed in reaction. She privately smiled and took her time painting him with longer, more licentious licks, offering hot and cool breaths in between. She waited until she heard a curse escape his gritted teeth before she enveloped *just* the tip in the fullness of her mouth.

His eyes closed and he released a guttural groan toward the ceiling.

She drew on him with firm purpose, smiling around the salty flesh that filled her mouth, rather liking the idea of bringing him off this way and getting the better of him when he was being so domineering.

As his tension increased and his breath grated with strain, his eyes snapped open. His hand arrived on her crown. "Stop."

Slowly she released him and brought the back of her wrist to her mouth to dry the dampness from her lips. "Did I do something wrong?"

"You know what you were doing. You think I'll let you control me, Bianca? You really are new to this, aren't you?" He sat up and cradled the back of her head as he plundered her mouth with a burning kiss, tongue thrusting between her lips, letting her know exactly what he wanted to do to her.

She was on her knees before him, helpless. Not from any force on his part, but from the inferno inside her.

When her thoughts were scattered all over again, he broke the kiss and cupped her elbows to help her rise, staying seated on the bed.

She was barely able to make her knees lock, muscles trembling with acute arousal.

"Tell me where you want my mouth. Here?" He pressed his lips to her forearm, then nuzzled his questing mouth across her stomach in the frame of her crossed wrists. His brow brushed the swell of her breast, but he didn't make any effort to find her nipple. He kept up those teasing kisses in innocuous places while his touch traced patterns on the backs of her thighs, down to her knees and up to the round curve of her behind.

"Everett," she begged.

"Are you so new to this you don't know what to ask for?" He drew her closer and made her bend so he could touch his mouth to her breastbone, branding the spot before tipping a look up at her. "Or are you too shy to say it? Show me."

Was he toying with her, or did he really want her to ask? Either way, it made her feel very defenseless when she twisted enough to touch her nipple to the seam of his lips. His hands on her arms firmed. He scraped his damp tongue across the taut bud and drew it into his mouth.

Her body shook. A helpless noise throbbed in her throat as lines of fire went from her swollen breasts to her center. Her sex felt heavy and dewy, ripe with need. It was almost too much, but she couldn't get away, not when his hot hands held her arms like this.

When his mouth released her nipple, she turned like a flower to the sun, giving him the other, lost to that thrum inside her that sought a hidden culmination. It remained frustratingly out of reach. Her inner muscles were clenching on emptiness. An anguished noise left her.

He tipped back his head. "Can you come like this?"

She shook her head, too inflamed to think of her role or anything beyond what he was doing to her. "No. I need you inside me for that. Please, Everett."

There was a hot, primitive flash behind his eyes, though. "Since you asked so nicely." He rose before her. "Stay right here."

She watched him disappear into the bathroom. When he came back, he wore a condom.

He retook his seat on the edge of the bed and motioned her forward, drawing her bound wrists over his head. She braced her elbows on his shoulders as he brought her to straddle his thighs.

"Slowly now. I don't want to hurt you." He gripped his erection in one hand and splayed his other on her hip to guide her. "You're still new to this and I have plans for the rest of the night."

She would have taken him in a greedy drop of her hips, but he kept his fist in the way, encircled around his member, allowing only his crown to fill her. She groaned at the exquisite torture of it.

"Hurt?"

"No. Everett, *please*. Stop teasing." She pressed her mouth to the side of his throat, sucking a mark there out of sheer frustration.

"Look at me, Bianca."

She picked up her head and forced her heavy eyelids to open.

"Don't look away. I want to watch as you accept that you're mine."

That didn't feel like part of the game.

His touch shifted and now he was allowing her to sink onto him, to feel his full length driving up into her. Stretching and filling. She was the one claiming him, she thought abstractly, but no, he was taking her as surely as if he had her on her back.

He shifted his hand to slide his thumb where they were joined. He stroked her sensitized flesh, circling where her most intense sensations gathered.

Climax was upon her in one, giant pulse, fogging her gaze and spearing intense sensations upward and outward. She was both melting and catching fire. Exploding and dissolving.

"Eyes open, lovely. Oh, that's beautiful."

She might have had her eyes open. All she saw was piercing blue and glittering stars. Powerful ripples rolled through her abdomen and joy shimmered into her extremities. Her lax mouth couldn't form words, but her throat was making trembling noises of ecstasy.

"Yes," he crooned, holding her hips tight in his lap while the waves went on and on. "Now you're mine, aren't you? All mine."

She was. Deep, deep in her soul. No other man would ever take her apart so tenderly, then put her back together with those smooth hands sliding across her back, encircling her in the safety of his embrace.

But he wasn't hers. He was still hard inside her, his self-discipline almost terrifying, it was so unbreakable.

As her orgasm faded and her breath began to even out, he kissed her chin. "Do you know what happens now, my darling?"

She couldn't imagine.

"You lie back and think of *me* while I show you all the other ways you belong to me."

The explosion was six blocks away, but it shook the floor of the fleabag apartment Everett stood in. He ran for the stairs, not frightened for himself. No, he knew what had happened and it was his fault. He even knew that he was already too late, but he had to get there. Had to stop it from happening.

Outside, the air was thick as molasses. No matter how hard he pumped his arms and legs, they were heavy as concrete. Useless. He couldn't get himself down the street.

A lucid part of his brain knew this was a dream, that his struggle was futile, but he still tried. He had to get there. Had to prevent it. To undo what shouldn't have happened.

In a whoosh he was standing next to the overturned wheelchair, its wheels bent. The man who used it was thrown facedown next to it. His body, already ravaged once by a horrific accident, had been damaged again. Because of him.

"Everett."

Freja? She shouldn't be here.

She was rattling his shoulder, hating him. Hating him so intensely for what he'd done, but no one could hate him as much as he hated himself.

"Everett, wake *up*."

His dream vanished and his eyes snapped open. His cotton-filled head was still in Dubrovnik, slow to catch up to his body in Miami.

He was in the bed of the hotel suite. Bianca was running her hand up and down his arm, crooning, "It's okay, it's okay."

He was coated in clammy sweat that turned to a blanket of self-contempt.

Damn it, why hadn't he realized this might happen? The replays always happened when he slept hard, and damned if he hadn't fallen into a near coma after wringing both of them dry with energetic lovemaking.

"Were you having a nightmare? Your heart is racing."

He brushed her caressing hand from his chest and mopped the edge of the sheet across his torso.

"Do you want to talk about it?" she asked with concern.

"No. Go back to sleep." He swung his legs off the side of the bed, doubtful he'd fall asleep again. Not for hours and not next to her. This was his own private hell and a well-deserved recompense for what he'd nearly done.

Her soft palm moved across his lower back. Her touch was meant to comfort, but it had the effect of reawakening his libido. How? That thing ought to have been run to death by now, but nope. He only had to recall how her thighs had clamped his ears and he was seriously considering a fresh seduction as pure distraction, but he would only fall asleep again and they'd be right back here.

He rose to pull on his pants.

"Where are you going?"

"I need a minute." He didn't look at her because he would only want to crawl back into bed with her.

In the lounge, he poured himself a double Scotch and stood at the window, noting stragglers at the bar by the pool, still partying despite the glow of pale gold condensing on the horizon.

He shouldn't have made love to her. So much for prom rules.

On the other hand, he was only human. When she had suggested taking things upstairs, his self-control had only extended to ensuring she was going into this with realistic expectations.

He'd thought playing out a fantasy would be less intimate, but oddly, it was more. It had forced both of them to reveal deeper aspects of themselves while trusting the other more fully. She had had to believe she was safe with him. He had put his faith in her calling a halt if he came on too strong.

He had reveled in his role. Letting himself imagine he was the only man to ever touch her, the only man who could make her scream in the throes of orgasm, was a kink he hadn't known was in him, but there it was. He hadn't been able to get enough of her. He'd touched and tasted every part of her, made her shake and moan and say, 'Please.'

In the end, he'd been so desperate for his own culmination, he'd pleaded with her to join him. *Once more, love. You can do it. Come with me. Let me feel it.*

She'd been flushed and glowing, lips swollen from their kisses, eyes unfocused as she arched beneath him. A fantasy come to life and the fantasy had been that she was *his*. Forever.

As the fine quivers of her sheath had begun to ripple around his thrusts, all the mutual caresses and kisses and strokes of pleasure that had piled up like sticks of dynamite had detonated.

He had sheltered her beneath him as the shock waves of orgasm shuddered through them. So many sensations had accosted him then—her soft body cushioning his, her crashing heartbeat against his own, her ecstatic cries and the clenching heat that matched his own pulsing release. Their voices had combined in ragged cries of ecstasy.

He had felt as though he had left a vital piece of himself inside her after he withdrew, even though he'd worn a condom. Whatever small shield that thin wall had afforded didn't extend to his psyche. He'd been the most unguarded of his life in those moments and he hadn't wanted to pick apart how he could feel so much more than the amiable gratitude he usually experienced after sex. He was always satisfied and thankful to his partner for sharing her body, but much like his first time with Bianca, he had been aware of a nagging sensation of *not enough*.

What would it take? he wondered. At this rate, they'd do themselves an injury trying to satiate their desire for one another.

There was a clink behind him. He turned to see Bianca

pouring herself a glass of Scotch. She wore a hotel robe, and her face was freshly washed, all traces of makeup gone.

She curled up in the corner of the sofa and sipped carefully, eyes on the contents of her glass.

"I don't want to talk about it," he told her.

"I don't expect you to. Sometimes it's nice to have someone sit with you when you're troubled, though."

The way he and Giovanni had sat with each other? The guilt that always dogged him caught up enough to nip at him.

He heaved a sigh at the ceiling, but the weight stayed on his chest. It belonged there. And it wasn't as if he hadn't talked about it to his superiors. When you nearly killed your best operative, you had to answer for it.

But his colleagues had all said, *You did what you had to*, as if that was a good enough excuse.

That's not what Bianca would say. She would be rightfully horrified and disgusted. She would berate him and give him the contempt he deserved.

"Giovanni worked for me," he said. "Technically. He's not the sort who needs a lot of direction, and the nature of the work doesn't lend itself to performance metrics. It was more of a partnership, but it was my responsibility to determine if he was fit for the things I was asking him to do. I could see he wasn't, but I let him continue anyway."

"Drugs?" she asked with astonishment.

"No," he snorted. "No, he was falling in love with Freja. Losing his focus. Shifting it, is a better word. Freja was becoming his priority. He didn't want to admit it. Not to me, not to her. Not even to himself," he said in dry recollection. "He swore she wasn't affecting his ability to be objective. I'd always trusted him, so I continued to trust him. I should have listened to my gut."

His chest was lined with spikes that were digging deeper on each heavy breath he took. He stopped short of revealing that Freja had been pregnant at the time. Her pregnancy and the loss of it were too personal to relay, but it added countless layers of anguish to the remorse Everett still carried.

"What happened?" Bianca asked softly.

"Giovanni was planning to retire, but he wanted to finish a job we were working on. That sort of work isn't something where you just promote someone else into a position. You have to take time, build trust. Even doing it myself would have set everything back months. That could have cost lives, but he was rushing things, trying to hurry a meeting. It literally blew up. He was nearly killed."

She gasped. "I saw something online about him being thought dead for a while. I couldn't find any details, though."

"It's all been scrubbed, but yes, declaring him dead was my decision," he said grimly. "I was protecting him from further attack, but that meant I had to let Freja believe it."

"That her husband was *dead*? You did that to her? But they love each other *so much*. That was really cruel, Everett." She was appalled and there was no satisfaction in hearing it.

"It was cruel," he agreed. Especially when she lost her baby and they couldn't be together. That's why Everett could barely look at himself in the mirror. That's why he couldn't accept that they still valued his friendship.

"But you did what you could to make it up to her," she recalled. "Freja said you put yourself in hospital to get a message to her foster mother."

"What I should have done was take Giovanni out of the field before it even happened. I knew something was off that day. Call it experience, call it intuition. I knew I shouldn't let him work, but I didn't stop him, and I should have."

"We all make mistakes, Everett."

"Not the kind that cost lives!" He rounded on her, refusing to accept any quarter. "Not the kind that causes months of suffering. If you had seen him in the hospital, wanting to get to her." His voice grew ragged, and he was right back to trembling in the aftermath of his nightmare. Back to trembling beside his best friend's broken body. He was a monster and deserved to be exiled to the farthest reaches of the universe for what he'd done. "If he hadn't been in traction, he would have crawled out to find her." He ran his hand down his face, trying to erase that day, that awful day when he had had to tell Giovanni that the baby was gone.

"Is that what the nightmare is about?" she asked gently. "The explosion?"

"Yes. It happens when I sleep too hard. I know he's about to be ambushed, I want to keep him from going to the café, but I can't get to him in time."

"Did you know that he was about to be ambushed?"

"Of course not." He brought his head up and scowled at her. "I never would have sent him into that. It was supposed to be a conversation with an informant, but I shouldn't have let him go to Dubrovnik at all."

"Because your instinct told you not to."

"Yes. And it never lets me down. It told me not to get involved with you, and look what happened when I ignored it then." That was a cheap swipe because he was feeling so damned exposed. Because she was being kind instead of hating him the way he wanted her to.

Her breath left her as though she'd taken a kick to the stomach. The tendons in her neck flexed before she lifted her glass and drank.

And that just made him feel worse. "I shouldn't have said that."

"It's fine," she said in a voice seared thin by the burn

of alcohol. "It's not like we're the kind of lovers who are mindful of each other's feelings."

His breath left him at the effortless way she delivered a body blow equal to his, but he had to admire that streak of toughness beneath her kitten-soft appearance.

"I think you should apologize to them," she declared.

"They know I'm sorry."

"You should apologize and ask for their forgiveness and let them forgive you." She drained her glass and leaned to set it on the coffee table. "The way you're pushing them away hurts them. Is that something you want to do? Continue to hurt them?"

"No," he grumbled.

"Then stop. Maybe the nightmares will stop, too." She rose. "I'm going back to bed. Good night."

I didn't ask for advice, he wanted to gripe, but the door closed without an invitation for him to join her. *Big surprise*, he thought ironically and turned his face back to the window. He'd been a complete ass.

He released a sigh that fogged the glass.

If Everett had come back to bed in the wee hours, he left before she woke.

Bianca was thankful. She wasn't ready to face him after their predawn exchange. It was true that she'd been a hurricane-level disaster in his life, but it had still hurt to hear how much he begrudged her for it, especially when she had gone out to him because she was worried about him. His nightmare had been causing his whole body to thrash, which was what had woken her. His breathing had been ragged, his face in the pale light tortured.

After everything they had shared in this bed, she had been compelled to try to comfort him. She had been touched that he entrusted her with what was a deeply personal and painful experience. She had thought it was a sign of closeness and had wanted to support him and help him work through it.

Then he had made that nasty remark, reminding her that all they shared was biology. Their lovemaking had not built an emotional connection. It had been a fantasy. Not real.

Which left her hollowed out and chilled despite a hot shower and a bright, sunny day.

She was still physically tender and emotionally exposed as she dressed, thinking of how much of herself she had shared. Yes, they'd started out playing a part, but the line had soon blurred. The pleasure of his touch, of feeling him against her and within her, had been very real. They had still been *them*. Hadn't they?

She had, but when she thought of it in the starkness of daylight, she didn't see where he had been anything more than titillated by their game. When he had suffered a moment of vulnerability, telling her the cause of his nightmare, he had lashed out right after, cutting off any more expressions of empathy.

Realizing how ruthlessly he could shut her out galvanized her into putting her own defenses back into place, otherwise she would suffer more than this sense of scorn in the time they were together. She would get her heart shattered.

She combed out her damp hair and put on a little makeup, then found Everett at the table on the balcony, pouring coffee.

"Good morning." She tried for a breezy tone, but his circumspect glance was enough to wash her in a fresh wave of vulnerability.

Aside from the dark circles around his eyes, he was his clean-shaven, sharply dressed self, but *she* knew how those masculine lips felt against her skin, how those strong hands could guide and caress. She knew he was both demanding and generous, powerful yet tender. She knew that *he* knew she couldn't refuse him anything.

"I heard you in the shower and took the liberty of ordering." He set aside the carafe and lifted the lids from the plates. Both held lobster Benedict with tomato and asparagus, fresh fruit and a small crepe rolled around a berry compote.

There was no particular warmth in his greeting. No sexy lingering glance or a sly *Sleep well*? Not even anything to suggest regrets over their talk, just a shuttered expression and that scrupulously polite tone.

She wasn't sure what reaction she had expected, but it wasn't this complete detachment, as if their lovemaking hadn't happened at all.

Biting her lips together to keep them from trembling, she sat, but her usually healthy appetite dried up. She refused to ask if everything was all right. She refused to be needy. This was exactly why her mother had instilled in her to hold herself apart from emotional dependence on a man. *Your worth is determined by you, not bestowed by anyone else.*

"The Catalanos will be here in a moment. They wanted to say goodbye before they fly to New York."

"Oh. Good." Her brain couldn't seem to catch up to his crisp, businesslike attitude. "Freja asked me why I was doing so many of my interviews and depositions here instead of there. I told her I didn't know." There were both a criminal and a class action civil suit being brought against Morris and Ackerley, not to mention a metric ton of media interest and a congressional committee hearing on how the scheme had gone undetected for so long. Miami wasn't the most convenient place for providing statements and evidence to any of those.

"That was my call. It made sense at the time."

"In what way?" She chased a blueberry with the tine of her fork.

"Inconveniencing Ackerley's people, mostly." He ate a morsel of lobster. "They'll be billing as much for travel as they do for legal services."

"Do I want to antagonize him like that?"

"I do."

"Why?"

"Because I don't like him."

She would have probed that remark, but she heard the ping of a doorbell. She rose to invite the Catalanos into the suite.

Everett followed her in, and Bianca executed a somewhat passive-aggressive move by saying, "Girls, help me count the people in the pool. You can teach me to do it in Sicilian."

She took them by the hands and pointedly closed the glass door behind them, locking Everett inside with Giovanni and Freja.

Fifteen minutes later, Freja came out with wet lashes and a big, trembling smile. She hugged Bianca extra hard.

"Thank you," she breathed. "We're not staying in New York more than a few days, but *please* come visit us in Sicily."

"If I'm allowed to leave the country, sure." It was a joke, but not entirely.

"Giovanni can help if you need it. But I'm serious. No matter what happens with Everett, you and I are friends now. I want you to come."

Moved, Bianca nodded, and they went inside where Giovanni waved her to bend so he could hug her and kiss both her cheeks.

"You'll come see us in Sicily," he informed her. "Soon. Let me know when you're free. I'll arrange it."

"I will," she promised, and waved the family off, heart full at seeing them so happy.

Then she apprehensively looked at Everett, half expecting a thunderous berating for interfering, but he was locked up behind his most inscrutable, flinty expression.

"Are you angry?" she asked.

"I'm going to shower, then we'll head back to the house."

"You're not going to finish your breakfast?"

"It will only taste like crow."

She ate the rest of hers alone.

Was he angry? Everett was still brooding on that hours later when he sat in on a meeting between Bianca and one of the producers from Freja's movie.

The entertainment sharks were circling, looking for the tastiest bite of her story before it was completely written. He'd warned her not to sign anything and was present to ensure they didn't pull a fast one, but he recognized she needed an income, and these sorts of offers could be very generous.

He listened with half an ear to the tedious attempt to seduce her into exploiting her private life. She kept politely rebuffing and they kept upping the ante.

Yes, Everett decided. He was angry, but not in the way she meant. He was angry that she had been right. He was angry that he had continued to hurt his friends without seeing the injury he was doing to them. He was angry that, instead of being an instrument of ruin, the way he wanted to pigeonhole Bianca, she had helped him fix a part of his life that he had broken all by himself.

He was angry that instead of walking around with a stab of righteous self-hatred turning in his gut, he was awash in an ache of humility. Apologizing to Giovanni hadn't been that hard. He had said those words before.

Being forgiven, however, had caused a pain that was not unlike a bone being reset. It still hurt like hell, but it was the dull throb of healing. It made him feel tender and tentative, and he didn't like that at all.

Bianca wasn't being smug about pushing him into reconciling with his friend, either, which would have let him resent her. No, she was holding on to some frost from his snarky comment last night, disappearing to do yoga the minute she got the producer out the door. He didn't see her again until they sat down for dinner, and she was still quiet and withdrawn.

"You were right," he acknowledged. "I should have done that a long time ago, and I'm glad it's not between me and Giovanni any longer. And you have a right to be angry with me about what I said. But it's not that I don't care about your feelings, Bianca. I do. I just don't want them to attach themselves to me."

"Yes, I got that memo," she said, her own voice cool, then easing to something more plaintive. "I'm not angry with you. I'm realizing why you were so angry with me. The way that producer was prying for details on my personal life made me realize how intrusive it is."

The stubble at the back of his neck stood up and his ears crackled. Immediately, his mind replayed the meeting, zeroing in on the way her jaw had grown stubbornly locked when she'd been asked about her absent father.

"We're conditioned to believe we should know our biological parents," he noted. "I was surprised to hear you didn't have any father figure at all in your life. Or were you protecting someone from being hunted down when you told him your mother never married?"

"No, that was true. Mom was a nurse and worked a lot of nights. It wasn't conducive to dating and she didn't want to confuse me with a string of men who might not stick.

She was determined to get me through college without loans, too. She worked a ton of overtime."

"You said she never told your father that she was pregnant. Why not?"

"Why should she?" A note of challenge entered her tone, but her voice quavered ever so slightly.

He was standing on a very raw nerve. What was that about?

"To give him a chance to step up?" Everett suggested lightly. "I would certainly like to know if I had a child out there somewhere."

"Would you?" Her spine snapped straight, and her fork went down with a clunk. "What if *I* become pregnant? What do you expect *me* to do?"

His shoulders hit the back of his chair and a churn of gravel arrived in his stomach.

"I expect you not to get pregnant." His teeth hurt, he clenched his jaw so tight. "That's why I wear condoms. I don't want children."

"Mom took precautions, yet here I am." She waved at herself, chiding, "Even fantasies can have consequences, Everett."

His heart was pounding so hard, his lungs were having trouble catching a breath.

"But don't worry," she muttered into the glass she raised. She took a big swallow of wine, then set it down. "Wanting children is a very personal decision. I wouldn't expect anyone to get on board just because I want them. I would deal with it myself."

"How?" The word shot out of him like a bullet.

A flash of shock bloomed behind her eyes.

"I won't know unless it happens, will I?" Her brows went up, but her mouth was trembling. "I would likely continue the pregnancy and raise the child myself. Alone. The way Mom did. It's not easy, but it's not impossible."

"And you wouldn't even tell me? I would want to know, Bianca." His own glass should have shattered in his hand, he was holding it so tightly.

"Why? What would you do?" she challenged.

"I won't know unless it happens," he said caustically. "But I want to know if it does." Ignorance was *not* bliss. It was ignorance. And even though this conversation was hypothetical, the idea she might keep something that profound from him thrust a wedge of deprivation into him.

"Noted." She threw her napkin onto the table and rose. "I'm going for a bath." She took her wine with her.

Bianca couldn't fall asleep. She kept thinking of Everett's emphatic, *I don't want children*. And the fact that the easiest way not to slip up and have a surprise pregnancy would be to not have sex at all.

She threw her arm over her eyes, hating that idea even more than having a child with a reluctant father. She'd been honest about not pressing a man to have a family if he didn't want one, but if that's what he would be, she shouldn't run the risk of pregnancy, should she?

She flipped her pillow to the cool side and stuffed her face into it.

That was only one of many reasons they didn't have a future ahead of them. Her whistleblowing would have repercussions for years. Not only was it unfair to ask him to stand by her through that, but he was underwriting a lot of her support. She had cornered him into that—unwittingly, but she had still done it.

And she hadn't fully appreciated how much he must resent the attention she had put on him until she had begun taking calls for interviews. Most of them had stuck to asking about her relationship with Troy, which was intrusive enough, but that producer today had wanted to do a memoir like Freja's. He had been taking notes about where she went to college and where her mother had worked. When he had asked about her father, Bianca had nearly snapped.

Yet again, she wondered if she should tell Everett who her father was. Warn him. But if she was the only one who knew, how could it affect him? No, as long as she kept it to herself, they were both safe from any ramifications on that front.

The door latch quietly clicked, and she instinctively held very still, trying to calm her breathing so he would think she was asleep.

He went into the bathroom to brush his teeth, and she clenched her eyes shut, willing herself to drop off, but she was still lying there stiff as a board when he slid onto the other side of the mattress. The bed was wider than the Great Plains and so well-made she didn't feel any dip or movement, but she felt his presence all the same.

His tension.

She hadn't moved one iota since he had entered the bedroom, but he said, "I thought you'd be asleep by now."

How was he so perceptive? She rolled onto her back.

"You're basically the most important person in my life right now. I don't like fighting with you," she said.

"Is that really what's keeping you awake? Because it didn't feel like a fight."

It wasn't. Whatever injury she had taken from the conversation had been disappointment that they were so different, not hurt at being attacked.

He clicked on the lamp on his side, then rolled to prop himself on his elbow, facing her. He was naked from the waist up, usually wearing boxers to bed from the few peeks she'd caught.

"But we could still kiss and make up," he suggested. "At least then we'll be able to sleep."

She rolled her eyes, then asked with mocking sweetness, "Are you sure you want to risk it?"

His face fell into grave lines. The sobriety in his voice left a chill across her skin. "That's why you don't want to have children with me, Bianca. I have a taste for risk that is higher than most can stomach."

He slid closer and loomed over her.

She pressed deeper into the mattress and set her hand on his chest, but he only reached to her night table and picked up the book she'd been reading in the bath. He read the back.

"Forced marriage." He slid her an amused look. "I think we could work with that." He continued to read. "I actually have majority shares in the shipping line that my great-grandfather started so I check the box for shipping magnate. That leaves you and what you're prepared to do for your grandmother's farmhouse." He set the book aside and held himself over her with his arms on either side of her. "Will you consummate this marriage?" His nose nuzzled hers. "It's in the will that we have to treat it as a *real* marriage."

He was big and solid, and his breath smelled like mint. The fine hairs on his chest were teasing her fingertips to pet him. If she did, she would bump into the hard bead of his nipple, and she really wanted to do that. She wanted to make his breath hiss and feel his body tremble and hear him call her *Mine*.

It's just a game. Harmless fun, she reasoned.

She turned her face to the side. "I'll submit to my conjugal duty, but I won't remove my nightgown."

"Oh? Why's that?"

"Scars. My grandmother believed I was too fearful of rejection to marry anyone. That's why she made this condition that I marry. Turn out the light."

"I've seen a lot in my rough life. I think I can handle it." His lips brushed hers.

She jerked her face to the side again. "And no kissing

on the mouth. My grandparents fell in love the first time they kissed. I don't want to fall in love with you."

He stilled for one pulsebeat, then drawled, "Lie back and let me have my way, then. I'll try not to bother you too much."

His mouth went into the crook of her neck while his hand searched beneath the covers, finding the hem of her nightgown and caressing the tops of her thighs.

She slid her arms over his shoulders and sifted her fingers into his hair, instinctually wanting to draw him to kiss her, but his tickling touch found her tangle of damp curls.

He made a rough noise of pleased discovery. "You have been lying here waiting for me, haven't you?"

She had. Shimmering pleasure swept through her pelvis as he casually pressed her legs apart and fondled her with a more proprietary touch.

"Poor neglected wife. Don't worry. I'll make it good for you." He set small kisses across her jawline as he swirled her dampness over her folds, parting and easily sliding one finger, then two, into her.

She groaned and dipped her chin to search for his mouth, but he shifted so he could find her nipple through the fabric of her nightgown. His hot mouth dampened the silk, and he used his tongue to rub it against the distended button.

Tension gathered across her abdomen. She instinctually lifted her hips, encouraging the rocking caress of his hand, clamping down as he found a spot that made stars appear behind her clenched eyelids. Very suddenly she was bucking in sharp, heady climax.

He was saying something to her in a gratified voice and slowed his caress to draw out her pleasure. She couldn't hear it through her shaken moans of joy.

His mouth came back to her neck and her cheek and her brow before he finally eased his touch away.

"You do want that farmhouse, don't you, darling? Will you do anything I ask?" He threw off the covers and dragged a pillow into the middle of the bed. "Let's try this."

She was still trembling with the final shivers of climax, muscles too lax to do anything but cooperate as he rolled her stomach onto the pillows and positioned her knees under her.

He kicked off his boxers and applied a condom, then brushed her nightgown up her buttocks, exposing her as he sought her still-molten entrance. He pressed into her, the wide dome of his erection forging where his fingers had been, reaching deeper, filling her more completely.

She closed her fists into the sheets, groaning at how good it felt to have him inside her.

When his hips were flat against her buttocks, he bent to cover her and kissed her neck and licked her ear. Then he dragged her hand down between her own thighs and said, "Let me feel it this time. Make yourself come again."

She couldn't deny him anything. He straightened and took hold of her hips, thrusting with steady power while she caressed herself and bit her lip and arrived at the crisis with embarrassing speed, practically screaming her sharp release into the mattress.

She could have wept, he made her feel so good.

He folded onto her again, crooning noises of approval and gratitude as he palmed her breast and suckled her earlobe. Carefully, he withdrew and rolled her onto her back, then slid inside her again, catching her up in his arms and drawing her into his lap as he rose to kneel on the bed.

"Do you know what kills me, Bianca?"

She clung to his shoulders and dragged her eyes open. "What?" Her lips were buzzing and her brain was too far away to imagine anything could bother either of them right now.

"That I left you to do that for yourself all those months when I could have been right here—" His hand flattened on her tailbone, and he shifted so he penetrated a fraction deeper. "Helping you, the whole time."

Her heart juddered to a halt in her chest.

Those words meant too much. They suggested things. They made her think she'd been on his mind the way he'd been on hers. They made her think he had missed her while they were apart and would later, when they were no longer together.

She didn't want to think of that. It made a scalded sensation rise in the back of her throat, one that burned all the way into the center of her being.

"I thought we only met and married this morning."

The piercing blue of his eyes reflected fiery heat and arctic ice.

She held her breath until his mouth curled into a self-deprecating line.

"Am I ruining the fantasy? Let me make it up to you." He eased her onto her back and began to thrust, sending her back into that golden place where nothing mattered but the fact they were joined. No longer two disjointed people, but one perfect entity. Whole.

She ran her hands over the landscape of his shoulders and back and buttocks, claiming all of him while she had the chance. He hooked his arm under one of her legs and drove deeper, making her writhe at the intensity of the sensations.

"There, Everett. There. Don't stop." She was straining for the pinnacle, hands going into his hair again, so she cradled his skull. "Never stop."

"Never," he vowed, muscles bunched as he thrust hard and fast, bringing her with him as he raced toward climax.

There it was. The horizon where she would tip off into

the sun. He was right there with her, gritting through his teeth, "Now, Bee, now."

As the quaking fracture tore across the earth toward them, he clamped his mouth over hers in a hot, passionate, claiming kiss.

They fell.

CHAPTER EIGHT

"SERIOUSLY, LOOK AT these two," Bianca said a week later when they were in the car. "Freja doesn't want me to go to Sicily. I'll kidnap her children and bring them home with me."

Everett glanced at the photo of Louisa and Theresa caught playing dress-up with Freja's sunglasses, jewelry, handbags and oversize shoes.

"Cute," he pronounced, because he wasn't a sociopath, but if Bianca was hoping for him to wax poetic with adoration and suggest they make a set of their own, she would be sorely disappointed.

"They are," she agreed. She turned off her phone and dropped it into her handbag, then turned her nose to the window.

She was disappointed. His conscience pinched.

Even fantasies can have consequences, Everett.

He kept thinking of that and how his brain had flatlined at the thought of her pregnant. Her suggestion of raising his child alone—*Don't worry about it*—had gone against every sense of decency he possessed.

He had gone to bed that night thinking, fine, they wouldn't have sex anymore. The chance of making a baby was one risk too far for even his nearly infinite threshold. He was still scarred from having to tell Giovanni that Freja had lost their first pregnancy. He could hardly bear recalling it, let alone contemplate experiencing it himself. He sure as hell wouldn't want to be responsible for Bianca going through that.

But when he got into bed, she'd been awake. The pull between them had been impossible to resist. He didn't *want* to control his desire for her. That was the problem. He wanted to revel in it no matter how self-destructive it might prove to be.

If she had stopped him, he would have backed off, but she had gone along with it. He'd never met a woman so greedy for orgasms. It made him want to spend all day, every day, giving them to her.

A review of their track record revealed he'd spent a week doing exactly that. Between meetings and social engagements, he'd been an Australian station owner, brushed up on his Greek for an island stranding, seduced his winemaker on his Chilean vineyard and skipped the stepbrother role in favor of being her brother's best friend holding a grudge over a broken career. An hour ago, he had been her ex-husband snowed in with her at their Whistler chalet.

When he had asked her why she read romance over anything else, she had said, "They keep me company, like friends. I lost touch with most of my real ones while Mom was sick. I made a few at work, but once I started gathering evidence, I was afraid I'd slip up if I went out for drinks with any of them. And they all had lives. Careers and marriage and families. I was taking a hatchet to my chances for all of that, so I insulated myself. I like that romance takes me out of the crater where my life used to be, and they always end happily, which gives me hope. I need that. It's really hard being alone."

Which was why she wanted a family.

That always put an ache in the pit of his stomach, but he had always thought of it the other way. It was really hard to care about someone. You worried for them. Hurt for them. He still had his mother, but she was thankfully healthy and lived a quiet life that caused him very little anguish. He cared about Giovanni and his family, but the worst of the responsibility for their welfare fell on his friend. Still, if something happened to any of them, Everett would be gutted.

There was a difference between preferring to stand on the sidelines of life and being pushed there by circumstance, though. Bianca obviously wanted to throw herself into that emotionally messy fray, foolishly brave soul that she was.

She couldn't have that with him, though, and maybe he owed her the real reason why.

"My father wanted more children. My mother refused." He ran his hand over his thigh, never finding it pleasant to talk about his childhood. "I think she wanted them, but my father was difficult to live with. She was afraid he wouldn't be there for her."

"Because of the brain injury?"

"Even before that. He got into automotive engineering because he loved speed. Any high-risk activity, really. That was really distressing for my mother, never knowing if he would come home."

"I've never understood how anyone gets a thrill out of being in danger. The whole time I was sneaking around behind Troy's back, my stomach was in knots." She rolled her lips inward before giving a small snort. "That doesn't bother you, though. Does it? The fear of getting caught."

It bothered him right now, when he glanced into her soft brown eyes and knew she saw straight into his soul. His chest felt unguarded. Exposed.

"It's a common misconception that daredevils are impulsive idiots with no sense of self-preservation. Some are, but my father was actually a control junkie. He believed he could anticipate all the risks and calculate all the variables and triumph over the fragility of being human."

"And you?" She already knew. He'd told her his tolerance for risk was more than she could stomach.

"I was blessed with his nature, and he nurtured it." His mouth twisted with self-deprecation. "I was seven when he first took me out onto a test track. He got us up to two hundred miles an hour. I freaking loved it."

"That's more than dangerous, isn't it?" she gasped. "I'm no physicist, but aren't there g-forces or something that would kill a small child?"

"If he had stopped and started too abruptly, yes. That's why my mother lost her mind over it. The more I followed in his tire tracks, the more she withdrew from both of us. To this day, she'll claim that she sent me to boarding school so she could be more accessible at work, but I think she was keeping me from seeing how distressed she was."

"That's sad." She studied him. "I'm sorry, Everett. That must have been very painful."

He shrugged it off. "People do what they have to, to protect themselves. Part of the reason I emulated him was a twisted attempt not to fear for him. If I could survive racing a car through Monte Carlo, he could survive whatever he was doing, despite catching fire on a closed track. My mother didn't have that outlook. She couldn't bear the tension and told him she wanted a divorce. That was right before he crashed."

"He crashed because he was upset?"

"Maybe. But I'm not saying the crash was her fault. You shouldn't punch the gas on eight hundred and fifty horsepower if your mind is elsewhere," he said crisply. "And if you don't want to take your family into consideration before you do things like that, then don't have one."

That was the crux of it.

She nodded solemnly. "I see your point, but you don't do those high-risk things."

"I want to. I took a job where I nearly got my best friend killed. I swore off doing that work and less than a year later, I'm rolling around with a white-collar whistle-blower, leaving myself susceptible to my secret life coming to light. I'm not a good bet, Bianca. You don't *want* me as a father for your children. I don't want to father children and be *that* father."

She looked straight ahead. In the flash of streetlights, he thought he saw a glimmer of dampness on her eyes. "That's what you meant when you called me a gateway drug and said your instinct told you not to get involved with me."

"I wasn't trying to be cruel. Hell, much of my desire to take risks is fueled by a hero complex. From the minute I realized what sort of enemy you had pitted yourself against, I wanted to back you up. It's arrogant, but I get off on getting the better of bad guys."

It hadn't been purely a white knight instinct, though. No, from the moment he'd looked across at her in the jet that day, he had wanted to know what was going on behind her alluring expression. His body responded to her, yes. Powerfully. But his mind was equally engaged. She fascinated him and challenged him and from those first moments, she had set a ticking clock inside him. He had decided long ago he would never marry anyone, never subject his own family to the fraught years he had suffered through, but there had been an urgency within him when he met her. They had a limited time, but he wanted to learn everything about her in the time they had.

"What happened with your father?" she asked. "Your parents didn't reconcile after his crash?"

"They tried. Mom blamed herself. My father couldn't get it out of his head that she hadn't wanted him when he was fully fit. How could she want him now? He wasn't capable of performing the sorts of calculations that had allowed him to excel in his field, so his career was over. He drank a lot, started having affairs. Eventually, they divorced. Dad's health deteriorated and he died from a heart attack a few years ago."

"I'm sorry, Everett."

"It was the consequence of living the way he did. That's why I don't want to lead you on. We won't live happily ever after, Bianca."

"I'm not a child, Everett," she said frostily. "I know happiness is fleeting. But you still have to chase it on the off chance you can catch hold of it for a minute or two. If you've already written off even trying to be happy, then yes, you're right. We don't have a chance and should probably quit while we're ahead."

"How did you and Everett meet?" a woman asked Bianca.

"I—" Shoot. That was a new one.

Bianca's mind was still on their altercation in the car. It sounded like Everett had had a difficult childhood where he identified with a man who had destroyed himself while his mother withheld her love for fear her son was turning out the same. She didn't blame Everett for being wary of repeating history with his own child, but his bleak view of things had laid waste to the tiny sprouts of hope she'd allowed to form.

All of that meant she felt terribly obvious when she sent a look of besotted adoration up to him, but her mind had gone completely blank. "Do you want to tell her, darling?"

He'd been wearing a remote mask. It smoothed into something more urbane.

"Bianca sat next to me on a plane," he replied without hesitation. "I couldn't take my eyes off her." His hand possessively came to rest at the small of her back. "She met me for dinner and moved into my home a few weeks later."

A pang struck her chest at how sweetly he reframed the truth into something that actually sounded as though they were smitten with one another.

This was how it went with every new couple or group they met. Bianca would try to remember that none of this was real, then Everett would touch her, and her body's reaction was *very* real. Her nerve endings came alive, and the rich timbre of his voice seemed to resonate in her chest. He would look at her a certain way and, for a few precious seconds, she would feel valued and desired and necessary.

"That's not as cute as I hoped." The senator's wife pouted in disappointment before an avid light came into her eyes. "But then you eloped, didn't you? Was that because you were hiding from the press? Or your fiancé?"

This was also how it went. They had a moment of accord, then reality smacked her in the face like a wet rag, reminding her why Everett was bothering to put on this charade.

Bianca smiled, pretending to find the remark as funny as the woman did, but Everett stiffened.

"We eloped because we're private people," Everett said bluntly. "Excuse us. I see someone I need to speak with." He led Bianca into the crush.

"That was rude," Bianca chided.

"Yes, she was."

Bianca had been talking about his behavior, but he wasn't wrong. That woman had been overstepping. She was hardly the first one, though.

They had fallen into a pattern where they sat in meetings all day with consultants and lawyers and advisors. Bianca carefully filtered every word she spoke and tried not to snap in half from the tension.

Then they would have an hour or two to themselves and always made love madly, dressing it up so it wasn't them. It was a part they played. A game. An excuse for her to lose herself in his touch and pretend she was keeping the most susceptible parts of herself protected.

That was the biggest lie in all of this because she was falling in love with him. How could she not? He was smart and sexy and protective. Passionate and wry and honest.

He was the man she wanted to father her children, but he didn't want to be that man so she would rise from the bed and pretend it had been nothing more than a bit of fun. She would truss herself into a designer gown so Everett could parade her around a dinner or gala. Most nights she didn't mind it. She could allow her true feelings for him to radiate out of her in what was probably the most unfiltered hours of her day.

Tonight, after how things had gone in the car, she couldn't reveal herself in that same way. She was peeled so raw, the judgy looks from people who were being fed lies by Troy and his ilk stabbed especially deep. According to Troy, Bianca was both a cheating fiancée and a scorned lover who had manufactured evidence to harm Morris and Ackerley. No one believed she was merely a woman who had exposed wrongdoing because her conscience demanded it.

It made for an interminable night, one where she felt more lonely and forsaken, surrounded by people with Everett's hand enfolding hers, than she had in the time before he had crashed back into her life.

She was tempted to drink herself into a stupor, but since she had to be so cautious in what she said at these things, she only ever carried a half-full wineglass around, barely tasting a drop.

Therefore, she didn't really need the ladies' room when she said, "Can I catch up to you in a minute? I need the powder room."

"Of course. Look for me near those windows. There's a man I'd like to speak to over there."

She nodded and hurried away, desperate for a break from the unrelenting tension of soaking in Everett's sex appeal while knowing his courtly gestures were only pandering to their audience. He was never going to feel about her the way she felt about him.

The attendant in the powder room was doing a brisk business in hemming and manicure triage, but she offered Bianca a glass of ice water that Bianca used to wash down a capsule for her dull headache. She lingered to fiddle with her hair and makeup, wondering how long she would have to pretend to be in a perfect marriage to a man who didn't want her.

"Lola! I didn't know you were here. Why aren't you sitting with us?"

It took Bianca a full three pulse beats to recognize that the sudden silence meant the remark had been directed at her. She turned from painting fresh lipstick on her mouth and watched a confused double take mar the other woman's flawless features.

As their befuddled silence stretched out, their spectators quit bothering to pretend they were washing hands or teasing their hair. They outright stared.

Betray nothing. Bianca was putting together that Lola might be short for Lolita, the name of the half sister she had never met. As her heart began to thud like running boots, she ruthlessly sculpted a bemused smile onto her face. She could feel the strain in her neck. Tension pulled her navel all the way into her spine. A cold sweat, sticky as tree sap, rose on her skin.

"I think you have me confused with someone else," Bianca managed to say.

"I do." The woman was frozen as she cataloged Bianca's face and hair and build. "I thought you were my brother's girlfriend. You look just like her."

Bianca tried to decide if it would do more damage than

good to say something about how she was mistakenly recognized a lot lately. After seeing her on the news, people were constantly asking where they knew her from.

"My date is an only child," Bianca joked. "I don't think he's your brother."

The woman gave a little laugh, but it was more skeptical than amused. "Let's take a selfie. I'll send it to my brother. But first…" She placed a hand on her pregnant belly and pointed toward the stalls. "I'll be right out."

"Of course."

Talk about rude, Bianca was far worse than Everett. The moment the woman's back was turned, she bolted from the room, certain several pairs of eyebrows went up as she did. She kept her head down as she hurried back to Everett.

"I was hoping you'd be here," Roman Killian, TecSec's founder, shook the hand Everett extended. "I wasn't sure if you would thank me or fire me for sending that video to Giovanni."

"I wasn't in a fit state to clean up my own mess. I appreciate your involving him." Everett asked after Roman's family, learning everyone was thriving.

"And *your* wife?" Roman asked without a hint of facetiousness.

"Bianca's here with me." Everett shifted so he could watch for her and tried to shake off the tension that had taken hold as they had arrived here. He didn't like discord between them, and he especially didn't like her disappearing from sight when there was. "She's in the queue for the powder room, I imagine."

Like him, Roman preferred to converse side by side so he could keep an eye on the room. "She handled herself well in that emergency."

It was an innocuous comment, but the hair on the back

of Everett's neck stood up. The back of Everett's throat dried and he wet it with champagne that now tasted sour.

"Why do you find that remarkable?"

Roman sent Everett a side-eye. "I may be overstepping again."

"Step," Everett commanded.

"Given that she nearly killed my client, I took it upon myself to run her name. At the time I only had the alias she had given your housekeeper."

"I ran Sandy Ortiz myself. There were several in New York, only a handful in her age group. No red flags. Her mother was clean, too."

"Which name did you use for her mother?"

"Isabel Palm—" Everett cut himself off. Swore. "She was Ortiz? Are you telling me that's Bianca's birth name?"

"I'm telling you that Isabel Ortiz gave birth to Alejandra Ortiz in New York on Bianca's birthday and the final instalment on her maternity bill was paid by Isabel Palmer a year later."

"Alejandra." Shortened to Sandy? His mind raced to find the implications, but so what if her mother had changed their names. That didn't mean Bianca was guilty of anything except hanging on to a piece of her family history. "Bianca doesn't know her father. Maybe her mother was hiding from him?"

"That's a good bet since there's an Alejandro Rodriguez in the Cuban Mafia here. They call him Sandro. Twenty-six years ago, he was heading into eight years for drug trafficking. His girlfriend, Isabel Ortiz, disappeared during court proceedings, but there was no follow-up, no missing person. Nothing from her family to raise an alarm."

Because Bianca's grandmother had known her daughter had gone to New York?

But if Bianca's mother had named her daughter after

her lover, that suggested warmer feelings toward the man than fear or hatred.

"Where is Sandro now?" Everett asked, prickling with suspicion.

"Here. He had his rival killed while he was still inside. Allegedly," Roman added dryly. "He got out in five and played the game smarter after that. On the face of it, he makes his money with convenience stores, nightclubs and ATM machines that specialize in crypto."

All well-known means of laundering illicit funds. Everett swore again.

"Even if Bianca has that sort of connection, she doesn't seem to be using it," Everett noted. "She's been staying in my house, not his." Unless she's been in contact with her father all this time. Unless she knew who Everett was, who he used to be, and was gathering as much information as she could on him.

The things he had confided in her began to churn like broken glass in his belly.

"Here she comes." Roman arranged his face into welcoming interest.

Everett couldn't manage anything beyond the poker face he adopted when stakes went through the roof and his world was avalanching toward a pile of rubble.

Bianca didn't notice. She kept her head down and grasped his arm, nails digging through his sleeve with urgency.

"Can we go? I don't feel well," she blurted.

Despite the gaping valley of distrust that had opened between them, his heart swerved with alarm. He reflexively took hold of her elbow and shot a glower back the way she'd come.

"What happened?"

"I don't feel well. *Please?* I'm so sorry." She barely glanced at Roman. "I just really... Please? Right now?"

Everett offered the briefest of nods to Roman and escorted her through the crowd to fetch her wrap from the coat check. He waited until the privacy screen had enclosed them in the back of the car to ask again, "What happened?"

Everett's voice was surprisingly sharp. They'd been slightly at odds since entering that party, given their conflicted exchange on the way there. His shuttered expression had hardened even more, though. There was a piercing quality in his gaze that seemed to already know answers to questions he hadn't yet asked, making her want to squirm at hiding anything from him.

She couldn't tell him she had been in the same room as someone who knew her sibling, though. She had never told anyone who her father was. Her mother had drilled into her that it was *their* secret. Bianca couldn't tell *anyone*. Ever.

"I told you, I don't feel well. I didn't mean to make a scene." Her insides were sloshing like a washing machine and there was a metallic taste under her tongue.

"Bianca—" he started to growl in warning.

"*No.*" She wagged a finger at him, tension igniting into temper. "You've been railroading my life since we *met*. I was going to do this whole thing on my own. You keep trying to make me feel guilty for dragging you into this, but *you* seduced *me*. *You* brought me into your house. *You* made me rely on you and you pretend you have my best interest at heart, but you *don't*. You're just using me for sex games and arm candy at your stupid parties! Why do I even have to do this?"

She could hear the hysteria climbing in her voice, but it was a cumulation of all she'd been through—abandoning her life, months and months of solitary confinement before being thrust into the limelight. *Him.* Taking over her thoughts and body and autonomy.

And now this. Putting her in danger of being discovered by the man her mother had gone to such pains to keep her hidden from.

"If being seen at parties was your main goal in life, you wouldn't be so bored out of your mind once you got there, so why are we going?" she charged. "Because I *hate* it. Quit making me go to these things. I don't want to meet a bunch of strangers for no reason. What do I even get out of it?"

His head had gone back as though buffeted by a strong wind.

"That's why you're upset? Because we went to a party and spoke to a few strangers? Did someone say something?"

"*Everyone* says something. I hate being on display like this." She was shaking, still freaking out at what a close brush she'd had. "Why did you even become involved with me? You're making my life worse, you know. I did the right thing." She jabbed at her chest. "I pointed out a crime. Why do I have to be questioned for hours and wear clothes that aren't even comfortable and get noticed wherever I go? Why do I have to have *my* life destroyed so you can keep yours?"

She clamped her mouth tight and sniffed back gathering tears, looking to the window as she tried to hold herself together. She never should have stayed in Miami. That was the problem. Nearly being recognized by someone who knew her father was her fault, not Everett's.

But there was a piece of her still standing in that powder room, wanting to beg, *Tell me more. What are they like? Take me to them.*

She heard the rustle of Everett's jacket and the subtle beep of him placing a call. "Bianca needs a break."

She jerked her head around. "Who is that?"

"What do you mean you 'can't dictate these things'?" Everett asked in a deadly tone. "Anything you can't do can be done by a better lawyer. Shall I find one? Because Ackerley's people are dragging this out to exhaust her, hoping she'll stumble. Quit playing into their hands."

"Is that my lawyer?" Bianca hissed. "Don't fire him!" She liked him.

"Cancel all of them," Everett said. "Tell them she'll be in New York at the end of the month. They can have one more meeting when we get there. Beyond that, they can wait until they're in court." He ended the call.

"By all means, keep taking over my life," she said scathingly. "Does it occur to you that I might prefer to get this over with?"

"It will take years before this is over. Perhaps never," he said bluntly.

She knew that. Deep inside, she had known that from the moment she had realized what was going on at Morris and Ackerley and that she was the only person who could stop it. She had known her actions would cause her to lose her job, her home, her friendships. Even most of her freedom.

It was still hard to accept. The fact that Everett was so pitiless about it made it a thousand times worse.

"It's my experience, Bianca, that when someone *appears*—I use that word deliberately." He tucked his phone away. "I'm not saying you're overreacting, but when someone *appears* to be overreacting— Quit prickling up."

She sat so straight all her hair was nearly on end. "You mean quit overreacting?"

"When someone *appears* to be reacting more strongly than a situation warrants," he continued in a firm tone. "For instance, when they run out of a building as though it's on fire and it's not, it means they have been pushed to their limit by factors I can't see. In your case, the ones that I *can* see are the long days of making statements and the long evenings talking to strangers who put you on the spot. By removing those pressures, I'm freeing you up to react however you must to some of the others."

His hand moved restlessly on his thigh before he added, "I didn't realize you felt used by our lovemaking."

"Don't call it *lovemaking* when you have no intention of loving me," she spat. Then she wanted to cringe into a ball of humiliation. Her throat was squeezed so tight, she could barely swallow, let alone talk. "I wish I could compartmentalize like you do, but I can't."

"So that's what this is really about? Our talk earlier? You're angry that I told you why we don't have a future?"

"I'm angry that you keep trying to shape my future when you don't even want to be a part of it."

Bianca went to bed as soon as they arrived home.

Everett poured himself a Scotch, then brought up his copy of tonight's guest list and examined it again.

She was angry at him and the things they'd discussed on the way to the party. He accepted that. But that wasn't the only reason she was upset. She had been withdrawn at the party until she'd gone to the powder room. Now that he knew she had more than a nascent connection to her father—she had been given a version of the man's first name, for instance—he had to wonder if she'd met with someone who had spooked her.

He had reviewed this guest list prior to their leaving the house. If he had seen anyone on there that concerned him, he wouldn't have taken her there in the first place. He still couldn't see who might have upset her so badly she would insist on cutting their evening short, then lose her temper with him.

He texted Roman and asked him to run the guest list through his database to identify known associates. The resources Everett had access to were good and he had the skills to fill in blanks manually, but that took time. Tec-Sec scraped social media and other ancillary connections with the push of a button.

While he waited, he mentally reviewed all that Bianca had said, searching for clues between the lines. A lot of air came out of a distressed tire, but not all of it. He addressed each of her indictments in turn, starting with the one that had kicked him in the teeth.

You're using me for sex games and arm candy.

He was using the *events*, not her, but it was true, she benefited very little from their appearances. Those pantomimes were PR events, and she was right. He mostly loathed them, but he'd been enjoying them more lately, mostly because when they were out like that, he could let others ask her questions and watch her smile and grow animated. God knew he stood taller having such a gorgeous woman beside him. He could hold her hand and smell her hair and react purely the way he wanted to without giving up anything of himself.

You keep trying to make me feel guilty for dragging you into this, but you seduced me.

He had. Against his better judgment, in fact.

I'm angry that you keep trying to shape my future when you don't even want to be a part of it.

That wasn't quite true. He was already dreading when this would be over, and they would have to say goodbye.

Don't call it lovemaking *when you have no intention of loving me.*

He rubbed the heel of his hand against his breastbone, unable to erase the burning ache behind it. His inhale and exhale scalded his lungs.

Thankfully, his phone pinged with the notification of a shared file from Roman, dragging him from a pool of rumination that was deeper than he was prepared to dive into.

He replied.

Thanks.

NP. I'm always looking for people with your skill set, FYI.

Everett snorted. He would get right on that, seeing as it had been working out so well for him lately.

He opened the file and clicked through it, searching for anyone with the last name of Rodriguez. Given the demographics in this city, it was no surprise he came across a dozen. Even more had associations to people with that same last name, but he soon drilled down to one guest who had a brother dating one Lolita Rodriguez, daughter of Sandro.

A quick flick to Lolita's social feed revealed her to be in her early twenties and a dead ringer for Bianca. Everett's brain exploded.

This was *exactly* what had happened to Giovanni. He'd let his fly do his thinking and missed some life-threatening details.

Swearing under his breath, Everett snatched up his phone to make a call. They were going off-grid and let's see Bianca dance away from his questions when she had nowhere left to go.

CHAPTER NINE

"Is THIS THE yacht you were coming to inspect when we met?" Bianca asked as Everett piloted the tender toward the stern of the *Abeona*.

The two-hundred-foot craft was named for the goddess of outward journeys, he had told her when he asked her to pack for a week.

She had agreed because it had seemed like a small peace offering and, after nearly being recognized last night, she was anxious to get out of Miami. A trip down the Keys would give her a little breathing room to figure out her next steps.

She never should have stayed in Florida. It was one thing when all her online photos had been dated corporate headshots, but now that she was constantly being photographed with Everett, something like last night had become inevitable.

"It is," he replied, maintaining the circumspect tone he'd been using all morning. He was being his inscrutable self, unfailingly polite and effortlessly sexy in his casual control as he lowered the boat from its top speed to smoothly guide it into place.

She bit back a sigh. She'd had plenty of time to regret her outburst while she'd been lying in bed alone all night. She was still distraught, but now it mostly centered around how embarrassed she was that she'd brought up the *L*-word.

She wished she hadn't revealed how much his detachment bothered her. He might have set the rules, but she had agreed to them. She had no right to complain.

"I guess I wouldn't have missed your arrival if you had pulled up in this," she joked, hoping to soften him a little, but he only cut the motor and moved swiftly to throw the line to a waiting crewman on the yacht.

Moments later, Everett helped her step onto the lower deck of the yacht where he introduced her to Captain Garcia, then the first mate and steward, Raj and Sheila.

Everett nodded for the yacht to get underway as soon as the tender was secured before offering Bianca a tour.

"It's a lean crew at the moment, since it's only us aboard," Everett informed her. "Crew quarters are on this deck and there are four staterooms for guests. We'll go up to the main deck here."

They took the stairs on the starboard side of the stern and arrived on a lido deck. Here the sparkle from the blue of the pool reflected off the underside of the blue-and-white awning that shaded nearby lounge chairs.

Bianca couldn't help gasp as they walked into the main saloon, which was all curved lines and gleaming chrome. Comfortable sectionals with silk tasseled pillows gave way to a glass-topped oval dining table that sat ten. A horseshoe-shaped bar was stationed beneath a tryptic of abstract paintings. That art seemed to be the inspiration for the color scheme of ivory and silver-blue with accents of deep navy and frosty greens.

She would have thought herself in a top floor penthouse in New York if not for the windows that offered unobstructed views of the Florida coastline and the open Atlantic.

"This is beautiful. No wonder you had to have it."

He started to say something but seemed to think better of it.

"What?" she prompted.

"Aside from my small obsession with cars, I'm not particularly attached to any of my properties, but I bought it after I'd met you and wondered what you would think of it."

She was momentarily befuddled by what sounded like an admission that she had held some importance in his decision. Maybe he wanted to smooth over things, too.

"I think it's beautiful, obviously."

He waved for her to move around the partition wall behind the bar, where a foyer accessed both the port and starboard decks.

On the wall between them, a pair of double doors stood open, allowing them to enter the master stateroom. It was also styled with chrome and curves and sumptuous comfort. Her gaze was drawn first to the skylight over the massive bed, then the desk on one side and S-shaped sofa on the other. A private deck with glass railings invited her to walk out to the bow. She sighed with reflexive bliss as she took in rippled water and endless sky and swooping gulls.

Everett joined her and set his hands on the edge of the Plexiglas rail.

"Last night, you accused me of trying to make you feel guilty for dragging me into your controversy."

"I shouldn't have agreed to dinner in the first place. I should have realized—"

"No." He held up a hand. "You were right. I knew something was up but pursued you anyway."

She was so relieved that they were clearing the air, all her defenses crumbled away. "I still could have been more honest."

"Yes. You could have," he said gravely. He turned his head, and his gaze was so impactful she grasped at the rail, feeling off-balance.

It's a boat, she reminded herself, and glanced around to catch her bearings. The breeze was picking up, rippling his shirt and the hem of her sundress. They had begun to move. That's why she felt off-kilter.

But his words had thrown her. She immediately felt pushed onto the defensive and now saw he was as composed and unassailable as always. She had thought they were both giving a little, but no. Only her. He was fully in command.

"I understand why you didn't tell me about the whistleblowing when we were only meant to be ships passing in the night," he continued in that voice that was ever so neutral. Why did that hurt more than if he had been angry and hard? "But you've had nearly two weeks to tell me the rest, Bianca."

"There is no 'rest,'" she insisted, but she couldn't hold his gaze.

She instinctually glanced at the narrow stairs behind him. They seemed to lead to an upper deck, but she decided against trying to brush past him and went back into the suite. She came up short as she realized he had closed the doors to the foyer when they had come in. Where did she even think she could run to? They were on a freaking boat, dry land growing smaller at a rapid pace.

She snapped a look at him as he came in behind her.

"I was only keeping Sheila from interrupting us. Leave the room if you want to, but this conversation will happen. We're staying aboard until it does. Alejandra."

Her knees nearly buckled, and her throat strangled on whatever words she was trying to form. Her muscles all began to twitch, the urge to fight or flee making her heart pound like a sledgehammer in her chest.

"That's just a name I used…"

"Don't embarrass yourself," he said in that voice so devoid of emotion. He leaned on the rounded corner of a wall. "I know that Sandy Ortiz is your birth name. I know who your father is. I know who you met last night. I want

to know what was said that had you running out of there
so fast. A threat? What have you told Sandro Rodriguez
since you came to Miami? What have you told him since
you moved into my *house*?"

Bianca threw her head back, astounded. And guilty.
Yes. But how had he learned all of that? Did it mean others knew as well? The adrenaline in her system intensified
and, because she felt so cornered, she went on the attack.

"So this isn't you trying to give me a break or patch
things up between us. You brought me onto a floating cell
for further interrogation. I hate your yacht, Everett. I think
it's a giant piece of litter owned by a lying, opportunist of
a man. Go soak your head." She started toward the door,
but what was she going to do? Jump overboard and ride a
dolphin to shore?

"I didn't hear a denial."

She spun around and came back. She was shaking so
hard it frightened her, but she was both scared and mad.
Scared that her secret, the one she had protected so carefully all these years, had been discovered and furious that
he was throwing it out at her as though she had any choice
in the matter.

"I told you I've never met my father. That's true. Yes,
Sandro Rodriguez conceived me with my mother, but he
doesn't know I exist. My mother never told him she was
pregnant. She didn't even say goodbye to him."

It felt strange to speak of it, as though she was top-
pling something sacred. Her mother could have taken the
identity of Bianca's father to her grave. Instead, she had
answered all of Bianca's questions, then had sworn her
to secrecy.

Telling Everett was like breaking that last bond Bianca
had shared with her mother. It made her feel as though
she was betraying her. It hurt and felt wrong, and she was
ashamed of herself for crumbling so easily, but once the

first trickle of truth spilled out, the rest swelled up, insisting on gushing forth.

"She realized she was pregnant while he was waiting to be sentenced. By then, people were trying to kill him. He couldn't protect her from behind bars, so Mom moved to New York and changed our name as soon as she was able to."

"Did she testify against him? Was she afraid of him?"

"She was *in love* with him." She hugged herself, cold despite the humid tropical air drifting in from the open doors to the bow. "They were planning to marry, but they kept it a secret because my grandmother didn't approve of him."

"Because he was a criminal?"

"Because he was *poor*," she said tersely. "And because it genuinely went against my grandmother's beliefs for Mom to have sex out of wedlock. She and my father were both very young and he wound up making some terrible choices trying to prove he could give Mom a good life. He was angry when he realized Mom had left. He called my grandmother and lost his temper. She wouldn't have anything to do with Mom after that because *she* was afraid of him."

That had weighed heavily on her mother. Bianca had seen it.

"And you?"

"Me? Oh, you care about me now?" Her throat was so thick she could hardly speak.

She resented that flinty look of his. It was exactly in line with all the questioning she'd undergone this week and told her exactly how little she or her situation was impacting him. He was turning her inside out while remaining detached as a lover, a friend, or even a pretend husband.

"By the time I was old enough to beg Mom to tell me about him, he was out of prison, married and staring his new family. Mom impressed on me that there would be no getting that cat back in the bag if I reached out to him, and there would be a lot of consequences if I did. I had to be very sure if I ever decided to take the step of trying to meet him. That's why I was upset last night." She paced a few restless steps, rubbing her bare arms. "A woman mistook me for m-my—" She cleared her throat. "My half sister."

"Lolita."

"Yes." The name scored across her heart deep enough to make her flinch. She had snooped on the young woman's social feeds in the past. It was like looking at her college self with a deeper tan and more fashion sense. There was a familiarity to her half brothers' features that made her wistful, too.

"If you're so afraid of running into them, why stay in Miami? Why use your *birth* name?"

"It's not exactly unique here," she scoffed, then swallowed, trying to ease the constriction that was causing her voice to quaver, but a corkscrew was lodged in her chest, turning and turning. "They're the only family I have. I had to walk away from every other part of my life, but that part still felt…possible."

His eyes narrowed. "So you *do* want to meet them."

"Of course, I want to meet them!" she cried, waving a helpless hand. "I always have, but I *can't*. I don't know how they would react. I don't want to destroy his marriage or ruin his relationship with his children. I can't imagine he'll want anything to do with me now I'm a whistleblower," she said with a broken, humorless laugh. "He would be suspicious as hell, and I wouldn't blame him. More importantly, who knows what his enemies would do if they found out he has another child? That's why Mom made me take a blood oath never to tell anyone. Not a best friend. Not a boss or a boyfriend or a *husband*."

His mouth tightened, telling her the sarcasm stung, but it wasn't the least bit satisfying. She was starting to cry, and it just made her more furious. She smacked at her cheeks to whisk the tears away.

"It's always been this huge, impossible balloon that sits inside me, making it hard to breathe. Sometimes it gets so big, I think it will burst and kill me. Other times, I think she was right to hide me from him. As long as we were the only ones who knew who I am, that part of his life couldn't hurt me."

"I'm the only one who knows," he said firmly, adding begrudgingly, "And Roman Killian, but he makes his living keeping secrets. It won't go any further than that."

"And we'll just assume that woman last night won't mention it to *anyone*? She wanted a selfie so she could text her brother." Bianca had been trying not to dwell on what might have happened after she left but given the fact her face was plastered everywhere these days, she thought the odds were good that her father would become aware of her and start to wonder. Others might, too.

"Just..." She sniffed and grabbed up a few tissues to blow her nose. "Let me off somewhere so I can...get lost."

His head went back as if she'd delivered an upper cut. The rest of his body stayed so still he seemed to be made of marble.

"I'm not dropping you on some island to fend for yourself," he stated grimly.

"Why not? You said this cruise would last until we had this conversation. It happened. Now take me back to shore." Her whole body was condensing with so much tension, she felt made of iron. Cold and hard and heavy and black all the way to her soul. If he dropped her overboard, she would sink straight to the bottom like an anchor.

"I need to make some calls." He pushed off the wall.

"We had an agreement!"

"Where would you go, Bianca? Hmm?" he challenged with impatience. "You know what's out there waiting for you. Now so do I. So no. You're not leaving this yacht. Not until I've arranged all those protections I promised you."

"I don't want you to keep paying for my problems!" She nearly stamped her foot like a child.

"It is my problem! Who took you to that party? I did," he snapped, thumbing into his chest. "I knew something wasn't right, but I put it down to our tiff in the car."

"Oh, my God, Everett." She choked on a laugh, genuinely astonished that she was coming to his defense when she was furious with him, but, "You can't actually predict every bad thing that might happen. You know that, don't you?"

He pinched the bridge of his nose, swearing. "It's the same damned feeling I had when I let Giovanni head straight into that ambush. I should have known."

"It's not the same," she cried, but there was a knock at the door, and he brushed past her to open it.

"Sheila. Go ahead and unpack Bianca. I'll sleep in another room." He took his bag from the startled steward and disappeared.

CHAPTER TEN

Everett found Bianca an hour later. She was reading in the shade next to the pool, wearing a bikini with a strapless top in neon yellow and tiny striped bottoms in yellow and lime green.

He swallowed and averted his gaze to the horizon as he lowered himself to sit sideways on the lounger next to hers. A glint on the water pierced into his brain.

"Do you ever sunbathe topless?" he asked abruptly.

"Dream on!" She glanced down at her top and that jerked his attention to where her nipples betrayingly poked against the cups.

Their gazes collided and her cheeks flushed.

"I'm advising you don't." He nodded at a flash of light. "Long lens camera."

"Ugh." For a moment, she looked like she would weep at yet another invasion of her privacy.

"Would you rather talk inside?"

"I'd rather read my book in peace," she muttered, closing it in her lap. "The king of a fictitious Mediterranean island had just kidnapped the heroine onto his yacht." She batted her lashes while her mouth wore a curl of irony. "Life imitates art yet again."

Don't, he ordered himself, but his body immediately conjured the sensation of her hands smearing suntan oil all over his body. He imagined working the fragrant oil into her smooth skin and flexing muscles before sliding their slippery bodies together as the afternoon sun burnished their skin to gold.

He took a gulp of the slushy drink on the table between their chairs, trapped ever deeper inside a medieval torture device, one that impaled him in a thousand places, making every movement and breath its own world of agony.

He had done this. He had seduced her against his better judgment and started all these dominoes falling. But...

"I stand by my decision to help you." He set down the sweating glass and dried his hand on the leg of his shorts. "Even if you'd managed to evade being tracked down, Ackerley was already destroying your credibility. The wheels of justice turn very slowly, and you would have been ground to bits in its gears long before it gets where it's going. I'll make no apology for providing you a fortress to hide in along with a team to represent you. I've ordered you a dedicated security detail and I have an agent finding you an apartment in New York—"

"I have an apartment in New York," she cut in.

"You *had* a sublet bedroom in a building that doesn't even have a doorman, let alone a proper alarm system."

"You can't keep buying me things, Everett."

"I can and I will. It'll take a week or so, but everything will be in place by the time we get back to Miami. I'll take you to New York myself then..." A searing pain bloomed in his chest. "Then I'll distance myself so I'm not drawing that extra attention onto you."

"And issue a statement that we're taking a break?" Her voice cracked and she turned her face away.

She must have immediately realized the camera was catching whatever emotions were on her face because she made a frustrated noise and abruptly rose. A moment later, she threw herself into a cushioned corner behind him.

He rubbed his hands together, fleetingly thinking of

Lady Macbeth failing to clean the stains from her hands. "It's for the best, Bianca."

"You don't know what's best for me," she snapped.

"I know what is *not* best for you." He rose so he could turn and face her. "Me."

"Is that your clairvoyant superpower telling you that? Did the government know you were bitten by a radioactive spider? Is that why they hired you?"

"They hired me because I am a dog with a bone. I don't quit until I've gnawed it clean, even if it means I'm surrounded by wolves who want to fight me for it. They hired me because I *like* being in that fight. Believe me when I tell you that you don't want to be with a man who is willing to risk everything for the high of proving he can come out on top. That's why we're in this mess right now."

"You really do think you're above the flaw of being human, don't you? You screwed up, Everett. We all do it, despite our best intentions. I did." She waved at herself, voice scraped raw. "I went ahead and fell in love with you, even though I swore to myself I wouldn't."

"Don't—" He held up a hand as if it could stop that bullet from piercing his chest, but bittersweet agony blossomed through his body anyway. "Why the hell would you do that? Now I'm going to hurt you even more."

"When?"

"What?" He dropped his hand.

"When are you going to hurt me? In a week, when you leave me in New York? Or while we're on this yacht? Because I will not let you spend a week turning the knife just so you can prove what a lousy man you are to love."

He flexed his hands, biting out, "Stop saying that."

"That I love you? Why? Does it hurt?"

"Yes."

Her shoulders sagged with defeat and her brow pleated.

"It's supposed to be a good thing, Everett. It's supposed to make you feel like you matter."

He looked away, aching from his scalp to his toes. *Don't say it.* He clenched his teeth, but had to say, "You matter. Okay, Bianca? You matter to me. That's why— *Oof.*"

Her body crashed into his and he reflexively caught her close as he staggered to keep his balance.

Then the reality, the *joy* of holding her, exploded within him. He told himself to let her go, but he couldn't. The best he could do was close his eyes and tuck her face into his neck while he smoothed his hand over her silky hair. She was shaking and so was he, both of them far more affected by their conversation than they were letting on.

"I am human. I do know that," he told her. "I don't have any superpower where you're concerned. It's more of a fatal weakness. That's why I'm trying to protect you. If you really understood who I am—"

"Show me," she insisted, tilting back her head to stare straight into his eyes. "I want that man. Not a tycoon or a spy or... I just want you. The *real* you."

Did she? Because that man snapped free of what constraints he had left. He released her, but only to stoop and throw her over his shoulder. He started to the master stateroom.

Bianca's breath left her in a squeal of shock. She grabbed handfuls of his shirt as Everett carried her through the saloon where one of the crew gave a cough of surprised laughter, then mumbled a daunted apology.

She didn't see who it was. Her hair was in her eyes and, as Everett entered the stateroom and pivoted to close and lock the doors, she threw an arm over her head in protection.

"I'm not going to let you bump your head," he muttered, sounding insulted. He swung her into the cradle of his arms before lightly dropping her onto the bed.

She caught fistfuls of the covers as she found her bearings again.

"So we're doing Tarzan and Jane?" she asked as he closed the doors to the bow and dropped the blinds.

"We're doing Everett and Bianca. This is who I am. I'm not as civilized as I pretend, Bianca. Now I want to see *you*." He came to the edge of the bed and caught her by the ankle, dragging her closer so he could twist his hand in her bikini bottoms and start to peel them off.

She gasped and thrust her hand down to cover her mound.

He froze. "No?"

"This feels really…"

"Frightening?" His hold on her bottoms loosened, and he drew back slightly, banking the lust that gleamed in his eyes.

"Intimate," she said. "Like we've never done it before." Like they couldn't come back from it. "I'm nervous."

The stern look eased from his face, and he flowed onto the bed, covering her and pressing her into the mattress, caging her as he propped himself on his elbows over her.

"But you know I'd never force you or hurt you. You trust me." It wasn't a question. He knew she did. Deep in his eyes, navy blue flecks gleamed like reverse stars in the sky blue of his irises, mingling with clouds of lust and possessiveness and something so tender, she began to shake inside.

She slid her hands from his chest around his rib cage to the indent of his spine. "I do."

She loved him. But she didn't say it. She showed him. She curled her legs around his waist and touched between his shoulder blades and relaxed beneath him, lifting her mouth to invite his kiss.

He swooped his mouth onto hers, hotly claiming. She welcomed the rake of his hungry lips, reveling in his ravishment. His whole weight pinned her a moment as he flattened himself on her, briefly dominating her before he pulled himself back under control with a hiss.

As he gathered his weight onto his knee and elbow, and tucked his tormented brow into her neck, she said, "Don't hold back, Everett. I want all of you. I can take it."

With a feral noise, he opened his mouth on her neck in damp suction, then licked up the throbbing artery to her mouth again. His kiss nearly smothered her before turning to something that tasted of agony and need and sweet, sweet veneration.

He slid down to kiss across her collarbone, over the swells of her breasts, then dragged the bikini top down to expose her nipple. When the hot cavern of his mouth enclosed the turgid tip, she groaned and slid her fingers into his hair.

He lifted his head and showed his teeth in cruel enjoyment.

"I like hearing that," he said grittily, dragging her hands from his hair and pinning her wrists in one hand above her head. "When you make those noises, I know you're feeling exactly the way I am, like you're going to die from the want." He licked at her nipple, blew softly. "Now come for me."

He began to suckle at her, drawing on one breast then the other, making her writhe beneath him. Hot runnels of desire flooded into her loins, again and again. She made all the noises for him, growing so aroused she was going mad with it.

"Everett, I can't. I can't," she cried, nearly weeping with sexual frustration.

"No?" He brought his head up to suck on her bottom lip, still palming one of her breasts. "You're so close, but

I don't want to bruise you. Tell me what you need." His hand trailed down to rub her bare abdomen, circling and circling.

She didn't know why that made her pant, but it did. Delicious tingles shot from her nape into her nipples, from behind her navel into her sex.

"You." She turned her wrists with protest in his grip. "Let me touch you. Let me feel you inside me."

He reared up on his knees and threw off his shirt, then yanked down the fly of his shorts. As he drew them off and threw them away, she peeled her bikini off. He tossed it off the bed once her feet were free and stayed on his knees above her, fiercely sexual with his bronze tan and sculpted muscles and erection thrusting blatantly from the nest of hair at the crux of his powerful thighs.

Propped on her elbow, she took him in her fist, compelled to hold and caress and shift to take him in her mouth. She was helpless before him, before *this*. She really was. That knowledge had been terrifying right from the beginning and would worry her now if she wasn't drowning in stronger sensations of sharp excitement and greedy desire. In a need to *show* him that she was his. Utterly and completely. She fondled his backside and felt his firm globes flex. Saw his abdomen tighten as a groan rattled in his chest.

She might have smiled with cruel delight then, but he cupped her cheek and pulled away.

He muttered something about trying to last and swept his thumb across her wet lips, hand shaking. "I want to do that to you, but I can't wait."

She dropped onto her back and bent her knees, opening her legs in invitation.

With a groan, he swept his hand down her body and combed his fingers into the tangle of wet curls. Another, deeper groan left him as his fingers drew patterns in the abundant moisture, making her arch and moan.

"Everett, *please*." She started to close her fist on him again, but with a tortured growl, he stretched himself across the bed and dipped into the night table.

A hard jolt went through her. She hadn't given a thought to protection, but of course he had.

That was good, she reminded herself. He didn't want children and she wouldn't force him to have any, but a poignant ache opened inside her when he swooped to cover her again.

His mouth sealed to hers as his hips pressed. His broad shape invaded. When his muscled thighs were hard where they held hers open, and the fine hairs on his legs scraped her inner thighs, she bent her knees and drew her ankles to his hips, tilting her hips to invite him deeper. He gathered her beneath him and let his weight settle heavily on her pelvis, ensuring they were as indelibly connected as they could possibly be.

I love you, she thought as she shaped his skull and caressed his neck and stroked over his bunched shoulders. She brushed light kisses across his mouth and jaw and cheekbone. If she couldn't have forever with him, she would remember every tiny detail of this moment when his spicy scent was making her drunk.

His eyes closed for the press of her mouth on his eyelid and a growl of pleasure reverberated in his chest. Inside her, he was hot and pulsing and his first shallow thrust made the world glitter.

"Look at me," he lifted his head to rasp.

She did, barely able to withstand the intimacy of their locked stare. This was raw and primal, and all her shields were gone. There was no hiding anything from him. Not now. Especially not her heart. It was there, offered freely, if only he would accept it.

His brow flexed in anguish, but he didn't hide from the light in her gaze. He studied her face as though memorizing it. His hand cradled her jaw and he kissed her softly, then with more heat, as though he couldn't help himself.

A small tension gathered in him, and he clasped her tight as he rolled them.

Startled to find herself on top, she adjusted her knees and arched with pleasure as his palms swept over her back and hips and buttocks.

"Better," he said with a tone of agreement. "Now take everything you need from me."

There was a pinch inside her heart. He must know what she wanted most from him, but as he gathered each of her breasts in his wide palms, fairly worshipping them in the way he gently cradled and brushed his thumbs against her nipples, and his gaze continued to stray over her as though she was the most glorious thing he'd ever seen, she thought maybe he was giving her everything he was capable of giving.

Her whole body throbbed with need. She wanted nothing more than for him to thrust with all his power, imprinting himself on her and taking her over the edge into ecstasy. But she leaned into that touch, lost to the bliss of it for a few breathless moments.

Then she let her hands roam over his muscled chest, luxuriating in the meatiness of his pecs, the ripples of his rib cage and the light line of hair down his abdomen. She did everything she could to pleasure both of them, stroking over his skin and licking at his nipples, making his chest swell and his breath hiss audibly.

She touched herself as she began to move on him. She rode him and watched through slitted eyes as his cheeks darkened and his lips drew into a grimace of tension. He made a noise of gratification, and his hands came to her hips, guiding her as he thrust up to meet her.

When he was a hard line beneath her and she was in danger of tipping over the edge into the abyss, she slowed and drew out each lift and return of her hips. She folded onto him so she could kiss him as she lived in the eternity of taking him to the edge of leaving her, then sinking back into the return so they both exhaled in relief.

His heart was hammering against her breast. His teeth caught at her lip. Her nipples scraped the hair on his chest and her insides quivered with tension. He was shaking beneath her, and she was trembling atop him. His breath was uneven as he fought to maintain control.

"I won't break until you do," she told him.

"Damn it, Bianca. Damn you." He wrapped his arms around her and thrust up, releasing ragged groans as he shuddered, and his erection pulsed hotly inside her.

She had no room in her for smugness. As his hips lifted hers off the bed, the sun exploded, and she was lost in the white-hot light of her own ecstasy.

She had completely unraveled him and continued to do so over the ensuing days. It was disturbing, opening places in Everett that had closed over like scar tissue, aching, but thick and protected. Now there was a sensation that was fresh and exposed, sensitive to each look from her. Each smile. Each kiss and caress.

He wasn't sure how he'd convinced himself he could make love to her and not feel her love as a gentle, persistent breeze that wore down all his hard edges. He hadn't, of course. He had been sure she would break off those pieces and leave him as a pile of moraine, but he hadn't cared. He was opportunistic enough to steal this time with her while he could. The later costs were negligible against the precious value these memories would hold for him.

He stored every moment in his mental vault as they made love and talked and swam and fished and strapped on tanks for scuba diving. It was like an enchantment to float in that blue, silent, timeless world, where the colorful fish had nothing on the graceful movements of her golden body and the delight in her eyes when she looked at him from behind her mask. Later, they would sit around reading and eating and behaving with unabashed hedonism, touching and teasing until they rose to find the nearest bed and make love again.

But he knew this was a new game they were playing, a new lie they were telling themselves. They wanted to believe they had forever, but they only had today and maybe a little bit of tomorrow. They wouldn't know until they got there. They talked about everything except that.

The clock wound down when they returned to Key Largo. They were mellow after a lovemaking-induced nap, sipping wine as the sun set. Flames of ruby and marmalade danced around them, reflecting off chrome and glass.

"I hate to spoil a moment," Sheila murmured as she topped up their glasses, "But your lawyer asked me to convey that he would very much like you to return his call at your earliest convenience."

"I saw there were a couple of messages from him," Bianca confessed with a wrinkle of her nose at Everett. She was snuggled under his arm, her bent legs tucked warmly against his thigh. "Do you mind?"

He did, but, "He wouldn't ask you to interrupt his dinner if it wasn't important."

She placed the call and held the phone so Everett could listen.

"Morris and Ackerley have negotiated a settlement," her lawyer said. "They will pay a fine and abstain from similar business for five years in order to avoid further investigation. There won't be any court proceedings or further charges. Bianca still needs to testify to a congressional committee, but that won't happen for several months. It's over."

"Over," Bianca said with disbelief.

Over. Everett had known that train was coming, but he still hadn't anticipated how quickly it would arrive. Or how it would travel through him and leave such a massive cavity.

"Are you still coming to New York as scheduled? I can give you all the details then, but I wanted you to know."

"Thank you. Yes, we're sailing back to Miami overnight and will fly to New York in the morning." Everett took the phone from Bianca's limp fingers and ended the call.

"They should have been arrested," she said with helpless anger. "I went through all of this so they could buy their way out of it and start doing it again in a few years? That's not *fair.*"

"It's not." But if he had a penny for every injustice he'd failed to right despite his best efforts... Well, he pretty much did, and he was pretty damned wealthy.

Everett didn't let his churning emotions engulf him, though. He snapped his mind to the practicalities.

"My concern is retaliation. You'll still need that security detail. I would suggest a visit to Freja as soon as possible. Their compound is very secure and big enough you won't feel cooped up. I'll make arrangements so you can fly to Sicily the minute you've finished with your lawyer." He reached for his own phone.

"*Stop it,*" Bianca cried, lurching to her feet so fast her stemless wineglass nearly toppled over.

He steadied it, then looked up at her, noting the misery gleaming in her eyes.

"Get it out then," he commanded.

"Don't you *dare* act as if this is a tantrum. I am not your pet project, Everett. I'm not your employee. I'm not even your *wife*. As evidenced by the fact you can't *wait* to get rid of me."

He clenched his teeth against saying, *That's not true.* But this breakup was necessary. A little hatred on her end would go a long way to making it quick and clean. To making it stick.

God, he could hardly bear to think of that.

"You're not even going to try to let me down easy?" Her throat flexed as she looked to the horizon. She was blinking fast, fighting not to reveal how badly he was hurting her, but he knew. He felt it inside him as a thousand turning knives.

"Look what I've done to you," he said with quiet anguish. "I've already caused you a lot of pain and it's been, what? Three weeks? You think that's going to change in another three weeks? In three years? If you give me the power to hurt you, I will. It's not even a risk. It's a given. Do you want that? I don't!"

"Neither do I," she said in a small, dignified voice.

Something in her tone caused a great hand to take hold of his chest, slowly closing into a fist, crushing his lungs into his heart until they were a ball of agony.

"But *love* is a risk," she said with a note of torment. "It hurts and terrifies and makes you feel worthless because how could you ever be as good as that other person wants you to be? Sometimes the people you love make mistakes and let you down and sometimes they even *die*. Love wrecks *everything*." She swept out a hand in emphasis. "But I'll tell you what, Everett. If you ever want to do something that makes you feel alive, genuinely alive and powerful and free, then fall in love." She stood tall and brushed the wetness off her cheek. "Until then, you go ahead and hide from it, so *you* don't get hurt. Thank you for your assistance. I can take it from here."

She walked away.

CHAPTER ELEVEN

BIANCA DIDN'T SLEEP a wink, nor did she shed a tear. Her devastation was too complete. She loved him and love was never wasted, but that would be her solace sometime in the future. For now, she could only lie still and suffer the pain while wondering when she had developed such a horrific taste for self-destruction.

While her mother had been alive, she'd been the ultimate good girl, earning straight As, rarely drinking, and never having sex on the first date. In the last year, she'd blown up her career, walked away from her life and had fallen in love with a man who refused to even try to make a future with her.

As if that wasn't the worst thing life could throw at her, when she rose in the early hours, she discovered she wasn't pregnant.

She didn't *want* to be pregnant, not really. Not if it would only trap Everett into sticking by her. She didn't want to lie to him about something like that either or exclude him from their child's life. He'd been super careful, so there hadn't really been a chance for her to conceive anyway. She hadn't had any genuine expectation that she would get pregnant, but as long as the possibility had been out there it had been that—a possibility. A tiny fantasy that could have sustained her a little longer.

But no. It was not to be and that felt like a death blow. They were definitely parting forever after this.

He appeared on deck when she did, having slept elsewhere. He must have slept at least a little because he didn't look nearly as much like dirty laundry as she felt. He was freshly shaved and wore a clean shirt and pressed trousers.

She didn't let herself take more than that snapshot of a glance, focusing on the travel mug of coffee Sheila handed her, but she felt Everett's gaze on her like a persistent hornet searching for a place to land.

"Your things from the house were packed and put in the vehicle that will pick us up from the marina," Everett said.

She didn't say anything, only sipped her coffee and watched Raj load their luggage from the yacht onto the tender.

Maybe she would speak to Everett once they were on the plane. That would have some symmetry. They could say their goodbyes in the air, the way they'd once said hello. She would tell him she was sorry she had called him a coward because who was she to accuse him of such a thing when she had never worked up the courage to meet her own father? Everett had done all sorts of brave, generous, forgiving things, including moving her into his house and paying for her upkeep, despite what she had eventually cost him.

Really, when she considered how much trouble she had been, was it any wonder he'd rather part ways as soon as possible?

Hide from it so you don't get hurt...

Good God, that woman knew how to throw out an insult, essentially calling him a coward, while also issuing a nearly irresistible dare.

Everett had been brooding all night, trying to logic his way out of the impossible position she'd put him in. He was trying to protect her, damn it, from himself. From his selfish impulses, the ones that were urging him to keep her and lock her into a lifetime of anguish.

Judging by how bruised her eyes looked, he'd already broken her heart. He hated himself for it, but if that was inevitable, surely letting her go now, so she could move on, was the kinder thing to do?

He averted his mind from thoughts of her with another man, of her making love and children with someone else. She'd be a really good mother, though. She was affectionate and funny and wasn't afraid to get her hair wet. She reacted well in an emergency. Kids were always scraping knees and falling out of trees.

She *deserved* to have the family she longed for. He couldn't hold her back from that.

It was a cold morning and she huddled in her windbreaker while Raj piloted them into the marina. It killed Everett to see her struggle to find a smile for the first mate as she thanked him and asked him to pass along her appreciation to the yacht's crew.

They were met by a bodyguard, Belle, whom Everett had already met online. She introduced herself to Bianca as part of Bianca's permanent detail. She was tall and had a wide jaw and a confident manner, but she shot a hard look off to her left as she was shaking Bianca's hand.

There was a small noise that could have been anything—a rub of a craft shoved hard against its mooring or something shifting and falling on the deck of a boat.

Everett's sixth sense was unbothered, which was the strangest thing. A few hours ago, he'd been prepared to keep Bianca on the yacht another day or two, his radar had been crackling so hard.

He had second-and third-guessed that impulse, wondering if he was merely finding an excuse to spend a little more time with her, but an hour ago, his tension had dissipated, leaving him with only the sick knot of having to say goodbye to a woman he was beginning to suspect he loved. Deeply.

"We used a decoy vehicle from the mansion to draw any followers, as you requested," Belle said to Everett in an undertone. "My partner is stationed at the top of the ramp and will let me know if he sees anything of concern." She touched her ear and smiled reassuringly at Bianca. "I swept the area before you arrived. It's a quiet day here."

Bianca looked at Everett, not the least facetious when she asked, "Do you think it's okay?"

He looked up the narrow leg of dock to where it joined the main stretch. Parts of it were cast in shadow by the luxury yachts in the slips on either side, but music drifted from some far-off craft and someone closer by was whistling tunelessly. There was a muted clink of equipment being moved around and the call of a gull.

"I do." He took her elbow and carried his own bag while Belle took Bianca's.

Walking up that swaying path felt a lot like slowly impaling himself on a spear. Was he being stubborn? Spineless? Or noble?

He wanted her to be safe and happy, and if he thought he could give her that, he would—

Belle touched her ear, dropped Bianca's bag and withdrew a gun.

Everett snatched Bianca into his chest and said with quiet urgency, "I love you."

She stumbled on the bag he dropped, but he held her upright, angling his body to shelter her from whatever bullets were about to rain down while he extended his other arm, pointing his own weapon at the men who appeared on the bows above them, all armed.

Six. Too many. Everett swore.

"You have a *gun*?" Bianca whispered into his chest, appalled.

"My partner has a clear shot," Belle warned them, but they all knew the men had the upper hand.

"No one will be shot today," one of the men said. "Let's put our weapons away, before someone calls the authorities and things become complicated."

"Did Ackerley hire you?" Everett demanded. He was like a granite statue, unmoving while his slamming heart bashed against Bianca's.

"No. We met him after he followed your car here from your home. We've removed him to another location. Your wife is perfectly safe, but my employer would like to meet her."

"Who is your employer?" Everett already knew and, judging by Bianca's muted gasp, so did she.

"Sandro Rodriguez."

She was shaking against him, but lifted her face to say, "I don't want anyone to be hurt. Can you please all put those away?"

The one who had been speaking tucked his gun into the back of his waistband and showed his empty hands. "*Hermana*. Come. Bring your husband. This will only take a minute."

"You're not going anywhere," Everett growled, holding her so tight he might leave bruises, but apologizing for that could wait until he got her to safety.

"I'll go alone if you don't want to come," she said, voice solemn. "But I have to meet him, Everett. I have to."

"You don't even know if it's really him," he said through his teeth.

Another man appeared next to the one who had put his gun away.

Both Everett and Belle pointed their weapons at the new arrival. He was unfazed.

"Alejandra. Come. We only have a few minutes. I want to say hello." He had the firm tone of a parent who brooked no disobedience.

"Everett, please." She reached to touch his arm, silently urging him to lower his gun.

What could he do? Shoot her father? Refuse her this one chance and break her heart in an even more unforgivable way?

This was why he had never wanted to fall in love. It *was* terrifying. It meant allowing someone who meant everything to him to do something reckless and foolish, just because it made them happy.

He lowered his gun and let her come even with him so she could look up at her father.

Sandro's dark brown hair was gray at his temples and he had the slight paunch of middle age pressing against the button of his tailored jacket. His eyes were a world-weary version of hers, shaped like her own and—Bianca caught her breath and her eyes started to well as a slow smile of pride dawned on her father's lips.

"Come." Sandro beckoned. "You have time before your flight for one cup of coffee."

Thirty minutes later, Bianca collapsed shakily into the SUV.

Everett slid in behind her, shoving her across the cushions as he growled, "Get us the hell out of here."

Bianca didn't really register his anger. Her mind was still echoing with gruff, accented phrases. *You are so like her, with her staunch principles. I left her no choice, but I wish she had told me about you. I wouldn't have let you fall in with such a man as you did.*

It was such a fatherly thing to say.

The SUV took a sharp turn that had her tipping toward Everett, snapping her back to reality.

"I'm sorry. I know that put you in danger, but I really wanted to meet him and—"

Everett brushed her hand from the seat belt she was trying to buckle and gathered her into his lap. His arms were so hard around her, he was back to crushing her breath from her lungs.

"It wasn't me I was worried about." He was shaking.

"Everett, I'm *sorry.*"

"Stop apologizing. I know why you did it. Just… Be quiet while I process that we're still alive." His hands were moving on her as if searching for broken bones, but she was absolutely unharmed and feeling startlingly whole.

"What happened to your intuition? Why didn't you know that was going to happen?"

"Because you weren't in danger?" he snarled, then pressed his mouth to her hair. "That was the worst moment of my life, realizing I'd missed catching that we were surrounded."

She snuggled into his warmth, still in shock at finally meeting her father and one of her half brothers.

Lola had brought her existence to Sandro's attention. He'd read up on Bianca and had had people watching Everett's mansion for their return. When Troy turned up and followed the car to the marina, they had quickly disarmed him and "had a chat."

He won't approach you again. His partner is also aware that you are not without protection. Of course, you also have your husband to look after you.

Everett had said in a grave, warning tone, *She does.*

Had he also told her he loved her or had that been a terror-induced hallucination?

"I always feared he would reject me or resent me," she murmured. Instead, her father had been regretful of the years they'd missed while accepting that they had been necessary. They had ended with an agreement that it was best if their relationship remained distant.

My other children want to meet you, but that should wait for another time. You will tell me if you ever need anything, though.

I will, she had promised, because Sandro Rodriguez seemed like a man you didn't refuse.

"I know you're angry with me," she said to Everett, cuddling her shoulder beneath his arm. "But I'm grateful you let me meet him."

"I didn't have a choice, did I?" He kept his voice low to keep their conversation private from Belle and the guard in the driver's seat, the one she had yet to properly meet. "But don't ever do anything like that to me again."

"I'll live a very boring life of healthy eating and gentle exercise from now on," she assured him. "You won't have to worry about me."

"This isn't funny. I love you and I thought I was going to lose you. Let's both promise not to scare the hell out of each other if we can possibly help it."

"I wasn't sure if I heard you right the first time. In fact, I might need to hear it a few more times before it sinks in."

"I love you," he said in the most belligerently endearing way, she started to laugh.

And since she had so much tension built up, and he was scowling with so much annoyance, she laughed until her middle hurt.

Maybe it was cramps. She gave a final wistful sigh and relaxed her head onto his shoulder.

"I need to say something," she said. "What happened today was important to me. Even if I can't have much of a relationship with them, I needed to know I had that connection. With Mom's family gone, I needed to know I was a branch on someone's tree. Now I do. If you don't want to make a tree of our own, if you don't want children, I think

I could live with that. I just want to be with you, Everett.
I want that very, very much."

His chest shook as he took a big breath and let it out.

"You humble me." He cupped her face, tilting her gaze
up to his. He caressed her cheek with his thumb and dipped
his head to press his lips to her brow. "I want you to have
whatever will make you happy, Bee, including the family you've always dreamed of. The stone-cold fact is, the
more I think of you making babies with someone else, the
more murderous I feel toward someone who doesn't even
exist. If you're having babies, *I* will be their father. Take
that to the bank."

Her heart was swelling in her chest, but it was catching
on small, sharp hooks of concern. "I love that you're saying that, but I don't want you to have children unless you
really want them. Don't say something like that to please
me. Definitely don't make babies to please me. That's not
fair to our imaginary children."

"I'm confident I would love our children a distressing
amount. I'm fond of those little monsters of Giovanni's.
I'm given to understand affection rises exponentially when
it comes to one's own."

"Okay, well, we don't have to make that decision right
now." She nuzzled her mouth into the warmth beside his
Adam's apple. "Maybe we should get married first?" she
suggested.

"There's an idea." He swore and patted for his phone,
taking it out and grimacing as he flicked through his
screens. "I already approved the press release that said
we were taking a break. I'll see if I can catch it before it
goes out."

"There's an idea," she mocked.

"I think that does it." He dropped his phone. "What
were we talking about? Oh, yes. I was proposing. Will
you marry me?"

"I asked you first."

"Then, yes. And soon. Very soon." He pressed their smiles together in a sweet kiss, one they kept reasonably PG on account of their audience.

After a moment, she said, "Maybe I should move into my own seat, now?"

"No, I'm not finished holding you. I don't think I ever will be."

That was convenient because she wasn't done being held.

EPILOGUE

One year later...

"I'm home!" Bianca called as she walked into their New York penthouse.

Miami was their permanent home, but they traveled a lot, now that Everett had a consulting job with Roman Killian. He also had majority shares in an engineering firm working on electric car technologies. There was enough risk and challenge to keep him interested without being a threat to his wife's peace of mind.

Bianca was also in a very good place. The hearings over Morris and Ackerley were behind her. She had discreetly and tearfully met her half siblings a few months ago, and she had recently launched a marketing and branding business for romance authors. She had thought she might pick up one or two accounts, but she was already thinking of hiring an assistant to help her meet the demand.

"How was your day?" Everett asked, coming into the kitchen where she was putting away the decaf coffee and vitamins she'd picked up on her way home. He looped his arm around her, kissing her temple.

"Good. Um—" She suddenly hit a wall of nervousness. She had told him she was meeting Freja for lunch today, which had been true, but she had also been to the doctor. Fortunately, she was able to delay spilling her news by pointing to the envelope on the counter. "You had a parcel downstairs."

"Oh, good. It got here in time. It's for you. I thought we might have a night in." He dragged the envelope across so it was in front of her, then leaned on the counter to watch her open it.

"A night in." She knew what that was code for and smirked as she pulled the tab on the envelope, amused excitement tingling through her.

Sometimes they still role-played and sometimes he liked to shop online for fresh story lines. Lately, he'd been going through a historical phase with a lot of pirates and dukes. It was a double win for her—great sex and something new to read in the bathtub when she had some downtime.

"Is it a werewolf? Because—" She grew speechless as she looked at the title.

"I thought I'd be the tech magnate if you want to—" he tapped the cover "—drop your secret baby bombshell?"

She dropped the book. "I wasn't keeping it a secret! I just wasn't sure yet. How did *you* know?"

"Your body is like a clock, Bee. We stopped using protection three weeks ago and you're four days late. What else would it be?"

"I don't know, but I didn't expect it to happen on our first try!" She hugged herself, still in shock.

He took her by the arms, dipping his head to catch at her gaze. "Are you okay?"

"Yes. Ecstatic. But I wasn't sure how you—"

"I'm sure," he said, smiling with amused tenderness while a light of wonder grew in his eyes. "I feel like I swallowed the sun and I'm floating. Are you really pregnant?"

"Yes."

"God, I love you." He wrapped her in his arms and kissed her with such emotion, her eyes stung with tears behind her closed lids.

His own lashes were wet, and he self-consciously drew back and picked up the book to divert her from noticing how emotional he was.

"I think we just skipped the good part and ended up at happily-ever-after."

"That is the *good* part, silly. But I know how thorough you like to be." She pressed into him, running her hands from his shoulder blades to his backside, giving his buttocks a suggestive squeeze. "Let's go make sure we didn't miss anything."

They got it absolutely right.

* * * * *

COMING SOON!

We really hope you enjoyed reading this book.
If you're looking for more romance, be sure to
head to the shops when new books are
available on

Thursday 14th April

MILLS & BOON ®

Coming next month

CROWNING HIS LOST PRINCESS
Caitlin Crews

"I don't understand this…sitting around in pretty rooms and *talking*," Delaney seethed at him, her blue eyes shooting sparks when they met his. "I like to be outside. I like dirt under my feet. I like a day that ends with me having to scrub soil out from beneath my fingernails."

She glared at the walls as if they had betrayed her.

Then at him, as if he was doing so even now.

For a moment he almost felt as if he had—but that was ridiculous.

"When you are recognized as the true Crown Princess of Ile d'Montagne, the whole island will be your garden," he told her. Trying to soothe her. He wanted to lift a hand to his own chest and massage the brand that wasn't there, but *soothing* was for others, not him. He ignored the too-hot sensation. "You can work in the dirt of your ancestors to your heart's content."

Delaney shot a look at him, pure blue fire. "Even if I did agree to do such a crazy thing, you still wouldn't get what you want. It doesn't matter what blood is in my veins. I am a farm girl, born and bred. I will never look the part of the Princess you imagine. Never."

She sounded almost as final as he had, but Cayetano allowed himself a smile, because that wasn't a flat refusal. It sounded more like a *maybe* to him.

He could work with *maybe.*

In point of fact, he couldn't wait.

He rose then. And he made his way toward her, watching the way her eyes widened. The way her lips parted. There was an unmistakable flush on her cheeks as he drew near, and he could see her pulse beat at her neck.

Cayetano was the warlord of these mountains and would soon enough be the King of this island. And he had been prepared to ignore the fire in him, the fever. The ways he wanted her that had intruded into his work, his sleep. But here and now, he granted himself permission to want this woman. *His* woman. Because he could see that she wanted him.

With that and her *maybe,* he knew he'd already won.

"Let me worry about how you look," he said as he came to a stop before her, enjoying the way she had to look up to hold his gaze. It made her seem softer. He could see the hectic need all over her, matching his own. "There is something far more interesting for you to concentrate on."

Delaney made a noise of frustration. "The barbaric nature of ancient laws and customs?"

"Or this."

And then Cayetano followed the urge that had been with him since he'd seen her standing in a dirt-filled yard with a battered kerchief on her head and kissed her.

He expected her to be sweet. He expected to enjoy himself.

He expected to want her all the more, to tempt his own feverish need with a little taste of her.

But he was totally unprepared for the punch of it. Of a simple kiss—a kiss to show her there was more here than righting old wrongs and reclaiming lost thrones. A kiss to share a little bit of the fire that had been burning in him since he'd first laid eyes on her.

It was a blaze and it took him over.

It was a dark, drugging heat.

It was a mad blaze of passion.

It was a delirium—and he wanted more.

Continue reading
CROWNING HIS LOST PRINCESS
Caitlin Crews

Available next month
www.millsandboon.co.uk

MILLS & BOON

THE HEART OF ROMANCE

A ROMANCE FOR EVERY READER

MODERN

Prepare to be swept off your feet by sophisticated, sexy and seductive heroes, in some of the world's most glamourous and romantic locations, where power and passion collide.

HISTORICAL

Escape with historical heroes from time gone by. Whether your passion is for wicked Regency Rakes, muscled Vikings or rugged Highlanders, awa the romance of the past.

MEDICAL

Set your pulse racing with dedicated, delectable doctors in the high-pressure world of medicine, where emotions run high and passion, comfort a love are the best medicine.

True Love

Celebrate true love with tender stories of heartfelt romance, from the rush of falling in love to the joy a new baby can bring, and a focus on th emotional heart of a relationship.

Desire

Indulge in secrets and scandal, intense drama and plenty of sizzling hot action with powerful and passionate heroes who have it all: wealth, statu good looks...everything but the right woman.

HEROES

Experience all the excitement of a gripping thriller, with an intense romance at its heart. Resourceful, true-to-life women and strong, fearless face danger and desire - a killer combination!

To see which titles are coming soon, please visit

millsandboon.co.uk/nextmonth

LET'S TALK
Romance

For exclusive extracts, competitions
and special offers, find us online:

f facebook.com/millsandboon

🐦 @MillsandBoon

📷 @MillsandBoonUK

Get in touch on 01413 063232

For all the latest titles coming soon, visit
millsandboon.co.uk/nextmonth

JOIN US ON SOCIAL MEDIA!

Stay up to date with our latest releases, author news and gossip, special offers and discounts, and all the behind-the-scenes action from Mills & Boon...

 millsandboon

 millsandboonuk

 millsandboon

t might just be true love...

MILLS & BOON
Desire

Indulge in secrets and scandal, intense drama and plenty of sizzling hot action with powerful and passionate heroes who have it all: wealth, status, good looks…everything but the right woman.

MILLS & BOON
MEDICAL
Pulse-Racing Passion

Set your pulse racing with dedicated, delectable doctors in the high-pressure world of medicine, where emotions run high and passion, comfort and love are the best medicine.